L. Joan Bradley was born in Perterborough, Ontario. She taught for many years in Northern Canada, where the aurora borealis dance and survival is a daily challenge. She has a degree in educational psychology and likes to paint, make drums, and play the tin whistle. She lives in Winnipeg Beach, Manitoba with her life partner Berty and a geriatric cat named Rockie. This is her first book.

This Book is dedicated
to my mother, P. Joan Bradley and
to Berty Jones, my forever friend and partner.

L. Joan Bradley

BEFORE THE SILENCE

AUSTIN MACAULEY PUBLISHERS™
LONDON * CAMBRIDGE * NEW YORK * SHARJAH

Copyright © L. Joan Bradley 2021

All rights reserved. No part of this publication may be reproduced, distributed, or transmitted in any form or by any means, including photocopying, recording, or other electronic or mechanical methods, without the prior written permission of the publisher, except in the case of brief quotations embodied in critical reviews and certain other noncommercial uses permitted by copyright law. For permission requests, write to the publisher.

Any person who commits any unauthorized act in relation to this publication may be liable to criminal prosecution and civil claims for damages.

This is a work of fiction. Names, characters, businesses, places, events, locales, and incidents are either the products of the author's imagination or used in a fictitious manner. Any resemblance to actual persons, living or dead, or actual events is purely coincidental.

Ordering Information
Quantity sales: Special discounts are available on quantity purchases by corporations, associations, and others. For details, contact the publisher at the address below.

Publisher's Cataloging-in-Publication data
Bradley, L. Joan
Before the Silence

ISBN 9781647509712 (Paperback)
ISBN 9781647509729 (ePub e-book)

Library of Congress Control Number: 2021918983

www.austinmacauley.com/us

First Published 2021
Austin Macauley Publishers LLC
40 Wall Street, 33rd Floor, Suite 3302
New York, NY 10005
USA

mail-usa@austinmacauley.com
+1 (646) 5125767

Thank you to:

Mae Vermeulen, for her encouragement and support during the writing process

And to

Susan Hammer, for teaching me that music has a place in every story

Kaylyn Reed 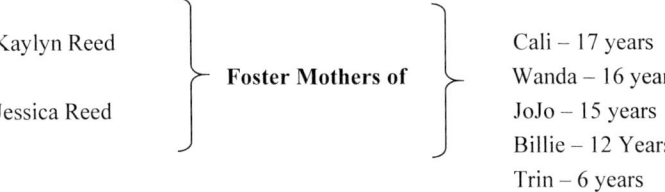 Cali – 17 years
　　　　　　　　　　　　　　　　　　　Wanda – 16 years
Jessica Reed　　　　　　　　　　　　　JoJo – 15 years
　　　　　　　　　　　　　　　　　　　Billie – 12 Years
　　　　　　　　　　　　　　　　　　　Trin – 6 years

The Grandmothers
Maggie – Jessie's maternal grandmother

Grace

Hanna – mother to Ingrid, mother-in-law to Harold
Kathleen – mother of Nadir
Lee – grandmother of Soo-Lee
Matibi
Megan

The Grandfathers
Jake
Zeke

Jake's Rescues
Bertha – alpaca farmer & sons
　　Aron – 12 years
　　Henry – 8 years
　　Kyle – 15 years

Grandma Lee's Students
<u>Female</u>　<u>Male</u>
Hua　　Bao
Lian　　Ji
Ling

Grandma Matibi's Students
Kwasi
Ibo

Earth Song
Tilly – matriarch
Andrew
Cassandra – sister of Jenny, Brit's aunt
Cerdwin – potter
Chloe – expert in edible plants
Greg – painter
Jeb
Jenna – sister of Mathew and Kevin
　　　Chloe's apprentice

Mae – weaver
Mark

The Little Ones
<u>Hanna's Grandchildren</u>
Jackson – 4 years
Lucas – 5 years
Maya – 7 years
Ria – 6 years

<u>Lee's Grandson</u>
Kim – 9 years

<u>Kathleen's Grandsons</u>
Adisa – 8 years
Benjamin – 6 years

<u>Mildred & Andy's Kids</u>
Amber – 7 years
Angela – 7 years
Byron – 6 years
Jill – 6 years
Kale – 7 years
Seth – 8 years

Cast of Characters
Before the Silence

Chapter One

Three taps were all Cali ever got before the bedroom door swung inward and Billie's round, freckled face appeared in the opening. Her youngest sister was already dressed for the day in jeans and a blue plaid, flannel shirt; her short red hair clung to her head like a helmet. "Momkay says it's time to get up, Sleepyead. Momjay has to leave for work soon, and Grandma Maggie's already started the waffles."

Cali yawned and stretched then lifted the corner of her blanket. "What do you say, Mouser? I bet there's sausage to go along with those waffles." The blanket twitched and a dark, furry head appeared followed by a yowl and a great deal of movement. Cali leaned back as the tiny calico leaped and landed on her chest.

Billie laughed. "I don't know why you call her mouser. Grandma Maggie says she's too small to catch anything bigger than a cricket."

"That's not what you say." Cali scratched behind Mouser's ear. "Is it, girl?"

"Not what you say?" Billie wrinkled her nose and took a step back. "You're just being silly, Cal. Cats can't talk."

"Are you certain?" Cali narrowed her eyes and tilted her head, waiting for an answer. She honestly didn't know why she'd been compelled to name a cat, hardly bigger than the palm of Grandpa Jake's hand, Mouser, but it had seemed like the right thing to do at the time. Maybe it was just wishful thinking on her part since mice seemed to be a standard fixture in this old house.

"Whatever." Billie waved a dismissive hand and took another step back. "You know I don't believe in that stuff. Now hurry up. Grandma Grace is here to take me to the shelter, and you know how much she likes Grandma Maggie's waffles." With that, she turned and disappeared into the hallway. The sound of boot heels followed her down the stairs.

Cali lifted Mouser from her chest to her pillow, swung her legs over the edge of the bed, and shoved her feet into her slippers. She shrugged her arms into the blue, terry cloth housecoat Momjay had given her for her last birthday and cinched the belt with a happy sigh. Eight years ago, lying in a hospital bed with her body covered in fist-sized bruises and her right arm in a sling, she could never have imagined her life turning out this way; she had her own room with an actual bed not a moldy pile of rags stuffed into a dark closet, decent clothes, all the food she could eat, and people who loved her and cared about her future. "And, on top of all that, I have the most amazing cat in the whole world, right?" Mouser mewed as Cali picked her up and cuddled the furry bundle to her chest. "How be we go get some of that breakfast?"

Mouser snuggled into her neck as she closed the bedroom door behind them. The aroma of sausage blended with the sweet scent of maple syrup and butter guided her down the stairs and into the kitchen. "Morning," she said as she lowered Mouser to the floor and took her seat beside Wanda; her goth sister raised a beringed eyebrow and stuffed another piece of sausage into her mouth.

"Good morning, Cali." Momkay set a plate heaped high with waffles and sausage on the table and ruffled Cali's hair as she passed by. "I told Jessie you'd be down in time to see her off."

Cali smiled across the table at the dark-haired woman with eyes the color of a late summer sky. "Good morning, Momjay. Sorry. I didn't know we were getting up early today, or I would have finished my paper this morning."

"I told Kat to let you sleep…" Jessie grinned at her partner. "But you know how she is about family breakfasts. Like a bear with a honey pot."

"Oh, you…" Kaylyn tossed her long red hair in feigned annoyance then took her seat beside Grandma Maggie.

"Well, I think it's a lovely idea…always have." Maggie gave Kaylyn's hand a comforting pat, but Cali knew that Momkay wasn't really upset by the teasing. They had all agreed years ago that sitting down to breakfast together was the best way to start off their day, and none of them had ever decided otherwise.

"Can't disagree with that." Grandma Grace adjusted her blue beret to better cover her thinning hair then looked down at her empty plate. "Those waffles were sure good."

Momkay laughed, and Jessie gave Cali a wink.

"I think there are some left, Gracey." Maggie pulled her grey braid over her shoulder and pushed her chair back. "How many would you like?"

"One would be good."

Thirteen-year-old JoJo giggled. "But two would be better."

"Well, fortunately, we seem to have quite a few left in the warmer." Maggie flipped two waffles onto Grace's plate with a smile. "Anyone else?"

Cali turned her attention to her own plate as everyone dug into second helpings and tiny paws batted at her pajama leg. She sliced a half sausage into tiny bits then reached for the small dish sitting above her plate as if by magic.

"I thought Mouser might be hungry, and we both know how Grandma Maggie feels about grease spots on her clean floors," Wanda said, then her black lips twitched up at the corner. "Just think of it as a favor you'll owe me at some point in the future."

"Right…" Cali nodded and scraped the sausage pieces onto the plate. "Wouldn't want anyone to think you might have a soft spot for…what did you call her…an annoying piece of toe jam?"

Wanda snorted. "I did, but only after she upchucked a hair ball in my slipper. And don't tell me she did it because she likes me."

Cali shrugged and set the plate of sausage on the floor. Mouser mewed then hunkered over the dish, making fast work of the food. "And don't forget to thank Auntie Wanda," she said, just loud enough for her sister to hear.

"I swear, Cal, if that cat leaves me another hair ball." Wanda nudged Cali with her shoulder, and Cali's knife clattered to the floor.

Momjay raised her head and frowned across the table. "Everything okay over there, girls?"

Wanda gave Cali another nudge then nodded. "Cali's just clumsy this morning because she's tired."

Jessie raised both eyebrows; when Cali didn't protest, she sighed and let it go. "So, what are the plans for today?" She glanced around the table then smiled down at Billie. "Since Grandma Grace is here bright and early, I assume you'll be spending your day at the shelter."

Billie swallowed a bulging mouthful of sausage and nodded. "I'm going to help make the soup today…black bean and vegetable."

"And if we have time…and flour…we might even whip up some biscuits." Grace wiped her mouth with a napkin. "We'll know exactly what we're working with, once we pick up the donation boxes."

"Well, you certainly have the right person to help you with the heavy lifting." Jessie winked at Billie making her blush. Cali's youngest sister spent two evenings a week at the 'Y' swimming laps and was quite proud of the muscles she'd developed. "And what about you, Jo?" Jessie asked turning her attention to the other end of the table.

"I'm going to the 'Human Rights Museum' with the other homeschoolers." Jo gave her signature one-shoulder shrug. "My next history unit is on World War II, and Grandma Hanna thought a visit to the museum would be a good place to start."

"I guess that leaves the computers to us for the day." Wanda gave Cali another nudge.

Cali nudged her back. "Nope. My next assignment is 'The life and times of Mark Twain as portrayed in the novels *Huckleberry Finn* and *Tom Sawyer,*' so I'll be spending the day reading."

"And Wanda and I will be going over her last algebra assignment." Maggie looked sympathetic as Wanda groaned. "I know it's the last thing you want to do, dear, but you'll need your math when you take the tests for your diploma."

"I know, but..." Wanda's shoulders slumped as she gave in to the inevitable. Then she brightened and turned to Kaylyn. "We're still going to the bookstore at four though, right? I have a new D&D avatar I want to try out."

Kaylyn smiled. "Wouldn't miss it for..."

"...all the tea in Grandma Maggie's cupboard." Billie giggled.

"Good one, Sprout." Jessie patted her youngest daughter on the back. "...all the tea in Grandma Maggie's cupboard. I like that."

Maggie smiled her appreciation. "So, what about you, Jessie? Heard anything back from that lawyer?"

Jessie nodded. "I got a text from her this morning. Apparently, she can't tell me anything beyond the fact that I'm supposedly related to this woman. Everything else has to be done face-to-face."

Grace looked up from her plate and frowned in Maggie's direction. "You don't suppose."

"Of course, you can have another waffle, Gracey," Maggie interjected. "Do you want one or two?"

Grace looked puzzled for a moment, then the frown lines disappeared, and she nodded. Cali didn't know what had passed between the grandmothers at that moment, but she was certain it had nothing to do with waffles. "On second thought," Grace said, "I think I've had enough waffles this morning, Maggie. Wouldn't want to ruin my girlish figure."

Jessie grinned then pushed her chair out from the table and stood up. "I'd best be going. I'm meeting with the lawyer at six so don't wait supper for me," she said as she picked up her briefcase. "I'll get something on the way home."

Billie clutched Jessie's sleeve. "But you 'are' coming home, right? Cause my dad went to see a lawyer, and he never came back."

Jessie dropped to one knee and covered Billie's hand with her own. "Hey, not all lawyers work with…"

"Criminals." Billie's lips quivered.

Jessie sighed and opened her arms. "That's right. Now come give me a hug." Billie swiped a hand across her eyes then leaned into that embrace. "You have a good day," Jessie said. "And I'll see you this evening. Okay?"

"Promise?"

"I promise."

Chapter Two

The sounds from below were loud and shrill; the inevitable squeal and crunch of metal against metal and the screams of fleeing pedestrians brought Andy out of her chair and to her window just as a third vehicle slammed into the intersection. It was the second major accident on Broadway since they'd replaced the traffic lights with stop signs.

"Obviously, someone missed the memo on 'turn-taking.' I hope no one was hurt."

Andy spun toward the voice. A tall brunette dressed in jeans and a wool turtleneck sweater beneath a red, thigh-length jacket stood in her open doorway. "Jessie! I was afraid…" Andy glanced at the carnage on the street below. "Well, never mind. I'm glad you're here now."

"I'm glad you got my message." There was a hint of wariness in Jessie's smile as she ran her fingers through her short, dark hair then joined Andy at the window. "I know four-thirty is kinda late for a meeting, but when you said it couldn't wait until next week, I figured I could kill two birds with one stone. Hope you don't mind."

"At this point, I'll take what I can get." Andy glanced at the clock above the door ignoring the look of concern her words had caused. She'd tried hard to keep Jessie out of this mess, but she'd run out of time and options, and the future was closing in too fast for one little girl. "What time's your appointment with the lawyer?"

"Six o'clock. Apparently, it's important that we meet sooner rather than later…sound familiar?" Jessie cocked one eyebrow then shrugged. "Anyway, that was the only time that suited both of us." She frowned out the window. "So what can I do for my favorite social worker?"

"Not here, okay?" Andy reached behind her and grabbed her jacket off the back of her chair. "Why don't we go get that coffee I promised you? And I'll tell you all about it."

Jessie didn't protest though she could feel the wasted minutes ticking by as she retrieved her bag from the desk and followed Andy into the hall. "And here I was all prepared for end-of-the-day coffee from the staffroom," she said lightly.

"It's better this way," Andy turned off the lights and locked the door behind them. "And we're not going far…just next door actually, so you'll have plenty of time to get to your meeting."

Jessie nodded and followed Andy toward the elevator. It was obvious that the younger woman had something important to say, and whatever it was, it had her wound up so tight that Jessie was afraid she might implode. 'You're a counselor, dammit. You can handle this.' It wouldn't be the first time she'd acted as Andy's sounding board, and it probably wouldn't be the last.

They turned left at the end of the hall and entered the reception area. Like most government offices Jessie'd been in, Child Services was the epitome of bland neutrality, a place of serious busyness where any hint of vibrancy was considered antithetical to its purpose. Jessie sighed as she ran her fingers through her bangs. She couldn't blame Andy for wanting to get out of there. "This place never seems to change," she said as she followed Andy past the scowling receptionist and toward the elevator. "A touch of color would be nice, don't you think?"

Andy stopped in front of a pair of matt grey doors and pressed the down button. She kept looking over her shoulder as though she was expecting someone to call her back. "It grows on you after a while. Like everything else, if you let it." She gave the button another impatient poke. "I suppose you're wondering why I want to talk to you away from the office. It must seem like I'm sneaking around behind someone's back." The doors opened, and Andy backed into the elevator. "Which is exactly what I'm doing, by the way. Just so you know."

"Whoa." Jessie stopped dead in her tracks; her body wedged between the two doors. She swallowed hard and tried not to look as concerned as she felt. Andy might stretch the rules to their limit when a child's welfare was at stake, but as far as Jessie knew, the younger woman worked very hard to maintain a professional relationship with her colleagues.

"Sounds serious," Jessie said as she gave the door a shove and stepped inside. The doors swooshed shut behind her.

Andy pressed the button for the main floor. "Serious enough that I'm about to break a promise I made to you three years ago even if it means the end of our friendship."

"Jessica Reed for Ms. Klein. I have a six o'clock appointment."

The receptionist glanced at her computer and nodded. "Just take a seat for a moment, please." She pressed a button on the side of the desk. "Ms. Klein's assistant will be right out."

Jessica nodded and sank into a faux-leather chair nestled beside a glass table; a small vase of red silk flowers held center place on the spotless surface beside a thick stack of magazines. Hoping that the proliferation of reading materials wasn't an indication of protracted wait times, she took two deep breaths, focused her attention on the painting of a lush, dark forest behind the desk, and let her mind drift.

Trinity…an interesting name for a six-year-old who couldn't…or wouldn't speak; a little girl who needed a safe home with people who would love her unconditionally. "Your home," Andy had said with such pleading, even though she'd promised not to make such a request ever again; even though Jessie's family had decided that four daughters were the perfect number. *I should have just said no then and there. I should have…*

"Ms. Reed. Ms. Klein will see you now."

Jessica blinked her eyes open and raised her head. A tall blonde in red blouse and navy slacks waited in the doorway to the right of the receptionist. Jessica nodded then gathered her bag and followed the assistant down the red-carpeted hallway to an open door at its end. A woman with short, grey hair and the greenest eyes Jessica had ever seen stood in front of a heavy oak desk clutching a red mug in her left hand. She wore a tweed jacket over a white blouse, and what Jessica suspected was a pair of casual day blue jeans. Jessica smiled and felt herself relax.

"Ms. Reed. I'm glad to finally meet you." The lawyer extended her right hand. "I'm Sara Klein. Your great-aunt was both a client and a friend. She'll be sorely missed."

"It's good to meet you too, Ms. Klein." Jessica did the polite thing though she usually avoided shaking hands, especially during flu season. "But I'm afraid you have the wrong person."

"Your aunt knew you would say that. And please, call me Sara." The older woman smiled and gestured toward three armchairs clustered around a circular table. A thin folder sat on the glossy surface beneath a carved, wooden box. "Hilda will bring you a coffee, if you like."

Jessica perched on the edge of the closest chair and lowered her bag to the floor. She'd planned to keep this visit short and sweet, but her plea of mistaken identity hadn't been the surprise she'd thought it would be, and she needed to know why. Besides, she was here now and her gut told her she should stay. What harm could it do to listen? "Coffee would be very nice, thank you."

Sara nodded to her assistant then took the seat across from Jessie. "Alice and her family have been clients of our firm for decades. A year ago, Alice came to me with that box…" She nodded toward the table. "…and a list of revisions to her will, among other things. She said it had taken her a long time to see you clearly, but now that she'd located you, it was paramount that the Sontheil legacy be placed in your hands." Her lips twitched upward. "She also instructed me to answer any questions you might have. And I'm certain you must have a lot of them."

"I do," Jessie said as she eased into the chair. If not for the nagging feeling in her gut, she might have chosen this moment to leave; she'd never heard the name Sontheil, and Maggie would have told her if she had a great-aunt named Alice. But maybe she didn't know. She cleared her throat and raised her head hoping that she didn't look as confused as she felt.

"I know this is a lot to take in," Sara said before Jessie could ask her first question. "But I promise you that even though Alice was considered to be an eccentric by most people who knew her, that was far from the truth. Your aunt was a freethinker, an astute businesswoman, and one of the most compassionate people I have ever known. It was your compassion that drew her to you in the end."

"That's…that's absurd. I told you that we'd never met."

Ms. Klein ignored Jessie's outburst. "Nonetheless, she knew you were meant to be her heir." The lawyer sighed. "Alice had a gift—one that is well-documented in your father's family." She cocked her head to the side. "How much do you know about the Sontheils, Jessica?"

"Absolutely nothing," Jessica said as she raised her mug to her lips with shaking hands. She'd have some harsh words with her gut when she got home.

Sara nodded. "That's understandable since your mother broke all contacts with them when your father died. She even took back her maiden name...O'Reilly."

Jessica stiffened. Her father had died before she was born; her mother two years later. "Why would she do that?" *And why has Maggie never told me any of this?*

Sara shrugged. "That's not for me to say, but rest assured that your father's surname was Sontheil and your aunt...and you...are distantly related to a woman known as the Yorkshire Sybil. Her married name was Ursula Shipton."

"Ursula." Jessie took a deep breath and tried to relax her fingers enough to pick up her cup. Lukewarm coffee splashed over her hand as she leaned back. *So much for calm, cool and collected.* "Ursula is my middle name," she shivered, "But you already know that, don't you?"

Nan Cave. No matter how many times Jessie read Cali's handcrafted sign, it always made her smile; tonight was no exception even though the smile was a little sad and frayed around the edges. The room behind this door was Maggie's domain: her classroom, bedroom, and library and the most likely place for her to be on a cold winter's night.

"Grandmother?" Jessie tapped three times on the heavy, oak door. "Grandmother, may I come in?"

Heavy footsteps made their way across the room beyond, and the door opened. The old woman frowned. "That was some long-winded lawyer you went to see, but no matter. We saved you some stew. Come in and warm yourself, and I'll bring you a bowl."

"Maybe later." Jessie stepped into the den and felt the warmth embrace her. A small fire crackled in the grate of the ancient fireplace and the soft strains of a Welsh air filled the spaces in between. "Right now, I just really need to talk."

Maggie nodded. "Thought you might. Take a seat, and I'll pour some tea, shall I?"

"After all the coffee I've been forced to drink today, that would be lovely." Jessie perched on the edge of the overstuffed chair to the right of the fire as Maggie poured hot water into two cups and tossed a handful of something brown and pungent into the fire. Steeping camomile and the scent of cedar added yet another layer of familiar comfort. "The house is awfully quiet," she observed to Maggie's bowed back.

Her grandmother's spine stiffened, just a little, but enough to be noticeable. "Kaylyn took the girls grocery shopping."

Jessie frowned. That never happened and for good reason; setting four teenagers loose with a grocery cart was a recipe for culinary disaster. She swallowed against the sudden knot in her throat. "So we can talk." Her chest heaved as she forced the words out. "…about Alice."

Maggie turned and pressed a mug into Jessie's hand. "Just breathe, Child, and when you're ready we'll say what needs to be said."

Jessie eased back in her chair and did as she was told, not as the child her grandmother named her, but as a woman answering a plea from one heart to another. She reached for all the calm Maggie had offered her and held it close as she set her cup on the hearth and turned to face her grandmother. "You knew her." It wasn't just a statement of fact, and they both knew it.

Maggie didn't flinch. "I first met Alice Sontheil…a very long time ago. She and I and Grace and the rest of the grandmothers went to university together." Maggie drew a deep breath and let it out slowly. "Alice and I weren't friends, but we did work together on a number of projects in our first year…then she just disappeared. Didn't even say goodbye."

"Then how…"

"…did she wind up being part of your…of our family?" Maggie closed her eyes and sighed. "I've thought about that a lot over the years. I'd like to believe that it was just a chance reunion in a coffee shop that brought our two families together, but I suspect that it was more than that." She raised her head; there was sadness and more than a little regret in those watery, blue eyes along with something akin to a deep sense of long-awaited release that made Jessie shiver. "I don't know what the lawyer told you about Alice," Maggie said. "But from the look on your face when you walked in here, I can make a pretty good guess that it wasn't anything you wanted to hear."

"It wasn't; not by a long shot." Jessie leaned closer. "In fact, she told me that I'm the heir, in more ways than one, to a woman with delusions of grandeur," Jessie didn't mean to sound sarcastic, but it was better than the alternative.

Maggie cocked her head, the way she did when she knew that what she was being given was more fiction than fact. "That's what I thought until Alice made her first prediction in my presence," she said without a hint of inflection. "It's very easy to label someone who claims to know the future as being delusional…at least it is until their predictions start to come true."

Jessie felt her jaw drop. "So what are you saying, Grandmother?"

Maggie gave her a sad, half-smile. "What did the lawyer really tell you, Jessica? Because I'm certain that your great-aunt wouldn't have retained someone in such an important role unless that person knew exactly who she was dealing with and had no compunctions about believing every word of it."

"She told me…" Jessica stiffened her spine. This time, she'd tell the unvarnished truth of her conversation with Sara, her grandmother deserved at least that much. But it didn't matter how much evidence Alice's lawyer had to ensure her compliance, Jessie refused to be bullied by the ramblings of a woman whose only claim to family was a few drops of shared blood. "She told me that Alice wasn't the only documented seer in our family, that our roots can be traced back over five hundred years to the mother of a woman known as the Yorkshire Sybil."

"The daughter's married name was Ursula Shipton." Maggie acknowledged Jessie's gaping mouth with a shrug. "I did my research. The mother's name was Agatha Sontheil. From what your aunt told me, your family is descended from Agatha's second child…a bastard son." Maggie brushed a wisp of white hair from her cheek. "She wasn't quite certain what his first name was."

Jessie reached for the calm and held on tight. "So you actually believe it…all of it."

"I do and for good reason." Maggie folded her arms in her lap and leaned toward the fire. "I was there, at your parents' wedding supper, when Alice very loudly and very clearly predicted your birth…" She drew a deep, steady breath. "…and your father's death."

Jessica swallowed the anger suddenly banging at the back of her teeth; Alice wasn't here, and Maggie didn't deserve it. "How could she do something that cruel?" She asked softly.

"According to your father, no one was more appalled by what she'd done than Alice was."

"So you're saying she couldn't control it."

Maggie shook her head. "I'm saying that she didn't know that it was happening. Her brother told everyone she'd had too much champagne and dragged her away, but there were a lot of Sontheils' and their kin at that wedding who knew that wasn't the case…including your father."

Maggie blinked the sudden moisture from her eyes then wiped it away with the back of her hand. "Eric was a good man, and he truly loved your mother. He managed to laugh off your aunt's words for Jennifer's sake, but the next day, he took out a huge insurance policy and had me put the papers in my safety deposit box." She sighed. "I really expected him to ask for them back someday."

Jessie blinked a sudden tear from her eyes. She'd never known her father. "So he just accepted what Alice said."

Maggie nodded. "The whole family did. But your father never let on to your mother, and I've always been grateful to him for that kindness. My daughter had eight happy months with him, and he gave me a beautiful granddaughter to remember the two of them by." Maggie sighed. "Your father died on the exact day at the exact time that Alice predicted he would. You were born five months later on a very cold, wet night at the end of March just as she said you would be. After that, it was hard not to believe that Alice was exactly what she claimed to be."

"So why didn't you tell me about her…about any of this?" At any other time, the whine in her voice would have been an embarrassment, but Jessie didn't give a damn about appearances right now. Her grandmother had lied to her by omitting her entire life and kept her from family, and she needed to know why.

"Because I promised your mother that I wouldn't." Grey brows narrowed beneath a shock of white hair, but there was no hint of repentance in Maggie's eyes. "And you know that I always keep my promises. Jen was terrified of your aunt after your father's death, and I can't say that I blamed her when she decided that she wanted nothing more to do with that side of your family. She let them know that in no uncertain terms at his funeral…and not surprisingly, they all seemed to know that it was coming." Maggie leaned back, reached into her sweater pocket, and tossed another handful of cedar into the fire.

Jessica felt the corners of her lips twitch upward as healing smoke wafted into the room. Maggie's pockets had always been a cornucopia of life's small necessities: tissues, foil-wrapped mints, safety pins, small change, paper clips…dried cedar leaves. It was comforting to know that some things never changed.

"The last time I saw Alice," Maggie said into the aromatic silence, "Or anyone else from that side of your family was at the funeral. Alice didn't come into the chapel. She sent an usher to fetch me."

A sigh and then, "Your mom blamed Alice for your father's death and demanded that I send her away, but I couldn't." One deep breath and then another. "Bad things happen in the universe every day, Jess, with or without someone seeing it on the horizon…especially if what's seen is only part of the story. Your father knew the when and how, but not the where, and I never believed that that was Alice's fault. So I went out to meet her. She looked like she hadn't slept in a week, and I knew she'd been crying. We just stood there staring at each other for a moment, then she asked me to take special care of her great-niece since she wouldn't be able to."

Maggie suddenly looked old and defeated. "You're not going to want to hear the rest of this, but she said the day would come when all your presumptions about the world would be tested, and you needed to be strong enough to meet that day head-on. Then she gave me these." Maggie retrieved a blue jeweler's box from her other pocket and opened the lid. Inside were five silver pins in the shape of a double spiral nestled in white cotton. "They're for your daughters. She said you would know when to give the pins to them."

Jessie forced air into her lungs, but she couldn't stop the hysterical laughter boiling up from her belly. "We have four daughters, not five."

Maggie shrugged. "A simple mistake."

Every fiber of Jessie's being wanted to let the laughter out, to reassure the quivering child within that her great-aunt wasn't infallible…that this was all a bad joke, but the mother who had listened to a social worker's pleas for the future of a helpless child knew better.

"Not a mistake." Jessica met Maggie's eyes as she took the box with trembling fingers. "Just a small glitch in the timeline."

"Are you going to open it, Child?"

Jessie stared down at the very official-looking envelope sitting in her lap. The blue box sat on the table beside her along with a half-eaten bowl of Irish stew and an empty package of tissues. Maggie had listened patiently while her granddaughter talked of pain and need and uncertainty then wiped her tears away and fed her belly as well as her heart. "What if I'm not strong enough, Grandmother?"

She watched the lines on Maggie's face soften as she pressed a silver broach into Jessie's hand. "Whatever Alice put in that envelope isn't intended just for you."

Jessie closed her fingers hard enough to leave a spiral imprint on her palm. The universe had no right to dump this on her family and that included a great-aunt forced to speak words that weren't her own. "But they're children," she said softly.

"Strong children with strong mothers and stronger grandmothers." The corner of Maggie's lips twitched. "I doubt that whatever you find in that envelope has a hope in hell of defeating such a formidable foe."

"Formidable foe." Jessie choked back a sudden burble of laughter. "You've been reading too many of Kaylyn's fantasy novels."

Maggie quirked a pale, jagged eyebrow. "Maybe, but it doesn't make what I said any less true. I think we both understand that whatever words Alice wrote down and put inside that envelope are going to affect your life…" Her eyes were drawn to the box sitting large between them. "…and probably the lives of everyone you care for, whether you read them or not." She paused and waited for the only honest response Jessie could give; she took a deep breath and nodded. "Then open the envelope, Child, so we know what we're facing before it steps up and smacks us in the jaw."

Jessica cocked her head then forced a smile. "If you say so, Grandmother." She ran her thumbnail along the flap and unceremoniously turned the envelope upside down; a single sheet of aged vellum wrapped in a clear plastic sleeve landed in her lap. Written across the shiny surface in red marker were the words: *As has been foreseen, I now deliver this to 'the barren mother of five cursed daughters.' Long have we awaited you. With love, Alice.*

Muffled laughter was the first thing Maggie heard as she closed the Nan Cave door behind her leaving Jessie with a crumpled piece of calfskin in one hand, a jeweler's box in the other, and a look in her eyes that was unfathomable even to someone who had known her since the day she was born. One reading was all it took for Maggie to realize that it would require a diversity of knowledge and many sharp minds to untangle the puzzle presented to her granddaughter; convincing Jessie that she didn't have to carry the burden of those words alone was a horse of a different color…one that was best wrangled by the person who cradled her granddaughter's heart with gentle fingers and offered her own freely in return.

Maggie bustled down the hall and turned left into the kind of loosely contained chaos that instantly eased her heart and made her smile. The kitchen was the largest room in the house, a cherished remnant of a time when families gathered around the woodstove to share food, warmth, and companionship after the day's work was done. She'd spent many happy hours in this kitchen as a child, and even though the woodstove was gone, this room with its large, round table and soft chairs was still a place of warmth and sharing.

"We're back, Gramma Maggie."

"I can see that, Child." Maggie grabbed the doorframe in self-defense as twelve-year-old Billie skidded to a halt just inches in front of her and waved a careless arm around the room. Her round, freckled face glowed with happiness.

"And look what we've brought with us." Billie crowed. "Have you ever owned so much food in all your life?"

"Can't say that I have." Maggie tried to avoid Kaylyn's look of utter defeat as she surveyed the room. Every flat surface was covered with colorful, cloth sacks packed to the brim with cans and bags and boxes of more food than they could possibly eat in six months.

"I honestly don't know where we're going to put it all." Kaylyn watched with weary eyes as Cali rearranged cans of tomatoes in the corner cabinet in a brave attempt to make space for a dozen more.

"Don't worry, Momkay. We'll find room." Maggie felt the brush of tiny fingers on the palm of her hand. Billie smiled at her as Maggie looked down. "Won't we, Grandmother?"

"Of course, we will." Maggie took a deep breath. "And while you and I and your sisters do just that, Kaylyn can take a break and put her feet up in the Nan Cave."

Kaylyn frowned as she scanned the kitchen. "I can't leave you with all of this," she said as her eyes met Maggie's. "Even with the girls' help, it's going to take ages to put it all away."

Sixteen-year-old Wanda huffed and stepped between her mother and her grandmother. She raised a black, beringed eyebrow in Maggie's direction. "Is Momjay home?"

Maggie nodded.

"Then you need to take that break Grandma Maggie offered you." Dark eyes, softened with genuine concern, turned toward Kaylyn. Wanda's dark exterior belied her bright mind and gentle heart, and as far as Maggie could tell, that was the way Wanda wanted it. Their goth child was a mystery she had yet to solve. "Cause if Momjay's home and she hasn't come out to say hi," Wanda said softly, "then something's wrong, and you need to fix it. Am I right, Grandmother?"

"How do you know things like that?" Jo exclaimed, then she pressed a hand over her mouth and ducked behind the table. Wanda scowled in Jo's direction.

"She's not wrong," Maggie said catching Kaylyn's eye over Wanda's shoulder. "You and Jess have a lot to talk about, and it's going to take a while. So the girls and I will finish up here…"

"And make the snack."

Maggie squeezed Billie's fingers. "And make the snack…while you go do what you need to do."

Kaylyn took a last, worried look around the kitchen as Wanda nudged her toward the door. "And don't come back until you bring Momjay with you."

The pressure on Maggie's fingers became almost painful as Kaylyn's lithe frame disappeared into the hall. "Is Momjay sad?" Billie asked in a voice so soft that it was barely audible.

"A little," Maggie said, all too aware of the four pairs of eyes turned her way. "But mostly she's confused. The people she went to talk to gave her a lot to think about today, and she needs Kaylyn to help her sort it out."

"Oh." Billie cocked her head to the side. "Grandma Kate says I'm good at sorting things. Maybe I could…"

Before the child could finish, Wanda yanked a box of Kaylyn's favorite sweet potato crackers from a bright red sack and pressed it into her youngest sister's hand. "Time to get back to work, Sprout. The best way we can help our moms right now is to get all these groceries put away." Wanda wiggled her bushy, black eyebrows up and down; Billie giggled. "So what do you say?"

Billie stared at the box in her hand for a moment, and everyone in the room held their breath. When their youngest had her heart set on something, it was almost impossible to change its direction without a fight…or a really tempting alternative.

"And when we're done, I'll make mini pizzas," Cali piped up from the other side of the room, "With extra cheese."

Maggie smiled. The concerted effort to divert and distract was quite impressive and very welcomed. It had been a long day for all of them, and the last thing anyone needed, including Billie, was a tempest in a teapot.

Billie took one final glance toward the door then released Maggie's hand and nodded. "Okay. I'll stay and help," she said as she headed toward the back cupboard with the box of crackers. "For a little while."

"I know it's a lot to take in and I wouldn't blame you…" Jessica gulped as a finger sealed her lips.

"You forget who you're talking to, my love. I'm a pagan, who has a master's in ancient history, plays Dungeons and Dragons with our daughter and spends her Thursday evenings with her sci-fi and fantasy book club." Kaylyn lowered her hand. "It's only a small step from there to accepting that your great-aunt was able to see into the future."

"And what about this?" Jessie held up the calfskin she still had clutched in her fingers. Kaylyn had half-expected it to wind up in the fire at some point during Jessie's tale and was relieved that it hadn't. "Even if Aunt Alice could see the future, what good is that knowledge if I can't understand what she saw?" She clenched her jaw and shivered. "If all it is, is gobbledygook written in rhyme?"

"Very Shakespearean." Kaylyn stifled an involuntary giggle as Jessie glared at her. "I'm sorry, love, but we can't start out believing we're going to fail at this." She drew a deep breath as Jessie continued to stare at her with eyes full of pain and doubt. "We'll figure it out…you and I, the girls and the grandmothers and anyone else who can help us…and then we'll do whatever we need to do to keep our family safe."

Jessie squeezed her eyes closed. "My father couldn't keep himself safe."

"I know love, but he kept you safe…you and your mom." Kaylyn closed the gap between them and tentatively offered Jessie her shoulder. Jessie's need to protect was strong. Her fear of failure was even stronger; it would immobilize her if they couldn't find a way past it. Kaylyn sighed as Jessie snuggled in.

"That's what Maggie said."

Kaylyn nestled her cheek in Jessie's hair; she smelled of woodsmoke and strawberries. "You mean that crazy old lady who sent me to the grocery store with four growing girls each harboring 'yet to be resolved' food issues."

Jessie giggled softly. "I think Gran feels bad about that."

"I'm still not going to forgive her." Kaylyn pulled Jessie closer. "So a fifth daughter, eh? I wonder how the girls are going to feel about that, especially since none of us really has a choice in the matter." She drew a deep breath as Jessie stiffened. "What's written on that piece of calfskin you're so determined to mangle doesn't just belong to you, my love. It belongs to every person who will be affected by it, including that little girl; we can't take that away from her even if we wanted to."

"You and Maggie are a lot alike," Jessie's voice was muffled against her shoulder. "You never turn away from a challenge no matter how crazy it is."

Jessie raised her head and sought Kaylyn's eyes; there was fear in those blue depths as Jessie drew her in, but there was also hope and the first stirrings of the indomitable spirit that fought every day to make the world a better place. "I love you for that, you know." Jessie chewed at her bottom lip then nodded to herself. "So when do we tell them?"

Kaylyn heard the doubt that still lingered behind that question and watched as Jessie smoothed the crumpled message against her leg with nervous fingers; hopefully, it would still legible when they needed it. "We'll talk to the girls tomorrow—after you and I meet with Andy and have finalized everything with the lawyer. Maggie can call the grandmothers…get them to come over." There would be no vote this time, no discussion of pros and cons; the future demanded a fifth daughter, and a fifth daughter it would get…as for the rest of it… "We'll lay everything on the table and go from there."

Kaylyn waited for Jessie's protest; when none came, she said, "Then we'll get everyone together Friday evening: our daughters, the grandmothers, maybe even a grandfather or two. I'll make copies of your aunt's predictions. We'll fill everyone in then put them to work." She pulled Jessie closer. "Don't worry, love, if I've learned anything over the past ten years, it's how strong and resilient this family is no matter how crazy things get. Everything will be fine."

There was a tense moment of silence. Kaylyn could almost hear the thoughts tumbling through Jessie's mind as she weighed the choices they both knew she didn't have.

"Sounds like a plan," Jessie whispered as she pressed the calfskin into Kaylyn's hand. "Take care of this for me…for us. Okay?" She gave Kaylyn a final hug and sat up. "Now let's go tell the girls that their curiosity is going to have to wait to be satisfied until tomorrow before I lose my nerve."

Kaylyn chuckled as she gently coaxed the calfskin back into its plastic sleeve. "It's okay, love. I'll have your back."

"It's not my back I'm worried about." *It's my sanity.*

Chapter Three

Gentle fingers tugged on Maggie's sleeve as she scraped the onions into the pot. She carefully laid the newly sharpened knife down on the cutting board and turned to find Jo hovering behind her. Maggie smiled at the rumpled child peering up at her from behind a messy tangle of hair the color of wet sand. Her dark eyes closed as she yawned then she shook herself and returned Maggie's smile. "Well, good morning, Josephine. You're up early."

Jo shrugged and peered over Maggie's shoulder. "What's that?"

Maggie turned back to the onion she'd been chopping when Jo walked in. "I'm making lasagna for supper. I should be done shortly, and then we can start breakfast."

Jo flopped down on the nearest chair. "I'm not really hungry."

"Is that so?" Maggie slid the finished pan into the oven, wiped her hands on the tea towel hanging off the fridge, and joined Josephine at the table. Breakfast was always Jo's favorite meal of the day; she'd have to be sick to refuse it. "Is your stomach upset?" Maggie pressed her palm to Jo's forehead. "You don't seem to have a fever."

The child's shoulders moved up and down as she sighed. "I'm not sick, Grandmother. I'm just not hungry. There's too much stuff in my head to think about food."

"Maybe I can help." Maggie folded her arms on the table and leaned forward. "I'm a really good listener. Ears like an elephant, so Billie says."

Jo pressed her hand over her mouth to stifle a giggle.

Maggie waited for the laughter to ease away some of the tension. "So what has you all tied up in knots?"

"I don't…" Jo drew a deep breath. Her lips quivered. "Secrets give me nightmares, Grandmother."

Maggie reached across the table and took Jo's hand. "I know, Sweetie, and no one can blame you for that." Secrets had destroyed Jo's family and killed her mother; her father was still on the run from the secrets he'd brought down on his family's head. "But this is only a half-secret…"

"Half-secret?" The dark eyes narrowed. "What's that?"

Maggie tried not to smile; sometimes a grandmother had to be quick on her feet and willing to break a few rules. "A half-secret is one you already know exists…so it can't sneak up on you. Like the secrets you're going to hear this evening. You already know they're coming, and when they arrive, your moms will make certain that those secrets can't hurt you."

Jo cocked her head to the side. "Is that true, Grandma Maggie?"

Was it true? She smiled to herself. Jess and Kat would do anything to protect their daughters; of that she was certain. "Absolutely!" She smacked her free hand down on the table for emphasis. "If I'm lying, I'm frying."

Jo giggled and Maggie eased her hand away. Maybe someday Jo would learn to trust enough that the nightmares would go away, but that would take years and a thousand baby steps along the way. "Now how about some breakfast? Cold or hot?"

"With six cereal boxes cluttering up the counter, we'll all be eating cold breakfasts for the next few days." Kaylyn ruffled her daughter's hair then smiled across the table. "Morning, Maggie. Whatever you have in the oven smells wonderful."

"It's lasagna," Jo piped up. "For supper."

"Mhmm. My favorite."

"Are you ready to go, Kat?" Jessie appeared in the kitchen doorway dressed in her red jacket and white boots. She looked almost as tired and anxious as her daughter. Maggie couldn't say that she blamed Jess for fearing what today would bring. Their lives were about to change; it was inevitable, and her granddaughter had yet to accept that deep down where it counted.

"Be right there." Kaylyn kissed the top of Jo's head. "Tell your sister's we're sorry we missed breakfast, but just this one time it can't be helped. Now mind your grandmother. We'll be home by lunchtime, okay?"

Jo nodded. "And I'll tell them about the cereal." She scrunched up her nose and giggled. "I bet Bryn makes her scowly face like she does when Momjay makes her eat broccoli."

"Now why would she do that?" Kaylyn demanded.

"She says that sweets give her pimples."

Kaylyn glanced at the door then back at Maggie. "I'll take care of it," Maggie said as she stood up and moved toward the entrance. Kaylyn followed her.

"Good morning, Grandmother," Jessie sagged against her as Maggie drew her granddaughter into a hug. "I wish we didn't have to leave right now, but…"

"It's only eight o'clock." Cali stood at the top of the stairs in her red plaid flannels and a 'Make Music Like No One's Listening' t-shirt; her dark curls stood up in soft, gleaming tufts all over her head. Maggie swore the child had ears like a bat or maybe an elephant. "I thought your appointment wasn't until ten."

Jessie took a step back as Maggie released her. "Kat and I are going out for breakfast first, and I'd really appreciate it if you looked out for your sisters…kept things as normal as possible."

Cali grinned. "No worries. Grandma Maggie has already given us a special project. It was on my pad this morning…something about shaman and seers."

Jessie raised an eyebrow in Maggie's direction. "Sounds interesting."

"Just a little background information." Maggie nudged Jessie toward the door. "And you can thank me for it later."

Chapter Four

A dragon's flame. A spear of light.
Rainbows dance across the night.
Silence falls upon the earth.
The ancient wisdom seeks rebirth.
The stone bound heart is deep and vast.
Your future lies buried in the past.
Barren mother of five cursed daughters,
Seize the day before life falters.
Flee to the forests and the fen.
It's here the child of light will ken.
Thirteen moons and thirteen more,
The stout of heart will hold the door.
Learn the secrets of the land.
Sustain your lives with your own hands.
And wait.

As usual, Hanna was the first to arrive, her long skirts flapping against her legs as she waited on the porch for the door to open.

"It wasn't locked," Maggie said as she waved the tall grandmother with the faintly mauve hair into the kitchen.

"Well, it should be." Hanna hung her coat on a hook by the door, took a seat, and pulled the tea tray toward her. "Where are the girls?"

"In the Nan Cave working on a project with enough snacks to keep them until lunch." Maggie set a plate of biscuits on the table. "Help yourself. I'll be right back."

"It's Matibi." Hanna smiled as Maggie peered at her over her shoulder. "I'd know the sound of that rattletrap anywhere. She probably brought the others with her."

"I hope so."

"And Maggie…"

Maggie paused with one foot in the hallway. She knew what was coming, but didn't want to belittle Hanna's efforts to keep them all safe. "Yes, Hanna?"

"Please, lock the door."

"I will," Maggie said just as a tall, black woman stepped into the hallway with Megan, Grace, and Kathleen hot on her heels.

"Already done." Matibi took off her jacket and stepped past Maggie into the kitchen. The three other grandmothers followed her.

"There was a time when no one locked their doors, at least during the day," Kathleen said as she poured four more cups of tea. "My grandparents never did; they considered it inhospitable."

Megan shrugged and pulled a steaming cup toward her. "So much for the good old days." She took a sip and turned to smile at Maggie; her chubby cheeks were still pink from being outdoors and wisps of white hair surrounded her face like a halo. The tail end of her braid brushed the table. "Camomile," she said. "Good choice since I suspect we're going to need its calming properties from what little you told us over the phone."

"I can't believe the nerve of that woman." Grace slammed her mug on the table, and Maggie winced; she should have known better than to use the good china when emotions were running high. "Hasn't she caused your family enough pain with her blathering?"

"It's not Alice's fault."

Kathleen placed her fingers on Grace's wrist and guided the mug gently back to the table. "We know that, Maggie. None of us ever blamed her for what happened. It's just that we weren't sad to see her gone. And now this." She lifted the top sheet from the pile sitting in the middle of the table. "I assume this is her latest effort."

Maggie shrugged. "I'm not certain that Alice is entirely to blame for this one."

"What do you mean by that?" Grace scowled then stared down at the paper in front of her. "Are you saying this isn't her work?"

"No. I'm saying that there seems to be more than one voice involved here." Maggie avoided the confused frowns and muttered comments as she pulled the original plastic-clad document from the leather satchel hanging on the arm of her chair and laid it in front of her. "As foreseen in ages past," she read, "I deliver this to 'the barren mother of five cursed daughters.' Long have 'we' awaited you."

"Barren mother…five cursed daughters, that's harsh," Megan said into the silence that followed, then she shrugged as all eyes turned her way. "I'm just saying."

"You're right, Meg, it is harsh," Matibi indicated the original. "But if Maggie's right, those words could have come from someone who lived in much harsher times and thought the phrase quite appropriate." She held out her hand and Maggie passed her the folder. "We have a few pieces of vellum like this in our archives; this was made quite recently…within the past two hundred years."

"Well, that certainly narrows it down," Meg quipped.

Kathleen leaned forward. "So those could still be Alice's words."

"Of course, they could. The writer didn't necessarily have to be alive when the vellum was still a calf…"

"Eww." Meg wrinkled her nose. "You have such a way with words, Mat."

Matibi shrugged. "Maybe, but all I'm saying is that anyone who lived within the past two hundred years could have had a hand in writing this."

"So what does it mean," Megan asked, "if these aren't Alice's words? If she was just the messenger?"

"Then they belong to someone else in that da…" Dark brows narrowed above faded blue eyes as Grace drew a deep breath. "…in that family, and since Alice delivered them, we're right back where we started, with a mess of mumbo jumbo we need to figure out before it jumps up and smacks us in the face."

Maggie sighed and raised her head. "I know it's a lot to ask…"

"Now you stop right there, Margret O'Reilly." Grace looked sideways at Kathleen and kept her mug on the table. "We were at Jen's wedding. We know firsthand what Alice said and what happened afterward." She tapped the pile of papers with her free hand. "So we're well aware that this thing is a ticking time bomb no matter which of Jessie's ancestors wrote it down, and we're here to help you disarm it the best way we can."

"I might have put that a little differently," Hanna gave Grace a wry smile. "But Grace is right. You're family, Maggie: you and Jess and Kat and the girls and we'll do what we can to keep you…keep all of us…as safe as possible."

Megan nudged Maggie's arm and smiled. "What she said."

"So now that we're all on the same page"—Hanna held up her copy of Alice's gift— "how are Jessie and Kat dealing with this? It must have been quite a shock."

"It was…for all of us, but I told Jessie everything last night…about the wedding and her father's death and her birth. I don't think she'll ever forgive me for not telling her sooner, but she seems to understand that there's no getting away from what's written there."

Hanna nodded. "And Kaylyn?"

Maggie let her smile spread across her face. "Jessie chose her partner well. Kaylyn didn't even flinch, but then she's always had a high tolerance for the strange and the extraordinary."

Megan giggled. "She'd have to have that to be part of this family."

"Grandma Maggie." Cali rounded the door into the kitchen and stopped. She blinked twice then smiled. "Hello, grandmothers. I thought you weren't coming until this evening."

"Change of plans," Maggie quipped. "What can I do for you?"

"I've finished my part of the project, and the others are doing fine, so I thought I'd come and see if you needed any help."

"Thanks, Dear." Maggie waved her over, took the sheaf of paper from Cali's outstretched hand, and laid them on the table. "But we're fine here," she said with as much nonchalance as possible. "Why don't you go practice your penny whistle until lunch?"

"Okay. If you're certain." Cali's turned and her brow furrowed as her eyes caught on the page sitting in front of Meg. "I know what that is. It's written in quatrains…just like this." She pulled her assignment toward her, flipped to the third page, and laid it beside the paper in front of Meg. "It's a prophecy, isn't it?" She turned to stare at Maggie. "The lawyer gave it to Momjay, didn't she? That why she was so upset when she got home."

Maggie met those dark eyes and nodded. The child was too smart for her own good sometimes. "That's right."

"And we're here to decipher it," Megan said, "to take some of the burdens of Jess and Kaylyn."

Cali plopped down on the empty chair to Megan's right. "Then I want to help."

"Cali, I don't think…"

"No, Grandmother." Cali shook her head. "You gave me that project for a reason; now let me use what I learned."

Maggie glanced around the table. Each of these women had had a hand in Cali's education; they knew how intelligent she was. Maggie would find no support there. She shrugged. "If that's what you want."

Cali nodded and picked a page off the pile.

"I'll read it out loud," Matibi said, "It will help us focus."

Cali closed her eyes and listened as Grandmother Matibi's soft, almost musical voice washed over her. Misty images and snippets of information gleaned from hours of study danced through her head.

"And wait," Grace's harsh tones shattered the sudden silence. "Bloody hell. Wait for what?"

Cali opened her eyes and glanced around the table. From the stunned looks on all those familiar faces, no one had an answer to that question.

Kathleen patted Grace's hand. "Maybe if we start at the beginning, we'll have more of an idea of what that means when we get there."

"I think that would be best," Hanna said. "But before we go forward, can we all agree that this prophecy is a warning about some future catastrophe? It might make a difference in how we interpret the information."

Cali felt a chill run up her spine as heads nodded around the table. She'd already guessed from the first few lines that something bad was going to happen, but hearing it said out loud just seemed to drive it home.

"Sounds sensible to me," Kathleen said. "Especially, since phrases like 'before life falters' and 'flee to the forests' would certainly indicate some sort of disaster. So, with that in mind, how would we interpret the first lines 'A dragon's flame…"

"I know what that is, Grandmother."

"Cali, please…"

Cali turned toward Maggie, shoving her anger down as she saw the hopelessness in those moist, blue eyes. "I really do, Grandmother." She pulled her iPod from its case and turned it on; it was her pride and joy, a gift from Maggie on her sixteenth birthday, and she never went anywhere without it. She turned to Grandmother Matibi. "Do you remember the aurora borealis project you gave me last year?"

Matibi frowned for a moment, then her face lit up. "The dancing rainbows."

"And they're caused by solar flares." Cali pointed to the first line. "Dragon's flame. Spear of light."

"That's very good, Cali," Hanna smiled across the table. "But solar flares happen all the time. They're hardly catastrophic."

"Unless they're large enough to shut down every piece of technology on and above the earth."

Cali turned on her iPod. "Listen to this. In 1859, a powerful solar storm, also known as the Carrington Event, burnt out telegraph lines in North America and Europe. Since a solar flare creates an EMP or electromagnetic pulse, if a solar flare in the magnitude of the Carrington Event were to hit earth today, it would shut down all power grids, satellites, communications, transportation…even knock out the cooling systems on nuclear reactors." She looked up and met Grandmother Matibi's eyes. "And silence falls upon the earth."

"'The ancient wisdom seeks rebirth.' She's right, ladies," Matibi said. "Such an event would thrust us back into the dark ages for a very, very long time."

Chapter Five

Two hours later, Maggie stretched the kinks from her neck and left her seat along with the rest of the grandmothers to silently begin lunch preparations. They'd deciphered as much as they could from the information Cali had given them and their own eclectic reservoir of knowledge, but understanding what needed to be done and knowing how to do it were two different things and would require a lot more thought. Simply put, a huge solar flare was about to boot the world back into the Stone Age, and to avoid all of the inhuman drama that would follow, her family would need to get out of Dodge and learn to live hand-to-mouth like their ancestors did.

She stared down at slices of bread lying untouched in front of her. Obviously, Alice and her ilk thought such a transition was possible, and if her family wanted to survive, they'd need to find a way to make it so. Except that, safe place didn't exist right now, and even if it did, the skills they would need to survive there were the stuff of theory, myth, and weekend hobbies.

A hand on her shoulder brought Maggie back to the moment. "It's not a mistake, is it, Grandmother?" Cali said softly in her ear. "I'm going to have a new sister, aren't I?"

Maggie nodded and spread butter on the first slice of bread. "I know we all decided that our family was big enough, but the prophecy…"

"You really believe it's going to happen, don't you?"

Maggie started on the second slice of bread. Cali's breath was warm in her ear. "We all do, for reasons I'm sure you'll hear about…" *Right after Jessie tears a strip off me for jumping the gun.*

Cali's fingers tightened on Maggie's shoulder. "I wouldn't mind having another sister. Maybe she'll be the child of light the prophecy talked about."

"Maybe."

"Or maybe it's Wanda." Cali laughed. "But don't tell her I said that."

Maggie chuckled. Of all the strengths the girls had manifested over the years, their resilience and their ability to laugh even in the direst of circumstances were the ones she cherished the most. No matter what happened, her girls would find a way through it together; she was certain of that.

Cali dropped her hand and turned away. "The moms are back," she said, "I'll go get the others."

Maggie nodded and applied herself to her task with a vengeance. Megan moved in with a bowl of egg salad, and between the two of them, they finished the sandwiches, separated them onto two plates, and put them on the table.

"Okay. I know it was a lot to take in and everyone's trying to deal with that, but this silence is driving me crazy." Meg flopped onto a chair as Hanna set out the plates and cups.

"What do you want us to say?" Grace joined Meg at the table. "That everything is going to be just tikety-boo or that one of us has a secret retreat in the country where we can all hang out?"

"Of course not, but…"

"Well, it looks like Maggie's put you to work already?" Kaylyn stood beside Jessie just inside the kitchen door. A large, brown leather bag dangled from Jessie's right hand.

Like children with their hands caught in the cookie jar, every eye in the room turned toward the papers piled neatly on the counter beside the fridge. Megan giggled. "You have no idea."

"You've been gone a very long time."

"I know. I was with the grandmothers." Cali shut the Nan Cave door behind her and returned Billie's glare with a smile. "And I'm glad you managed not to come looking for me."

"But they weren't supposed to be here until lunch."

"I know, but…" Cali drew a deep breath and took a seat on the couch beside Jo and a scattering of hastily scribbled notes. Wanda and Billie took the chairs across from them.

"But what?" Wanda demanded as Cali continued to gather her thoughts.

"Okay." Cali ran her fingers through her bangs. Her sisters deserved to know what they'd be facing when they left this room.

"Okay, what?" Wanda slid to the edge of her seat. "Come on, Cal. You're making me nervous. What did you find out?"

"We're going to have a new sister."

Billie shook her head. "We already decided…"

"I know we did, Sprout." Cali shrugged. "But it can't be helped."

"But where will she sleep?" Jo glanced from Cali to Wanda and back again.

Cali met Wanda's eyes and saw the hint of panic quickly buried. Their goth sister had spent too many nights feeling unsafe in her own bed; she deserved a space of her own and a door that locked even if Grandma Maggie held the spare key. "I'll share with her."

Jo stared at Cali wide eye. "But you're the oldest…"

"So, I get to decide."

"Thanks, Cal. I really appreciate it." Wanda's dark lips twitched into a smile then her brow furrowed and her head tilted to the side. The image of an inquisitive crow flitted through Cali's mind. "You said it can't be helped. Why?"

Cali glanced at Jo's notes. "There's a reason Grandma Maggie wanted us to learn about people who can see the future."

"Like Nostradamus." Jo turned and pointed at the image of a stern-looking man wearing a squashed black hat and a long grey beard on her computer screen. "He wrote a whole lot of little four-line poems…"

"They're called quatrains," Wanda said.

"Yeah. That's right." Jo straightened in her seat and gave Wanda a grateful smile. "But they're like some kind of code or something, so no one is ever absolutely certain if they've got the meaning right."

"So, what does Maggie's project have to do with our new sister?" Wanda narrowed her eyes.

Cali took a deep breath. No sense beating around the bush. "Great-Aunt Alice, the woman who named Momjay as her heir, could see the future; she left Momjay a prophecy in her will. That's what the grandmothers and I have been working on. It talks about a fifth daughter."

"Barren mother of…" Billie's eyes widened, and she slapped her hand over her mouth.

Cali glared at her youngest sister. "You were snooping, weren't you? After you promised Momjay that you wouldn't do that anymore."

"And she didn't." Wanda pulled a familiar sheet from her study folder and passed it to Cali. "I found this on the floor under my computer after you left. I thought it was part of the project, so we worked on it for a while, but we didn't get very far."

"Yeah." Billie glared in Cali's direction. "We were waiting for Brainiac to come back and help us figure it out."

There was a lot of hurt behind those words. Cali swallowed her pride and shrugged apologetically. "I'm really sorry, Sprout. I shouldn't have accused you of snooping."

"Maybe not, but you didn't know about this." Wanda waved the offending paper in the air then narrowed her eyes in Billie's direction. "And we weren't going to bother you with it until tomorrow in case we came up with something more on our own." Her shoulders slumped. "We didn't realize that it was real."

Cali shrugged, "At least you've had a look at it, so it won't be a big surprise. There are a lot of things I still don't know, but Grandma Maggie said they'd explain everything after lunch…"

"Mmmm. Food." Billie rubbed her stomach.

Wanda laughed. "You just ate half a plate of biscuits."

"What can I say?" Billie shrugged. "I'm a growing girl."

"And on that note." Cali stood up and headed toward the door. "I'll race you to the kitchen."

"Sounds like the hordes are about to arrive." Kaylyn took her place at the table beside Maggie and squeezed the grandmother's hand. "I want to thank you." She looked up and smiled at each grandmother in turn. "…for what you've done. It'll make what comes next that much easier."

Maggie caught Jessie's eye and held it. "Are you going to tell the girls about Alice and her predictions?"

"I was hoping you'd do that, Grandmother…since you were actually there."

Maggie glanced up as Cali tumbled around the door frame and skidded to a halt. She took three long steps forward and turned just as Billie rounded the corner, the other two girls hot on her heels. "That wasn't fair," Billie said, "You had a head start."

"Girls." Maggie clapped her hands to get their attention. It was good to see them still smiling after what she was certain Cali had told them, but manners were important no matter what else was going on. "Come take your seats so we can begin."

"Mmmm. Egg salad," Billie said as she sat down between Jessie and Grace. "My favorite."

"I'd wager that anything edible is your favorite," Grace said with a broad smile.

Billie shook her head but returned the smile. "There're lots that I won't eat: like raw turtle eggs," she giggled. "Or mealy worms."

"Even if they're fried?"

"Eww. Grace." Megan wrinkled her nose. "What are you teaching the child?"

Grace winked at Billy. "Just some good, ole, army survival skills. You never know when they might come in handy."

Billie smiled up at the old woman in the tattered, blue beret. "Grandma Grace and I read a book about a boy who survived alone in the woods for almost two months with only a hatchet. He ate raw turtle eggs."

Megan cocked an eyebrow. "And fried worms?"

Billie giggled and shook her head. "That was a different book."

"I know that one…"

Maggie helped herself to another sandwich while her family diverted themselves with culinary excerpts from their favorite books…the stranger, the better. She didn't want to consider the prospect that this might be a useful exercise, that a plate of fried worms or sautéed ants might someday be the only thing between them and starvation, but the possibility was there along with the other frightening alternatives to complete annihilation that kept flitting through her head. *I'm too old for this.* She shook her head and muffled a self-deprecating laugh as Grace ruffled Billie's hair and Matibi raced Jo to the last sandwich. *And when has age ever stopped any of us.*

"You finished with that." Hanna stood at Maggie's elbow holding a stack of dirty plates in both hands. She chin-pointed toward Maggie's partially eaten sandwich.

Maggie stuffed the last bit of crust into her mouth and set her plate on the top of the pile. She looked over to where Kaylyn was loading the dishwasher with Wanda's help. She wondered whether they'd miss that little convenience when it was gone. "I'll put on the kettle." She stood up and pushed in her chair.

"Irish breakfast would be good," Hanna said over her shoulder. "I could use the pick-me-up."

Fifteen minutes later, Maggie, set the tea tray in the middle of a spotless table and took her seat. An expectant silence hovered around them.

Jessie cleared her throat as Kaylyn reached for her hand beneath the table. "I'm certain that you're all aware by now that Kat and I have agreed to add another daughter to our family. I hope you will come to understand why we did so without asking for your advice…"

"Cause Aunt Alice said…"

"Billie, hush." Wanda glared at her youngest sister then turned to face Jessie. "We found a copy of Aunt Alice's prophecy on the floor of the Nan Cave. We thought it was part of our project so we read it, and it mentions five daughters." She raised her dark eyebrows and shrugged. "I guess you must think that the prophecy has some val…val…"

"Validity."

Wanda turned her glare on Cali. "Thank you, Ms. Dictionary."

Cali grinned. "Glad to help."

"Whatever." Wanda turned her attention back to Jessie. "…and that makes you believe that you had no choice in the matter, but even though we didn't understand most of it, that prophecy said some pretty scary things." Wanda's lips quivered, and she took a deep breath to steady herself. "I know it was your aunt who gave it to you, but I'd like to know why you think it's real. A lot of prophecies…"

"I've got this."

Wanda turned at the sound of Maggie's voice. Jessie tightened her fingers on her partner's hand and nodded. "Thank you, Grandmother."

Maggie had hoped to spare her granddaughters her own pain, but the question had been asked and needed to be answered for them to go forward together. She spoke of the grandmothers as young women not much older than Cali, Alice's inclusion in and ultimate disappearance from their study group, and the years that passed before the ill-fated reunion.

Jessie watched the faces of her children as Maggie talked. Cali's eyes glowed at Maggie's description of the friendship that had grown between the grandmothers over the years until they became more family than friends; her eldest daughter had always considered herself lucky to have so many elders in her life. Descriptions of Alice's sudden reappearance in their lives and her nephew's proposal to Maggie's daughter followed, then Maggie took a shaky breath and reached for her tea.

Kathleen touched Maggie's arm. "May I?" Maggie nodded and Kathleen folded her hands on the table. No one, not even Billie, made a sound. "I was a guest at the wedding of Jessie's parents." She made an elegant gesture toward the grandmothers. "We all were. We were there when Alice stood up during the meal and made two predictions: one of them was very sad, but the other one was very happy." She smiled at Jessie. "Both of those predictions came to pass, and that's why all of the adults around this table believe in the validity of Alice's message to us."

"But what happened?" Billie demanded.

"It's not necessary that you know that, Little One," Kathleen said kindly. "It happened a long time ago."

"I'm not little," Billie slouched back against her chair and narrowed her eyes. Jessica held her breath waiting for the storm to break.

"Aw, don't mind Kathleen," Grace said. "She still calls Jessie 'Little One' at times."

Billie's eyes flew open. "Really?"

"If I'm lying…"

"…you're frying." Billie giggled.

Jessie exhaled and smiled at Grace over Billie's head. She retrieved the brown bag and deposited it on the table with a loud thump ensuring that the divert and distract maneuver was complete. Cali and Wanda both noted Billie's reaction to the sound then exchanged a knowing glance. "This is what Kaylyn and I picked up at the lawyer's office this morning…"

Jo leaned forward in her chair. "What's in it?"

"A box." Kaylyn steadied the bag as Jessie reached inside and pulled out a heavily carved wooden cube about the length of her forearm.

"And before you ask," Jessie said as she turned the lock toward the middle of the table. "The key didn't come with it."

"And why is that?" Grace demanded. Then she waved a dismissive hand. "Let me guess. There's another hoop we have to jump through…some kind of twisted treasure hunt."

"It's not a very sturdy lock." Megan shrugged as all eyes turned her way. "I'm just saying."

Hanna frowned at Meg then returned her attention to Jessie. The tension in the room was almost palpable. "Did the lawyer tell you why it couldn't be opened at this point in time?"

Jessica winced as Kaylyn cleared her throat. They weren't going to like the answer. "First of all," Kaylyn began as she glanced around the table, "We are not going to pry this box open. No matter what your feelings are toward Alice, she was Jessie's great-aunt, and it would be disrespectful." Whether it was her tone, the fierce light in her eyes, or her words, everyone, even Billie, seemed to get the message. Jessie felt an overwhelming sense of love and gratitude at that moment. "Why Alice decided to do things this way is beyond me," Kaylyn continued, "But she had her reasons, and Jess and I need your support to see this through to the end."

"Of course, we support you." Grace's gravelly voice held an edge of contrition. Heads nodded around the table. "So, what's our next step?"

"Tomorrow our family welcomes our newest addition. Her name's Trin, and she's six years old. The next day, we're going to find the key that will open this box. Sara has a map to its location…"

"I'll be here tomorrow," Grace said as she shrugged her arms into the long, navy coat Billie held up for her. "But I'm not certain I can make it on Saturday unless I can find someone to take my shift at the soup kitchen."

"But you have to come, Grandmother."

Billie stepped back as Grace turned toward her. "I'll do my best, Sprout," the old woman said, "But I don't want you making a fuss if I can't. You're much too grownup for that. Right."

Billie took a deep breath and her face scrunched up for a moment then, with great effort, she nodded.

Kaylyn muffled a smile behind her hand. "So, we'll see you tomorrow, Grandmother." She wrapped her arm around Billie's shoulder and felt the sturdy body relax against her.

"I'll be here with bells on," Grace said eliciting a giggle from Billie as she disappeared into the night.

One by one, the other grandmothers followed Grace. "I just love treasure hunts," Matibi said as she pulled the door behind her. "Wouldn't miss it for the world."

"As if we didn't know that," Maggie said as she turned the lock.

Cali giggled. "Do you think she'll wear a brown fedora on Saturday?"

"Oh, I wonder if she has a whip."

"Okay, Wanda…Cali, that's enough." Kaylyn gave them her not-so-stern glare and motioned everyone back into the kitchen. "I know it's been a long day," she said. "But we have some house things we need to talk about, and they can't wait until tomorrow."

"Can we have a snack first?" Billie flopped into a chair. "I'm famished."

"Why don't I dig out some of those cookies someone snuck into the cart last night," Maggie stared at Jo who would live on nothing but sweets if she could.

Their third child dropped her eyes to the table before Maggie could see her smile. "They go really good with milk."

Maggie huffed and threw up her hands. "Cookies and milk it is then."

"Thank you, Grandmother," Kaylyn said then turned her attention back to the table. "I'm really proud of all of you," she said as all eyes turned toward her. "I know it's been a little scary…"

"…a lot…" Jo pushed her shoulders up around her ears. "…a lot scary."

Jessie covered Jo's hand with her own. "I know what you mean."

Jo raised her head. "Are you scared too?"

"Of course, I am, but we can't let the fear stop us from doing what we need to do. Right?"

Jo sat up straight. "I'll try, but…"

"And I'll help you." Wanda wiggled her eyebrows.

"We'll help each other." Kaylyn smiled. "Just like we always do. And with that in mind, we need to make your new sister—"

"Trin," Billie interjected.

Kaylyn nodded. "We need to make Trin feel welcome. So how do we do that?"

"We've already talked about this a little bit," Cali said. "And if it's okay, she can share my room."

Kaylyn met Jessie's eyes and shared her relief. They'd talked about this all the way home and hadn't come up with a solution that would keep everyone happy. They'd never even considered putting an eight-year-old in with their soon–to-be adult daughter. "You're certain that's what you want?" Kaylyn said.

Cali nodded. "There's enough room for another bed, and it's not like I spend much time there." She smiled. "It'll be fine."

"Thank you," Jessie said wholeheartedly. "You've just taken a huge weight off of our shoulders."

"That doesn't solve the bed problem, however." Maggie put a pitcher of milk and a plate of cookies on the table.

"I'll get the mugs," Wanda said.

Maggie nodded her thanks and eased herself into a chair. "She'll also need somewhere to store her clothes. So, what I propose is a shopping trip."

Jessie frowned. "It's almost ten o'clock."

"This is the twenty-first century, love," Kaylyn grinned. "You can buy anything in Winnipeg at any time, if you know where to look."

Jessie groaned and shook her head. "I've got to get out of the office more often."

Chapter Six

"She's so tiny," Grace said as Andy and Trin approached the house, "like a little elf."

"Grandmother!" Jessie protested.

"I didn't mean anything by it, Jess."

Jessie took a deep breath. "I know you didn't, Grandmother. It's just that I'm so worried that we won't find a way to help her heal. And with all this other stuff going on…"

Grace's hand came to rest on Jessie's shoulder. "We'll find a way. Now take a deep breath and smile."

"That's it, Trin," Andy said, as they struggled up the steps to the porch. "We're almost there."

Trin looked up and met Jessie's eyes. That one glance spoke louder than words. "Welcome to your forever home, Trin."

"Ho…mmmm."

"That's right, Trin," Andy said with a broad smile. "Home."

"Here let me help you with those. I'm Grace by the way." The grandmother took the reusable shopping bags from Andy so she could help Trin out of her coat. "Jess…" Jessie blinked as Grace cleared her throat. "Kaylyn and the girls are waiting for the two of you in the kitchen."

Jessie held her hand out to her youngest daughter. Such incredible green eyes; perhaps Grace was right. Perhaps there was an elf child in there waiting to get out. "I bet you're hungry," she said as tiny fingers tightened around her own. Trin nodded.

"I knew it." Andy breathed from behind them as they entered the kitchen. "You can sit here."

"Ho…mmm." Trin said as she let go of Jessie's hand and limped toward the chair Billie indicated.

Jessie turned toward a beaming Andy. "I think she's going to be fine. Why don't we get Trin's stuff settled in her room while Kat and the girls introduce themselves? And then you can meet the grandmothers. They're all here today, including Grandmother Lee."

Andy glance over at the table where Wanda was putting a plate of cookies in front of Maggie and Cali was pouring milk into Trin's glass. "You know, that's only the second time I've her Trin speak. The first time was at the hospital when they were putting the casts on her legs, and she told them to stop."

"And I take it that no one listened to her."

"Well, how could they? She had breaks in three…" The defensiveness left Andy's tone. "I see what you're getting at."

"Well, we'll be sure to listen to her. Now come on." Jessie picked up one of Trin's bags; Andy took the other and followed Jessie up the stairs. "We worked half the night to fix up her room, and I'd like to get her stuff put away before she sees it."

"Home," Andy said as she stuck her head in the door Jessie indicated. "This is beautiful, Jess. She's going to love it."

"Kat and Cali and Billie bought the bed and dresser last night. Wanda and I put it together and JoJo and Maggie made the finishing touches. The quilt is the first one Maggie ever made, and the posters and the stuffed dragon are from Jo's stash."

Andy raised a bronze eyebrow. "Jo has a stash?"

Jessie smiled. "What can I say? She's a collector…like Maggie."

"So, who sleeps in the other bed?"

"Cali." Jessie dumped one of Trin's bags on the smaller bed and held up a pair of green pants with holes in the knees; she tossed them on the floor. "It was her idea."

Andy watched as a faded red t-shirt joined the green pants. "What are you doing?"

"When was the last time someone bought this child new clothes?" Jessie pointed at the growing pile. "From the looks of it, I'd say never." She kicked the pile over by the wall and dusted off her hands. Andy was grinning at her when she raised her head. Jessie took a deep breath and smiled back. "We'll go through them tonight and see if she wants to keep anything for sentimental reasons. Then Kat and Maggie can take her shopping while I'm at work. I had to reschedule a lot of my appointments, and it's going to be a full day for me tomorrow."

Andy sank down on the edge of Trin's bed and cuddled the dragon to her chest. "I never really thanked you." She looked up, and there were tears in her eyes. "Every year, it gets harder to find foster homes for kids like Trin…let alone ones where they'll flourish. Sometimes, I just feel like giving up, and then people like you and Kat come along." She swiped at her eyes with the back of her hand. "So, thanks."

"You're welcome." Jessie dropped the last tattered shirt into the pile. There wasn't much else to say. She didn't know Andy very well outside of their professional relationship, but she knew a kind and caring heart when she saw one, the kind of heart that would fit right in with her family if that kind of friendship was allowed. "You were right," she said. "She's an amazing little girl."

Andy raised her head and smiled through her tears. "You really think so?"

"I do," Jessie smiled. "We'll take good care of her…"

"Momjay, are you up there? Easy, Trin, one step at a time. Momjay?"

"Come on up, girls." Jessie pointed to the door on her right. "Bathroom's in there," she said just loud enough for Andy to hear. The young social worker gave her a grateful nod and escaped the room just as Cali and Trin appeared on the threshold.

"And this is our room." Cali pointed toward the bed Andy had just vacated. "And that's where you'll sleep."

"Ho…mmm."

Cali raised her head and grinned in Jessie's direction as Trin let go of her hand and limped across the room. If she didn't know her oldest daughter so well, Jessie might have missed the hint of uneasiness buried behind that smile. She moved to her daughter's side and took the hand Trin had held. "If home is the only word she ever says," Jessie whispered, "then we will make the whole world feel like home…you and I and every member of this family." She gave Cali's hand a gentle squeeze as their eyes met. "We'll be her home."

Cali nodded. "No matter where we are."

Chapter Seven

In all her sixteen years, Wanda had never seen so many trees: tall ones, short ones, straight ones, crooked ones, grey, black, white, yellow, prickly green, and between each one, wiry bushes with grasping fingers or hidden thorns. They'd been following this overgrown trail for what seemed like a long time, though she knew it had only been moments, skirting deadfall and clumps of wild roses bare except for a few wizened rose hips and a smattering of dry leaves, hoping that their destination was just around the next bend.

She adjusted her pack to distribute the weight more evenly on her shoulders and barely missed the low-lying branch coming straight at her head. When Momjay asked her to carry the box, she'd accepted the responsibility without a second thought never suspecting how heavy that extra weight would become.

"I think we've lost the others," Cali said from close behind her. Her older sister's voice was tight with worry. "Maybe we should ask Ms. Klein to slow down. This is an awfully long hike for people who aren't used to it. Who knows what might've happened?"

Wanda started to turn her head then thought better of it. "They'd blow their whistles if they were in serious trouble."

"Yeah. I suppose. It's just that this place makes me feel...I don't know." Cali huffed out a breath. "Like it's watching me."

"It just makes me feel claustrophobic."

"Maybe that's it." Cali glanced over her shoulder and shivered. "Do you think we'll ever get used to it?"

Wanda shrugged. "When the time comes, we won't have much choice, will we?"

Jo clutched Billie's shoulder and closed her eyes as they approached the path leading into the trees. "Just hold on tight," Billie said. "I'll get you through this."

"Thanks, Billie. I thought I could handle being in the woods again, but..."

"Hey, nothin' wrong with being afraid. Now we're going to start with our right foot," Billie snickered, "as soon as Grandma Meg zips up her pants. You ready?"

"As I'll ever be."

"Well, that's some treasure chest." Grace stood in the middle of the narrow opening into a large, sun-swept meadow, both fists couched firmly on her hips.

Cali peered over her shoulder. "What are they, Grandmother?"

"Quonset huts or quonsies as we used to call them when I was a recruit. Spent a lot of time in one of those." Grace took a step into the clearing as Sara brushed past her. The lawyer looked like an aging model for a soldier of fortune catalog in her camouflage fatigues. "Is this Alice's doing?" Grace demanded. "Is this key we're looking for inside one of those or is this just another diversion like the box?"

Sara turned toward Grace and cocked her head to the side. "You never did care for Alice, did you, Ms. Long?"

Graced sighed and shook her head. "Never cared for the games she played."

"What's the holdup, Grace?" Maggie pushed her way past the bottleneck and looked around. "And where are those two…" Her eyes followed Cali and Wanda's trajectory. "…going?"

"To find the treasure, I suppose," Grace readjusted her pack, took Maggie's hand, and started across the clearing at a quick march. Sara was already moving in the right direction. "Come on. Goodness only knows what they're going to find in there."

Maggie pulled her hand free. "You go ahead. I'll wait for the others…make sure everyone finds their way out."

"Good thinking." Grace gave Maggie a curt nod and continued on her way. If her stamina held out, she'd catch the girls before they found a way inside, then they'd have a nice long talk about responsible behavior in the middle of a frigging forest.

Maggie listened to the distant sound of twigs snapping, muffled curses, and the occasional words of encouragement as the remainder of their party followed the overgrown path toward the clearing. The entire inner circle had shown up bright and early this morning dressed in gum boots and hiking clothes and carrying bulging knapsacks; that meant seven grandmothers, two mothers, five daughters, and their guide, a total of fifteen people had started along this path, and ten of them were still back there looking for a way out. Maggie cleared her throat and put all the energy she could muster into her voice. "Billie! JoJo!" Young ears were the most likely to hear her. "Billie! JoJo! Trin! Can you hear me?"

"We hear you, Grandmother." The thrashing grew louder as one-by-one her family spilled into the clearing with Billie and JoJo bringing up the rear.

"My goodness," Hanna exclaimed as she pulled tiny twigs and dried leaves from her hair. "Grace warned me to keep my hat on. Guess I should have listened."

"How'd you get so far behind?" Maggie asked as Jess lifted Trin down from Kaylyn's back. They'd obviously taken turns carrying their youngest daughter and seemed none-the-worse-for-wear despite the extra effort. When she had a moment, she would be certain to thank Lee for keeping the family in such good shape over the years.

"That would be my fault." Megan blushed. Then she looked at Maggie and shrugged. "When you've gotta go, you've gotta go."

"Alright. Enough said." Maggie turned and pointed to the pair of silver buildings in the distance. "The others are waiting for us over there."

"We'll take Trin," Jo said as she boosted the little girl onto Billie's back. Trin giggled and wrapped her arms around her sister's neck.

Kaylyn nodded and Jessie took a deep breath. "If you're sure she's not too heavy."

Billie grinned. "She ain't heavy," she sang as she took a step forward. "She's my…"

"…sister," Jo held the last note as the three of them moved off across the clearing.

"It seems that the new addition to the family has made quite an impression." Grandmother Lee fell in beside Maggie as everyone followed the musical procession. "Do you think it'll weather the coming storm?"

Maggie gave a tentative nod. "We can only hope, can't we?" She glanced sideways and saw the diminutive grandmother's frown. Lee was a tai chi master, her teacher and one of the most astute people she knew; that look could only mean one thing. "Why? Do you think maybe it won't?"

"I'm not certain of anything right now," Lee said. "When Kathleen came to the dojo last night for her lesson, she brought me up to date and gave me a copy of Alice's gift to our granddaughter." She turned and pulled Maggie to a halt. "I read it to my zumu. She said that the fire dragon comes from the west; its breath can bring great pain upon the world, but zumu also said we must remember the cleansing power of fire. It will burn away the barriers to the sacred energies and allow us to rediscover our true nature…if we survive."

Maggie shivered. Lee's respect for her ninety-eight-year-old grandmother's wisdom would be endearing if the old woman's words didn't add yet another disturbing dimension to Alice's predictions. "I certainly hope those flames are metaphorical and I don't know much about sacred energies beyond what you've tried to teach me, but one thing I am certain of is that, if anyone can survive what's coming, it's us…you and me and every other member of our family." She took a deep breath and smiled. "So, I guess the answer to your question would have to be yes, the bonds between our children are strong enough to survive anything a dragon can throw at them because anything else would be unimaginable."

Lee took a step back and bowed her head. "It makes my heart glad to hear you say that." She smiled and nodded toward the cluster of people waiting impatiently for them to catch up. "We'd better get a move on before Matibi blows a gasket."

Maggie waved the others ahead then turned to follow. "I'm hoping that finding the key will give us some answers though I don't understand why we had to come all the way out here to find them." She let her eyes drift around the clearing to the forest beyond. "It is beautiful though. I wonder who owns it."

Lee chuckled. "I have my own theory about that." She lengthened her stride. "Let's see if I'm right."

Sara dropped the large, grey key into her vest pocket and nodded to Cali to open the first door. "You'll find the treasure you're looking for in the fire pit."

Cali blinked. "Fire pit?"

"Indentation in the concrete. Used for building fires." Sara pushed the door partway open and nodded Cali forward. "Go ahead. It's about fifteen steps from the door."

Cali peered inside the building. A small window set far above the door cast a patch of weak sunlight on a grey, concrete floor directly in front of her; the rest was shadows upon shadows. A circle of darker shadow about six feet in diameter showed the location of the fire pit. She took a step back, turned toward her family waiting expectantly behind her then shook her head in Sara's direction. "The box and the key belong to Momjay. She should go in first."

"You heard the girl." Grace nudged Jessie toward the door. "The sooner you get that box open, the sooner we can get on with the important stuff."

Cali reached into the outside pocket of her knapsack, pulled out her self-powered flashlight, and gave the crank a dozen turns. "It's pretty dark in there," She placed the flashlight in Jessie's hand. "You're going to need this."

"I'm coming in with you." Kaylyn moved to Jessie's side then turned and opened her mouth to address the family. Most of the grandmothers had spread out their emergency blankets and were sitting in a semicircle about ten feet away conserving their energy until it was needed. Trin sat with her head on Maggie's shoulder half-asleep. Wanda and JoJo hovered just out of Kaylyn's line-of-sight hoping to remain inconspicuous. Cali couldn't see Billie anywhere.

Before Kaylyn could open her mouth, Sara stomped forward. "I don't have all day, Ladies, and I can't leave until I can certify for my firm that the box has been opened and my duties have been discharged." She huffed out a deep breath. "So, will someone, please, go in…"

"Got it." Billie pushed past Sara and held the key out to Jessie.

Kaylyn closed her eyes and took two deep breaths. Billie's grin started to fade. "I know you meant well," Kaylyn said as she opened her eyes. "But what you did wasn't safe, Sprout. Abandoned buildings in the country can become home to any manner of wildlife and an angry raccoon or even a skunk can be just as vicious as Mr. Tully's dog."

Billie's face blanched; she still had the scar from poking her hand through Mr. Tully's fence.

"I'm sorry, Mom." Her lip quivered. "I just wanted to help."

"I know." Kaylyn opened her arms and Billie stepped into her embrace. "Just give yourself a count of ten next time to think about what you're doing. Okay."

"More like a count of thirty," Wanda said as she popped out from behind Kaylyn's back, hoisted the brown bag she'd been guarding since they left the city, and passed it to Jessie before anyone could respond. "Here you go, Momjay. Time to find out what's in the box."

Jessie hugged the box to her chest and waited for Kaylyn to spread her blanket on the ground facing the grandmothers. Their daughters filled in the spaces between them. The sound of a door closing was an unwelcome reminder that at least one of their number was impatient to leave.

She waited for her partner to sit down then handed her the box. "We'll do this together," she said as she lowered herself to Kaylyn's side. There was a rustle of Mylar on dead grass as she inserted the key and the lock popped open. When she looked up, the circle had shrunk to half its previous dimensions.

Kaylyn lifted the lid and peered inside. "Oh, my goodness. You're never going to believe this, Jess."

Billie leaned across Wanda. "What is it, Momkay?"

Kaylyn pulled out a slender sheath of paper and handed it to Jessie. "It's the deed…to this land. And it's in your name."

"Well, that takes care of that little problem," Grace chortled, "Now when we flee we'll know where we're going."

"And it's such a beautiful place." Maggie grinned at Lee. "You knew, didn't you? But how?"

"You must remember that Alice was my student for a time." Lee's dark eyes came to rest on the box. "Despite the burden she carried, I found no malice in her heart; she wouldn't have brought us all the way out here just to find that key. There had to be more to it than that; an opportunity to make amends perhaps."

JoJo cocked her head to the side. "I know what that means. This land is her way of saying sorry."

"You've got it, kid," Sara smiled at JoJo then took a knee beside Jessie. "There should be an envelope in that box addressed to me."

"You're right." Kaylyn pulled out a plain white envelope and handed it to Sara. "But that's not all. There's also one for Maggie…" She pulled out three more envelopes and shuffled through them. "One for Jess…and one for me." Kaylyn frowned at the final envelope. "But I didn't even know her."

"Not relevant where Alice is concerned." Sara smiled at Kaylyn then handed Jessie a pen and the contents of her envelope. "Read it then sign beside each ex. Basically, it says that you have received the box and its contents: one deed to six hundred and forty acres of forested land and four sealed envelopes addressed to Margret O'Reilly, Jessica Reed, Kaylyn Reed, and Sara Weiss." She pulled two large keys on a piece of string from her pocket. "And these. Don't forget to lock up before you leave."

Kaylyn said goodbye to Sara then tipped her letter back into the box; Maggie and Jessie followed suit.

"Aren't you going to read it, Momkay?" JoJo moved to Kaylyn's side. The youngster had leaves in her hair and a scratch on her chin.

Kaylyn pulled a clean wipe from her pocket, tore off the wrapper, and dabbed at the spot of blood. "Does that hurt?"

Jo shook her head.

"Good." The tiny square of cloth disappeared into Kaylyn's bag. "And to answer your question, no, I'd rather use this time to do some exploring."

Billie giggled and clapped her hands. "Can I come?"

"Me too." Wanda scooted closer. "Maybe I can find a new rock for my collection."

"I think a little exploring would be a great idea." Matibi's singsong voice drew everyone's attention. "We must check out those silver edifices…"

Grace laughed. "They're made of steel not silver and they're called quonsies."

"You're spoiling my fun, Gracey." Matibi glared at the older Grandmother. Kaylyn stifled a giggle as Grace pretended to cringe. "Now where was I?" Matibi tapped her finger on her chin. "Oh, yes. We need to find out what is in those buildings…or what isn't, so we have an idea of where to go from here." She grinned. "And because it will be fun."

"Well, I'm all for the fun part." Megan raised her hand. "Count me in."

"Alright then." Kaylyn closed her bag and stood up. "Let's break into two teams. JoJo, Wanda, Trin, Grandma Hanna, and Grandma Kate will come with me and Maggie and the rest of you can go with Matibi and Jess. Keep your eyes open for interlopers. We'll take the building on the right. Any objections?"

"Why can't we all go together?"

"If we had more time, Sprout, we would." Kaylyn tousled Billie's hair. "But we need to be back at the cars before dark. We wouldn't want anyone to get lost, would we?"

Billie shook her head, but the disappointment lingered in her eyes.

"Besides, there will be lots of time for exploring in the future." Kaylyn grinned. "Oodles and noodles of it. So many noodles that you'll never be hungry again."

Billie grinned back. "You promise?"

Kaylyn nodded. "I promise."

Maggie stirred the embers to life, placed a fresh log on the fire, and closed the screen.

"You're so lucky to still have a functioning fireplace," Megan said from the armchair to Maggie's right. "When we bought our house, Steve had the big fireplace in the living room bricked up. He said it was old and draughty and we'd probably end up burning the house down if we tried to use it." She gave Maggie a wry smile. "He was probably right."

"He was a smart man," Maggie said as she took a seat between Grace and Kathleen on the saggy, old couch. Matibi and Hanna had volunteered to help with dinner. Lee sat lotus style on a cushion beside the hearth.

Megan nodded. "That he was."

They sat in silence for a moment, watching the fire; each lost in her own thoughts. They'd gone through a lot together over the past forty odd years: marriages, births, deaths, good times and bad, but the last few days had been what Maggie considered the final test; the icing on a cake that never fell. These women weren't just her family by choice, they were also the bravest, smartest, and most compassionate people she'd ever known; if anyone could handle this crisis without being overwhelmed by it, they could…together.

"I've been thinking about what Sara said before she left us." Kathleen's soft voice pushed through the silence. "Despite all the heartbreak and deception it's taken to bring us to this point, I think Sara was right. I think that what Alice has given us is truly a gift…a gift of life."

Grace made a growling sound in the back of her throat. "Oh, yeah."

Kathleen nodded. "Just think about it for a moment. We've all heard the warnings about the effects of climate change on the food and water supply. We've even talked about it, but like most people, we've done nothing to prepare for a time when the wells run dry or the food runs out. Except for Maggie and Hanna, none of us even have a garden."

"So, what's your point?"

Kathleen smiled. "I think you know, but I'll say it anyway." She caught Grace's eye and held it. "How likely do you think it would be that we'd all be so completely involved in trying to avoid possible extinction by a rogue solar flare, if we didn't know, beyond a shadow of a doubt, that Alice could see the future?"

"I…" Grace blinked and shook her head. "You're right. As much as I'd like to believe that this is just a bad dream, I can't." She huffed. "So here we are, facing the end of the world as we know it with six hundred and forty acres of land, two empty quonsies, seven old ladies, two moms, and five children…"

Megan giggled. "It sounds like the lyrics to a country and western song."

Grace flung her hands up in the air. "Fine. Laugh if you want, but…"

"We need a plan," Lee said calmly. "And more people to fill in the gaps, people who are going to be able to live and work together under primitive conditions."

"How are we going to tell?" Meg shivered. "I don't even know if I'm one of those people."

Kathleen leaned over and placed her hand on Megan's knee. "You'd do anything for the people in this house right now, wouldn't you?"

"Of course, but…"

Kathleen gave the knee a pat then sat back. "Then you're one of those people."

Cali waited for Wanda to put the extra leaf in the table then gave her end a gentle nudge. Grandpa Jake and Grandpa Zeke were joining them for supper and they always took up a lot of room.

"I'll get the placemats," Wanda said.

"And I'll get the hot pads." Cali opened the cupboard next to the stove and pulled out six, red calico rectangles neatly stuffed and quilted to protect the wooden table from the heat. She spread them around the table so the food would be within easy reach. Even when she was small and not yet willing to trust, she'd found comfort in these family dinners; at that time, she'd never seen so much food or heard so much laughter and no one had made her feel like she had no right to be there, that she was just a waste of space like her father always said she was.

"You alright, love."

Cali blinked at the hand on her shoulder…Kaylyn's hand.

"You looked like you were a thousand miles away," Kaylyn said as Cali looked up at her.

"I'm fine, Momkay. Just a little tired, I guess."

Kaylyn nodded. "Well, supper's just about ready and I think I heard the grandfathers come in, so why don't you go round everyone up and we can get started before the food gets cold."

"I'll come with you." Billie slid her hand into Cali's.

Cali smiled at the pile of utensils waiting to be distributed. "Nope. You need to stay here and finish your job before everyone ends up eating with their fingers."

Billie clenched her jaw and her eyes narrowed.

"And before you even think about having a tantrum, I want you to remember what we talked about." Cali looked over her shoulder to make certain Momkay couldn't hear her. "The grandmothers and our moms are going to need our help now more than ever before, so we're all going to have to do whatever they ask us to do without making a fuss. Okay?"

"But I..."

Cali cocked her head and frowned.

Billie reached for a handful of spoons. "Oh, alright. The sooner this gets done, the sooner we can eat I suppose."

"Good choice." Cali gave the younger girl a brief, tight hug. "See you in a few minutes."

Chapter Eight

"Where is everyone?" Jessie stretched her arms over her head and yawned as she entered the kitchen. The loose t-shirt and sweatpants she wore on Sundays had definitely seen better days.

"Here and gone already." Maggie spooned oatmeal into a bowl and set it on the table. "Kaylyn and Trin went for a walk to the park. But if you're looking for the older girls, they asked to use the Nan Cave for the day. Said they needed to work on a project. I suspect it has something to do with everything that's happened over the past few days."

Jessie dug a spoon out of the drawer and sat down at the table. "Should I be worried?"

"To tell you the truth, I'd be more worried if they weren't in there searching for answers." Maggie eased herself into a chair. "Maybe they'll be the ones to figure out how we're supposed to move forward with all this." She pushed the honey pot toward Jessie's end of the table. "Truth be told, they seem to be handling this a little better than the rest of us."

"Except for Kaylyn." Jessie downed a second spoonful of cereal then licked a drop of honey from the corner of her lips. Maggie caught the hint of confused regret in her granddaughter's tone and sat back to listen. "I've always loved to listen to her when she talked about the earth like it's a living, breathing entity, but I never took it as seriously as perhaps I should have…until last night."

"So the voices and the footsteps weren't in my head." Maggie gave the younger woman a lopsided smile. "Good to know."

"Shit…"

"Swear jar."

Jessie closed her eyes and sighed. "I forgot that our room is right above yours. I'm sorry, it's just that I've never heard Kat speak so passionately about her beliefs. It's like everything that's about to happen is some sort of a blessing in disguise…a way for humanity to reconnect with the earth and each other. As far as she's concerned, that section of forest and everything that our living there will entail is a dream come true. She's not afraid of the fact that the world as we know it may well disappear overnight or that we have no idea how to survive when that happens. She said that the forest will take care of us…" She drew a deep breath and continued before Maggie could speak. "…and then she proceeded to show me her proof."

Maggie watched as Jessie shoveled another spoonful of porridge into her mouth. She'd learned years ago that silence was often her best offense when this granddaughter had a story to tell and emotions were running high. Unlike Jessie, Maggie had lived long enough to appreciate those who still saw the earth as more than a means to fill their pockets or as a receptacle for their garbage, though she had never held on to any hope that those attitudes would change as long as there was a dollar to be made.

"Have you ever heard of 'forest bathing,' Grandmother?" Maggie shook her head as Jessie put her spoon down and wiped her mouth with a napkin. Some of the tension was gone from her voice. "The Japanese call it shinrin-yoku. It's part of their country's preventive health strategy."

"So they've done studies on it."

Jessie nodded. "Kaylyn showed me some of them last night. Apparently, spending time in the forest reduces stress, lowers blood pressure, boosts the immune system, frees up creativity and who knows what else." She shrugged. "And that's all great news, but I don't see it as a solution to our problem or proof that we'll be safe there. We're not going out there as weekend visitors. We're going to need to feed and protect ourselves in an environment that most of us know nothing about."

Maggie reached over and patted Jessie's hand. "You're right, but that doesn't mean that Kaylyn is wrong or that she doesn't realize the difficulties that lay ahead. She just wanted you to know that those difficulties aren't insurmountable as far as she's concerned. From what I can tell, she gave you a piece of scientific evidence…something she thought you might be able to come to terms with, but that isn't the whole picture, Jess. In her own way, your partner is a very spiritual person. That t-shirt she wears that says "The earth is my mother" is truly the foundation of her beliefs…"

"I know, but…" Jessie drew her hand away and let it fall to her lap. She sighed as she raised her head and met Maggie's eyes; there was sadness there and a struggling acceptance that gave the old woman hope for the future. "There is no but, is there? I should just be happy that at least one of us doesn't feel completely overwhelmed by this whole back to the wilds thing."

"A little faith can go a long way, especially when you're out of your depths and dry land is nowhere in sight." Maggie smiled and reached for Jessie's bowl. "Let me warm that up for you. Kaylyn should be back soon. Maybe the two of you can do something fun together this afternoon. Take a break from all the drama and go to that little coffee house you like. I'll keep an eye on the girls."

Jessie tilted her head as the corners of her mouth twitched upward. "Thanks, Gran. I owe you one."

Maggie grinned. "That you do, Love. One dollar…in the swear jar. Grandma needs new oven mitts."

"So, where do we start?" Cali let the question hover in the air between them for a count of five then fixed her eyes on Wanda. "Any ideas?"

"Seriously?" Dark eyebrows disappeared beneath a mat of jet-black hair. "It's Sunday, Cal. My brain doesn't even wake up until lunch on Sundays."

"But you agreed…" Cali saw the beginnings of a smile as Wanda lowered her head. "You're messing with me, aren't you?"

"Well, somebody has to if it will keep you from asking any more stupid questions." Wanda gave an exasperated sigh. "We all know that you already have this planned out in your head; it's what you do best. So just tell us what you need us to do and we'll do it." She raised her head and the smile became a grin. "And we promise not to be upset because you didn't make us feel included in that part of the decision making process. We don't have time for that today."

"But I…"

"What she said." JoJo pointed at Wanda as Cali turned toward her. Then she grinned. "Just don't make it a habit."

Cali closed her eyes and sighed. Involving everyone in the day-to-day decisions that kept their family running smoothly was something her mom seemed to do as naturally as breathing. It was a skill she hoped to master someday…but it wouldn't be today.

"Okay." She said as she raised her head. "We need to approach this like it's an actual research project and we're starting out at square one. Which means…"

"Brainstorming." Billie chortled. "Grandma Grace and I brainstormed my project on polar bears. She said every successful project starts out with a good brainstorming to shake out the cobwebs. It was fun." She hopped up and headed toward the back cupboard. "I'll get the paper and the markers."

Cali smiled. "Thanks, Sprout."

"So what's the working title of this project?" Wanda mused then she blinked and sat forward. "Maybe *The Bare Necessities*."

"Isn't that a song?"

Wanda nodded in Jo's direction. "It is, but I think it still applies. From the way everyone has been talking that's what we need to focus on…the things we need to keep us alive. Nothing more…and nothing less."

"Here's the stuff." Billie stood behind Wanda's chair. "Where do you want them?"

"Let's move the chairs over by the fireplace and we'll put the papers on the floor." Cali stood up and pulled her I Pod out of her bag as the others rearranged the furniture. A few minutes later they were all sitting on the floor around a large white sheet of poster paper.

Jo leaned over and wrote *The Bare Necessities* in the middle of the sheet in red marker then drew a circle around it. "I did a paper for Grandma Kate on human needs about a year ago," she said as she sat back, "There are a lot of theories, but the basic needs…the bare necessities…" She grinned at Wanda. "…are easy. You just need to think of things that you have to have so you stay healthy and you don't die."

Billie rubbed her stomach. "Like food."

Wanda drew a short line from the circle and handed the marker to Billie. "Go ahead and write it down."

Cali typed 'basic human needs' into her computer and chose the first web site. Ten minutes and three more websites later their diagram also included: air, water, food, shelter, clothing, sleep, reproduction, sanitation, medical care, protection, a sense of belonging, and opportunities for learning.

Billie sat with her chin propped on her fist while she followed the circle of words with the index finger of her other hand. "No internet." She looked at the iPod cradled in Cali's lap then raised her head. "What are we going to do without the internet?"

Cali looked up and shrugged. "I guess we'll need to take lots of books with us."

Wanda drew a short line and wrote books under 'opportunities for learning.' "The internet isn't the only thing we're going to have to do without."

Billie folded her arms across her chest. "What's that supposed to mean."

"It means no more hot showers or flush toilets or Friday night movies or trips to the grocery store…"

"That's enough, Jo." Cali glared across the circle.

"But it's true."

"No." Billie clenched her fists and her face turned as red as her hair. "It can't be true. It's not…" Her chest heaved and tears streamed down her cheeks. "I…I don't want…it to…be true."

Wanda wrapped her arm around Billie's shoulder and drew her close. "Neither do I kid. It's scary and I don't want to think about it, but you know what would be worse?"

Billie shook her head against Wanda's shoulder.

"If we don't do this, if we don't prepare ourselves, we end up out in the woods with nothing and no idea of what to do to keep ourselves alive…"

Billie raised her head her eyes filled with genuine tears. "We could die," she said softly.

"Yes, Sprout. We could die."

Jessie rolled her grandmother's cherished tea trolley into the family room and parked it just outside the circle of chairs. It had only taken a single phone call from Billie to Grace to rally the grandmothers for an impromptu gathering and for the past two hours they had listened respectfully while her girls explained the chart tacked to the wall and fielded questions and suggestions from the floor. Now it was time to regroup, digest the information they'd been given, and share their thoughts over a cup of calming tea.

"Well done, Girls," Maggie said as she gave the nod to Jessie. "You've given us a lot to think about. What say we take a short break, give our old brains time to catch up." She winked at Billie. "I believe I saw a plate of double fudge cookies…"

Trin popped her head out from behind Cali's chair. "Cook…ees."

Cali smiled down at her youngest sister while everyone else tried not to laugh. "I think you're right, Grandmother. Time for a break." She held out her hand. "Come on, Little One, let's go get you and Sprout a cookie."

Grace stood up and headed toward the door mumbling something about young bladders while Meg and Jake distributed mugs of tea around the circle. Jessie leaned over the back of Kaylyn's chair as her partner scrolled through various web sites on her iPad and transferred prices to a spreadsheet. "Why don't you take a break from that and have some tea?"

Kaylyn glanced over her shoulder. "The girls have done a wonderful job of keeping our needs to a bare minimum, Jess, but it still tallies up to tens of thousands of dollars that we don't have…" She glanced around the circle. "And after the stock market bottomed out the last time, I doubt that anyone else has it either."

"Then we'll have to get creative." Jessie realized how ridiculous that sounded as soon as the words were out of her mouth. She took a mug from Meg, pushed a chair aside, and wiggled through the gap to take her seat beside Kat. She held the mug out. "Here. Drink up. It'll help."

"I doubt that," Kaylyn said as she accepted the offering and took a sip. Jessie had never seen her partner look so utterly defeated by anything, even when she'd lost her government job to downsizing and accountants were a dime a dozen on the unemployment line.

"So, what are you going to tell them?" Jessie snagged her own cup and put it to her lips.

"The truth." Then her lips twitched into an almost smile. "Then we get creative."

"That's my girl."

"So, Kat," Maggie said loudly enough to draw everyone's attention. "What do you have for us?"

Jessie squeezed Kaylyn's knee as her partner took a deep breath and focused on her iPad. "Even with everything reduced to the bare bones, it's going to be costly." She brushed a stray wisp of dark hair from her cheek. "Just as an example, the least expensive bunk bed I could find that isn't likely to fall apart is about four hundred dollars. To buy sixteen of them…"

"We can't build a sustainable hunter/gatherer community with just sixteen people."

"What are you talking about Matibi?" Grace demanded. "We've already decided to extend an invitation to immediate family. We're just trying to get some numbers here."

The anthropologist scowled. "We'll try these numbers on for size. Fifty to sixty which is the optimum range of members for a cohesive and sustainable hunter/gather band; any less than that and there aren't enough hands to sustain the community especially if you add gardening to the mix." Matibi shook her head and looked away. "Which means that it will cost a minimum of twenty thousand dollars to provide beds for the numbers we're going to need if we're actually going to survive this. And that doesn't include the money for food for the first year or tools or…"

"I think we get the picture, Mat," Kathleen said softly. Jessie followed her eyes as she glanced toward the girls.

"It's okay, Grandma Kate," Cali said catching the grandmother's eye. "We already know that the most important things on that chart are the food and the woodstoves. If we have those, we can make do." She looked over at the other girls huddled on their chairs trying to look brave. "We've all slept on the floor before. We can do it again."

"Hell, yeah."

"Billie!"

"It's okay, Jo. I think we can let the swearing go this time." Maggie said. She squared her shoulders and looked around the circle. "We've certainly been given a lot to think about today and I'm going to suggest that we take the next few days to mull it over and see what shakes out. I'd also like to suggest that in the meantime, those of us, who have a family to talk to, do so before our next meeting. The more people we have on board from the beginning, the easier it'll be down the line. So, if there isn't anything else…"

"I'd like a copy of that spreadsheet that Kaylyn's been working on," Grace said as she stood up. "If that's possible."

Kaylyn pressed the print icon in the top left-hand corner of her page. "Already done, Grandmother. You can pick it up in the Nan Cave."

"I'll show you." Billie jumped up from her chair and followed the grandmother out the door.

"You know what, Love," Jessie said as the grandmothers did their usual round of hugs before leaving the room. "It's just a feeling, but despite everything, I believe you're right. I believe we're going to be okay out there."

Kaylyn gave her a lopsided grin. "Is that your gut talking or are you just trying to make me feel better?"

"A bit of both maybe." She took Kaylyn's hand and returned her grin. "I am the great-niece of a seer however, so it might behoove you to believe me."

"Behoove. Who talks like that anymore?" Kaylyn protested as she followed Jessie down the hall toward the kitchen.

Jessie grinned over her shoulder. "Our oldest daughter. You know, the one who treats the dictionary as leisure reading."

Billie leaned her elbows on the red, plastic tablecloth and cupped her chin in her hands; her eyes darted around the kitchen as though she was looking for a place to hide. Maggie rested her free hand on one bowed, flannel-clad shoulder as she set a glass of Billie's favorite juice on the table. She understood the reasoning behind Kaylyn and Jessie's decision to involve the girls in all discussions pertaining to the prophecy from the very start; each of the children had come from situations where they had been made to feel helpless and excluded and both Jess and Kaylyn had vowed that that would never happen again, but the past few hours had been difficult for all of them and even she was wondering exactly how much control they actually had over their future. "I made your favorites for supper," she said into Billie's ear, "Black bean and sweet potato soup with biscuits and chocolate pudding."

"With whipped cream?" Billie whispered back.

Maggie straightened and gave the shoulder a pat. At least the child still had her priorities straight. "Nice try, Sprout, but Momjay hasn't lifted the ban on spray foods since you and Jo decided to create your own game of paintball."

Billie giggled and removed her elbows from the table as the rest of the family took their seats.

"Before we eat, I have some things that I'd like to say." Jessie waited while Maggie turned down the heat under the soup and lowered herself to her chair; supper would have to wait. "I can't begin to tell you how proud I am to be part of this family. What you girls did was simply amazing and because of it we now have a direction and a goal."

"Ho...mmm." Maggie watched lips twitch into full-blown smiles all around the table and allowed herself to relax...just a little.

"Yes, Trin. We're going to make ourselves a home in the woods..." She smiled at Kaylyn. "And we're going to be happy and healthy and protected.

We're going to learn new skills and get to know new people…and we're going to have everything we need to create a good life for ourselves."

"But how?" Cali asked her eyes bright with a mixture of hope and disbelief.

"That's not important right now," Kaylyn said coming to Jessie's rescue. "What is important is that we all keep moving forward with this, and part of that process is learning the lay of the land."

JoJo frowned. "What's that mean?"

"It means we're going on a camping trip." Wanda smiled across the table. "Right, Momkay?"

Kaylyn nodded.

"First I heard of it," Maggie grumbled though she secretly thought it was an excellent diversion while the adults got their shit together and figured out a way to pay for everything.

"We could go tomorrow…" She looked pleadingly at Jessie who was trying not to look surprised. "…and be back in time for your first client on Wednesday."

Jessie shook her head and shrugged; her lips twitched into an almost smile. The girls drew a collective breath. "Sure. Why not?" She held up her hand before anyone could say anything. "But only if we bring some people along who actually know what they're doing."

Kaylyn frowned then the light bulb went off. The smile she gave Jessie was bright with love and gratitude. "I'll phone Cerdwin and see how many Earth Song members are willing to come on short notice." Kaylyn turned her attention back to the girls. "So who's up for some exploring?"

Maggie pushed her chair back to cheers and random comments about what they needed to take with them. She hadn't been on a camping trip since her camp cot finally gave up the ghost ten years ago. Old women weren't meant to sleep on the ground. She lifted the lid off the soup and gave it a stir then ladled it into the bowls lined up beside the stove.

"Let me help you with that, Maggie." Kaylyn reached for the first bowl.

"Nice save, Dear," Maggie said as she filled the second bowl.

Kaylyn shrugged. "I believe in Jess," she said softly, "Every part of her…including her gut."

Maggie smiled. "I think the feeling's mutual."

Chapter Nine

Kaylyn stood on the porch of the three-story, late Victorian-style manor house that had provided a studio, living space, and meeting space for the Earth Song Collective for almost forty years and waited for the door to open. Until she'd met Jess, this had been her home, her spiritual center and the only place where she'd actually felt that she belonged. She still came here during meeting nights sometimes, but it had been a long time since she'd picked up a paintbrush in the studio upstairs, bugged out on a weeklong wilderness camping trip, or spent an afternoon in the kitchen discussing environmental issues over tea. Sometimes she missed those moments more than she wanted to admit.

"Kaylyn?" The door squeaked open and a short, grey-haired woman with twinkling, blue eyes smiled up at her. "Come in. Come in. It's so good to see you." She stepped aside and waited for Kaylyn to enter. "What brings you out at this hour?"

Kaylyn hovered on the threshold. "I tried to call, but it just kept going to voice mail." She ran her fingers through her long, red hair surprised by how awkward this felt. *Shouldn't have missed the last two meetings.* "I know it's late, Tilly. But this is kind of a last-minute thing. And I could really use your help…if you're willing to give it."

"You're family, Kat. If we can help, we will. You know that." Tilly spun on her heels and started down the hall. "Greg was just putting on a fresh pot of tea. Go on in and I'll go up and get the others."

"But…" Kaylyn shrugged as she made her way past the stairs toward the grand, old kitchen behind the parlor. She hadn't intended to disturb the entire house, but she supposed that the more people who heard her story the first time around, the fewer times she'd have to repeat it. Whether they'd believe her or not was an entirely different matter. They might be the most open-minded, 'outside the box' thinkers she was ever likely to meet, but even she'd had a few moments of doubt when confronted with their new reality.

"You're just in time." Greg grinned as Kaylyn took a seat at the table; it was old and scarred, but it had served its purpose for many years and was an integral part of Earth Songs history. A lot of truths had been shared around this table; a lot of lives made better for the sharing. "Tea's ready and Mae baked oatmeal cookies this afternoon."

"Sounds good." Kaylyn leaned back and took a moment to look around as Greg covered the pot with a bright red cozy and set it and a loaded plate of cookies on the table. Except for a few updated appliances, this room hadn't changed since the day the collective had inherited the house from their founding member, and Tilly was put in charge of its preservation. There was a lot of Katlyn's history in this place: years of learning to trust that her life had a purpose, that she was part of something wonderful, something truly magical despite all evidence to the contrary.

"Kat. Good to see you. Sorry about the mess up with the phone. I was talking to my sister." Cerdwin shrugged. Her blue jeans and navy t-shirt showed evidence that she had been pulled away from her wheel and there was a smudge of clay on her pugged nose. The redhead took the seat beside Kaylyn and gave her knee a pat with a freshly washed hand. "Tilly says you need our help with something."

Kaylyn nodded. "I hope I didn't interrupt the process."

"Hell, no. I needed a break. Haven't thrown a perfect pot in days and it costs so much to get them fired that it's not worth my while unless I can be certain that they'll sell."

Cerdwin reached for a cookie as Tilly entered the kitchen with four other members in tow. Kaylyn recognized Chloe and Mae and Tilly's son, Mark, but the fourth member of the group was a stranger to her.

"That's Jenna Weiss," Cerdwin said nodding toward the tall blond standing by the door. "Apparently, her grandmother was one of the original five and wrote about this place in her journal. Jenna came by to check out the house, found us still here, and decided to stay after she talked to Tilly. Nice kid. Knows a lot about plants, including the wild ones."

Kaylyn smiled as Jenna approached. "That's more than I knew when I showed up at the door."

The young woman stopped and held out her hand. The scent of lavender filled the space between them. "You're Kat, right."

Kaylyn took the offered hand. "And you're Jenna. Welcome to Earth Song. I'm certain your grandmother would be proud that you're here."

"I never knew her, but I'd like to think so." Jenna took the seat to Kaylyn's left and reached for a mug. She looked to be the same age as Cali and was dressed in a similar style: blue jeans, a generic light blue t-shirt, and running shoes that had seen better days. "My mom gave me this before she died." She pulled a small, black notebook from her back pocket. "Said I should check it out if my dad didn't come back for me."

Not a runaway then. Kaylyn thanked Cerdwin as she poured tea for the three of them. She raised her mug and sniffed. "Camomile and…"

"…rose hips with a dash of lavender." Jenna smiled. "It's my special blend."

Kaylyn took a sip and nodded. "It's delicious."

Two pots of tea later, Kaylyn finished explaining the history of Jessie's family up to and including Maggie's promise never to reveal any of it to her granddaughter. "Now comes the really weird part," she said as she passed around copies of the prophecy including all of the notes Cali had made concerning their interpretation. "This was Alice's final gift to Jessie. Long story short, it predicts that a solar flare will cause a technological blackout of the world and send us back to the dark ages for a very, very long time."

She placed the deed to the land that Jessie had given her with her blessing in front of her and folded her hands around her mug giving everyone the time they needed to digest the information she'd given them. It felt good to know that Jess trusted her enough to let her run with this.

"I've been gathering information on solar flares from the net for the past few months," Greg's soft voice rippled through the lingering silence a few minutes later. All heads turned his way. He shrugged. "Earth Song has been tracking changes in the climate and preparing for the tipping point for years. But this could be just as devastating, at least in the short term, and with all the government hype about solar flares lately, I didn't think it would hurt to keep an eye on things."

Tilly looked down at her copy of the prophecy then raised her head and stared at the faces around her. "So you believe that we should pay attention to this prophecy…that it might have some validity." She said as her eyes came to rest on the man beside her. Kaylyn held her breath; Greg was a highly respected

Earth Song elder and his answer would hold a lot of weight with the other people around the table.

Greg turned to Kaylyn. "Before I answer that question, I'd like to hear why this was brought to us in the middle of the night…"

"It's hardly the middle of the night," Cerdwin scoffed.

"No. It's okay," Kaylyn wiped her sweaty palms on her jeans. "I understand that it's late and that this has been a bit overwhelming. I probably would have handled the whole thing better if I'd had the time…"

"You said you needed our help, Dear." Tilly smiled kindly across the table. "Let's go with that. Shall we?"

Kaylyn nodded and pushed the deed toward Greg. "Alice also left Jessie six hundred and forty acres of old forest." There was a loud intake of breath from around the table. Kaylyn smiled. "And when we flee to this forest, we'd like you to come with us. You have the attitude and a lot of the skills we're going to need out there if we're going to thrive and…" She cocked her head and her smile brightened. "…it will be a chance for me to have all of my family around me. As for why I had to do it this evening, I need some volunteers to join me and my girls on an impromptu camping trip to get the lay of the land and to keep them distracted while the adults figure out how to do what we need to do on a very limited budget." She drew a deep breath and sagged against the chair. It was out of her hands now.

"Then my answer is that we should seriously consider both requests," Greg gave Kaylyn a broad smile. "As for myself, I'd just like to say thank you to you and your partner for making an old man's dream come true." He glanced around the table. "I think that this is one of those times when the final decision on this opportunity we've been offered is going to have to be on an individual basis."

"I agree," Tilly said, "We've been working toward getting out of the city and onto the land for a long time, but now that the opportunity is finally here there may be some who have second thoughts." She frowned as Jenna prepared to say something. "I will set up a meeting for the end of the week." Jenna nodded and sagged back in her chair. "In the meantime, we'll need volunteers from the people around the table to join Kat and her girls…"

"I'll go," Jenna blurted. She gave Chloe a pleading look. "Jim said I did really well on our last trip to Riding Mountain. Didn't he, Chloe?"

The dark, heavyset woman nodded. "He was quite impressed and so was I." She smiled at Kaylyn. "I'd like to come too. It seems like ages since I last saw your girls."

Kaylyn tried not to grin. "Then you're in for some surprises."

"Count me in. What about you, Mark?" Cerdwin asked with a slight smirk, "I could probably talk Andrew into coming with us so you're not the only guy."

Mark tossed his long dark bangs out of the way of his equally dark eyes and scowled when his mother caught his attention and nodded. Kaylyn knew he was about the same age as Cali and probably longing for the day when he could make all of his own decisions. "Okay, but only if Andrew comes and we have our own tent."

Cerdwin smiled and nodded. "Of course."

"I'd love to come, but I have other commitments this week," Mae said. "Maybe next time."

"I'm afraid I'll need to bow out too…just this time," Greg said as he passed the deed back to Kaylyn. "And not without regret, but I have a gallery showing at the WAG on Wednesday and…well."

"Greg, that's wonderful."

The old man grinned. "Lots of dreams coming true this week."

Tilly squeezed Greg's hand. "Amen to that."

Chapter Ten

Grace parked her ancient VW in front of the real estate office on Monday morning, grabbed her shoulder bag, and clambered out onto the pavement. It was a point of pride with her that she made the exit seem effortless despite the twinge of pain in her hips and the weakness in her knees. She'd considered getting a new vehicle, one with slightly more ground clearance and wider doors, but she'd bought her little, blue beetle the day she'd earned her third chevron, had even named her Sarge to commemorate the occasion and hadn't been quite ready to give her up. She gave the hood a pat. "Guess that's a moot point now. Can't say that I mind that the decision's been taken out of my hands."

A young man with a take-out coffee in his hand stopped on the sidewalk and gave her a thumbs up. "Don't see many like that anymore." He grinned. "Best damn car ever made as far as my grandpa is concerned."

"He's not wrong." Grace returned his smile with a twinge of regret as he continued on his way. So many good people just going about their lives totally unaware of what the future had in store for them.

She gave the car another pat, squared her shoulders, and made her way inside. A young woman with frizzy, brown hair sat behind the reception desk reading a training manual. Grace ignored the twinge this time; she had a family to save. "I have an appointment with Terry Lawson," she said as the young woman looked up. "Names Grace Long."

The young woman nodded then pointed over her shoulder. "She said to send you back as soon as you arrived. Straight down that hallway. Third door on the left."

"Thanks," Grace took a step then paused. "Could you tell me where the ladies' room is?"

The young woman smiled. "We only have one washroom. Second door on your right."

Grace nodded her thanks and made her way down the hallway. The washroom was clean with plenty of tissues and soap that smelled like lavender; the smell followed her as she entered Terry's office.

"Grace. It's so good to see you again. It's been a long time." Terry stood up and walked around her desk. She tossed her long, silver braid over her shoulder and gestured toward the armchairs beside the window. "Let's sit over here. The light is better."

"Looks like you've done well for yourself." Grace relaxed into the cushioned seat and put her bag on the floor. Kaylyn's spreadsheet peeked out of the side pocket. Grace had spent a whole day going over the numbers, searching the internet for alternatives or inspiration, and finally, it had come to her. "I need to sell my house, Terry, and I need to sell it fast." She watched as Terry's eyes narrowed in concern. "And no, I'm not dying…not yet anyway…and I haven't taken up gambling."

"Good to know." Terry smiled and eased back in her chair. "We'll need to do a walk through before I can give you anything definite, but given its location, the number of bedrooms, and the fact that I can't imagine it being in anything but a pristine condition, I'd say you're looking at an asking price somewhere around two hundred and fifty thousand."

"Dollars…" Grace snapped her mouth closed and gave her head a shake. Of course, they were talking dollars. "That's ten times what I paid for it."

"That was forty years ago, Gracey. A lot has changed since then."

Grace was relieved to see Kathleen's bike parked outside their favorite greasy spoon as she pulled into the parking lot. Not only had she just agreed to put the only real home she'd ever had up for sale for a shitload of cash but she could also no longer ignore the niggling feelings of guilt that made themselves known at the most inopportune moments.

Kathleen looked up from the menu as Grace approached the table and smiled. She had the kindest eyes of anyone Grace had ever known; at times like this, it made it difficult for her to maintain her composure. "Hi, Katie. Hope I didn't keep you waiting."

"Just got here actually." Kathleen nodded at the chair across from her. "You going to sit down?"

Grace pulled out the chair as a glass of ice water and a bundle of utensils wrapped in a red napkin landed on the table in front of her. The young waitress took a step back as Grace glared over her shoulder. The youngster drew a deep breath then started her spiel. "Today's special is fried chicken with mashed or baked potatoes and coleslaw. The soup of the day is cheese and broccoli and our chocolate desserts are half price with a meal. Can I get you anything—"

"Coffee," Grace snapped. "Cream and sugar."

The youngster spun on her heels and disappeared into the kitchen. Kathleen folded her arms across her chest and sat back. "So, what's put the bee in your bonnet?"

Grace let out a long sigh and reached for her water. "Look around you, Katie. How many of these people do you think will still be alive two years from now?"

"Survivor's guilt."

"What?"

Kathleen raised her eyebrows at the tone. "You're the second person to say something like that in my presence in the past two days and I doubt you'll be the last." She took a sip of her tea; the cup rattled against the saucer as she put it down. "Since I'm the resident psychologist for our motley band, I've decided to call it survivor's guilt…sort of a pre-emptive strike. And all I can tell you is that it's only going to get worse unless we can reconcile ourselves to the fact that we can't save everyone, but we can save a few." She patted Grace's hand. "And we're going to do our very best to make that happen. Right?"

"Damn straight." Grace finished her water and plastered a smile on her face. "I'm selling my house, Katie. It goes on the market tomorrow for ten times what I paid for it; more than enough to get everything on the girls' list and then some."

Kathleen smiled at the news. "Grace, you never cease to amaze me. When did you come up with this idea?"

"About three o'clock this morning when the damn dog next door woke me up. I spent all yesterday evening skirting around the issue. I think a small part of me still didn't want to believe that this end of the world thing was really going to happen…and then that damn dog started barking…kinda like she was telling me to wake up and smell the coffee."

"Well, there was no dog involved in my epiphany," Kathleen grinned. "But it suddenly occurred to me that the bonds I had squirreled away for a rainy day…" She shrugged. "I cashed them in this morning. They weren't worth near as much as your house, but every little bit helps. Right?"

"We should tell the girls," Grace pulled out her phone. "Put a smile back on their faces. Poor little tykes."

Kathleen laughed. "Don't let Wanda hear you call her that; she might take offense. Besides, the girls aren't home right now."

Grace set the phone down and picked up her water. "Then I'll give them a call later."

"One coffee." The young waitress put a steaming mug carefully on the table and took a tentative step back. "Are you ready to order?"

"No thank you," Kathleen said before Grace could answer. "Just bring us the bill, please."

"I thought we were meeting for lunch." Grace watched as the young woman disappeared behind the swinging doors. Too late to call her back. Her stomach rumbled as she took a mouthful of coffee.

"We are. Just not here." Kathleen tossed a toonie on the table and stood up. "I talked to Maggie a couple of hours ago. The girls left on a camping trip first thing this morning with Jess and Kaylyn and some of the members of Earth Song."

"They're good people according to Kaylyn. Know what they're doing out there." Grace drained her mug and followed Kathleen to her feet making a concerted effort to keep her disappointment from her voice. She would have enjoyed a couple of days in the woods with her granddaughters, especially since their biggest problem at the moment had been taken care of.

"I'm glad you feel that way, since they've been asked to join us and, as far as I know, they've accepted." Kathleen walked toward the cash register.

Grace picked up her bag and followed. "They have a lot of skills that will be useful, so why not." Her stomach grumbled again. "So just where are we going for lunch."

"Our favorite diner."

"Huh?"

"Maggie's Kitchen."

"Hail. Hail. The gang's all here." Grace stopped in the doorway to the kitchen and grinned. Kathleen wasn't wrong; this truly was her favorite place to eat. "Do I smell Irish stew?"

"And rhubarb crumble." Megan patted the seat beside her. "Maggie says we're celebrating, but she won't tell us why."

Grace's brows came together as she took the offered seat. Kathleen must have told Maggie about the bonds; that would be enough of a reason to celebrate. She chuckled to herself as she surveyed the smiling faces. Wait until they heard her news.

"There you go, Gracey," Hanna said as she placed a steaming bowl on the table. "Help yourself to the biscuits. Matibi made them."

"Thanks," Grace pulled the bowl closer and drew in a deep breath of warm air redolent with the scent of mutton slow-cooked with potatoes, carrots, parsnips, and peas. Her stomach rumbled so loudly Meg heard it across the table.

"Dig in. Eat your fill." Maggie cocked an eyebrow in Grace's direction and took her seat as the last bowl hit the table. "Then we'll talk."

Grace didn't need any more encouragement: her news could wait until her stomach was taken care of and, apparently, so could Maggie's.

"This is delicious, Maggie." Lee said, "Well worth an afternoon away from the dojo even if I have to pay Gerald extra when I'm not there. But not for much longer. Kim Soo will be joining me next month…" She shrugged one shoulder. "At least until we close the doors for good."

"Is your granddaughter coming with us when that happens?" Hanna asked.

"She will come to the gathering this weekend; then she will decide."

Megan reached for a biscuit. "She has kids, doesn't she?"

"A girl and a boy…" Lee's lips pinched into a frown. "…and a husband who is a bully and would not be compatible."

"I guess that's why we've never met him," Meg said. Then she smiled. "Don't worry. If your granddaughter wants to come with us, we'll find a way to make that happen. It's not like her husband will be able to find her once we leave. Right?"

"We will see," Lee said as she raised her spoon.

"Let's leave dessert for later." Hanna rubbed her stomach. "I'm too full to eat anything else right now and I really want to know what we're celebrating."

"Agreed," Matibi said.

"Anyone not in agreement?" Maggie glanced around the table. No one spoke. "Alright then. As you all know, the rest of my household has taken an impromptu camping trip. Kaylyn thought it would be a good way to take the girls' minds off last night's meeting."

"Very wise," Kathleen said.

Maggie nodded. "But, according to Jessie, having the children otherwise occupied should give the rest of us time to do some brainstorming of our own and figure out how to pay for the things we'll need."

"I spent all night thinking about just that," Hanna said. "And I've come up with some ideas."

"Likewise," said Matibi. "It was hard not to after the brave front the children put on."

"Alright then…"

"You finally found that pot of gold at the end of the rainbow," Hanna narrowed her eyes. "That's what we're celebrating, right. Come on, Maggie spit it out."

"Not a pot of gold, but close to it." She turned to Kathleen. "Go ahead. Tell them."

"I think Grace should go first." Kathleen smiled across the table. "What she's done for the sake of all of us is truly phenomenal."

Grace felt the heat rise to her cheeks as everyone turned her way. Kathleen nodded and Grace cleared her throat. "I've put my house on the market. It should sell for at least a couple of hundred thousand."

"But you love that house," Megan blurted.

Grace shrugged. "I do." She caught Kathleen's eye stifling the rising feeling of guilt. Someone would buy that house, plan a life around it not realizing how short that life might be. One of the many they couldn't save. "But I love you guys more."

"I want to thank you, Gracey." Matibi raised her mug in salute, "All I could come up with was the few thousand in my savings account." She grinned. "I thought about selling my car…"

That brought a round of laughter from everyone at the table.

"I did sell my car…well Jim's car," Hanna said.

"You sold the Cruiser?"

"Yes, Meg, I sold the Cruiser; haven't driven it since Jim passed." Hanna propped her chin on her fist. "Got back more than we paid for it too, so I don't think he'd mind."

Maggie went to the drawer beside the fridge and pulled out a pen and a pad of paper. She handed the paper and pen to Hanna. "Write down what you're able to put into the pot, then we'll add it up. I'll get the dessert." She looked up and smiled. There were tears in her eyes. "Best, damn celebration ever."

Maggie scraped the bottom of her bowl and shoveled the last dregs of cream-soaked rhubarb crumble into her mouth. She was still having trouble believing the problem that had seemed so insurmountable less than twenty-four hours ago had been so easily solved.

"Three hundred and sixty-seven thousand dollars," Megan chortled, "Who would have thought that we're such an affluent bunch."

"Grapes come in bunches, Meg," Hanna said as she spooned a second helping of dessert into her bowl. "We're family. Something we'll need to keep firmly in mind going forward."

"Well, that shouldn't be too hard since we're going to be living together pretty soon…" Megan grinned. "…just like the good old days."

Hanna met Maggie's eyes over Megan's head and gave her a sad smile. Sharing a house when they were students had been fun and exciting for the most part, but they were much, much older now, more set in their ways. How long would it take for the lack of privacy alone to erode the bonds they'd formed over the years? Maggie sighed. "Meg, you do realize…"

"Saved by the bell, Mags." Hanna stood up and walked across the floor. "Someone's at the door. Be back in a sec."

Maggie groaned. "I completely forgot in all the excitement." She stood up and started gathering bowls. Meg leaped up to help her.

"Who's at the door, Maggie?" Grace demanded as she passed Megan her bowl.

"A friend of Kaylyn's from Earth Song…"

"Names Tilly…like the hat." A short woman with pewter grey hair, wearing jeans and a red, wool sweater stood on the threshold with Hanna at her side. "Sorry, I'm late."

"Not a problem." Maggie held out her hand. "Nice to see you again."

"Likewise." Tilly took the chair Maggie offered and looked around the table. "So you're the grandmothers Kaylyn has told us so much about."

"I'm Grandma Meg and this is…" Meg turned to her left.

"Grace…just Grace except to the children."

"And I'm Matibi."

Maggie waited for everyone to introduce themselves then brought a fresh pot of tea over to the table. Kathleen got clean mugs from the cupboard.

When the tea was poured, Maggie took her seat and turned toward Tilly. "Jessie told me that Kaylyn visited Earth Song last night: she said that Kat told you about the prophecy and the land Jessie's great-aunt left her."

"She did." Tilly set her mug on the table and straightened. "She also extended an invitation with Jessie's blessing, to the members of Earth Song. She asked us to join you when you move on to the land. I'm here today…" She glanced around the table. "…to ensure that that invitation meets with everyone's approval and that there aren't going to be any uncomfortable surprises going forward when it's too late to remedy the matter."

"That sounds wise," Kathleen tipped another helping of tea into her mug. "Kaylyn says that Earth Song has a very interesting history." She said with too much nonchalance. "Why don't we start with that?"

"Do you want the long or the short version?"

Kathleen raised an eyebrow in Tilly's direction. Maggie couldn't help but feel that the counselor knew something the rest of them didn't, but that only made sense. Kaylyn had spent a lot of time with Kathleen before she and Jess decided to become foster parents. Who knew what they'd talked about during those sessions? "The long version, of course," Kathleen said. "I believe it will be quite enlightening."

Tilly gave Kathleen a long look, sucked in a deep breath as the counselor smiled at her and nodded her assent. "Okay. Here goes."

Chairs creaked and teacups were refilled as everyone settled back, ready to listen. Maggie didn't know much more than most of them about Kaylyn's other family except that they were artists with a deep sense of connection to the earth.

"Our founder was a psychologist by trade, a self-professed pagan by choice, and one of the most brilliant minds I've ever known…" Tilly pushed her glasses up on her nose. "…and, believe me, I've known a few in my time. She was also an artist in her own right."

Tilly took a sip of tea and clutched the mug to her chest. "Helka and I met during a series of Arts Council workshops in the early eighties and, over a week's worth of free lunches, we learned that we shared many interests. At the end of that time, she invited me to attend a discussion group for like-minded people that she hosted in her home. It was from that group that the concept of Earth Song was born."

"It is amazing how a group of creative minds searching for answers to life's greatest questions can weave strands of knowledge, desire and conjecture into whole cloth. It started with a shared belief that the earth is our source and our sustenance…our progenitor so to speak…and worthy of our reverence and gradually evolved into a physical manifestation of our desire to further explore the gifts the earth has given us."

"Helka's family home was in the Wolsey area of Winnipeg, a neighborhood of aging hippies, new-age sycophants, and young families just trying to get by. It was the perfect location for a pagan artists' collective and we thrived there until gentrification crept in and the cost of living sent us scrambling for ways to make ends meet. The year the taxes tripled, a third of our members jumped ship for less uncertain climes while the rest of us struggled to come to terms with what we perceived to be the end of a dream, but not Helka. She resurrected bits and pieces of our earliest conversations; our acceptance of our true nature and our determination to someday be fully connected with this planet that we love and with them she laid a path for those who were courageous enough to walk it. For over a decade, we have tightened our belts, taken odd jobs to fill the coffers, and turned our creative minds and hands to learn the skills we will need to follow in the footsteps of our most ancient ancestors, to fully divest ourselves of the trappings of modern society, and become truly human in an inhumane world."

"Helka believed that the farther we strayed from what made us truly human, the more certain areas of the brain fell into disuse or were violently shut down. And before you ask, to be truly human means living in absolute harmony with the earth…the way our most ancient ancestors did before the ten percent of our brain that craves conflict and change for its own sake took over, before the connections were willfully broken and greed superseded compassion." She cleared her throat and looked down at her hands. "It was Helka's premise that the only way to access that unused portion of our brain and reconnect with our mother was to deliberately return to humanity's natural state."

"And you hope that by joining with us you will have the opportunity to prove her theory." Maggie finally understood why Kaylyn found it so difficult to share certain details of her beliefs with her more pragmatic partner or her children; the last thing Kat would want is for her girls to grow up as part of a scientifically motivated spiritual experiment.

Tilly nodded. "Over time…yes, but we're not quite there yet. There is still so much we need to learn before we take that final step backward."

"A psychological experiment with an anthropological bent." Matibi nodded. "I like it."

"So you continue to pursue your founder's wishes even now," Kathleen said, "I remember Kaylyn mentioning that Helka passed quite a few years ago."

"She did, but promises were made at her bedside and I intend to see that those promises are kept wherever possible." Tilly turned and gave Maggie a wry smile. "Kaylyn mentioned that you're just realizing how costly it can be to choose a simpler way of life…especially when you're trying to ensure that your basic needs are fulfilled every step along the way. We may be determined to follow in the footsteps of our ancestors, but we're not there yet, and ensuring that we remain alive and healthy until we can walk that path with confidence is of the utmost importance." She glanced around the table meeting every set of eyes on the way past. "That being said, should you still find our inclusion in this grand adventure to be acceptable after what you've heard here today, we will be able to help in regard to the funding. The Forest Fund is not huge, but it's big enough to cover some of the basics."

Hanna leaned forward. "Everything you just told us about the path your members have chosen to follow…Kaylyn knows all of it, right?"

"She does." Tilly raised her chin. "She's part of our family even though she no longer lives among us. She knows everything we know."

"But she doesn't know you're here."

Tilly shook her head. "Kaylyn grew up at Earth Song and, as far as I know, has never questioned our beliefs, but she can be naive at times." She smiled. "I wanted to make certain that this wasn't one of those times."

Maggie's lips twitched into a smile. "It seems that we all have our granddaughter's best interests at heart."

Chapter Eleven

"The camp is all set up." Kaylyn rested her hand on Jessie's shoulder and gave it a gentle squeeze. Cerdwin's insistence that they sleep in tents for the weekend hadn't been intended as a slight, but Jessie seemed to have taken it that way. She'd been sitting on the gentle rise in front of the second Quonset hut, her knees tucked up to her chin for almost an hour. The ring of large, grey keys dangled from the first finger of her right hand. "Cali's making tea. Why don't you come and have a cup with us?"

"They really are grotesque, aren't they?" Jessie dropped the keys in the grass. "Like soup cans, someone cut in half and stuck in the ground." She raised her head and smiled softly. "I don't want our girls to spend the rest of their lives living in a soup can. It just seems wrong somehow."

Kaylyn tried not to smile at the images Jessie's words brought to mind as she lowered herself to the ground. "Maybe it doesn't have to be forever, Jess, but I don't know how we can avoid it right now." She chin-pointed over her shoulder. "Those tents are fine in the warmer weather, but one good snowfall and splat…no more tent. And it's not like we have the money for anything else or the skills to create something different right now."

"Don't I know it?" Jessie sighed and took Kaylyn's hand. "Guess I should have listened more closely when you tried to share the things you believe in with me. Maybe I wouldn't feel so out of my depths right now." She shook herself and scrambled to her feet before Kaylyn could pursue that thought with her. She loved Jessie; had accepted right from the start that there were some things they would never see eye-to-eye on. She didn't know whether to feel happy or sad about Jessie's possible change of heart. "We should get back before someone…" Jessie squinted across the field. "…or five someones decide to find out what's going on."

Kaylyn glanced over her shoulder and grinned as their children moved relentlessly toward them. "You have to admit that our girls have great instincts…"

"…even if their timing leaves a lot to be desired."

"At least you're not pouting anymore," Kaylyn grinned then the smile disappeared as quickly as it had come. "Seriously, Jess, they don't need to know about the soup can thing. At least the quonsies are something they can depend on right now and they need that after yesterday's debacle."

"I know." Jessie bent and retrieved the ring of keys. "Let's go get some tea."

Kaylyn took a seat on the ground close to the fire and pulled Jessie down beside her as Cali poured tea into tin mugs and passed them around. It would be summer in a few short months, but there was still a winter chill in the air. She hunkered closer to the fire and felt the steaming liquid warm her to the core.

"You have no water source here," Cerdwin said into the silence. She drained her tin mug and hooked it onto her army surplus web-belt. Kaylyn saw the envy in Billie's eyes and tucked the information away for another time. "So I suggest that we spend the afternoon looking for a pond or a stream or even a swamp nearby."

"Yuck." JoJo suppressed a shiver. "I'm not drinking swamp water. There're all kinds of nasty things in there."

"You'll drink it if that's all that's available." Cerdwin smiled as Jo shook her head, horror and disbelief written all over her face. Kaylyn squeezed Jessie's knee as her partner appeared ready to intervene; they'd invited Cerdwin and the other members of Earth Song on this trip because they could teach them the things they needed to know to keep themselves safe. It would be unwise to interfere in that process now. "But not until it's boiled," Cerdwin raised her eyebrows at Jo. "And that goes for any other groundwater whether it's a stream, a pond, a puddle, or a lake. Bring the water to a rolling boil for one minute and your good to go."

"Unless it's full of polliwogs…" Mark ducked as Cerdwin made a swatting motion at his head. "I was just going to tell them about the filters." He fumbled in the bag beside him, pulled out a bundle of coffee filters, and passed them to

Jo. "If you strain your water through one of these before you boil it, then it will be cleaner than most bottled water."

"Even if it comes from a swamp?"

"Swamps are really special places actually," Mark grinned as Jo wrinkled her nose. "But yes, even if it comes from a swamp."

Jo nodded and held out the filters. She looked somewhat relieved; at least for the moment.

"You keep those," Mark said, "I have lots."

"Can I have some?" Billie asked as Jo tucked the bundle of filters into her pack.

"Trin…too." Kaylyn held her breath as Mark hesitated.

"Of course, you can." Cerdwin ruffled Trin's soft curls then raised her head to take in everyone around the fire. "As a matter of fact, you should all have one or two in your pack."

Jenna stood up from her seat beside Chloe. "Geoff gave me an extra package before we left the house. I'll go get them." She crossed the short distance to her tent and ducked inside.

"I'm going to be making supper while you're gone," Chloe said as they waited for Jenna to return. "So if anyone wants to stay behind…" She glanced at Trin nestled in Jessie's lap then looked away. "I could use some help gathering the ingredients for the pot."

Kaylyn bumped Jessie's shoulder, looked down at Trin then chin-pointed toward Chloe grateful for the older woman's foresight. Carrying their youngest daughter on their backs along a relatively clear path was one thing; trying to keep her safe while crawling over deadfall and navigating through thickets of thorn bushes was quite another. "That's your out," she whispered as understanding dawned in Jessie's eyes.

Jessie lowered her head so she could see Trin's face. "Chloe needs help finding the flowers to put in the soup and I'd really like to know how she does that," Jessie said just loudly enough for everyone to hear. "How about you?"

Trin narrowed her eyes in Chloe's direction.

"I can show you some of the plants you can eat so you'll never go hungry," the older woman said. "What do you say, Trin. Will you help me?"

Trin looked at Jessie then turned back to Chloe. The older woman gave her a broad smile; Trin returned it with one of her own. "Maa…k flow…er soup," she said and giggled.

"Are we really going to eat flowers for supper?" Billie asked as she fell into line with her sisters.

"I guess we are." Cali adjusted her pack so it rode firmly on her hips. Their legs made swishing sounds in the tall grass as they followed the others toward the trees. "Jenna pointed out some of the edible plants to me when we were gathering the wood. She said her mom taught her how to find them. They'd go to the riverbank and the parks on her mother's day off. She said that even when they had no money, they always had food." Cali pointed toward the stand of birch trees up ahead. "She said you can make flour from the inner bark of those trees…or from acorns. And you know those plants with the burrs."

"The ones that stick to your pant legs." Wanda scowled. "I hate those things."

"Maybe so." Cali grinned remembering the last time Wanda took a walk by the river. It had taken hours to get all of the hooks out of her tights. "But you can eat their roots…the same with dandelions."

"I wish I'd known that when my mom would use the food money for…other things," Jo said softly.

"Do you think Jenna…or Chloe…will teach us more about the plants," Billie drew a deep breath and her eyes grew distant. "Then if we can't afford to buy enough food to store away, we won't go hungry."

Wanda draped her arm across her little sister's shoulder as they ducked beneath a low hanging branch and the ground grew uneven. "Don't worry, Sprout. Momkay says we're all family now. So we're going to share the land with Chloe and the rest of the people from Earth Song and they're going to teach us everything they know about how to survive here because that's what real families do…they take care of each other."

JoJo giggled; there was a high, almost hysterical pitch to it. Jo had assured them that she would be fine on this trek through the forest, but given the way she was acting, Cali suspected that show of confidence was more bluster than reality. "Well listen to you, Ms. Goth, getting all philosophical." Jo skipped ahead as Wanda turned to glare at her. "You sound just like…"

Cali saw the twist of roots an instant before Jo went tumbling forward. She skidded across the carpet of pine needles, coming to a stop just inches from Andrew's heels. He turned and took a knee beside her. "That was quite a tumble," he said as Jo rolled over and sat up. Her jaw was clenched as she tried to avoid his eyes. "Are you alright?"

"I'm fine…thanks." She refused his hand as she struggled to her feet and brushed herself off. There was a hole in the knee of her borrowed jeans that hadn't been there before. She caught Wanda's eye and her shoulders slumped. "I should have been more careful."

Andrew smiled and looked around. "This is a very old forest; there's going to be lots of things to trip you up…or smack you in the face." He grabbed a nearby branch. "So keep your eyes open. Okay?"

Jo nodded.

"Good. Then we'd better catch up before we lose the others." Andrew turned and started down the trail, looking back once as he disappeared into the shadows.

Jo stared after him for a moment then fell into step beside Wanda. "I'm sorry. That was stupid of me, but I…I just…" She drew a deep breath as Wanda stared straight ahead. Her voice quivered. "I just don't trust any of this right now. I mean, we're frigging traipsing through a bloody forest looking for water that may or may not exist with people we don't even know, worrying about being hungry because some old woman predicted that the world is going to end." Her tone rose an octave. "And when that happens…"

"It's okay, Jo." Wanda pulled JoJo to a stop and drew her into a hug. "We're city girls. Traipsing through the woods and drinking swamp water aren't things we would ever have chosen to do and it's so damn scary that it twists your stomach into knots and makes you say and do stupid things just so you can not feel like a coward…even if just for a moment."

Billie took a step toward her sisters, nodding her agreement.

"Let Wanda handle this," Cali whispered. She placed a hand on Billie's shoulder, holding her in place as a sob shuddered through Jo's body. Sometimes JoJo was like Grandma Maggie's pressure cooker letting everything build up without talking about it until the lid blew off splattering everyone around her…often at the most inopportune times.

JoJo continued to sob, her face pressed against Wanda's shoulder. "Do you want to go back to camp?" Wanda rested her chin on Jo's hair. "I could take you back if that's what you want."

"No." JoJo took a step away and shook her head. She swiped her hand across her eyes and squared her shoulders. "That won't change anything or make any of this…" She moved her arm in a broad circle. "…go away. Will it?"

Wanda shook her head. "No. It won't."

Jo closed her eyes and took a deep breath. Her lips were a tight line of determination as she started down the path. Her fingers brushed against the hole in her jeans. "Then let's get on with it before we can't catch up. Then we'll really be lost and I'll have another thing on my conscience."

"We're not going to get lost." Billie slipped her hand into Cali's. "Are we?"

"Nope." Cali squeezed Billie's hand and pointed toward the woman stepping from the shadows. "Because she would never let that happen."

Kaylyn took a step then planted her feet as Billie came barreling toward her. She'd been watching them from the shadows since Andrew told had her what happened; giving them time to regroup before making her presence known. She knew JoJo was struggling, that the woods had been a scary place for her since her mother's death; that they remained the stuff of nightmares after all these years was something Kaylyn had come to regret. She could have shared her love of the wild places with all her daughters years ago, taken them into the backcountry to experience the beauty and power of nature, helped Jo come to terms with her fears, but she'd been determined to wait until they were old enough to truly appreciate the spiritual nature of the experience on their own terms. *And how did that work out for you…for them?*

"Momkay." Billie took a final step and launched herself into Kaylyn's arms. The impact sent them both backward into an immature birch tree. Dried leaves rustled overhead. "You found us."

Kaylyn smiled as the others approached. "Were you lost?"

"I don't think so." Cali shrugged. "JoJo fell and by the time we got that all sorted…well, everyone just seemed to disappear."

"And that must have been very scary." Kaylyn tucked Billie under her right arm and held her left hand out to JoJo. "Are you alright?"

Jo nodded and took a tentative step closer. "But I don't like it in here, Momkay. It's dark and cold and it seems like everywhere you turn something's reaching out for you, trying to grab you or trip you up." She reached out her hand until their fingers touched. "I'm sorry…"

"No. You have nothing to be sorry for." Kaylyn took the offered hand and drew JoJo into her other side. "You've been thrust into something you're not prepared for and that's not your fault. But I promise you…" She raised her head and forced a smile. "…all of you…that it will get better. You may never love the forest as I do…"

"You love this." Jo's tone was incredulous as she struggled to meet Kaylyn's eyes.

"Of course, she does." Wanda quirked a beringed eyebrow. "*Daughter of the Earth* ring any bells?"

"But that's just a t-shirt."

Kaylyn gave her middle daughter a squeeze. "No, Jo, it's not. I wear it to remind myself of who I am. I'm a daughter of the earth: we share the same energy…the same magic."

"Whoa, Momkay!" Wanda took a step forward. "That…is…sick. And I mean it in a good way," she hurried to add.

"It's what I believe," Kaylyn said softly, "But it's not the only reason that I love the forest. There's so much life here…so many things to see if you look hard enough." She pulled Jo closer. "But you don't have to take my word for it. Just give it some time."

"We really don't have any other choice, do we, since we'll be living here?"

"You're right, JoJo. We don't."

"And on that note…as Grandma Maggie would say." Cali stepped away from the oak tree she'd been leaning against. "It's probably a good time for us to get going…before we really do end up lost…and stranded in the middle of nowhere."

"We found it." Jenna bounced up and down on the balls of her feet. "We found it, Kat, and oh…my…goddess, it's beautiful. There're a lake and a tiny creek." She grinned at Jo. "And a swamp…but not a very big one. And there's a rise to put the tents on. Come on. It's not far."

Cali watched Jenna turn and bound away, her blond braid bouncing between her shoulder blades. "She must be part deer. It's like her feet just know where to go."

Kaylyn squeezed Cali's shoulder. "It might look like that, but I bet she's had her fair share of tumbles. Let's just stick to a fast walk, shall we."

Cali nodded and turned to follow Jenna. The trees grew thinner as they moved ahead and clumps of grasses and early wildflowers filled in the sunny patches in between.

"I can hear them," Billie said, brushing past Cali to take the lead. A moment later, they were standing on the edge of a small, slate-blue lake, and Mark was pressing a steaming mug into Jo's hand.

"Your swamp water, my lady." He smiled. "Filtered and boiled and steeped to perfection."

Cali held her breath, waiting for Jo to refuse the offering, but instead, she wrinkled her nose, brought the cup to her lips, and took a sip. "It tastes like…like a Christmas tree."

"It's good, right?" Andrew tilted his head to the side as Jo gave him a puzzled stare. "We make it from fir needles. It's easy…"

"…and it's good for what ails you." Jenna said as she came up behind Jo and gave her a nudge. "Lots of vitamin c and other good stuff. Just might save your life someday."

The look Jo gave Jenna made Cali's heart freeze in mid beat. She took a step forward, ready to intervene as Jo closed her eyes with a groan and her narrow chest rose and fell beneath her sky-blue t-shirt in the short, sharp pants that usually preceded a burst of temper. Then a hard-won smile twitched at the corners of her younger sister's lips. "Thank you," she said ignoring Jenna's presence to raise her cup to Andrew, "It really is quite lovely."

Wanda muffled a snort. "Any idea what just happened?" she whispered. "I was sure Jenna was a goner."

Cali shook her head as Jo followed Andrew toward the fire. "But whatever it was, I think Grandma Kate would call it a turning point. I'll talk to Jenna…"

"No. I'll do that," Kaylyn said coming up behind them. "Why don't you girls go get some of that tea?" She nodded toward Cerdwin as the redhead waved them over. Billie was already seated at her side munching on the apple Momjay had put in her pack that morning and sipping tea from her new tin mug; she looked quite at home at the moment.

Jo nodded to them as they took their seats then continued to poke at the fire with a long, smooth stick. Andrew sat quietly by her side.

"Not bad for city slickers," Cerdwin said as she passed them each a cup. "The first time Tilly took me into the woods, I turned tail and ran back to the car the minute she took her eyes off me. My hair kept getting caught in the overhanging branches and I swore that the trees were out to get me; I didn't want to have anything more to do with them."

Billie giggled. "That's just silly."

"Billie!"

"It's okay, Cali." Cerdwin patted Billie's knee. "It was silly. Why would the trees want to hurt me? I'd never done them any harm."

"So...how did you get over it?" Jo rested her chin on her knee. "...being afraid, I mean."

Cerdwin turned in Jo's direction. "I adopted a tree." She nodded as Jo narrowed her eyes. "It was an old oak that grew in Earth Song's back yard. When we got back from our trip, Tilly marched me right up to it and introduced me."

Billie giggled. "The tree had a name?"

"No, but it certainly had a presence and I could feel it right down to my toes." Cerdwin smiled. "I spent hours sitting under that tree after that: thinking about life, sharing its nuts with the squirrels, and sketching the patterns in its bark. It took me a while to realize how calm I felt when sitting under that tree...like everything was right with my world. It was then that I understood how much that tree had taught me."

Jo raised a skeptical eyebrow. "And you weren't afraid anymore?"

"I wouldn't say that. There's a big difference between one old tree and a forest full of them, but it allowed me to push that fear aside long enough to open myself to what the forest had to offer." Cerdwin's eyes grew distant. "The trees gave me the most amazing gift the day I finally screwed up the courage to walk among them; they made me feel at home and I'll never forget that moment for as long as I live."

"Can you teach me to love the forest as much as you and Momkay do?" Jo asked softly. "I don't want to be scared anymore."

Cali saw the slight nod Kaylyn gave the red-haired woman as their eyes met. Cerdwin smiled and gave Jo a wink. "I will certainly try my best...that's all I can promise."

"Thanks," Jo said and went back to poking the fire.

Kaylyn finished the last sip of her pine needle tea and tossed the dregs into the fire. It had been a long day and the heat of the fire was making her feel drowsy. Being forced to carry four liters of water through a mile of forest had certainly brought Cerdwin's concerns home to roost. *Maybe a well...*She stifled a laughed and cleared her throat. *Add it to the list of unaffordable necessities.*

Cerdwin glanced her way and smiled. "More tea?"

Kaylyn returned the smile and shook her head. "I'm good, thanks. I just…" She turned her gaze back toward the fire not wanting her long-time friend to see her guilt. "I just wanted to thank you…all of you…for what you did today. I really thought I still had time to share this part of my life with my girls…"

"Water under the bridge," Chloe said, "From what I've seen today, you've raised strong, compassionate children who aren't afraid of a little hard work; the rest will come with time."

"You really think so?" Kaylyn raised her head and saw the truth in the older woman's eyes. Chloe had been like a mother to her when she'd needed one the most; she knew that look of unveiled pride.

"I do. They pay homage to the source just by being who they are and you…and the other women in their lives…have taught them that." She glanced around the circle. "We've talked it over and if you agree, we'd like to join you in expanding their knowledge."

"I…I would like that…but it's not just my decision to make."

"I understand." Chloe nodded and glanced over her shoulder; the soft sound of singing came from the tent behind her. "We've decided to celebrate our good fortune tomorrow morning. We leave for the lake an hour before dawn. You're welcome to join us."

Kaylyn smiled her thanks and pulled her knees up to her chest as Jessie backed out of the six-person tent and zipped it shut. She smiled as she took a seat beside Kat and stretched her hands out toward the fire. "They're all dead to the world…including Cali," she said as she accepted a mug of tea from Mark.

"Fresh air and exercise will do it every time," Chloe chuckled.

Mark groaned. "Especially when the exercise includes lugging four liters of water along an overgrown game trail."

Kaylyn flexed her shoulders. "Can't argue with that."

"Which brings us back to the lack of water in this area and how invested the two of you are in using those Quonset huts as the primary means of shelter." Cerdwin raised her eyebrows and smiled. "Now that you know where the closest source of water is."

"If there was a better alternative…" Jessie sighed and shook her head. "But there isn't…not on our limited budget."

Cerdwin nodded thoughtfully then drained her mug. "Well, I'm for bed. See you all in the morning."

"What was that all about?" Jessie whispered as the others said their good nights and disappeared into their respective tents.

Kaylyn stared into the fire. "Maybe they don't want to live in a soup can any more than you do." She hugged Jessie's shoulder. "Besides, we have more immediate problems that need to be solved."

Jessie leaned into Kaylyn's embrace. "But not tonight," she said as her eyes drifted shut.

"No, love. Not tonight."

Chapter Twelve

Ghosts. That was the first thought that came to Jo's sleep-addled mind, but she knew it wasn't true. There was no such thing as ghosts. She huddled in the partially opened tent flap watching the pale, moonlit shadows float silently toward the trees; none of them seemed to notice the tiny child following in their wake. *Trin.*

She reached behind her and gave Billie's foot a hard shake. "Billie, wake up the moms; tell them Trin's gone into the woods." And with that, she was barreling toward the deer trail, fear riding on her shoulder like a well-trained falcon. If she moved fast enough, she should reach her littlest sister before she entered the trees, but Jo had never been fast, or strong…or courageous. "Trin! No!"

Jo's legs turned to mush and she fell to one knee as Trin disappeared into the shadows. A glance over her shoulder revealed nothing. There was no one behind her, no family to lend her their strength, no one else to keep Trin safe from the dangers hidden in the darkness…just like the night her mother died.

She struggled to her feet, trying to ignore the child huddled in the deepest shadows of her mind, screaming at her that nothing good lurked beneath those trees. Five years had passed since the night the men had come to her home looking for her father; finding her mother instead. Jo still remembered the sound of wood splintering as a gentle hand pressed against her lips silencing her questions. "In the closet and don't come out until I come for you." Jo had obeyed that voice even as muffled screams drifted through her window then faded away until there were only darkness and the faint ticking of the clock in the hallway downstairs. Ever the obedient daughter, she'd waited as she had been told too until a band of sunlight seeped beneath the door and she knew that to stay there any longer would be futile. She'd sucked back tears as she'd fumbled for shoes and a jacket, determined to find her mother or die trying, not understanding that the time to be brave had already passed her by. She'd known where she'd needed to go. The patch of forest behind their house had been her mother's private concert hall for as long as Jo could remember and the memory of a fiddle's plaintive cry had woven itself around her mother's screams drawing her forward, pulling her into the sun-dappled darkness until she'd stepped into a brighter clearing and found her mother's naked and lifeless body, tied to a tree, blood pooled at her feet. Grandma Maggie told her that a hiker had heard her screams, but Jo remembered nothing past the moment she'd realized that her mother had died while her only child had huddled in her closet like the coward she was.

Trin. With a final glance over her shoulder, Jo forced herself to her feet and ran. The canopy of branches rattled, showering her with the crumpled remains of last year's foliage as she fled the coward lurking beneath her heart. *Momjay loves the forest. Cerdwin talks to trees.* She drew those thoughts around her as she pressed forward, eyes straining in the grey speckled darkness. The ghosts had disappeared, but a tiny shadow that could only be her sister lingered in the middle of the trail, one arm outstretched. "Kit...tee."

"Trin. No!"

Greg made his way toward the kitchen stove and the pot of freshly perked coffee sitting on the back burner. "I didn't hear you come in last night," he said watching Tilly from the corner of his eye as he filled a heavy china mug.

"Maybe because I didn't want you to."

"That bad, eh?"

Tilly looked up from the paper she'd been staring at since he'd walked into the kitchen. "No. As a matter of fact, they were quite receptive to everything I said. They want their granddaughters, including Kaylyn, to have the best chance they can get to survive the prophecy and they see what we have to offer as important to that goal."

Greg nodded. "They'd be fools not to. So why so glum?"

Tilly let out a soft chuff of coffee-scented air then leaned back her eyes focused on a point above Greg's shoulder. They'd been friends for a long time and he recognized the signs; there was a battle going on inside of her and she wasn't certain what side she was on. "I've waited half my life for an opportunity like this, to leave this polluted world behind and become one with the source as humans are meant to be." A tear trickled down her cheek. "But I was never truly honest with myself. I always knew, in the back of my mind, that the world we were leaving behind would still be here in case we needed it along the way…in case the experiment failed."

Greg reached for her hand and drew it toward him. "That doesn't sound like the Tilly I know."

She dropped her eyes to their hands but made no move to pull away. "It wasn't me until Helka left us and I suddenly found myself forced into her shoes." She shook her head, still not looking him in the eye. "Don't get me wrong. I don't regret one moment of the past few years. And my faith is still strong. It's just…"

He felt her fingers go limp as if she'd somehow given up. "It's just what, Tilly?" He gave her hand a squeeze. "Come on. Talk to me."

"Damn it, Greg." She straightened and pulled her hand away. "Don't you understand? This isn't just about finding the source anymore. This is about survival, pure and simple, and we're going to be flying without a net."

Maggie woke to sunlight, and the faint scent of bacon wafted in from beneath the door. She smiled. Katie had said something about making breakfast this morning when she'd decided to keep Maggie company while the girls were away; apparently, she was intent on keeping that promise. Maggie glanced at the clock on the mantel then threw back the covers and sat up. It had been a long time since she'd slept in past seven o'clock and she didn't know whether to feel guilty or elated; either way, she was well-rested and that would be important over the days to come.

"Maggie, you up?"

"Yeah, I'm up, Kate. Come on in."

The door to the Nan Cave crept open and the smell of coffee preceded Katie into the room. "I know you usually have tea for breakfast, but I thought this might be a treat. And I fed Mouser the rest of the salmon. I hope you don't mind." She handed Maggie a steaming mug and took a seat on the pullout couch. "How did you sleep?"

"Like a baby. And you?"

"I've slept better."

Maggie took a sip of the dark, fragrant liquid and put the cup down. "And what's that mean."

Kathleen grinned. "Really, Maggie. Has no one ever told you how badly you snore when you're tired?"

Maggie shrugged and took another sip of her coffee. "Maybe a time or two." She tried to look contrite. "Sorry."

"Don't be." Kathleen drained her mug and set it on the table. "I doubt I would have slept much anyway after our conversation with Tilly." She waved her hand as Maggie open her mouth to respond. "Don't get me wrong. I have no problem with the members of Earth Song treating this as a spiritual quest, especially since it comes coupled with good, old fashion know-how. I might even be tempted to join them eventually."

Maggie laughed. "This from the quintessential atheist."

Kathleen nodded. "Remaining neutral isn't necessarily a bad thing, especially in my profession. You'd be surprised how many people blame their problems on God or some holy doctrine that requires them to act as they do. But that doesn't mean that I can't change my mind if I find something I can truly believe in." She shook her head and sighed. "That doesn't alter the fact we're going to be bringing people who have been preparing for this for a long time together with those of us…"

"…who know next to nothing about living anywhere except the city." Maggie nodded. "And you're wondering how we're going to pull all those people together…at least fifty including family if we follow Matibi's criteria for a stable community…and ensure that they're able to survive without automatically giving Tilly's crew the upper hand." She shrugged as Kathleen's mouth dropped open and the counselor nodded slowly. "Don't look so surprised. I've been having the same thoughts and I've come to the conclusion that we…as in you and I and the rest of the grandmothers…don't."

"Don't…what?"

"Have the final say in any of this when it comes right down to it." Maggie smiled as Kathleen's eyes narrowed in confusion. "This is Jessie's prophecy and by extension, it belongs to Kaylyn…and the girls."

"And you really believe that we should foist it all onto their shoulders."

Maggie sighed. "We're getting old, Kate."

"Now you sound like Grace."

"And she's not wrong…as much as we like to deny it." Maggie sighed and pulled a mauve envelope from under her pillow. "But you don't have to take my word for it."

A frown wrinkled Kathleen's brow. "Is that your letter from Alice?"

Maggie nodded. "With everything that's happened, I forgot all about it until I found the box under Billie's jacket when I was tidying up the mudroom yesterday morning." She pointed to the wooden case sitting on the corner of the desk. "Jessie's and Kaylyn's letters are still in there as well."

"I'm surprised none of the girls said anything considering how curious they were." Kathleen held out her hand. "May I?"

Maggie removed the letter from the envelope, smoothed out the creases, and passed the single page across the table. "Read it out loud, would you please...in case I missed anything."

The corners of Kathleen's lips twitched up. "Lost your glasses again, eh?" She cleared her throat, not waiting for an answer. "To Margaret Siobhan O'Reilly, Matriarch...Matriarch?"

Maggie shook her head as their eyes met. "This is Alice, remember."

"Right." Kathleen nodded then dropped her eyes to the letter. *"The world is about to change, Maggie,"* She read. *"In ways, we never foresaw in our generation's innocent belief that progress would be our salvation. We were wrong, as well our children will soon discover, and with that, discovery must come the understanding that they are the last, best hope for humankind. Though it will be difficult, my friend, you must not interfere in that process as those you love the most follow their future into the past. In the spirit of sisterhood, Alice."*

"As much as I hate to admit it, it sounds like good advice," Maggie said as Kathleen lowered the letter to her lap. "Maybe it is time to let the younger generation take the future into their own hands since none of us can guarantee that we'll be around long enough to see everyone settled into their new lives."

Kathleen closed her eyes for a moment then nodded. "It makes sense that whatever decisions are made should be made by those who will have to follow through with them when we're gone." Kathleen sighed. "I get that, but how are we going to convince our granddaughters that it's time for them to step forward? Because even with this..." She ran her fingers across the page. "...they're going to have their doubts. And frankly so do I, to an extent."

"So we don't show them the letter." Maggie gave the counselor a wry smile. "We do what we always do with the girls to build their confidence; we start with the small things and work our way up."

Kathleen frowned. "Do we have time for that?"

"We'll make time," Maggie sighed, "There's really no other option that I can see."

"Well, Ms. Matriarch…" Kathleen grinned as Maggie swatted at her. "Now that we've got that sorted for the time being, what would you say to my famous bacon and cheese omelet?"

Maggie took a last look at Alice's letter then shoved it under her pillow. "I'd say 'lead on McDuff.'"

"You realize that that's a misquote, right?"

Maggie grinned. "Tell that to my mother."

"Grandma Maggie, we're home."

Maggie stepped from the kitchen into the front hall just as Trin followed Billie through the outside door. Their youngest raised her head and grinned. "Ho…me."

"You're not going to believe it, Grandmother," Billie said as she slid her backpack to the floor. "But Trin made us flower soup and JoJo…"

"…conquered her fear of the forest." Kaylyn planted a kiss on Maggie's cheek as Jo followed her inside.

Jessie stood behind her middle daughter. "And almost gave me heart failure." Jo smiled sheepishly and ducked her head.

Maggie took a step back as her other granddaughters piled into the hall. Everyone seemed to have something important to say. "It sounds like you have a lot of stories to share. Why don't we continue this in the kitchen? I have a pot of stew on the stove…"

"I knew I smelled something." Billie took a step then turned and picked up her bag. "Wouldn't want someone to trip," she said as she slid past Maggie into the kitchen.

"Well that's new," Maggie raised a questioning eyebrow in Jessie's direction.

"Oh, you'd be amazed at the changes a couple of days living with five people in a four-person tent can make." Jessie turned toward the four girls standing behind her. "Why don't we all stow our packs in our rooms then we can tell Grandma Maggie everything that happened while we eat."

"Sounds good. I'm starving," Cali said as she took Trin's hand and headed toward the stairs. She and Wanda each gave Maggie a quick hug on the way by.

"And don't forget to wash your hands," Maggie called after them, "You're in the civilized territory now."

Maggie sprinkled dried cedar over the gently burning logs then took the seat beside Jessie on the couch. The girls had retired to their rooms without any fuss after the meal, talking about hot showers and soft beds like they'd been without those comforts for weeks not just a couple of days; she found that realization strangely disturbing as she pushed it away for another time. "That must have taken a lot of courage on JoJo's part…" she said as she leaned back against the cushions, "…following Trin into the woods by herself after what happened to her mother."

"I couldn't believe it myself until I found the two of them huddled in the middle of the trail. I thought maybe one of them was hurt until I got close enough to smell them." Jessie laughed. "Apparently, Trin wanted her own kitty. It's a good thing Chloe carries her skunk spray kit with her when she goes camping. It took a whole bottle of hydrogen peroxide and dish soap plus a full box of baking soda to get the smell off their bodies and their boots." She shrugged. "We ended up burying their clothes."

Maggie choked back a laugh. "No wonder Jo doesn't want to talk about it."

"I agree that the whole thing was quite the ordeal for her, but I shudder to think what could have happened if Jo hadn't gotten to Trin when she did." Kaylyn frowned and moisture pooled in the corners of her eyes. "I don't know what I would have done if either of them had been hurt since it was my fault…"

"You have to stop thinking that," Jessie said softly. "You couldn't have known that Trin would follow you."

Maggie frowned. "Follow you?"

"Cerdwin asked Kat to join them at the lake to greet the dawn," Jessie said, "And I was supposed to be back at the camp when the girls woke up, but I fell back to sleep, so actually, it was my fault…"

"Stop it, both of you." Maggie huffed as they turned to face her. Non-interference be damned. "Playing the blame game isn't helpful and both of you know that. Trin and Jo are safe in their beds upstairs and we've been gifted with a very valuable lesson at little expense, so learn from it and move on."

Jessie closed her eyes and nodded. "Sorry, Grandmother."

"Good then," Maggie said taking Kaylyn's silence as agreement. "Time to get down to business. I debated whether to bring this up at supper, but I figured that if I did the girls wouldn't get any sleep tonight and from the looks of them…"

"What are you talking about, Maggie?" Kaylyn sounded more tired than annoyed.

Maggie grinned. "The money we need to make this happen, we have all of it and then some."

"You didn't rob a bank did you?" Jessie sounded as though she was only half-joking.

"Of course not," Maggie sniffed and that got her a smile from both her eldest granddaughters. "Grace sold her house this morning. With that money and all the bits and pieces the rest of us have squirreled away over the years, we've managed to put together over three hundred and fifty thousand dollars."

"Wow." Was Jessie's only response as she flopped back against the cushions.

Kaylyn cleared her throat. "I don't know what to say."

"You don't have to say anything, dear. We were glad to do it, but a thank you would be nice."

"Well, of course, but…"

Jessie leaned over and took Kaylyn's hand. "No sense arguing. What's done is done and the grandmothers will only be annoyed if you question their decision. You know that as well as I do."

Kaylyn sighed then raised her head and caught Maggie's eye. A weary smile tweaked at the corner of her lips. "What you and the other grandmothers have done is wonderful, Maggie, and the rest of us will be forever grateful." She yawned. "You said you had two things you wanted to talk to us about."

Maggie let the undercurrent of disappointment she was feeling rise to the surface then pushed it away as quickly as it had come. It had been a long few days for these two and their lack of enthusiasm over her news made perfect sense. "Well, there were three things actually, but I'll keep it short. I can see how tired you are." Maggie ran her fingers through her hair and sighed. "We had a visit from Tilly yesterday."

"Did you invite her?" Kaylyn demanded.

"No. Actually, she invited herself. Most of the grandmothers were here celebrating our good fortune and I didn't see the harm in getting to know each other a bit better. She told us a little about the history of Earth Song and the spiritual nature of their quest." Maggie touched the back of Kaylyn's hand. "She said she just wanted to make certain that there were no misunderstandings."

Kaylyn shook her head and gently pulled her hand away. "I wonder when she'll realize that I'm all grown up. If I'd thought that there'd be a major problem, I wouldn't have approached them in the first place."

Jessie nodded. "We know that love." Her gaze drifted to Maggie. "But it's not a bad thing to have people looking out for you…even if they can get a little overzealous at times."

"And on that note…" Maggie stood up and walked toward the desk. *Overzealous at times…but not all of the time?* She filed that bit of information away, opened the box, and turned with the two remaining letters in her hand. "Remember these?"

Chapter Thirteen

"This is the last one," Wanda said as she dragged Grandma Maggie's desk chair into the overcrowded family room. "Twenty chairs and seven cushions, do you think it'll be enough?"

"It'll have to be. It's not like we have time to round up anymore." Cali finished tacking *The Bare Necessities'* chart to the sidewall and turned around just as Wanda sagged into the chair by the door. "Everyone will be here in two hours and Grandma Maggie is frantic that there won't be enough food since the moms didn't give her the time she needs to do a proper shopping."

"Don't you think that's weird?" Wanda frowned as Cali seemed to shrug the question away. "You have to admit that it's not like our moms to rush into things. If this meeting is such a big deal, why didn't they talk to the grands…or us…about it? We just got home last night. It would have been good to have a few days to recuperate…maybe get things back to normal for a little while."

Cali laughed. "I think we left normal behind the moment Momjay came home from the lawyer's office." Cali turned the seat of a kitchen chair toward her and sat down with her arms draped over the back. "But if it makes you feel any better, the grandmothers have a whole pile of projects lined up for us starting next week."

Wanda's shoulders sagged with relief. "That means we'll have access to the internet again"

"And why is that suddenly so important?" Cali tilted her head to the side.

Wanda forced herself not to look away. "It's not."

"Good. Because you remember what happened the last time you used the computer to play that game you're so enthralled with when you were supposed to be working on a project."

"I just wanted a peek at the online version." Wanda shrugged; the little she'd learned hadn't been worth a week confined to library use only without any access to the internet at all. "But I'm not foolish enough to do that again."

"So what's the big deal?" Cali leaned her chin on her hands. "You're not generally this enthusiastic about doing project work."

Wanda sighed. "You're not going to let this go, are you?" She stood up and moved toward the door not waiting for her sister's response. "I'll meet you in my room in five," she called over her shoulder as Cali made no move to follow her.

"You really should tell the girls about that before the others get here." Maggie pointed to the purple envelope sticking out of Jessie's jacket pocket. "They deserve to know what all the kafuffle is about."

"I know. They've been so good about helping to get things ready without asking a whole lot of questions. But how do I tell them…"

"…that their usually sensible moms panicked because of two simple words." Maggie shook her head and turned back to cutting cookies. She could almost hear Alice chuckle. *I should have left those damn letters in the box.*

"Tick tock." Jessie tossed the letter on the table. "Those words can mean only one thing…that our time is running out."

"But you already knew that." Maggie wiped her hands on a tea towel then leaned back against the counter. If she'd been thinking clearly, she would have kept a chair for herself when the girls came to clean her out. "I'd say there's a good chance that those letters are nothing more than Alice's way of keeping her finger in the pie while it's baking."

Jessie frowned. "What's that even mean, Grandmother?"

"It means that your great-aunt never did know when to butt out." Maggie pulled her own letter from her pocket. She must have reread it a dozen times last night, trying to get rid of the doubts that kept gnawing at her stomach whenever she let her guard down. Of course, there would come a time when the granddaughters would need to shoulder the responsibility for what was to come, but that didn't mean that they shouldn't have people to look out for them for as long as that was possible. *And I'm going to be one of those people, Alice, for as long as I have breath in my body…even if I do get overzealous sometimes.* "Just think about it for a moment, Jess. Your great-aunt guarded that prophecy for a long time, maybe her whole life, knowing that she wouldn't be around to see it to fruition."

Jessie looked at the letter in Maggie's hand then down at the one laying on the table. "So you think this is…what? A way to take back some of the control? Make us jump through hoops?"

"Maybe both of those things. Or maybe she sincerely thought that she could see a better way for us to move forward and wanted to make certain that we got the memo."

Jessie frowned. "What did your letter say, Grandmother?"

"That I…" Maggie drew a deep breath and let it out slowly. *Sorry, Kate, but they need to know this now, not later.* "…that the grandmothers should back off and let the younger generation lead us into the future…that we should stop interfering."

Jessie grinned. "Well, it's a good thing you knew better than to take her seriously." Maggie stifled the urge to wince as Jessie continued. "We all know that the only way we're going to survive this is by working together as a family…young, old, and in between."

"Even if some of us get a bit *overzealous* at times?"

"Yeah…well…about that…" Jessie squirmed. "Kat and I…"

"It's okay, Jess. The two of you are just trying to protect the family." Maggie tucked her letter back into her pocket. "But I wasn't talking about you and Kat. I don't doubt that there've been times when I…or one of the grandmothers…stepped in when we didn't need to and I'm not going to apologize for that." She locked eyes with her granddaughter letting all the love she felt for her daughter's only child flow through that contact. "But I will promise to count to thirty the next time that I think you need my help."

"Or you could just ask."

Maggie smiled. "Now what would be the fun in that?"

Cali sat on the edge of Wanda's bed sorting through the pile of cards spread across the quilt. "So these are part of the game you've been talking about."

"I've called it 'Dragon's Flare' and underneath that it will say 'This Game Could Save Your Life.' I thought that with a title like that people might take a second look."

Cali nodded. Dragon's Flare had a nice ring to it. "And the cards?"

"The blue ones are things we need." Wanda pulled a blue card from the pack and read it out loud. "Your canteen is empty. You will need a source of water and a way to purify it."

"And the white cards?"

"They're the things you have to find or the skills you have to have to fulfill those needs." Wanda shuffled through the cards until she found one that said "swamp" and another that said "fire." "When I do up the proper cards there will be a lot more information on them, but it's a start."

"And this is why you wanted the internet turned on." Cali picked up another card. "Food Source, burdock root."

"I want to put a picture on there so it can be easily identified, also the instructions on where to find it and how to eat it." Wanda swept the cards into an old shoebox and shoved it under the bed. "But that's as far as I've gotten. I wanted to show it to Momkay today…get her input, but…" She shrugged.

"Maybe after this meeting, things will settle down." Cali smiled. "I think Momkay would really be interested in what you want to do; especially if you can figure out a way to get it out to people; it won't do them any good if it's on the internet."

"I've got some ideas, but…" Wanda shrugged. "…it would take some money…maybe a lot of money."

"You're probably right about it being costly if you want to do it right, but since the grandmothers liquidated their assets, they're rolling in the stuff. They would probably spare some for a worthwhile project."

Wanda's eyebrows disappeared beneath her bangs and the ring in her lip quivered. Cali hated when her goth sister got all emotional, especially when Cali was the cause.

Wanda drew a deep breath and let it out slowly. "You really think this is a worthwhile project?"

Cali fought down the urge to say something glib and simply nodded instead. "But I'm not the one you need to convince."

"Convince about what?"

Wanda's head swiveled toward the door. "Geez, Sprout, don't you know how to knock?"

Billie grinned. "I do, actually." She wrapped her knuckles three times on the door jam. "See. But Momjay said to hurry and…well…I guess I forgot."

"And why does Momjay want us to hurry?" Cali demanded before Wanda could say something she might regret.

Billie shrugged. "The moms want us to meet them in the family room…immediately if not sooner. They didn't say why. Maybe they have some last-minute chores for us to do."

Wanda swung her legs off the bed as Cali stood up. "Or maybe they're finally ready to tell us what's going on."

"Run and tell Momjay that we're coming," Cali gave Billie a gentle nudge. "Go on. We'll be right behind you."

Kaylyn took the middle cushion on the couch between Jessie and Maggie and waited for their eldest daughters to join them. Billie wiggled her way between Jo and Trin on the smaller sofa and slung her arms over the back; the pose looked uncomfortable and Kaylyn tried not to smile.

Billie was in tough mode and who could blame her; it had been a hell of a day for all of them.

"Pull up a chair, girls," Maggie said as Cali followed Wanda into the room, "Your moms have something to say to you before everyone else arrives."

Kaylyn nodded as the two girls turned to look at her and Jessie.

"I think I'll just sit right here." Cali assumed the lotus position on the carpet in front of the couch. Wanda joined her. "Wouldn't want to miss anything."

Kaylyn ignored the edge of sarcasm in Cali's tone; she and Jess had made a lot of demands on their family since sunup this morning without a word of explanation and probably deserved a good comeuppance for the turmoil they'd caused. She rubbed her sweaty palms on her jeans then took a deep breath. Jessie gave her shoulder an encouraging nudge. "I…we would like to start with an apology," she said meeting Cali's eyes then extending her gaze to include everyone else in the room. "We forgot something very important when we woke up this morning. We forgot that the people in this house must never be kept in the dark because that's the realm of distrust and disappointment and we're deeply sorry for that."

Cali scooted forward; there was still a hint of skepticism in her eyes, but the concern in her voice was genuine. "So what made you forget?"

"I believe it was a combination of stress, a lack of sleep, and some ill-conceived advice from someone who lacked a solid understanding of how families function." Maggie glanced sideways at Jessie and shrugged. Jessie just gave her head a slight shake and smiled.

"Whose advice?" JoJo demanded.

"I can't…"

"It's okay, Grandmother," Jessie said as she pulled the envelope from her pocket. "From now on we do everything above board and in the light; it's the only way we can stay strong going forward."

Billie pumped her arm. "Yes."

"That's your letter from Great-Aunt Alice, isn't it? I recognize the envelope," Wanda said softly.

Jessie nodded.

"Was it her bad advice that made you so…"

"…crazy." JoJo shrugged as all eyes turned toward her. "We all know it's true."

"Jo's right. Momkay and I were acting crazy and this is what started us down that path." She handed the letter to Wanda. "Read it out loud, please."

Wanda stared down at the paper for a moment then furrowed her brow. "Take the bull by the horns and do it quickly. Tick. Tock. Tick. Tock."

"Tick. Tock. Like in the Hunger Games?" Cali peered over Wanda's shoulder then looked up at Kaylyn and Jessie. "Can't blame you for freaking out. Tick. Tock. Only ever means one thing; that your time is about to run out." She sat back and blinked. "But how can that be? The prophecy said we had a year."

"But the prophecy was never really clear on that. Was it?" Wanda stared up at Jessie with frightened eyes.

"Clear enough," Maggie said, "So you all need to calm down. We've already had enough craziness for one day."

"Trin…not…cra…zee."

"Of course, you're not." Billie pulled her youngest sister onto her lap. Kaylyn filed the moment away for later.

Jessie cleared her throat. Maggie had warned her this might happen. Their girls were too smart not to make the connection. "Grandma Maggie explained it to me like this." She went on to talk about Alice's relationship to the prophecy, how hard it must have been to let it go, and how writing the letters probably made her feel that she still had some control over what happened going forward. "But we're not going to ignore the letters completely."

Cali glanced around the room full of chairs. "Obviously, not." She shrugged. "But maybe a little haste isn't a bad thing now that we have the money to do what we need to do."

Kaylyn nodded. "The sooner we get the camp set up, the sooner we can start practicing the skills we're going to need to live there and stay alive."

"Is that what you're going to tell the people from Earth Song?" JoJo demanded, "Or are you going to tell them the truth?"

"The truth," Billie said as she raised her chin and caught Kaylyn's eye; there was a fierce determination in that look. "You said we're all going to be a family and families share. Right. So it wouldn't be fair not to tell them about the letters."

"I agree with Billie," Jessie said as she patted Kaylyn's knee. "If we're going to do this, we need to do it right...clear the air so to speak and move forward."

Kaylyn squeezed Jessie's hand. *One big, happy family.* Was that even possible with so many strong personalities already in the mix? "I agree."

Chapter Fourteen

"M'in."

Tilly smiled down at the tiny person standing proudly in the doorway. She'd heard the tale of the two sisters and the skunk and had recognized this one immediately. Cerdwin was right; she looked like a tiny, china doll with her wheat-colored hair and big, blue eyes. "Why thank you, Trin," she said as she stepped over the threshold. "My name's Tilly."

"TIL...eee."

"Glad you could make it," Maggie said from the door to the kitchen. She raised an eyebrow in Trin's direction and the little girl turned and scampered away. Maggie shook her head at the child's retreating back.

"We had the same problem with Kaylyn when she was little," Tilly said as she held out the container of muffins Mai had insisted that they bring. "Always wanted to be the first one to answer the door."

"Well, that's interesting." Maggie took the box and turned back toward the kitchen. Tilly followed her. "So how did you handle it?"

"We finally had to put on a chain." Tilly smiled as Maggie's eyebrows rose. "On the door, not Kat. Greg told her that the day she could undo that chain with her feet flat on the floor would be the day she could answer the door by herself."

"And it worked?"

Tilly laughed at the memory. "It did...until she realized that the door would still open enough for her to see who was on the other side."

Maggie nodded. "Then it certainly won't take Trin long to figure that one out. Still might be worth considering," she said more to herself than to Tilly as she set the container on the counter and pulled off the lid. "Chocolate chip muffins. Billie will be ecstatic." She turned and a soft smile tweaked at the corners of her lips. "Thank you, but..."

Tilly waved the rest of that all too familiar disclaimer away. "I know, we shouldn't have, but Mae insisted. She's very much of the mindset that food is the glue that binds people together." Tilly glanced at the covered trays on the counter and the pot simmering on the stove. "I get the feeling that the two of you have that in common."

Maggie nodded. "I never gave it much thought, but I guess we do."

Tilly gave the kitchen a cursory glance then folded her arms across her chest and leaned against the table. "I take it that the chairs are elsewhere."

"I'm sorry." Maggie reached over and turned the heat down on the stove. "Just give me a second and I'll take you to the family room. The older girls must still be upstairs getting ready." She glanced at the clock on the stove then back at Tilly. "You're early."

It wasn't an accusation; there was no rancor in Maggie's tone, just a touch of weariness and a great deal of relief that the error wasn't hers to claim.

"Yes, I am," Tilly said. "And don't ask me why, because I don't really know." She shrugged as Maggie leaned back against the counter. "It just felt right that I should be here when the others arrive…just in case."

Maggie choked back a laugh. "I suppose I'd feel the same way if I was in your shoes, but I can assure you that there's nothing for you to worry about. As to the sudden urgency, I'll let Kat and Jess explain that."

"That's good to hear. Cerdwin and Chloe both fell in love with that piece of forest and couldn't stop talking about how perfect it is. Everyone else is quite anxious to get things moving…especially since we've been working toward something like this for so long" Tilly smiled. "It's good to know they're not going to be disappointed."

Kaylyn stood just inside the door of the family room, extending a heartfelt welcome to everyone as they filed in and found their seats. The girls had moved the chairs and couches into a loose semicircle with a small table sitting beneath *The Bare Necessities* chart that hung at a slight angle on the far wall. "The girls did a good job of getting things ready," she said as Jessie came to stand beside her, "Looks like we're going to have a full house."

"The people from Earth Song are quite impressed with our home," Jessie said with a hint of pride, "I'm glad we got the yard cleaned up; the place hasn't looked this good since last summer." Jessie sighed. "But I'd gladly give that up if Jo would just stop glaring at me every time we meet each other in the hall."

"It's been a hard few days for her and you know how she hates getting her hands dirty. It'll pass…eventually."

Jessie nodded. "I know, but I've been thinking…I'd like to do something special to show how much we appreciate what they've done. Maybe we could take Maggie and the girls out for supper and a movie. We haven't done that in a long time and it would be a nice way to say thanks…"

"…and maybe get you out of the doghouse." Kaylyn gave Jessie's hand a squeeze. "I think that's a wonderful idea, love. Let's just get through this and we'll talk about it. Okay?"

"Momkay." Billie suddenly appeared at Kaylyn's elbow; she was wearing a yellow button-up shirt; and her red hair was brushed back from her face. She looked quite pretty, but Kat wouldn't dare tell her that; Billie's father had raised her to be the son he'd always wanted and Billie still clung to that identity, especially during times of stress.

"Looking good, Billie." Kaylyn reached to brush a strand of hair from her daughter's cheek then thought better of it. She let her hand fall to her side and smiled. "What can I do for you, Sprout?"

"Grandma Maggie says it's time to get this show on the road."

Kaylyn glanced toward the small sofa tucked between two kitchen chairs on the right side of the room. Maggie and Tilly had claimed this place of honor and were staring in Kaylyn's direction, arms folded across their chests as they waited expectantly. "I think we've inherited another grandmother," she whispered in Jessie's ear. "Look." She chin-pointed toward the sofa.

Jessie followed her gaze and smiled. "And so it begins."

"Can't say I blame you for…" Greg frowned down at the letter laying on the table. "How did Kaylyn put it? Freaking out?"

"I'm glad you feel that way. I can only guess what people were imagining when they got the call this morning." Jessie nodded to Grace as the grandmother came to stand beside the table; the old woman looked smug and Jessie hoped this wasn't a prelude to another 'Alice' rant.

"I personally think that getting together so quickly is a good thing, Jessie, despite the impetus behind it." The tense moment passed as Grace shook her head and continued. "The sooner we get the camp ready, the sooner we can start honing the skills we'll need to survive there." Grace addressed her next comment to Greg. "And I'm very intrigued by your suggestion to build yurts beside the lake. I actually spent a week in one a long time ago and found it quite cozy."

"Grandmother?" And here I thought I'd heard every tale she had to tell.

Grace smiled. "I'll tell you all about it someday, Jess, but right now I'd like to hear more about Greg's ideas for the sleeping and storage arrangements." She smiled up at Greg. "Why don't we get some of those lovely looking snacks, then we can talk."

"I do believe Grandma Grace is flirting," Kaylyn said from behind Jessie's left shoulder.

Jessie turned her head only slightly as she watched the elders cross the room. Kaylyn might just be right. "How long have you been standing there?"

"Long enough," Kaylyn folded her arms and grinned. "I think it's kind of sweet."

"I dare you to tell Grace that."

"Yeah, not going to happen." Kaylyn moved around Jess to take her seat at the table. Her brow furrowed as she took Jessie's hand. "So, how are you holding up?"

"I'm good actually." A burst of laughter drew Jessie's eyes to the ring of people hovering around the snack table. Her two eldest daughters looked quite comfortable ensconced between Cerdwin and Grandma Meg as the conversation flowed around them. "I might even hazard a guess that most of these people are happy to be here." She shrugged. "Maybe it's reassuring for everyone to know that things are going to start happening sooner rather than later."

Kaylyn nodded thoughtfully then patted the chair beside her. "Well, at least now we know why Cerdwin kept questioning us about the Quonset huts. If you think about it, the yurts make a lot more sense, especially with the water issue."

"I can't disagree with that. I read somewhere that people in Tibet still live in yurts all year long and I'd hazard a guess that their weather is at least comparable to our own." Jessie glanced at the picture Greg had stuck to the wall. "And we definitely wouldn't be living in a soup can."

"Now that's a blessing if I ever heard one." Kaylyn grinned. "No more Campbell's Kids doing the backstroke through my dreams."

Jessie shook her head. A smile twitched at the corners of her lips and she swallowed it back. "You're ridiculous sometimes. You know that, right?"

"Me. You're the one who put the image in my head in the first place." Kaylyn laughed then picked the letter up and handed it to Jessie. "I think everyone has had a chance to look at this, so maybe it's time to call the meeting back to order."

Jessie blew Kaylyn a kiss, shoved the wrinkled page into her pocket, and stood up. "If everyone would take their seats, please, we'll finish up with today's agenda. The grandmothers have prepared a feast for us for later on and everyone is invited to join us."

There was a rumble of agreement and encouragement from the grandmothers as everyone found their places and turned their attention to the front of the room.

"Again, I'd like to thank you all for making room in your busy schedules to join us here this afternoon. I think that we've made great strides so far. The decision to build yurts and to use the Quonset huts as storage is definitely a step in the right direction." Jessie shared a smile with Kaylyn. "We've also managed to put names to faces, share ideas for the future and discuss concerns. And even though we've only scratched the surface, I'm certain we will all leave here tonight with a sense that the coming days and weeks and months will be both exciting and productive. There is only one problem." She paused and glanced around the room satisfied that she had caught everyone's attention. "This family we're building is incomplete; that means that there are voices that aren't being heard and this is unacceptable as we go forward." Scattered murmurs rippled through her audience. "As you may remember from Grandmother Matibi's presentation, a hunter/gatherer band needs at least fifty to sixty people to be sustainable; there are only twenty-seven people in this room, barely half the number that could guarantee our survival. In my opinion, we need to fix this sooner rather than later."

Maggie raised her hand and Jessie nodded. "I agree that it's of the utmost importance to bring all of the potential members of this family together right from the beginning, but we must be cautious. It's very fortunate that Kaylyn's two families." She directed her smile to the head table and the woman at Jessie's side. "…share many of the same attitudes and values, but we all know that there are those, even among our own relations, who do not."

Jessie watched as one head after another gave a reluctant nod. Maggie paused and her eyes flitted toward Grandma Lee.

"So what are you trying to say, Maggie?" Greg asked in his deep, soft voice.

"Only that I think it might be worthwhile if we took some time before we start adding people to our list, to create a clear picture of the community we want to live in and the values we wish to uphold because when the silence falls, we will only have our shared values and the people around us to depend on."

Kathleen put up her hand and Maggie gave her a nod. "I think that's an excellent idea," the counselor said addressing the room. "Choosing the people who will join us in this venture will be difficult; having a clear picture of what we want for our community will make the hard decisions a little less painful."

A middle-aged woman with close-cropped brown hair and green eyes stood up. "So, if my brother-in-law is a misogynistic asshole, does that mean my sister and her daughter can't join us?"

"May I speak?" With fluid grace, Grandmother Lee stood up and bowed toward the head table.

Jessie automatically returned the sign of respect. "Of course, Grandmother."

Lee bowed again and turned toward the woman who had just spoken. "Your name is Cassandra?"

The woman smiled. "It is."

"My name is Lee," the grandmother offered, "And you and I have something in common. My grandson by marriage believes that he is the center of the universe. He is selfish and can be cruel when things don't go his way. He is not the type of person who would bring harmony to our community."

"But what about your granddaughter?"

Lee offered Cassandra a soft smile. "She is a good and caring person and my great-grandson is too young to yet be infected by his father, so, when the time is right, we will steal them away." She squared her shoulders. "I will help you do the same for your sister if need be."

There was a moment of stunned silence as brows furrowed and glances were exchanged, then one by one, heads began to nod and soft words of comfort and support rippled through the room. Jessie heaved a sigh of relief.

"Compassion. That is my wish for our community." Maggie's voice filled the room as she pointed toward Jessie. "Write that down Granddaughter…nice and big so everyone can see it. Compassion…for ourselves and for each other."

"*Compassionate. Communal. Conscientious. A community that cares, shares, and always strives to do the right thing.* I like it." Cerdwin filled a bowl with stew and passed it to Cali. "Good job."

"I agree," Mae said as she passed Cali a biscuit. "It's short and sweet and says everything that needs to be said at this point. You should be proud of yourself."

Cali tried not to blush. "Thank you. But it wasn't just me. Our group sifted through a lot of ideas, but they all seemed to revolve around those three words. Grandma Maggie talks a lot about how important it is to have compassion for others and Chloe gave us the word communal..."

"And Cali, the wordsmith, put it all together." Wanda grinned at Cali as she reached past her to snag a biscuit. "It's okay, big sister, your secret is out. You don't have to hide your talents any longer."

Cali shook her head and sighed. "Thanks for the stew and the biscuit," she said to the smiling women, ignoring Wanda's twitching eyebrows as she turned and made her way to the table. It was always best just to walk away when Wanda was in one of her moods.

As always, the stew smelled delicious; Cali nodded to the people around the table then lowered her head over her bowl and turned all of her attention to her meal. All she wanted right now, besides the opportunity to fill her rumbling stomach, was to find some peace and quiet, but that wasn't going to happen any time soon; it would be rude to sneak away before their guests had taken their leave, so she kept her head down and hoped no one would talk to her...at least for a little while.

"What necessity did you sign up for?" Cali ignored the question and shoveled another piece of stewed beef into her mouth; surely the query wasn't intended for her.

"I put my name down under Food, Year Two and Beyond," the speaker continued without missing a beat, "I found a lot of edibles just in the areas I've seen; some medicines too. I want to explore that further, maybe put together a guidebook and a map. It'll be important to have a way to locate the plants we can use once our initial food stores run out."

Cali looked up through her bangs just as the speaker paused and filled her mouth with a heaping spoonful of stew. *Jenna. I should have known?* The young woman was a lot like Grandma Meg, all bubbly and oblivious, especially when she was excited about something. Cali swallowed her last spoonful and wiped her mouth with her napkin. "I signed up for 'Opportunities for Learning.'" She stifled a grin at Jenna's momentary look of confusion. "My necessity category, that's what you wanted to know, right?"

A smile stuttered across Jenna's lips. Her head nodded gently up and down as her eyes brightened and the tension eased from her shoulders. "Right. Sorry about that. It's just that today has been so exciting my minds a little scattered. Did you know that Trin signed up for my group?" She shrugged. "Well, actually Billie wrote her name down when she kept pointing at it. Chloe said she was glad to have Trin on the team; apparently, she learns quickly."

"When she wants to," Cali said remembering the way Trin conveniently forgot how to make her bed or fold her clothes.

"Chloe also talked to your moms about teaching Trin sign. Chloe's brother was deaf and her whole family learned to sign so that they could communicate with him." Jenna picked up her spoon then put it down again. "I think it would be great if Trin could really talk to us. Don't you?"

"Absolutely." A ball of warmth settled in Cali's stomach. Maybe someday Trin would be able to tell them about the nightmares that plagued her rest and caused Cali's heart to break on almost a nightly basis; maybe then they could help make the terrors go away. "Sign me up," she said just as Tilly walked into the kitchen with her empty plate and bowl in hand. The elders had eaten in the Nan Cave to free up space at the table and Cali couldn't help but wonder what secrets had been shared in that cozy little room.

"Finish up, people, and let's hit the road," Tilly said as she handed her bowl to Jessie. "It's been a long day and this old woman needs her rest."

"So does this young woman," Cerdwin nodded to Jessie, and Kaylyn then headed toward the door. "The Earth Song express leaves in five minutes, so say your thank yous and get your butts out to the van. The last one in gets to sit on the floor."

Cali frowned. "Isn't that illegal?"

"She's not serious." Jenna grinned. "It's just something she says to get us all moving." She pushed her chair back and gathered up her dishes as she stood. "Thanks for everything, Cali. See you soon."

"Yeah. See you soon," Cali said. There was a slight twinge of anticipation that came with those words. Maybe next time everything wouldn't be so overwhelming. Maybe next time she'd have a real chance to get to know these new people in her life…these recently acquired members of what Wanda was now calling their "Dragon's Flare" family.

The room smelled vaguely of dried cedar, woodsmoke, and beef stew with just a hint of camomile emanating from the tea Maggie had put to steep on the corner of her desk. Kaylyn yawned as she leaned into Jessie's side, grateful for the support. Her girls were sprawled on the Nan Cave carpet like so many kittens after a hard game of chase the mouse; it brought a smile of contentment to her lips. She shared that smile with the grandmother, who had taken up her usual post in the armchair beside the hearth, gave Jessie a nudge to get her started then cuddled back to listen.

"Time to touch base everyone; that was a very trying, eventful day and I'm certain that we all have something we'd like to say about the experience?" Jessie smiled expectantly at the children. Sharing their day was something they usually did around the supper table, but that hadn't been possible tonight, so tea in the Nan Cave was the next best option. "Who'd like to go first?"

"I would." Cali sat up and nestled Mouser in her lap. The little cat had been quite indignant when Kaylyn had let her out of the pantry and had stayed by Cali's side ever since. "But it's hard to know where to start."

"Why don't you start with the things that made you feel really positive about today?" Kaylyn said, "Something that made you smile?"

"When Gregory said he'd be honored if I'd call him grandfather," Cali beamed at the memory. "That was when I told him that I really like the idea of living in a yurt. I don't know why, but the thought of spending my life in a Quonset hut made me feel uncomfortable." She shrugged. "Besides, now we won't have to lug water jugs through the forest and, although sharing a sleeping space with five other people instead of thirty may not be perfect…" She offered Wanda a sympathetic look. "…it will certainly be a lot less crowded."

Kaylyn's heart went out to Wanda as her daughter struggled with the idea of not having a locked door to keep the nightmares at bay. Sharing a tent with her sisters for two nights had been difficult enough; sharing a yurt with them for the rest of her life would be Wanda's ultimate challenge and neither Kaylyn nor Jessie knew what to do about that. Maybe Kathleen could help.

"There's just one thing that bothers me," Cali continued as she scratched behind mouser's ear. "It's going to take a long time to order the yurts and get them set up and there's already so much to do." She took a deep breath and her eyes filled with worry and determination. "I know that we're not supposed to dwell on Great-Aunt Alice's warning, but what if our time runs out before we're ready."

"We'll starve, that's what." JoJo leaned up on her elbows.

"No, we won't. I promise you that." Maggie stood up and made her way over to the teapot, certain that she had caught their attention. "Us old folk didn't spend our time in here just gossiping and filling our faces," she said as she poured tea into the mugs lined up beside the pot. "We had a very serious discussion about the possibility that the timeline might actually be skewed and we came up with a plan."

Kaylyn watched, as anxious to hear the end of this tale as everyone else, as Maggie took her teacup over to her chair and sat down. "Better help yourselves before it gets cold," she said with a hint of a chuckle. No one moved.

Maggie rolled her eyes for dramatic effect and put her cup down. "Alright then. I'll make this fast." She flashed a smile. "The elders, which is a better name for us than the old folk..." Billie giggled; Maggie narrowed her eyes until the child whispered an 'I'm sorry' then continued. "The 'elders' have decided to spend the next month buying the dry goods we will need for the first year and getting them transported to storage in the Quonset huts. We'll also make certain that the mattresses are put on rush order along with a grate for the fire and three cords of wood." She gave them a satisfied smile and leaned back in her chair. "And that's all I'm going to say until you each have a cup in hand."

"Everyone just stay where you are," Kaylyn said as she pushed herself to her feet. "I'll pass them out." She watched Maggie from the corner of her eyes as she worked. The Grandmother was obviously enjoying being the bearer of good news and who could blame her. No matter how much they might want to discount Alice's letters, she had been a woman with a window into the future and who truly knew what she saw there in the final days of her life.

"Thanks, Kat," Jessie said as Kaylyn passed her a mug and resumed her seat; she nodded at Maggie.

"Does this mean that things aren't going to get back to normal?" Wanda blurted out before Maggie could collect her thoughts.

The grandmother shook her head. "No. Not at all. The elders will be getting together tomorrow to set up a schedule and it will be built around our normal, day-to-day activities. So you'll be hitting the books again starting on Monday."

"Thank goodness." Wanda grinned at Cali then ducked her head as she realized that Kaylyn was watching.

"And I will be heading back to work before my clients think I've deserted them for good," Jessie said. "But I'd like to help out as much as I can."

"That's good because we're going to need drivers and strong backs to get everything transported." Maggie nodded. "We have to plan for sixty people and that's going to make for a heavy load. But I'll know more about that after tomorrow."

JoJo yawned and Billie followed suit.

"Drink up, everyone," Kaylyn said, "Unless there are any more pressing comments or questions, maybe we can continue this tomorrow evening. You were up pretty early this morning…"

"At dawn, you mean."

"Not quite, Jo, but if you're as tired as I am, I imagine it feels that way." Kaylyn gave Jo a commiserating smile and raised her eyes to take in all of her daughters. "Alright then off to bed. I'll be up in twenty to say good night."

"And I'll be up in ten," Jessie said with a smile in Trin's direction, "Just in case someone can't find her toothbrush."

Chapter Fifteen

Wanda sat with her back straight, her arm resting lightly on the kitchen table as the pen moved smoothly across the page. Twice a week for the past six years, she'd joined her sisters in what Grandma Maggie referred to as the lost art of penmanship, the precursor to the keyboard and the printing press. Wanda was glad that classes had resumed for the time being. She enjoyed the artistic nature of the writing exercises and was quite pleased that she no longer needed guidelines to keep her letters straight. Typing was faster and easier however and she'd never seen much actual use for the handwritten word until this past weekend. No computers. No printers. No reams of paper or cartridges of ink. The scale of what they were about to lose still made her shudder. She put her pen down and flexed her fingers. Maybe writing with a quill will be easier.

"Finished already?" Grandma Maggie's voice came from over Wanda's right shoulder.

Wanda shook her head without looking back. "Just working the kinks out."

"Still holding your pen like it's about to run away." A hand patted Wanda's shoulder. "Try a lighter grip."

"Yes, Grandmother."

Maggie continued her trek around the table. She looked tired and Wanda wondered if she was sleeping poorly; not that Wanda could blame her. The Grandmothers had shouldered a heavy load when they'd agreed to ensure that no one would starve if their time actually did run out before the deadline. The boxes of dried beans and other non-perishables stacked in the family room were evidence of a week's worth of shopping trips, and they'd only scratched the surface apparently.

The grandmother finished her rounds then took the empty seat next to Trin; the little girl grinned and held up her sheet of carefully execute A's. "Excellent work, Trin." The Grandmother gave the little a hug then pushed her chair back. "Who else is finished for the morning?" When no one answered, she stood up and took Trin's hand. "Well, since we're both done for now, we're going to have some quiet time in the Nan Cave. You can join us when you're finished."

"Yes, Grandmother," Cali said. Jo and Wanda echoed her reply. Billie covered her work with both arms and mumbled something under her breath.

Wanda waited for Trin and the grandmother to leave the kitchen then leaned toward her younger sister. "You've been awfully quiet, Sprout." She nodded toward the paper Billie was trying to protect. "What ya working on?"

"Nothing."

Wanda reached out her hand as Billie glowered at her. "Then you won't mind if I have a look."

Billie's face scrunched up; before anyone could intervene, she threw herself back against her chair and sent the papers skittering across the table. "Go ahead," she growled, "Look all you want."

Jo frowned as she pulled the top paper closer. "It's a letter to someone called Sophia."

Cali glared at Wanda then patted Billie's hand. "Isn't she the little girl who called the cops on your dad?"

Billie swiped angry tears from her eyes and nodded. "She was my best friend and now she's…she's going to die."

Wanda swallowed against the guilty knot in her throat. She should never have invaded Billie's privacy, but perhaps it was for the best; a friend's impending death was an awful load for a twelve-year-old to carry by herself.

"You don't know that, Billie," JoJo said; though there was an edge to her tone that belied her words.

"Yes, I do." Billie's voice rose an octave and her whole body shuddered. "I heard Grandma Grace tell Momjay that even if we told everyone what's going to happen, it wouldn't save them because they wouldn't believe us." A tear trickled down her cheek. "But Sophia…"

"…might believe you," Cali said softly.

Jo dropped her pen on her paper. "And then what? We just take her with us when we go?"

Billie's nostrils flared. "She's family, isn't she? She's the only reason I'm here safe and sound and my dad is in prison. Maybe if I add her name to the list we could rescue her like Grandma Lee's granddaughter."

"But that's different?" Jo scoffed, "Soo Lee is an adult."

Billie's nostrils flared. "Sophia's mom is a bitch and a druggie," she spat. "Her daughter shouldn't have to suffer for that."

"I agree." Wanda felt the heat rise to her cheeks as everyone turned to stare at her. She closed her eyes, drew a deep breath then turned to Billie. "I'm sorry for not minding my own business, Sprout, but you've given me a lot to think about and I want to help." If they found a way to rescue Sophia, maybe she could do the same for her friends at the bookstore.

"But we can't go around kidnapping children." Jo shook her head and sighed, "The moms would never agree to it."

Wanda wiped her sweaty hands on her pant legs and raised her fist; before she could knock, the door to the Nan Cave swung open and Trin peered up at her. "M'in."

"Ah…thanks." Wanda walked inside as Trin stepped out of her way. Sometimes she almost believed that the little girl was psychic, but Wanda wasn't about to tell anyone.

"So, you've finished your lesson for the morning. Maybe…" The grandmother paused as Wanda shook her head.

"I promise that I'll finish it this aft, but I needed to talk to you about something." Wanda raised her chin. She was here to make amends to Billie, but she needed the grandmother's help.

"Go ahead," Maggie said as Wanda slid into the seat across from her. Trin leaned on the arm of Maggie's chair.

"Billie has a friend. Her name is Sophia."

"I know of her," Maggie said after a moment's thought. "She lived in the house next to Billie's. I took Billie to see her once, but the mother didn't want anything to do with us." Maggie gave her a wry smile. "I imagine it was because of all the attention the police were paying to her daughter."

Wanda sighed as Maggie waited silently for her to continue. Maybe this was going to be harder than she thought. "Billie wrote Sophia a letter. She wants to warn her about what's going to happen."

"And you want me to help her deliver it."

Wanda flashed back to the surge of hope in her younger sister's eyes when she'd promised to help her. Even though she knew that nothing would come of it, she had to try. "There's more to it than that. Billie claims that Sophia is family…and she wants us to rescue her when the time comes."

Maggie closed her eyes for a moment and Wanda wondered what the grandmother was thinking. Of course, she'd say that it wasn't possible, probably for the same reason JoJo had given them. When that happened, Wanda was afraid that Billie would try to take matters into her own hands; to tell the truth, Wanda wouldn't blame her younger sister if she did just that. She had friends of her own that she intended to save…she just hadn't thought it all through yet.

"I'll take her to deliver her letter," Maggie said, "But past that I won't make any promises. And you're coming with us."

"M…eee to," Trin piped up.

Wanda shrugged as relief flowed through her. "Sure. Why not?"

"Tell me you're not seriously considering this, Grandmother?"

"I won't know that until we've had our visit, Kat, but I'm of a mind to believe that Billie should be given the same consideration as Lee or Cassandra or anyone else who has family they want to rescue."

"But that's different."

Maggie shrugged. "Maybe. Maybe not. I'll know more when we get home." She paused with her hand on the door to Kaylyn's office. "But while I'm gone, I'd like you to consider the fact that Billie cares deeply for her little friend. It will be devastating for her if she's forced to leave Sophia behind, and we haven't done everything within our power to prevent that from happening."

"I understand that." Kaylyn gave Maggie a pleading look as she ran her fingers through her hair. "And I don't want Billie to be hurt any more than you do, but I can't see any way around it."

Maggie smiled. "Why don't we cross that bridge when we come to it? For now, I'm just going to take my granddaughter to see an old friend and deliver a letter. We'll talk more when we get back." With that, she stepped into the hallway and pulled the door closed behind her. Billie and Wanda met her at the bottom of the stairs.

"Cali and Trin are in the family room watching a movie," Wanda said, "Cali made popcorn, so Trin is okay about staying home. Jo's going to join them when she's finished her assignment, so we're good to go."

"Do you have your letter, Billie?" Maggie asked as she pulled on her jacket.

Billie pulled a white envelope from her pocket. She was grinning from ear to ear. "It's right here. I even drew her a map to our house…in case she wants to visit."

Maggie drew a deep breath and forced a smile. "I know you meant well, Billie, but it's probably not a good idea for Sophia to have a map to our house…just in case."

"But how will she find me?" Billie demanded. Her eyes narrowed and her hands balled into fists.

Wanda sighed. "It's not Sophia she's worried about. Is it, Grandmother?"

"No, it isn't." Maggie gave Wanda a grateful smile then turned to an obviously angry and confused little girl. "Do you remember the last time we went to see Sophia?" Billie nodded. "Do you really want Sophia's mother to have access to a map to our house after all the things she said to you? Because I don't." She gave Billie a one-arm hug. There was moisture in those big, blue eyes as the import of what Maggie said sunk in.

"That bi…that witch isn't going to let me talk to Sophia, is she?" Billie pulled away from Maggie and wiped her eyes on the back of her sleeve.

"But that doesn't mean you can't deliver your letter…" Wanda's eyes widened and she smiled. "That's why I'm going with you, isn't it, Grandmother? 'Cause Sophia's mom doesn't know me."

Maggie smiled. "You always were a smart one."

"So you see, Sprout." Wanda turned to Billie and held out her hand. "I'm your courier. I'll deliver your letter…just not the map. Here…" She wiggled her fingers. "I'll take out the map and write our phone number on the bottom of the page."

"I can do that." Billie grinned as she tore open the flap and let the envelope and the map fall to the floor. "I just need a pen."

"And a new envelope," Wanda said with a smile in her voice as she scooped up the garbage and headed for the kitchen, "Be right back."

"Last one," Jenna grunted as seventy pounds of cardboard and metal landed in the back of the truck. She and Mark had spent the better part of the morning tracking down every deck storage box currently available at the multiple CT outlets around the city. It was heavy work and she was looking forward to a hearty lunch and a hot bath.

Mark grinned as he slammed the hatch. "Last one for now, anyway." He chuckled as he disappeared around the side of the truck and his door creaked open.

"What do you mean…for now?" She demanded as she followed him into the cab and fastened her seat belt.

The truck groaned as Mark shifted into second gear and turned onto the highway. "Greg figures we'll need at least fifty more of them; he says they can be used to store more than just food and can double as benches and beds if we need them to." He shrugged. "It'll make the Quonsets slightly more comfortable…"

"…if we can even get to them." The words were out of her mouth before she could pull them back; they'd been on the tip of her tongue every moment of every day since the nightmares started, nagging at her as everyone threw themselves into completing the elders' emergency plan.

Mark frowned at her then turned his attention back to the road. "Care to explain?" The furrow between his eyes deepened. "Why wouldn't we be able to get to them?"

"Because our timeline isn't as solid as we thought it was." She drew a deep breath and let it out slowly. "We thought we had a year to prepare and get everyone situated before the flare happened. Easy-peasy. Right. But it isn't so easy anymore."

"Maybe not," Mark said. He pulled to a stop at the next red light and gave her his full attention. "But we'll have all the essentials out there within the next few weeks…"

"Except for the people." She blinked as the car ahead of them started to move forward. "It's green. Go." She pointed as he continued to stare at her. "Go."

"I'm going." He drove across the intersection, pulled right into a tiny, strip mall, and turned off the engine. "Not to sound dense," he said as he leaned back against the seat, "But what the hell are you talking about?"

"I think part of you already knows," she said, matching her words to the hint of panic in his voice, "But let me spell it out for you. It's over a hundred miles to that piece of property which means most of us…all of the elders, the children, and maybe even some of the adults…will need to be taken there by car. The rest of us could bike or even walk that far, but our cars depend on technology, right? And if we haven't gotten the others out there before the flare happens…" She left that thought hanging in the air and turned her face toward the window. He needed to process what she'd said, draw his own conclusions.

"Have you told anyone else about this?" Concern was written all over his face as she finally turned toward him.

"I wanted to." She raised her head and looked him straight in the eye, hoping he'd understand why she hadn't. "But everyone's been working so hard, thinking we'll all be safe as soon as the elders' plan is completed…"

"And you didn't want to be the bearer of more bad news." It was a statement, not an accusation and for that she was grateful. The corners of his lips twitched upward at the beginning of a smile. "I can understand that."

"You can."

"Yep." He brushed a strand of dark hair from his eyes and turned the key. "But this is important stuff. Tilly and Greg are the only ones at home right now. How be we tell them together and let them take it from there?"

She felt the weight lift off her shoulders as he waited for her answer. "Let's do it," she said as they pulled onto the street. "And Mark…"

"Yeah?"

"Thanks."

"Any time, little sister." He gave her a cockeyed grin. "Any time."

"Smells good." Jenna kicked her shoes off at the door and followed her nose into the kitchen; Mark padded quietly behind her. He'd known Tilly and Greg his entire life and, after noting her heightened anxiety as they pulled into the drive, had offered to take the lead on the impending revelation. She was more than grateful to him for the rescue and was determined to back him up as best she could…if she could.

"Jenna. Mark. You're just in time." Tilly set a green and gold tureen in the middle of the table. "Greg made lentil soup…"

"…easy on the hot sauce." The old man chuckled as he noted the look of cautious relief on Jenna's face. The last time Greg had made the soup, it had literally taken her breath away and left her mouth on fire for a good hour afterward.

"Go ahead. Sit down." Mark nudged her gently in the back as he made his way toward the fridge. "I'll get us some milk." He turned and grinned at Greg. "Just in case."

Tilly lifted the lid off the tureen and gave the soup a stir as Jenna took her seat. "I kept a good eye on him," the older woman said. She ladled out a bowl and passed it across the table, "So I think we should be okay." She gave Greg a look of fond exasperation then caught Jenna's eye and smiled. "So how was your morning?"

Jenna froze with the spoon halfway to her lips. "Ah…"

"Backbreaking and boring." Mark smiled at Greg then winked at Jenna. She forced herself to relax and winked back. "But we did manage to find twenty of what you wanted," Mark continued. "We packed them in tight. So, they're all ready for delivery tomorrow."

Greg swallowed a spoonful of soup and nodded. "Twenty benches should be enough for the food stacked in Maggie's family room, but we'll need twice that number for the rest. I put in an order for fifty this morning. They should be here in ten days…plenty of time to get all of the basics out there and stowed away by the deadline."

"And what about the people?" Mark shrugged beneath the weight of Greg's frown. "Those supplies aren't going to do anyone any good if we can't get to them."

"What are you talking about, Boy?" Greg demanded.

Jenna flinched at the harshness of his tone; he was obviously as tired and wound up as the rest of them. He didn't need another problem thrust into his lap, but he and Tilly were the only people she and Mark had to turn to at the moment. If they didn't get the transportation problem out in the open now, they might not be able to deal with it before it was too late.

"I'm not a boy," Mark growled, "And I'm talking about the fact that most of our people need to be transported to the property by car…"

"Well, of course, they do," Tilly said without a hint of condescension. "And we've already lined up enough vehicles to get all of us there as quickly and as safely as possible."

Mark nodded. "And that's great, Tilly, but those vehicles are as vulnerable to EMP disruption as your computer and won't do us any good if we don't get our people out to the property before the flare hits."

"But we don't know…" Tilly took a gulp of air. There was fear in her eyes as she turned to Greg. Then her spine stiffened and her jaws clenched. "You need to contact all of your suppliers and light a fire under them. Offer them a bonus, if it'll help. Then take a look at those websites you've been tracking. Find out how much lead time we'll have between when the superflare is spotted and when it'll hit."

Greg stared at her for a moment then raised his hand in a mock salute. "I'll get right on that."

Tilly shook her and sighed then turned toward the door. "Mark, help Greg. Jenna, you're with me. We're going to talk to Maggie and her granddaughters."

"Grandma Maggie. You were gone a long time." Jo stood in the doorway to the family room with a large, white mixing bowl in her hands. "We've watched the whole movie and half of the sequel since you left."

Maggie smiled. "And how many bowls of popcorn did you eat?"

"Just two." Jo eyes slid to the left. It was her tell when she chose to subvert the truth.

Maggie narrowed her eyes and the smile disappeared. "Are you certain?"

"Ah…" Jo screwed up her face in a look of deep thought then took the way out that Maggie had given her. "Come to think of it," she said refusing to meet Maggie's eyes. "Maybe it was three bowls."

"You guys ate three bowls of popcorn…" Billie ducked around Maggie and peered into the bowl. "…and you didn't save us any."

Jo shrugged. "Sorry."

"It's okay." Much to Maggie's amazement, Billie smiled. "I had cookies at Sophia's. Her granny made them." She pulled a large, paper bag from behind her back and held it up. "She even sent some home with us to share."

"Why don't you take them into the family room and pass them around." Maggie encouraged then plucked the bowl from Jo's arms and took a step back. "I'll put this in the kitchen on the way upstairs. Wanda?"

Wanda appeared from around the corner. "Yes, Grandmother."

"Keep an eye on things until I get back. Okay? I need to talk to Momkay." She turned into the hallway as Wanda nodded and wrapped an arm around each of her sisters. "And ask Cali to make a pot of tea, please. Black. Four bags."

"Four bags?" Wanda raised an eyebrow then shrugged. "Of course, Grandmother."

Maggie nodded and turned down the hall. The day was barely half over and all she wanted was to get into her chair and take a nice, long nap. The tea would help alleviate some of the weariness, but there was no tonic she knew of to stop this roller coaster they were on.

She deposited the bowl beside the kitchen sink, grabbed two bottles of orange juice from the fridge, and headed upstairs to Kaylyn's office. She rapped twice to get the younger woman's attention then walked in, took a seat, and held out a juice bottle as a peace offering. "I thought you might be thirsty."

"Well, you thought right. Thanks." Kaylyn took the bottle with a smile and twisted off the lid. "So…how was the visit?"

"Enlightening." Maggie took a drink, set the half-empty bottle on the desk, and sat back. "Sophia's Grandmother is taking care of her right now, so getting into the house was easy as soon as Sophia recognized Billie." Maggie smiled. "It was a very loud and tearful reunion."

Kaylyn sighed. "I'm so glad things worked out that way." A crease appeared between her eyebrows. "Sophia's mother…"

"…was in a car accident. She's in a coma and the doctors don't give much hope that she'll come out of it," Maggie settled deeper into her chair, "Stephanie…Sophia's Grandmother…is the child's legal guardian right now. Nice woman. Was a high school science teacher for years apparently. Spent her summers visiting out-of-the-way places with her husband until her daughter was born. He died a few years ago. She gave her daughter the house and moved into a seniors' complex; she's been living there ever since."

"Seems like the two of you really hit it off." Kaylyn smiled. "And I'm assuming that Billie got to spend some quality time with Sophia. How did that go?"

"According to Wanda, Billie told Sophia everything."

Kaylyn nodded. "I suspected as much. And what did you tell the grandmother?"

"That once she talks to Sophia about her visit, she should give me a call." Maggie took a long drink and cupped the bottle in her hands. "Billie wrote her letter on the back of her copy of the prophecy…the one with Cali's notes…so Stephanie has all the information she needs to make a decision." She shrugged. "That's the best I could do given the situation. The woman doesn't know me from Eve, Kaylyn, and I wasn't about to give her a reason to ask me to leave before Billie finished her visit." She smiled and raised both eyebrows. "You have to admit, this would all seem pretty crazy if you were looking at it from the outside."

Kaylyn snorted. "It looks crazy even from the inside, Maggie, but I want to thank you for what you did for Billie even so. Do you think Stephanie will call?"

Maggie cocked an eye in Kaylyn's direction. "Would you?"

"Grandmother!" Footsteps pounded down the hall. Maggie's head snapped up just as JoJo appeared in the doorway. "Grandmother, Tilly's downstairs. She wants to see you and Momkay right now. She says it an emergency."

Maggie glanced at Kaylyn then sighed and pushed herself to her feet; she could see her own fear and confusion echoed in the younger woman's eyes. "Tell her we're on our way," she said as Kaylyn shut down her computer and pushed her chair back. "Then take her into the Nan Cave. Tell Cali to bring in the tea when it's steeped."

"But Grandmother…"

"I haven't had tea this good since the youngsters convinced us to go herbal." Tilly took another sip of the hot, dark beverage then put the cup down. Some of her previous sense of urgency seemed to have dissipated and her hands no longer shook, but she had yet to reveal the true reason behind her visit.

"So we're on track for the end of the month," Maggie prompted, "That's good news. Isn't it?"

Jenna inched forward on her chair as Tilly's brow furrowed. "I could tell them if you like."

Tilly gave the young woman a fond smile. "Thank you, dear, but this is my…" She raised her head and her eyes locked with Maggie's. "… 'our' oversight and we need to correct it. You see, Maggie, us old folks didn't take into account one very important element in our emergency plan. We didn't consider the technological aspects of our transportation and that oversight could prove to be a more devastating problem than not having enough food." She went on to describe her conversation with Mark, her instructions to Greg, and the conclusions she had reached on her way over. "We need a full group meeting, Maggie, including all of the people on our lists, and we need to have it within the next few days."

"But that's almost fifty people," Kaylyn protested, "We don't have enough room for that many. And if we're bringing in everyone, the meeting is going to have to be in the evening since some people still have jobs to go to."

Tilly nodded. "Two very good points, Kaylyn, but neither of them are insurmountable. There is a housing co-op not far from Earth Song. They have a large, multipurpose room that they've given us access to in the past for a minimal charge. And I know it's available in the evening."

Maggie heard the door behind her open and close and tried not to smile. She'd suspected that Cali had remained behind after serving the tea, but hadn't wanted to draw attention to the young woman's presence by searching her out. In a few moments, the girls would know the reason behind Tilly's visit. "I'll get ahold of the grandmothers. Most of them are dropping by tomorrow with food boxes, so we can make certain that the list is complete. Once you've got word on the room, let us know and we'll make the calls."

Jenna pulled a wrinkled slip of paper from her jeans' pocket. "I want to add these two names."

Maggie took the offered list and scanned it. "Mathew Shepherd and Kevin Shepherd."

"They're my younger half-brothers." The young woman looked down at her hands, but Maggie could see the glimmer of tears at the corner of her eyes. "Their father took them when he divorced my mom."

Tilly frowned sympathetically. "But you've never talked about them."

"They were so little the last time I saw them." She shrugged. "I didn't think they'd remember me…"

"…but they did. Didn't they?" Kaylyn gave Jenna's hunched shoulder a gentle squeeze.

"Yes." The young woman accepted a tissue from Maggie and dabbed at her eyes. "I waited for them outside their high school and introduced myself. Apparently, our mom sent each of them a picture of the two of us and a letter shortly before she died. Probably around the same time that she gave me their address."

"So you've spoken to them about what we're doing," Tilly's tone was soft and tentative. "And they've agreed to come."

Jenna raised her chin. "I know what you're worried about, but Mathew is seventeen and Kevin is a year older. And yes, they've agreed to come."

"Then we'll add them to the list," Kaylyn said before Tilly could make another comment.

Maggie nodded. Family was family, either by blood or by love or by both if you were lucky, and it was too late in the game to second-guess what that meant for the community they intended to build.

"Thanks." The smile Jenna gave them was broad and warm and full of gratitude. Then she pointed to the paper in Maggie's hand. "You know, I could probably come back tomorrow and help you make some of those calls…even help get the food boxes repacked." She turned to Tilly. "Mark and I have done everything on the list Greg gave us and you don't need me to arrange for the room."

"That sounds like a great idea," Kaylyn smiled at Tilly and gave Jenna's shoulder another squeeze. "Especially since we need to get those boxes into Hanna's truck for our move on Saturday."

"Then I guess that's settled." Tilly stood up abruptly, gave Kaylyn a hard stare then turned to Jenna. "We should get going, Jen," Tilly said gruffly. "It's getting late and I still have supper to make."

Maggie stood up as Jenna scrambled to her feet, her face a mask of confusion.

"No need to see us out," Tilly said as she headed toward the door. Jenna looked back over her shoulder and waved as they disappeared into the hallway.

"What was that all about?" Kaylyn mused as Maggie took her seat and reached for her cup.

"It would appear that Tilly's not used to sharing." Maggie sat back and smiled as Kaylyn weighed the veracity of that statement and how it might apply to this situation.

"You mean she hasn't had a half-dozen meddling grandmothers to contend with." Kaylyn grinned. "Not that I'm complaining, mind you." Then the grin disappeared and frown lines appeared between her eyebrows. Maggie sipped her tea and waited. "This not sharing, is it going to be a problem?"

Maggie smiled. "Why don't you let the 'meddling grandmothers' worry about that? Tilly just needs some time; she has a long history at Earth Song and is, I'm almost certain, the reason it still exists."

Understanding dawned in the younger woman's eyes. "You're right. When I lived there, Tilly was always the one who made sure that things got done. The rest of us just followed her lead."

"Now, she needs to learn to share the responsibilities she taken on over the years. It won't be easy for her, but we can help her with the transition. It will just take some time." Maggie sat back and raised her cup. "Here's to 'meddling grandmothers.' Now drink up. We have a long week ahead of us and there's no time like the present to get started."

Chapter Sixteen

Wednesday and Thursday had gone by in a whirlwind of activity: making phone calls, sorting and packing boxes of supplies, loading the vehicles for Saturday's trek to the property and seemingly endless hours of food preparation. No one could convince Grandma Maggie that snack trays weren't necessary for the upcoming meeting and the fridge and the freezer were stuffed full of bags of rhubarb scones, plates of sliced cheese, and tins of oatmeal cookies. The kitchen smelled so good it made Wanda's mouth water in anticipation.

"Nice work today." Grandma Mat patted Wanda's shoulder as she made her way toward the front door. Smears of flour stood out in sharp contrast to the grandmother's dark skin. "I'm off for a hot bath and a long nap. See you tomorrow evening. Take care."

"I will," Wanda said to the grandmother's retreating back then closed the door and headed toward the stairs. Momjay would be home for supper soon and Wanda needed to speak to Momkay while she was alone. She skidded to a halt in front of the closed door, drew a deep breath, and knocked. Momkay had retired to her office an hour ago to make the last few calls on her list; she should be free by now.

"Come in," a muffled voice called from inside the room. Wanda opened the door just as Kaylyn shoved the last of an oatmeal-chocolate chip cookie into her mouth and downed it with a sip of tea. "I couldn't resist," she said as she put her mug down and turned to face her daughter with a smile. "Come on in. Take a seat."

Wanda nodded and made her way to the chair beside the desk. "It's Thursday," she said without preamble. "D&D night at the *Second Time Around*. We're still going, right?"

Kaylyn blinked twice then sighed and shook her. "I'd love to go, but…"

Wanda's nostrils flared. "No! No buts. This is important, Momjay. I need. I need..." The words caught in her throat and a tear trickled down her cheek. She needed to talk to her friends, tell them everything before it was too late.

Kaylyn reached over and wiped the tear away. "Okay. What's this all about?" Her voice was soft as she rolled her chair closer.

Wanda drew a deep breath and withdrew a small plastic bag from her pocket. "Mel and the boys have been helping me with these." She dumped the contents on the desk: four, quarter-page bundles of handmade cards in green, blue, white, and yellow; a rough map; a folded copy of the prophecy; and an instruction sheet landed in front of Kaylyn. "When I thought we had a year, it was going to be a teaching game. Then we ran out of the time; we needed to do it up right. I guess it could still be played with a little imagination, but now it's really just a bag full of important information."

Kaylyn picked up the empty bag and peered at the label. *Dragon's Flare, This Bag Could Save Your Life.*"

Wanda drew a deep breath to steady herself. "The cards contain information about edible plants, how to purify water, how to snare and clean a rabbit or a squirrel, green spaces outside the city. There's even one on packing a survival bag. It could have been a really good game," she finished sadly. She picked up the white cards then put them down again. "Mel and the boys have been passing them out at the high school and Caroline has a stack of them at the bookstore."

"And this was your idea...to help save lives." Kaylyn didn't wait for a response. She opened her arms and drew Wanda into a tight hug. "What an amazing project. Why didn't you tell me sooner?"

Wanda sat back as Kaylyn released her. She felt all warm inside after her mother's reaction and didn't want to make her feel bad; it really wasn't anyone's fault that their lives had been overtaken by one setback after another. "You had enough on your mind and the guys were happy to help. We've been doing it all by email and they're excited to learn more. I told them we'd discuss everything tonight."

Kaylyn nodded then ran the fingers of her right hand through her hair. Wanda sat very still while her mother processed everything she'd heard. "I suppose we need to go then." Kaylyn raised her head and met Wanda's eyes. "Have you invited them to join us?"

"No. Not in so many words. I…" Wanda stared down at her hands. "I didn't want to get their hopes up, but now there's no more time and…and they're my friends. How can I just leave them behind without at least giving them a choice?"

"You can't." Kaylyn was staring at the stacks of cards laying on her desk when Wanda looked up. "It would break that gentle heart of yours." She picked up the plastic bag and started to refill it. "And I'm not going to let that happen."

Jessie woke early on Friday morning. She'd spent all day yesterday cleaning out her office and closing her files. Being a life coach had been both a rewarding and lucrative career choice for her while giving her the flexibility she needed as her family seemed to grow by leaps and bounds. She liked to believe that her efforts had been helpful, that her clients had gone on to lead healthier, more productive lives, that maybe they'd even learned something about themselves that would help them in the times to come.

As if anyone's ideal goals included surviving the end of the world as we know it. She drew a deep breath and pushed that thought to the darkest recesses of her mind and bent over to dig a dozen eggs, a half bag of grated cheese, and a green pepper out of the fridge. The girls loved cheese omelets and Maggie would probably appreciate having breakfast made for her after all the cooking she'd done yesterday.

"Need any help?" Kaylyn yawned and swiped her fingers through her mop of auburn curls as Jessica turned toward her.

Jessie smiled. "Are you up for making coffee? I could use the pick-me-up."

"No argument here." Kaylyn brushed past Jessie and gave her a quick hug on her way to the drip percolator at the end of the counter. "After the day we had yesterday, I think we could all use a pick-me-up. The girls worked so hard and Maggie was all but run off her feet. Maybe today, we could just kick back, watch a movie, make some popcorn."

Jessie nodded. "Sounds good. A little R&R before the coming event." Jessie listened to Kaylyn's breathy chuckle then poured milk into the bowl of eggs and picked up the whisk. "I wonder how many people are actually going to be there tonight."

"There were forty-eight on the list at last count, but that doesn't include Wanda's friends or Sophia and her grandmother…if they all come." Kaylyn put a pile of plates on the table and went back for mugs. Jessie watched her from the corner of her eyes enjoying the fluid grace of her movements. "Caroline…that's the bookstore owner…will definitely be there. She didn't seem at all surprised by what she was hearing."

"Well, at least that's something. Wanda seems to really like her." Jessie gave the bowl a final stir. "Omelet's ready for the frying pan. Should we wake them or wait for a little while…let them sleep."

Kaylyn grinned and poured coffee into two mismatched mugs. "Why don't we let them sleep?"

The street was different…more traffic, less trees, but the long, single-story building they'd parked in front of was oddly familiar. "I think I've been here before. I…" Maggie felt the pull of distant memory as she stood and closed the car door behind her. "Of course. I used to come here on Fridays to Circle Dance. How could I have forgotten that?"

Jessica stepped up beside her. "You never told me you were a dancer."

"It was a long time ago." Maggie sighed. "But the essence of it still lingers I think…at least I hope it does. It was a very spiritual time in my life…the music, the movement, the feeling of connection it gave us to the original dancers, to our distant and not so distant ancestors…I think it changed me in ways I'll probably never fully understand."

"Then why did you quit?"

Maggie gave her granddaughter a rueful smile then moved toward the trunk. "That's a story for another time. Now let's get the food unpacked and inside before someone comes looking for us. Cali?"

"Right here, Grandmother." A shadow straightened on the other side of the car.

"Grab some bags and follow me." Maggie hefted two reusable, shopping bags from the trunk and headed toward the central door. If she remembered correctly, the multi-purpose room was just across the hall.

Cali scooted up beside her. "I have something to give you once we get everything inside. Jo and I put the finishing touches to it just before we left. We think it will help make this meeting…more productive."

"You don't say." Maggie recognized the seriousness of Cali's tone and tried not to smile. Her younger granddaughters had always been clever and over the years that raw intelligence had been nurtured and refined to the point where critical thinking was as natural as breathing to them.

Maggie handed her bags to Mae at the door to the kitchen with a promise to return in a moment then stepped aside. Cali gave her a puzzled frown.

"Put the bags on the counter," Maggie said, "then we'll find somewhere quiet to sit."

Cali grinned. "Yes, Grandmother."

Maggie turned and made her way to the table tucked beneath the familiar *Bare Necessities'* chart and the list of task groups assigned to each need category. It felt like an eternity since her girls had provided that starting point for all of the conversations that followed. She took a seat at the table and waited for Cali to join her. Kaylyn smiled in Maggie's direction as she followed her daughter out of the kitchen.

"I asked Momkay to join us since she'll be welcoming everyone to this meeting and it's important that she knows about this," Cali said as she and her mother joined Maggie at the table. Kaylyn raised one eyebrow in Maggie's direction; Maggie shrugged. A battered brown messenger's bag landed on the table between them; Cali reached inside and pulled out a stack of vibrant orange sheets and smiled. "JoJo picked the color."

"What is this?" Kaylyn reached for the top page and turned it toward her. She squinted at the heading: *A Synopsis of the Dragon's Flare Project to Date.*

"You know." Cali shrugged. "It's like what Grandma Hanna taught us to do with all the novels and stories we've read." She tapped the top of the pile. "Remember when Grandma Kate said that this would be a difficult meeting because we wouldn't all be on the same page and we should probably be prepared to spend a lot of time doing catch-up."

Maggie nodded. "I remember. That's why we're starting the meeting so early."

"From the looks of this," Kaylyn glanced up and smiled at her daughter, "The time we'll need for catching up and making certain that everyone is on the same page just got a lot more manageable."

Maggie scanned the synopsis in front of her: it was done in point form starting from the day Jessica visited the lawyer's office and ending with the final preparations for tonight's meeting. A copy of the prophecy was printed on the back of the page. "I think you're right, Kat." She smiled at Cali. "Whose idea was it to name the project *Dragon's Flare*?"

"Let me guess?" Kaylyn said, "You got it from Wanda."

Cali nodded. "It just seemed so…"

"…amazingly appropriate." Kaylyn smiled as Cali nodded again. "That's what I thought the first time I heard it."

"I agree," Maggie said setting the paper down, "But it's not just our decision to make. Names are important and everyone should have the opportunity to weigh in on this one."

"We could have a vote. Take suggestions from the floor." Cali pulled a notebook from her bag. "I could even make tiny ballots."

"Well, it would certainly get everyone involved right from the start," Maggie grinned. "What do you think, Kaylyn?"

"I think both the synopsis and the vote are great ideas." She turned to Cali. "When Jo and Grandma Kate get here with the rest of the food, get your sister to help you set things up for the vote. There are some large sheets of paper beside the table to write suggestions on."

"And I'll arrange to have the synopsis passed out. Now if you'll excuse me." Maggie ignored Kaylyn's look of confusion as she made a beeline toward the head-on collision about to happen just inside the door. "Billie! Billie, stop!"

Billie slowed and glanced over her shoulder. "It's Sophia, Grandmother. She's here."

Maggie took two more quick steps and grasped Billie's arm interrupting her forward momentum. "I know she is, dear, but you need to take a couple of deep breaths and slow down before you run into someone. Okay?"

Billie inhaled loudly then nodded. "But how is she here, Grandmother?"

"Her grandmother phoned me last night. She wanted to know if what you told Sophie was real, so I invited her to join us tonight." Maggie took a step forward and released Billie's arm. "Let's go welcome our guests, shall we? Then I have a little job for you and your friend."

"Thank you all for coming tonight." Kaylyn paused and waited for the murmur of voices to fall silent. She smiled at Wanda and her friends from the bookstore; somehow the boys had convinced their mother to come with them and Kaylyn hoped it was a positive sign. "Does anyone still need a copy of the synopsis?" She held up an orange sheet and waited for a count of five: nobody moved. "Good. If you have any questions about the contents of this sheet, please hold them until after the break. We've set aside time to address any questions or concerns you might have."

Kaylyn put the paper down and stepped to the side so that everyone could see the wall behind her; a large sheet of white paper with the words Dragon's Flare sprawled across the top appeared in the gap. "You might have noticed the name Dragon's Flare at the top of the synopsis page. That was my daughters' idea," She smiled at Cali and Jo then nodded at Wanda. "But naming something as important as this project is a very special act and should involve everyone." She noticed various heads nodding, including Tilly's, and her smile broadened. "So we're going to give everyone the opportunity to weigh in. If you have a name you prefer, please add it to the list during the break; we'll take a vote as soon as the meeting recommences. Now I'd like to call on Tilly to explain the reason behind this meeting."

"It's all about the technology we've become so dependent on that we don't even think about it anymore," Tilly said as she took Kaylyn's place behind the table. "In the beginning, we thought we had a year to prepare for the main event..."

"You mean the solar flare?"

Tilly nodded to a woman Kaylyn didn't recognize sitting in the second row. "Exactly. But we've since been given cause to doubt the timeline." Tilly went on to describe the warning from Alice, the grandmothers' emergency plan, and their oversight concerning the vehicles and the technology they operated on. "So we're here tonight to build a new timeline, one that will get most, if not all of us, out of the city as soon as possible." She pointed to the task groups and the list of names beneath each designation. "As you can see, we have our work cut out for us if we are to ensure the survival of our community. Each of these groups is already creating lists of necessary supplies and researching possible sources. The *Food (Year One)* committee has already purchased over half of the dry goods we'll need..."

"Excuse me." Maggie watched as Stephanie waved her hand in the air. "Before we go any farther, I'd like to know how you're paying for all this."

Tilly huffed, but before she could answer, Jessie stood up and approached the table. "I'd like to take that question. I think it's important that I do," She turned to address Sophie's Grandmother as Tilly gave her a grudging nod. "When my great-aunt first gifted me with the prophecy and the grandmothers confirmed through prior knowledge of Alice's abilities that it was most likely a true seeing, one of the first questions Kat and I asked ourselves was how we could possibly afford to take our girls out of the city when we had no forest to flee to and no money to get the things we would need to keep us safe and alive. Fortunately, Alice solved the first part of that problem with a subsequent gift of a section of old-growth forest and two Quonset huts; the seven women I have called grandmother since I was old enough to talk…" She smiled at Maggie and the women seated beside her in the back row. "…took care of the rest of the problem. They sold possessions, cashed in bonds, raided their savings accounts, and came up with enough money, along with a donation from the people at Earth Song, to cover the basics."

Stephanie frowned. "So you're not going to charge the rest of us to be a part of this?"

Jessie took a deep breath and scanned the faces around her. "You are all ripples in a pond of friends and family and you're here today, not because of what you have, but because of who you've proven yourselves to be to someone in this room. We need strong, compassionate people who are willing to take on the responsibility of creating a future where all of our members are valued and respected and all of the tasks of daily living are equally shared, more than we need your money. So, no, we're not going to charge you for being a part of this."

"If you were, I wouldn't be staying." Stephanie stood up as the room fell silent. Sophia held Billie's hand and watched her grandmother with wide, hope-filled eyes. "I guess I don't need to tell you how fantastical this all seems, but my Sophia wanted to come and now I'm glad we did. I have some money and since you're not asking for it…" She chuckled. "…I'm more than willing to add it to the pot. I'll write you a check during the break. How would that be?"

"That…that would be wonderful. Thank you." Jessie gave Tilly a nod and made her way back to her seat. Her granddaughter looked both stunned and pleased by the results of her impromptu speech; Billie would have her best friend with her when she left Winnipeg; and Maggie knew that that rather than the offered money was the source of Jessie's pleasure.

"Thank you for clearing that up, Jessica," Tilly said flatly, "Now I'd like to ask Greg to come up and tell us how the Shelter committee is progressing."

For the next hour, each committee spokesperson delineated their progress to date and what still needed to be done to complete their list. It was obvious that everyone was struggling with the truncated timeline and the scope of each of their tasks.

In the end, Greg got up and addressed the group again. "I'm certain that by now you all realize the magnitude of the task at hand and how important it is for 'all' of us to roll up our sleeves and pitch in." He cocked his thumb over his shoulder. "If you aren't signed up for a task group, please do that over the break. Tomorrow will be our first dry run at getting supplies up to the property and into the Quonset huts and we're going to need all hands on deck to make that happen. I know it's short notice…" He said as a couple of hands went up, "…but this is a matter of life or death; think about that while you're eating the lovely lunch the grandmothers have provided. We'll discuss the particulars when we reconvene."

"That was beautiful, Jess. Ripples in a pond of friends and family." Jessie blushed as Kaylyn hugged her tight. "I'm so proud of you."

Jessie returned the hug and took a step back. "Thanks, but it just seemed to pop out of nowhere. Everything has been so organic up to this point that I didn't realize how hard it would be to explain how we all came to be here together until I was standing up there."

Kaylyn brushed a loose strand of dark hair from her partner's eyes and nodded her understanding. It had been a brave move on Jessie's part to stand up in front of these people with no idea of what she was going to say. "I don't think any of us have given it much thought," she said as they moved toward the food table, "but it wasn't just Sophia's Grandmother who was interested in what you had to say. A lot of the new people seemed either intrigued or relieved. I wouldn't doubt that they'll be giving the synopsis the girls did a good read now that they know exactly why they've been asked to be here and what's expected of them going forward."

"Good job," Grandma Kate said as she poured Jessie a cup of tea, "What you said really hit home with a lot of people. The gentleman who came in just before you got up there"—she nodded toward Sam and Ian's father— "just handed Maggie a sizeable check because of what you said. He told her that he'd had a lot of doubts when his boys asked that they be allowed to come tonight, but what you said convinced him that we truly believe in what we're doing. He said that he would be honored to join us if it would keep his family safe and even if the event never happened, his boys will have had the opportunity to experience life at its most basic."

Kaylyn grinned as she accepted her tea. "You been eavesdropping again, Grandmother?"

"I believe you have me confused with someone else." Kathleen returned the grin. "Now get on with you before the foods all gone."

Kaylyn moved to her right behind Jessie and grabbed a paper plate; even the grandmothers couldn't justify the hours cleanup would take to use the available china when the meeting was scheduled to run so late. She buttered two scones and added slices of cheese plus two cookies from the closest tin. Following Jessie toward the row of empty chairs at the front of the room, she watched as people added their names to the task groups and wrote down alternative names for the project.

"World's End. That an interesting one," Jessie said around a mouthful of cookie.

"Too negative. New Dawn's not bad…though it is a bit overworked…if you're a science fiction reader," Kaylyn ducked her head. "But at least it's positive."

"I suppose, but I still like Dragon's Flare the best."

Kaylyn nodded. "Sort of says it all, doesn't it?"

Chapter Seventeen

"What if they don't come, Momjay?" Wanda leaned against the van's front bumper and wrapped her arms around her chest. Instead of her usual black on black, her goth daughter had opted for blue jeans and a faded green t-shirt this morning, her "down and dirty working clothes" as she called them. "What if their parents changed their minds?"

"They'll be here. They're just running a few minutes late." Kaylyn gave Wanda a one-arm hug and pulled a ten-dollar bill from her pocket. "Now why don't you go and get a chocolate milk for you and Trin. I'll keep an eye out while you're gone."

Wanda took another look at the road that ran beside the gas station then leaned over and took the money. "Thanks, Momjay. I'll be right back," she said as she disappeared down the side of the van.

Kaylyn took Wanda's spot and stifled a yawn. As expected, last night's meeting had stretched into the wee small hours of the morning as task groups used smartphones and tablets to flesh out their lists and plan their next steps. It had come as no surprise to Kaylyn that the whole project was now officially named Dragon's Flare or that the new recruits they were waiting for at this moment had all but seamlessly fit into the mix. Lisa, Sam, and Ian's mother had turned out to be a nurse practitioner with ten years of experience and was genuinely welcomed by the members of the Medical Care committee while the boys' father, Robert, with his background in construction, had been an easy fit with the shelter committee along with his two sons. The entire family had stayed to the bitter end last night seeming to enjoy the camaraderie and the challenge; there was no doubt in Kaylyn's mind that they would be here soon no matter what the reason for the delay might be.

"The cashier wanted to know whether we were all headed for the festivities in some place called Arborg," Wanda said as she reappeared at Kaylyn's side. "I didn't know why she'd ask me that or what to tell her, so I just said yes."

Kaylyn smiled. "I'm sure she didn't mean anything by it. She was probably just being friendly."

"Oh." Wanda wrinkled her nose and glanced back over her shoulder. "Friendly's good, I guess. She didn't even seem to notice my piercings."

Kaylyn let the comment pass and stuck out her hand. "Any change left over?"

"Yeah." Wanda's eyes drifted past Kaylyn's outstretched hand and her face brightened. "They're here, Momkay. I wonder what's in the truck."

Kaylyn wondered the same thing as the rented three-quarter ton pulled up beside them and Lisa climbed out. "Sorry, we're late. Robert wanted to bring his grandfather's little tractor along. He thinks it might be useful, but we needed a truck to do that…" She shrugged and scanned the parking lot. "I suppose that everyone else has gone ahead."

"We've been sending them off in batches. We're the last." Kaylyn caught Wanda's sleeve as she moved toward the truck. Ian was waving at her through the window. "If you're ready, we should go."

"Just give us a sec to use the bathroom," Lisa said, "Maybe get something to drink."

"If the woman in there asks, we're going to Arborg," Wanda said as Lisa turned away.

"I'll keep that in mind." The short, blond woman smiled over her shoulder as if she understood.

"I like her," Wanda said. She waved to Sam and Ian and followed Kaylyn into the van. Trin was still fast asleep in her booster seat.

"I do too, love." Kaylyn patted Wanda's hand. "Now put on your seatbelt. We'll be leaving as soon as they come back."

"Bout time," Grandma Grace said as Kaylyn pulled the van in behind Jessie's car on the gravel road. The old woman had obviously been waiting for them and looked genuinely relieved. "I was about to send out a search party."

"It was our fault," Lisa said. She climbed down from the truck and held out her hand. "I'm Lisa. I don't believe we met last night." She thumb-pointed over her shoulder. "And that's my husband Robert."

Grace took the offered hand and introduced herself. "Well, you're here now; that's what matters," she said gruffly and stepped back. She gave Robert the once over then nodded. "Greg's waiting for you in the red truck upfront. Andrew and Mark are with him."

Robert thanked her and called to his boys; they quickly climbed down from the truck, smiled as Wanda stuck her head out the van window, and promised to find her when they were done before running off after their father.

"I don't think any of them, including my husband, slept a wink last night that's how excited they are to be here." Lisa pulled her bag off the seat, closed the door, and turned back to Grace. "I must admit, the feelings mutual, so if you'll just point me in the right direction…"

"Here to work, are you?" Kaylyn stifled a smile as Grace couched her fists on her hips. Lisa took a small step back and tilted her head to her side as though puzzled by the old woman's reaction.

"Of course, she is," Kaylyn said then cocked an eyebrow in Lisa's direction. "Grandma Grace has no patience for tardiness or shirkers. I think it has to do with her military background." She gave the elder an unrepentant grin. "Isn't that right, Grandmother?"

Grace humphed and Lisa stifled a smile behind her hand. Kaylyn returned Grace's glare with one of her own and was relieved when the older woman's eyes softened. "I suppose," she said gruffly then turned to Lisa. "I owe you an apology…"

"No, you don't." Lisa shook her head. "We were late and made you worry. You had a right to be upset." She shouldered her bag then gave the grandmother a nod. A pleased smile twitched at the corner of Grace's lip; Kaylyn suspected that Lisa had just made herself an ally for life. "Shall we go?"

"I…" Grace stammered then turned on her heels. "I'll take you down to the Quonsets. We're building benches and unpacking…"

"Trin's awake," Wanda called and Kaylyn heard the van door open.

"Ho…m." Trin chortled and a moment later the grinning six-year-old had attached herself to the grandmother's side.

The older woman's face lost all its remaining hardness as she took the small hand. "That's right," Grace said just as three green, garden wagons trundled onto the road. "We're home."

"Momjay," Cali called as she veered toward them. Jenna and Mel took two more steps onto to road and stopped; all three girls wore jeans and t-shirts under light jackets and were rosy-cheeked from their exertions. "Grandma

Maggie's waiting for you guys. Momjay took a group down to the lake to get water and the ones who stayed behind need help putting the benches together and unpacking boxes. Chloe and some of the others from Earth Song are busy setting up camp. Mae's going to make stew for dinner."

Kaylyn grinned at her oldest daughter's detailed report. "It sounds like everyone is spread out pretty thinly." She'd noticed the wistful look in her second daughter's eyes. Babysitting her little sister didn't hold a candle to being with her friends even though she'd volunteered for the job and wouldn't ask to be relieved of a commitment once it was made; it was one of the things Kaylyn admired most about her goth daughter. "I bet you could use Wanda's help up here." She heard the sharp intake of breath and glanced over her shoulder. "Go ahead. I'm certain one of the grandmothers will keep an eye on Trin."

Wanda gave Kaylyn an unexpected peck on the cheek. "Thanks, Momkay."

"And if you see my boys," Lisa smiled at Wanda's obvious attempt to look like that wasn't her plan all along. "Tell them where they can find me when they're finished helping their father."

Wanda nodded seriously. "I will."

"Well, don't let us hold you up," Grace said then turned on her heels and walked purposely toward the path into the meadow. Lisa grinned at Kaylyn and fell into step behind the older woman.

"I can see why we're putting the shelters here." Ingrid, Hanna's daughter and mother of five children age seven and under, stood on the edge of the lake, a broad smile on her freckled face; with her flashing blue eyes and strawberry blond hair she reminded Jessie of her fourth daughter, Billie. "And not just because of the ridiculously long distance between the Quonsets and the lake."

"Beautiful, isn't it?" Grandma Lee said. She waved her students forward and pointed toward the ridge. The three young women and two young men formed a line to Lee's right; they were all wearing the new jeans and hooded sweatshirts she'd bought them to supplement their less than sturdy wardrobes. "That's where the yurts will be. Why don't you go have a look while we fill the water jugs?"

Lian bowed to Lee. "Thank you, Sensei."

"Not, Sensei. Grandmother," Hua admonished, "We're family now. Right, Grandmother?"

"That's right." Lee turned and smiled at Lian; at nineteen going on twenty, she was the youngest of Lee's students and the least secure in her present situation. "And I would be honored if you would call me Grandmother as the others do." She felt a twinge of sadness at Lian's continued look of distress. Of the fifteen Chinese exchange students she'd accepted into her dojo at the behest of their sponsoring agency, these five had chosen to remain in Canada over the summer break. She couldn't, in good conscience, just disappear out of their lives without an explanation. She sighed. Now here they were, willing participants in the near-impossible expectations of the Dragon's Flare prophecy, content that their Sensei would never steer them wrong. Should she feel guilty about that? Only time would tell. "Now go ahead. Take a look at what will soon be your new home."

"Yes…Grandmother." Lian gave Lee a shy, half-hearted smile and hurried after the others.

"Hanna says they were your students," Ingrid observed as they watched the young people sprint up the hill.

"They still are," Lee said. She tugged at the hem of her denim jacket then picked up her discarded water jug, "Only now their lessons will be much harder on all of us I believe. Shall we?" She forced a smile and turned toward the lake.

"I'll be with you in a moment," Ingrid said. She took two steps toward the ridge then smiled over her shoulder. "I'm just going to have a peek."

Jessie fell into step beside Lee where the mixed sand and gravel verge…she couldn't really bring herself to think of it as a beach…eased its way toward a well-trodden path between the cattails. "Jenna says this swampy area is full of good food," she said as she and the grandmother eased their way toward the water; the ground was wet and muddy and Jessie wished she'd worn her galoshes instead of the steel-toed boots Kaylyn had insisted that she buy when they'd decided to renovate her great-grandmother's garden shed. "A lot of deer come through here." She pointed to the mishmash of prints. "Coyote too, from the looks of it."

"Or wolves." Lee glanced back over her shoulder, but she didn't seem worried. "My zumu told me when I was young that watering holes are neutral territory for the most part. I'm certain she believes it, but I think we'll need to find a safer spot to draw our water from, one with less traffic and more visibility."

Jessie giggled; she couldn't help it. She was feeling a bit unsettled at the moment. "Like the back lanes, you make me take during rush hour," she said lightly in an attempt to hide her nervousness behind a joke. She was going to be living here soon; she'd have to get used to the fact that they would be sharing this forest with creatures that might well see her as their next meal. She shivered. *And how are we any different?*

"Just like those back alleys, but with less rubbish." Lee smiled, placed her jugs on the ground, and bent to untie her laces. "So keep your mind calm and your eyes and ears open."

Jessie frowned. "What are you doing, Grandmother?"

Lee kicked off her left boot and bent to untie the right one. "What I'm not doing is walking back to camp with wet feet."

Jessie glanced down at the water seeping toward the seam between her rubber soles and the leather uppers. "Damn."

The inside of the first Quonset hut wasn't quite as grim as Kaylyn remembered thanks to the dozen battery-powered lanterns scattered about the room, but it was still cold and damp…and grey. She was glad that Grace volunteered to get Trin settled in the children's play area near the camp and keep an eye on her. Surprisingly, there were almost a dozen young children being watched by two of the grandfathers and three of the grandmothers.

"Well, it doesn't seem 'so' bad," Lisa said with a grimace as they stepped across the threshold and into the semi-dark interior. "But you're right. Even if it had a well, I wouldn't want to live in here for very long. It really feels more like an empty hangar than a possible home."

"Jessie says they look like two halves of a soup can and she doesn't want our girls growing up inside them." Kaylyn winced at the memory. "Something about that image gave me nightmares for a week."

"I can understand that," Lisa said softly. She met Kaylyn's eyes then cocked her head to the side. "We always want the best for our children don't we; it's hard when we fear that that won't happen. I guess that's the real reason Robert and I showed up last night." Her shrug was almost apologetic. "We've known for years that our children and grandchildren will live in a world very different from what we have now, but we didn't know how to make certain that it would be a world they could survive and, ultimately, thrive in. We belonged to the Green Party, went on marches to save the environment, even stopped using our car, and started buying local, but none of it really made a difference. It was like we were well and truly stuck until our boys came home and showed us the package you'd put together. I guess it didn't matter that it was a solar flare instead of global warming that was about to change everything, we were being offered a way to keep our children safe and healthy; we would have been fools to turn our backs on it without checking it out."

Kaylyn put her hand on Lisa's shoulder and smiled. "Thanks for sharing that," she said sincerely. "Sometimes Jess and I worry about whether we're doing the right thing by dragging everyone into this; for all we truly know, the prophecy might be totally bogus."

"And if it is, we'll soon find that out." Lisa made no move to step away. Instead, she raised her own hand and covered Kaylyn's. "But this place and these people will still be part of our children's lives. No matter what world-changing event happens in the future, our children will still have this to fall back on. As far as I'm concerned, that's all that matters."

Kaylyn nodded and stepped away. "You're right." She glanced toward the group of men and women busily sorting bags of dried beans and brown rice into metal boxes and waved a hand in their direction. "And all of them would agree with you, so let's go give them a hand. Then we can all get out in the sunshine while it's still there."

Lisa nodded and followed Kaylyn toward the south wall where Maggie was kneeling on the cement struggling to attach the lid to a two-by-three metal storage bench. The grandmother smiled over her shoulder as they approached and struggled to her feet. "Just in time," she said. "These benches aren't as easy to put together as Greg thought they would be." Her forehead creased. "Mind you, they're perfect for storage or for sitting on and Stephanie figured out that if we push three of them together they'll support a mattress…if it comes to that."

"It's always good to have a backup plan, isn't it?" Lisa tucked her bag behind a finished bench then pulled her hair back in a ponytail with an elastic band from her wrist. "So, how can I help?"

"Well, that part was relatively easy," Greg said as Ian and Mark closed the door to the second Quonset hut. The second-hand yurt the grandfather had bought a year ago, just to get the feel of how it would suit Earth Song's purposes, had fit quite nicely on the tractor's homemade trailer. The trip from the road to the meadow had taken some time because of the rough terrain and the weight of the load, but it certainly beat packing the individual pieces in on their backs. "Shouldn't take much effort at all to bring the others in when they arrive."

"Well I can guarantee it's not going to go so smoothly at the other end," Mark mumbled as he pulled off his gloves and tucked them into his belt.

"Then maybe we should go take a look-see." He suspected that Mark might be right having made the trek twice beforehand, but Greg needed to see it for himself, set his mind to solving the problem, if there was one, with all the facts on hand. "Who's up for a walk?"

"Maybe we should have something to eat first." Mark nodded toward the table set up beside the fire pit on the other side of the camp; three large coolers sat side-by-side on the ground in front of it. "Mae and Tilly brought stuff for sandwiches and bottles of juice." He grinned at Sam and Ian. "I bet there're even some of those cookies you liked so much."

"I could use a bite to eat myself," Robert said as his boys turned hopeful eyes toward the long, green, folding table and its stack of tin plates and utensils. "What do you say, Greg?"

Greg looked at his team's hopeful faces and sighed. They'd worked hard this morning and deserved a break. Couldn't have them losing their momentum just because he may have bitten off more than he could chew. "I suppose we need to keep our energy up," he said just as his pocket started to vibrate. He pulled out the smartphone Cerdwin had bought him for his winter solstice gift and glanced at the caller ID. "You fellows go ahead. I need to take this call."

"I'll make you up a plate," Mark called over his shoulder as he led the others between the rows of tents and toward what passed as the camp's kitchen.

Greg made his way to an old folding chair sitting forlornly beside a sapling birch just outside the camp's perimeter, pressed the button to return the call, and sat down. With all the goings-on lately, he'd forgotten that he had two yurts due in next week. "This is Greg Smyth returning your call," he said as Tim Young came on the line and introduced himself. "Are the first two yurts ready to be delivered?"

There was a heavy pause on the other end of the line. "About that," Tim Young said finally. Greg clenched his teeth waiting for the shoe to drop.

"We've had a bit of a cash flow problem and our accountant has ordered us to clear our inventory before we start on any more custom orders and that could take months."

Greg swallowed hard and thought he might be sick. "So you can't fill our order."

"Well, here's the thing, Greg. Can I call you Greg?"

"Do you mind if we join you?" Robert held out a cheese sandwich and a ripe pear resting on a tin plate. "Lisa thought you might like this. She'll be along with tea in a minute."

Greg stretched out his hand for the plate of food though he felt like he couldn't stomach the thought of eating. "That was the yurt company on the phone," he said as he met Robert's gaze with dull, watery eyes. "They can't fill our order…at least not the way we wanted them to." He couched the plate in his lap and waited for Robert to sit down in the mishmash of dead grass and new shoots. Lisa appeared at Robert's side, handed both of the men a mug, and took a seat beside her husband.

"It appears we have a bit of a dilemma," Robert said as Lisa raised a questioning eyebrow in his direction. "The yurt company wants to change our order."

"Cash flow problems." Greg looked down at his plate then set it beside him on the grass. "I'll eat that later," he said as Lisa gave him the eye; the same one Tilly used to express her displeasure. He took a large swallow of his tea, sat up as straight as possible on the rickety old chair, and prepared to spill his heart out. He had promised shelter that wasn't dark and dank and overcrowded, had found what he'd thought was a reputable firm…one known for its craftsmanship and punctuality. He'd even negotiated the delivery dates so that each yurt could be carried to the lake and put up before the next load came in. But what the company had just suggested…

He sighed, shook his head, and pulled the rough list he'd made from his jacket pocket. "We ordered twelve twenty-foot yurts. They have four fourteen-footers, seven sixteen-footers, two twenty-footers, one that's twenty-four-feet, and one that's thirty. They also have two twelve-footers they'll throw in for good measure and they'll sell us the lot for the price we already agreed to if we'll take delivery within two weeks." He scrubbed the fingers of his left hand through his thinning hair. "If we don't, the contract gives them six months to fulfill their end of the deal or return our deposit."

Robert nodded and stared down at his hands. Greg knew what he was thinking. If they were to avoid living in the Quonsets and still meet their protracted deadline for getting everyone safely situated, they would have to take the deal and make the best of it. From the look in Lisa's eyes, she'd come to the same conclusion. "We don't have much choice do we," Robert said as he raised his head. "As far as the square footage goes, we're going to come out way ahead and at least the yurts will be here. We won't have to worry about coming up short if the worst happens. I think we should do it."

Greg closed his eyes and propped his head in his heads. "How are we going to handle that many crates a one time?" he moaned. "It took half the morning to get the one loaded and down to the Quonsets and if the path to the lake isn't wide enough…"

"We could fly them in," Lisa said softly.

Robert almost laughed aloud at the look of horrified disbelief on Greg's face as he raised his head. "Lisa's sister and her partner were helicopter pilots in Afghanistan," the younger man said by way of explanation. "Now they have shares in a company that does everything from sightseeing tours to heavy construction."

Greg shook his head. He didn't quite believe what he was hearing. "We couldn't afford that." He looked up sharply. "And even if we could, they'd have to agree to join us. We all decided right at the beginning that the only people who can know the location of this camp are the people who are going to live here. It would be too dangerous otherwise."

Greg heard Lisa's sharp intake of air and watched as Robert reached for her hand; of course, they both knew the danger he was talking about, the people who would feel entitled to take this place away from them without a second thought to anyone's welfare but their own.

"We were going to talk to someone today about bringing Kim and Juno on board," Robert said, "They're really our only living family…"

"And they'd probably do it for the cost of fuel." Lisa looked so hopeful there was no way Greg could ignore it even if he'd wanted to.

The old man nodded then returned his attention to Robert. "We need to take the changes to the building committee, but first we need to find Jess and Kaylyn and the grandmothers." He gave Lisa a wry smile. "Not that they'll say no, mind you, but it's best to run potential members by them since they're the ones with the list of names." He chuckled. "Makes them feel on top of things, you know."

Sitting on an upturned log beside an open fire pit with her plate resting on her knees and her closest friends all around her reminded Maggie of her summers at Girl Guide camp. Of course, her bottom had been well-muscled at the time and her limbs were much more supple. "Could use a lawn chair right about now," she said to no one in particular and saw a couple of heads nod.

"Mine finally fell apart at the end of last summer," Kathleen said, "Never got around to replacing it. Didn't see any pressing need."

Grace chortled and waved her arm in a broad circle. "Didn't see all this either, did you?"

"No, I suppose I didn't." Kathleen shrugged and took a bite of her cheese and mustard sandwich; thinking about that combination always made Maggie's teeth ache.

"I think we have visitors."

Maggie followed the direction of Tilly's nod. Lisa waved as their eyes met then quickly closed the gap between them. "I'm glad we found you all together." She smiled at Kaylyn as she took a seat and waved Greg and Robert over to join them. "Robert and I have a request to make and we've been told you're the people we should bring it to." She glanced at Greg as though waiting for confirmation; the grandfather shifted uncomfortably on his log and looked away.

"We'll do what we can, dear." Maggie tried to keep the hesitancy from her voice. Whatever promises Greg had made to the young couple, he was obviously having second thoughts. "Go ahead."

Lisa heaved a sigh of relief and raised her head to take in the whole group. "I have a sister…her name's Kim…she and her partner flew helicopters in Afghanistan."

"Helicopters. Now isn't that something?" Maggie put her empty plate on the ground and rested her hands on her knees. She met Kathleen's eye across the fire pit and knew that her friend was as intrigued as she was. "Let me guess. You'd like to ask them to join us and you want us to give you the go-ahead."

Lisa nodded.

"Well, we can't really do that." The young woman's face fell. Maggie scowled at Greg and hurried to explain. "You remember Jessie talking about ripples in a pond of friends and family."

Lisa gave a resigned nod.

"Well, your sister and her partner are yours and Robert's ripples. You're part of this family now. If you think Kim and…"

"Juno," Lisa said hesitantly as she tried to process what Maggie was saying.

"…Juno will be good additions to the project. Then who are we to say otherwise?" Maggie sat back and let her words sink in.

"But Greg…" Lisa scowled at the old man then a huge grin spread across her face. "Where do we sign them up?"

Kathleen's head came up. "So you've already told them about us."

"No, but I know that when I do they'll be all for it," Lisa smiled. "What's happening here is exactly what they've been looking for since they were discharged. We plan on asking them tonight. It's just that"—her eyes slid toward Greg and back again— "we were told there are only four places left on the list…"

"…and we can't take the chance that those spaces will be filled by someone else." Greg scrubbed his fingers through his hair then gave Lisa an apologetic shrug. "That's why I brought them here, so we could be certain that they were penciled in right away."

Robert snorted. "Maybe you should start at the beginning," he said somewhat gruffly.

"Yes, maybe you should," Maggie agreed.

Greg looked down at his hands; they were folded into loose fists in his lap. "I suppose you're right."

"Whoa. When did this all come about" Kaylyn scooted from her log to the ground and tucked her knees up to her chest; she saw the momentary envy in Maggie's eyes and decided right then and there to find the money for folding chairs for each of the elders.

"A little more than an hour ago," Robert said.

Maggie pulled the crumpled list of members from her jacket pocket and spread it out on her lap. She raised her head and met Lisa's eyes. "I want you to know that Kim and Juno are welcome here, helicopter or no helicopter; they're your family; and by extension, they're mine and everyone else's."

Lisa nodded. "I'll tell them that." She said softly. She reached for the pen and paper Maggie held out to her.

"Well, go ahead," Kaylyn said as Lisa stared down at the page. "We can always use more strong women to keep things going around here. I, for one, am looking forward to meeting them."

"Thanks, Kaylyn," Lisa said as she scribbled the names on the bottom of the sheet and gave it back; Maggie folded it and tucked it carefully into her pocket.

It felt strange and a little frightening to have the success of their entire project rest in the hands of two women she'd never met and Kaylyn could see that concern writ plain on the faces of those around her. She finished the last bite of her sandwich then raised her eyes to meet Lisa's. "Are you staying for a while?"

"Well, of course, I am." The blond woman frowned. "We still have four benches to put together. Right? And Kim and Juno aren't coming by the house until this evening. I already called them and they're bringing supper with them." She smiled sheepishly. "I kinda knew you wouldn't say no to our request."

"Good." Kaylyn grinned, more relieved; then she'd expected to be by what she'd just heard. She really liked Lisa and was glad to hear that a level of trust had been established between them. She also desperately needed help to finish the benches; they were a two-person job and the grandmothers lacked the upper body strength to manage easily; Jessie was still hauling water and her older girls were busy collecting wood for the evening campfire. "I'll get us both a tea and then we can go."

"There is one more thing I'd like to mention," Lisa said.

Kaylyn lowered herself slowly back to the ground and waited.

"I heard you tell Grandma Hanna that we'd be lucky to afford half of the equipment we need, so adding anything new to the list wasn't really feasible at the moment. I wasn't trying to eavesdrop," she hurried to add, "But it got me thinking. We shouldn't have to put out good money for things that we probably already have in the garage…"

"…or the kitchen, or the attic." Maggie laughed. "I never thought about it but you're absolutely right."

Lisa looked pleased when she turned to Kaylyn. "Do you have a copy of the equipment list with you?"

"No," Kaylyn grinned. "But I'm certain Cali has one in her bag of tricks."

"Then let's go find her, shall we?" Lisa stood up abruptly. "Maybe, if she has one, we could read the list at supper and everyone can start thinking about what they have to pitch in." She smiled at her husband. "I'm certain that Robert wouldn't mind donating his snowshoes and fishing poles to the cause."

"And Lisa has this humongous soup pot that belonged to her aunt," Robert laughed. "You could feed an army out of that thing."

"Sounds like a plan…and a good one," Grace said, "I've got a storage locker stuffed with good things." She waved her hand dismissively. "Don't ask me why, but some things are too useful just to be tossed aside."

Megan giggled. "Never pegged you as the sentimental type."

Grace gave her a mock frown. "There's a lot to me that you don't know about me."

"I'm sure there is, Gracey." Meg looked unapologetic. "And whose fault is that?"

"If I could have your attention while the final touches are being made to this evening's feast, we have a bit of business to attend to." Tilly waited as one by one, the members of Dragon's Flare found a place to sit around the fire. When a hush fell over the gathering, she smiled. "First of all, the suggestion has been made that many of the items we've deemed necessary to our survival might already be in our possession…things like fishing poles or skis or snowshoes…"

"I have a complete set of gardening tools," Hanna said, "But we could use more."

"I have a still." Jake smiled sheepishly. "It was my granddad's…kinda an heirloom."

Tilly scowled. "And just what does your granddad's still have to do with our survival?"

"Maybe nothing." Jake shrugged. "But it can't all be about surviving, can it?"

"That's exactly what it's about." Tilly fought down the desire to put Jake squarely in his place and squared her shoulders. "Anything that has to do with preparing, cooking, storing, or producing food needs to be on that list as well as blankets and bedding. We'll be ordering bunk beds from what I've been told and the yurts are too small for any other furniture."

"We'll also need tools: axes, saws, hammers, chisels," Robert said, "And cooking utensils."

"I'd like to bring my paints." Greg smiled. "Buy a few canvases."

"And where are you going to keep them?" Tilly demanded, "The paints will freeze in the Quonsets." She shook her head as Greg's smile faded. "Listen, people. I know it sounds harsh, we have very little time to get the essentials out here and stored away. Room in the vehicles is at a premium and every non-essential item we bring out here is taking space away from something we truly need."

"So what do you propose?" Maggie asked.

Tilly squared her shoulders. "We need a 'no frills' list from each committee…just the bare essentials…and we need to stick to it; at least until we have the necessities taken care of."

"Makes sense," Grace said, "My committee will have a list of kitchen utensils and gardening tools ready for tomorrow…with the stipulation that we revisit all this once the essentials have been taken care of."

Tilly smiled. "Of course."

Cali pulled a sleepy Trin down into her lap and smiled as Momkay tucked a blanket around them. "Jenna said just to put it in her tent when you're done with it."

"Where is Jen?" Cali looked over her mother's shoulder. She hadn't seen her new friend or her other sisters since they'd finished eating.

"Scrubbing pots." Jessie grinned. "Wanda and Jo volunteered to help…without any encouragement. Billie's with Stephanie and Sophia straightening out the woodpile and sorting the logs from the kindling; most of the people who are staying over are helping them. We'll be leaving as soon as everyone's finished."

"I wish we could stay." Cali tried not to sound petulant, but she knew that they weren't coming back for a few days and she didn't want to miss the excitement when Ian and Sam's aunts flew in their helicopter.

"So do I," her mother said as she lowered herself to the ground, "But we have to be home when Andy comes for her mandatory visit and Grandma Maggie and Momjay and I have shopping lists a mile long that we're going to need to get done as soon as possible." She wrapped her arm around Cali's shoulder and pulled her in tight. "And you and Wanda have perhaps the most important job of all waiting for you to get back to it."

"I suppose." Cali hadn't forgotten the huge binders of information sitting beside Grandma Maggie's computer back at the house full of do-it-yourself instructions from the internet on everything from building a proper outhouse and making your own bow and arrows to tanning a hide with urine. She stifled a giggle at the memory of Wanda's face when she'd read that one then sighed in resignation. "Will we at least be here to help when the yurts are brought in?"

"Of course, we will." Kaylyn nodded thoughtfully. "And once everything is here, we'll have a better idea of how long it will be before we can move everyone on site permanently, but I promise you, solar flare or no solar flare, we'll be living out here this summer."

"Do you think we'll have the yurts up by then?" Cali hugged Trin tighter. "There's an awful lot of them. What if Ian's aunts can't chopper them in?"

Kaylyn raised a dark eyebrow. "Chopper them in. Where did you hear that?"

"From Sam."

"Well, Lisa and Robert are certain that Kim and Juno will be willing to help us," Kaylyn said. She pulled a corner of the blanket over Trin's shoulder. "And I believe them. Now, why don't you…"

"Momkay!" Billie's frantic shout brought Kaylyn immediately to her feet. The red-headed dynamo, her fourth daughter, sprinted from between two tents and stopped.

"Over here."

Billie turned toward her mother and grinned. "I've been looking all over for you."

Kaylyn took a deep, calming breath as her daughter closed the gap between them. Cali buried her smile in Trin's soft hair. "You scared me half-to-death," Kaylyn said. "Unless it's an emergency, use your inside voice next time."

"But we're not…"

"I wouldn't argue, if I were you," Cali warned knowing full well what her younger sister was about to say.

Billie narrowed her eyes then glanced over her shoulder. "I'll be back in a minute," she said with a huff and headed toward the tents.

"Thank you for the ride home," Stephanie said as she climbed into the van. "When Cerdwin offered to pick us up this morning, she didn't mention that she was staying the night."

"I'm sure it never occurred to her that you weren't." Maggie slid over to make room in the front seat. "Well, no harm done."

"Thanks to Billie…and the rest of you," Stephanie couched the oversized shoulder bag she was carrying in her lap and smiled. "Not that we couldn't have made do, mind you. One night in the quonsie wouldn't have been so bad and I brought along extra clothes just in case, but…"

The smile faded. "…I need to see my daughter, talk to her doctors."

"Of course, you do." Maggie recognized the resignation in Stephanie's voice and could sympathize with her quite easily; it was gut-wrenching to lose a child as Maggie well knew and even more so when that child was about to leave another behind. She gave Stephanie a few moments to collect herself then smiled into the review mirror as Kaylyn appeared on the road behind them followed by Billie and a widely grinning Sophia. "Your granddaughter seems to have had a good time today."

"Oh, my goodness, she loves it out here. And everyone is so kind to her. Of course…" Stephanie frowned and shook her head. Maggie sensed that something important had just gone unsaid. "I think we'll both be happy here."

Maggie smiled. "That's good to hear, especially since everything is so up in the air right now."

"Or not," Stephanie said with a sudden grin. "I certainly hope those young women choose to help us out with their helicopters. I really don't know how we can do it all if they won't."

"Momkay says that if Lisa and Robert are certain that Kim and Juno will help us," Cali said over the back of the seat, "That's good enough for her."

"Then I guess it's good enough for me too." Stephanie turned and smiled over the seat just as her granddaughter climbed inside with Billie. She gave Cali a nod then settled back and pulled her seat belt over her shoulder as Kaylyn opened the driver's door.

"Are Cali and Trin in here?"

"We're here, Momkay," Cali called from the back seat.

"Good." Kaylyn climbed in and closed the door. "Wanda and Jo are going back with Jessie, so that means everyone is present and accounted for."

"Maybe we could stop at the gas station on the way," Maggie kept her tone light, but after using that plastic barrel with the tiny seat that passed for a toilet earlier in the day, her decision not to do so again was finally catching up to her. Somehow they'd need to get a proper outhouse set up soon.

"No problem," Kaylyn said with a knowing grin. "I could use a bathroom break myself."

Chapter Eighteen

Maggie handed Billie a clean pair of pj's from the mound of laundry that hadn't been put away for days then sat down on the bed and patted the mattress beside her. JoJo would be in the shower for a few minutes yet…just enough time for Maggie to do some gentle probing. "That was quite the day, wasn't it," she said as Billie accepted her invitation. "Did Sophia enjoy herself?"

Billie's eyes lit up. "She said it was the best day she's ever had."

"I'm glad to hear that. Her grandma said people aren't always kind to her." Maggie knew she was stretching the truth, but from what Stephanie had said…or didn't say…she knew she wasn't far off.

Billie hugged the pajamas to her chest and nodded. "Sophia's different…" Frown lines appeared amidst the sprinkling of freckles then disappeared as quickly as they'd come. "Kinda like Aunt Alice."

"Is that right?" Maggie wasn't certain what to make of that revelation, so she schooled her face and kept her tone light. "So…Sophia can see the future."

"No…not the future…not really. But for a while." Billie sighed and shook her head. At that moment, she looked more world-weary than any twelve-year-old ever should. "When we were little," she said softly, "Sophia used to tell me stories about the kids at school. She'd say Kevin is going to steal Ryan's ball glove, or Janie's going to run away from home. I thought she was just making things up at first…"

"…but she wasn't…making them up."

"Nope. All those things actually happened exactly the way she said they would." She raised her head and met Maggie's eyes. "It was the voices, you see."

"The voices?"

Billie nodded. "She can hear what people are thinking…like they're talking to her inside her head."

"Did she ever tell this to anyone else?" Billie looked stricken by the question as though it brought back painful memories. Maggie hugged the tiny body close and kissed her forehead. "It's okay. You don't have to tell me."

"It's not that, Gran. It's just…she tried a few times…to warn people when she knew that something bad was going to happen." Billie sighed, scrubbed her eyes with the back of her hand, and sat up. "But no one wanted to listen to her; they thought she was crazy. Only a sick person hears voices in their head, right? When her mother learned about it, she took her to the doctor and had her put on pills."

"But you didn't think she was sick."

Billie gave her head a savage shake. "She was my friend and those pills did bad things to her. So one day I crawled in the kitchen window and threw them away. Sophia's mother was too high most of the time to notice much…" She took a deep breath. "I told Sophia what I'd done and made her promise never to repeat what the voices said anymore to anyone but me."

Maggie nodded. "Did she keep that promise?"

"Yeah…well, mostly. But everyone already thought she was crazy." Sadness thickened her voice and brought tears to Maggie's eyes. "Kids can be really mean sometimes, but Sophia's got guts. No matter how much the things they said hurt her, she just pretended to ignore them until they backed off and found someone else to bully." Her jaw clenched. "Good thing too or they would have had to deal with me."

Maggie didn't doubt that for a moment. "So Stephanie knows that Sophia is still hearing the voices…that they're real."

"How…" Billie gave Maggie a sideways glance then shrugged. "Sophia had to tell her, Gran. She was at Sophia's house the night…" The narrow chest heaved as Billie choked back a sob. Maggie found the tiny hand fisted on the bed between them and gave it a gentle squeeze. She knew that her granddaughter believed every painful word she said, but Maggie needed to hear the end of this tale before she made up her mind. "…the night my dad decided to off himself and take me with him. Sophia heard me in her head begging him not to and phoned the police. Her gran overheard her and asked what she was doing."

"And Sophia told her."

"Yep. And when the police came to talk to her, her gran backed her up. Said they were on the back porch and heard yelling." She gave Maggie a tentative smile. "Sophia saved my life, Grandmother."

Maggie heard the edge of fear behind those words; as much as Billie had come to love and trust her new family, in this case, at least, that trust needed reassurance. "I know she did, love,"

Maggie said softly, "And I think it's a good thing that Stephanie found out about the voices and the pills that night…" Though Maggie suspected that Sophia's Grandmother had already had an inkling about what was going on. "At least Sophia had someone to talk to when you weren't there."

Billie nodded sagely. "I never thought about that."

"And, don't you worry," Maggie said as another sigh wracked the tiny body, "Sophia and her grandmother will always have a place with us." And she meant it. Though she would definitely have a good long talk with Stephanie; the more she knew, the better it would be for all concerned.

"Thanks, Gram," Billie smiled. "Never doubted it for a moment."

By the time they'd dropped Stephanie and her granddaughter at their north end bungalow, eaten the takeout pizza Jessie ordered on the way home, and managed to get all of the girls cleaned up and into bed, Kaylyn could barely keep her eyes open and it was only nine o'clock. "I really need a shower and a good night's rest," she said knowing the first would be lukewarm and the second would be impossible. How could anyone sleep with so many unknowns running around in their head, chasing their tails like a litter of overexcited puppies?

"You go ahead," Jessie said as she filled the kettle. "I'll just have a wash down here before I get ready for bed."

"Practicing for the future," Kaylyn said with a wry smile.

Jessie frowned then shook her head obviously confused.

"Boiling water. Washing up in a bowl." Kaylyn groaned. Sometimes Jessie could be so obtuse. "I'll see you upstairs." She said. She could feel Jessie's eyes follow her as she walked out of the kitchen, but she didn't look back. Jessie had always been stronger than she was, more able to adapt to new situations. Kaylyn had no doubt that her partner would thrive at Dragon's Flare, happily bathing in a bowl and waking up in the cold to stoke the fire...even if they were forced to live in a soup can, but Kaylyn wasn't certain she could do the same and that scared her more than she wanted to admit.

She stepped into the shower and turned on the hot water tap; the water was barely warm enough to get a decent lather. She washed quickly, rinsed the soap from her hair with cold water, and turned off the tap as she reached for her towel. She was in bed with her back to the door when Jessie came in.

"Want to tell me about it?" The bed sagged as Jessie crawled under the covers; she smelled like lavender and woodsmoke.

Kaylyn took a deep breath and rolled over. "I'm sorry," were the first words out of her mouth; her little tantrum hadn't been Jessie's fault. "I know that it was childish of me to get upset, but boiling water so you could have a wash just seemed to come so naturally to you. It's not that I haven't done the same thing on camping trips...or that time when the power went out." She knew she was babbling, but she couldn't stop herself. "It's just that hearing you be so nonchalant about it seemed to trigger something."

"Go on." Jessie propped her head on her hand; there was real concern in her eyes.

Kaylyn nodded. "I'm not brave, Jess." She pressed a finger to Jessie's lips to keep the denial at bay. "I thought I was once, but not anymore. Not that I'll let it stop me from doing what I need to do, but lately it's made it hard to breathe at times. Downstairs...tonight...what you did without a second thought made me realize how unprepared I truly am for what's about to happen." She closed her eyes and took a deep breath.

"Ah, now I understand." Jessie smiled as Kaylyn turned to look at her. "This has more to do with what's happening at Robert and Lisa's than it is about my bathing habits. You're all at loose ends right now..."

"I am not," Kaylyn said belligerently.

"Yes you are, Kat," Jessie said calmly. "It feels like our whole future is hanging by one of those tiny threads that you can't seem to grasp; you have no control over what happens next and that's making you feel uncertain and helpless. And can you guess how I know this?" She didn't wait for Kaylyn's answer. "Because I feel the same way."

Kaylyn flopped over on her back and rested her left arm on her forehead. "I don't know how you put up with me sometimes. Of course, you feel the same way; I imagine everyone does and here I am moaning about bathing bowls and how brave I'm not."

"So what are we going to do about it?" Jessie glanced pointedly at the clock. "It's just nine-thirty. I know Lisa said they'd call tomorrow, but…"

"Are you sure this is where we're supposed to meet them?" Jessie asked as they turned off the road.

The tiny café huddled between a computer depot and a hair salon in an aging and grimy strip mall that had definitely seen better days; there were only two other vehicles in the parking lot. Kaylyn took a second glance at the paper in her hand and nodded. "This is the address. Doesn't look like much, does it?"

"Oh, I don't know. Maybe it has really good coffee." Jessie climbed down from the van and waited for Kaylyn to join her. "Lisa didn't say why she couldn't tell us over the phone?"

Kaylyn felt a shiver of dread run up her spine and breathed into it; she'd made enough of a fool of herself already without giving vent to her fear in a dark and dirty parking lot. "I'm sure she had a good reason," she said tightly as she opened the door and stepped inside. Lisa waved to them from the far corner.

"I'll get the coffee," Jessie said heading left toward the front counter. "Be with you in a minute."

Kaylyn took a deep breath, pulled down the zipper of her burgundy windbreaker, and headed for the far table. A dark-haired woman with caramel skin and large brown eyes perched on the bench beneath the window; a blond who could only be Lisa's sister sat beside her.

"Glad you could make it," Robert said as Kaylyn took the chair beside him. "We would have asked you over to the house, but the boys have had enough excitement for one day and we didn't want to wake them."

"Besides, this place serves better coffee." The dark-skinned woman grinned at Robert then reached across the table. "Hi. I'm Juno." She glanced at the woman beside her. "And this is Kim."

Kaylyn nodded toward Lisa's sister then took the offered hand and shook it. "I'm Kaylyn." She gestured over her shoulder. "Jessie's getting the coffee."

"Actually, it's good that you called," Lisa said as her eyes tracked Jessie's progress. Kaylyn forced herself to breathe. "These two wanted to speak to you and Jess in person before they make their decision."

"Here's your coffee, Kat." Jessie handed Kaylyn a white mug and slid into the chair to her right. She'd obviously heard the last bit of the conversation. "So, how can we help?"

Kim smiled thinly. "Lisa and Robert showed us all the information you gave them, but you have to admit that it all seems pretty…"

"…far-fetched." Jessie supplied into the elongated pause. "Believe me. We know what that feels like."

"I'm sure you do." Kim drew a deep breath and her shoulders noticeably relaxed. She leaned back against the cushioned seat. "Then you understand why we needed to meet with you. Not that we don't trust Lisa and Robert's judgment…" She smiled at her sister. Lisa returned the acknowledgment with a wry smile of her own. "…but Juno and I have put a lot of time, effort, and money into building our company and we can't just give it up without being absolutely certain that we're doing the right thing." Kim glanced sideways at Juno. "So what we really need…"

"…is to hear the story from the horse's mouth."

"Like Mr. Ed." Jessie grinned then sighed and shook her head when no one seemed to understand the reference. She shrugged. "He was a talking horse in one of those fifties reruns my grandmother used to enjoy." Kaylyn gave Jessie's hand a sympathetic squeeze beneath the table; growing up in a household of old women had distinct disadvantages at times. "So…what can we tell you," Jessie asked, "that you don't already know?"

"Your aunt was a bona fide seer?"

"Great-aunt and according to eyewitnesses, she was."

Kim nodded thoughtfully. "You inherited the land…and the prophecy from her." She glanced sideways at Juno then looked away. "So say that this time, your aunt—great-aunt was wrong" She tilted her head to the side, obviously letting the idea sink in. "If that happens, what are you going to do with the land and everything else people have helped to build?"

Kaylyn felt Jessie stiffen then very slowly relax. "I asked Grandma Maggie that same question not long ago." She smiled at the memory. "She said that there's maybe a one percent chance that Alice was wrong and even if she was, with things going the way they are in the world, only someone with less than half a brain would be willing to walk away from what we're in the process of reclaiming."

Juno frowned. "And what would that be?"

"A future for ourselves and our children."

Kaylyn saw Robert give Kim a small nudge and smiled. "I can understand where you're coming from," Kaylyn said, "It must seem odd to you that we would give up any proprietary interest in the property so easily, but our lives have never been particularly insular. Jess was raised by seven well-educated grandmothers who, by the way, sold their possessions and raided their bank accounts to fund this project." She saw the flicker of interest in Kim's eyes and smiled. "Those seven women are now helping to raise our five foster daughters and I basically grew up in an artist's commune surrounded by people intent on leaving this materialistic world behind as soon as possible, so it's only natural for us to share what we have unconditionally…but how would you know that?"

"You wouldn't." Jessie leaned forward in her chair. "And all I can tell you is that the welfare of our family is the most important thing in the world to Kat, and I'm talking about the kind of family bound together by mutual respect and love, not necessarily by blood." Kaylyn felt Jessie's fingers tighten around her own as Kim and Juno seemed to draw closer together. "Pretty soon the people who are working so hard to build a viable community for themselves and each other will realize that they're a family." Jessie grinned across the table. "And on Lisa and Robert's recommendation, we'd like you to be part of that…with or without your helicopter."

"Whoa." Juno leaned across the table. "But without the chopper, you won't be able to accept the deal the yurt company has offered."

"Not much of an offer if you ask me," Robert muttered.

Jessie gave Robert a sharp nod of agreement. "We'll also lose a great deal of money we can't afford to lose, but we can't leave the yurts on the side of the road and it would take months for us to move them to the building site…even if the trails…" Jessie took a deep breath. "But we still have the Quonsets…"

"Hell, no," Kim blurted, "Lisa told us about them. They might be fine for a bunch of grunts to hole up in for a while, but not as a permanent home for my nephews." She grinned at Lisa. "Or my sister."

Kaylyn let out the breath she hadn't known she was holding as Kim turned to Juno. Do or die, this was the moment. "So what do you think? It'll get us out of this godforsaken city. Fresh air. A fresh start. Wide opened spaces." Kim's smile broadened into a full-blown grin. "It'll be an adventure, Junie, and we haven't had one of those in such a long time."

Juno glanced around the table then turned to Kim and grinned. "You always get your way, don't you?"

"So, is that a yes or a no?" Kaylyn shrugged as all eyes turned her way; it wasn't like she was the only one who wanted to know.

Juno sighed dramatically. "It's a yes, of course…the chopper too."

Lisa stifled a laugh as Jessie reached across the table and shook Juno's hand. "Thank you," Jessie said, "You've just made a lot of people very happy."

Kaylyn glanced at her watch as Robert dialed Greg's number; the woman behind the counter was giving them very noisy hints that it was closing time, but there was still so much that needed saying, plans that needed to be made. "I know it's getting late," she said, "And I, for one, am exhausted. So what do you say to brunch tomorrow…around ten-thirty." She turned to Lisa. "You could bring the boys. I'd just…I just think it would be good if we could hash some things out before everything gets crazy again."

Robert laughed. "I'm all for that."

"So will you come?" Kaylyn swept the table with her eyes. "Grandma Maggie loves to cook…"

"We'll be there," Juno said then gave her partner a cheeky grin. "And so the adventure begins."

Juno chewed and swallowed her last bite of Grandma Maggie's cheese and green pepper omelet then washed it down with freshly ground coffee. "Lisa told us that, at first, you thought you had a year to prepare for this."

"We did." Jessie put her fork down and stifled a contented sigh. Grandma Maggie had outdone herself this morning and Jessie was comfortably full of fried ham, omelet, and buttery garlic bread; it gave her a warm feeling inside and that made her slightly sleepy. "Thirteen moons…essentially a year…was the only time frame we were given." She shrugged. "I know it sounds pretty vague, but how else could we interpret it?"

"But that all changed."

"You're talking about Alice's tick-tock notes." Jessie acknowledged Juno's nod then picked up her coffee mug and cradled it in her hands. She didn't need to look around to know that everyone was watching her; the kitchen had become ominously silent. "I have to admit that they sent us off the rails there for a while."

JoJo giggle. "For a while?"

"More like forever," Billie said with a cheeky grin.

"Eat your breakfast, girls." Maggie's tone was light, but there was no mistaking the look in her eyes; Jo and Billie bowed their heads over their half-empty plates and tucked in with a vengeance. Sam and Ian shared a glance then followed suit.

"As ill-mannered as they might seem," Jessie said, ignoring the sharp intake of breath from her middle daughter, "In some ways, the girls are right. There's a big difference between believing you have months to get something done and suddenly finding out that you may have mere days."

"Days!" Kim coughed and reached for her coffee.

"There's really no way to know how long we have," Maggie said reasonably, "So there's no sense getting your knickers in a knot. What we do know is that there is no major activity taking place on the sun right now thanks to the websites Greg and some of the youngsters are monitoring."

Kim didn't look convinced. "But essentially it could happen at any time."

"That's why it's so important that we get everything to the site as soon as possible," Kaylyn said around a mouthful of omelet. "Once that's done, we'll get everyone moved into tents, and then it won't matter to us when the flare happens. We'll all be safe and we'll have months to get things set up for the winter."

"Unless we're up in the air when the flare happens," Kim deadpanned.

There was a moment of heavy silence then Juno laughed. "Don't worry. If that happens, it won't be the first time we've crashed and walked away."

"What!" Lisa gasped and turned angry eyes toward her sister. "You never told me that happened."

Kim just smiled and shrugged.

"So what needs to be taken to the site," Juno said coming to her partner's rescue, "Besides the yurts."

"The woodstoves," Cali piped up, "They're the next most important thing."

Juno grinned at the young woman. "I would tend to agree with that."

Cali smiled and ducked her head; Kim and Juno had obviously had an effect on her oldest daughter; she'd been watching them very closely since they arrived. "We also have to purchase sixty bunk bed frames," Jessie said trying to picture the list Kaylyn had shown her, "Lumber for the outhouses. Cement blocks to support the yurts."

"And the commodes," Maggie added.

Robert frowned. "Commodes?"

Maggie huffed. "Not everyone can just pee out the door if it's the middle of the night."

The boys giggled and Robert turned a pale shade of red. "Ah. I see," he said and stuffed a piece of garlic bread in his mouth.

"Well, as part of our business agreement, we can sign the Snow Eater out for two weeks. We just need to put it down as holiday time," Kim said thoughtfully. Then she turned to Kaylyn. "Lisa says that you're part of the Equipment Committee. How long do you think it will take to get the woodstoves and everything else out to the property? Can you do it this week? We'll need to get the small stuff into the site and packed out of the way before we fly in the yurts."

Jessie watched as Kaylyn closed her eyes and took a deep breath; they both knew that they'd be starting from scratch, that not one stove or bed frame had been ordered so far. "Winnipeg's a big city," Jessie said by way of encouragement.

Kaylyn opened her eyes and nodded. "We'll do our best to get it all up there by next Sunday."

"Good enough," Juno said and poured herself a third cup of coffee.

Chapter Nineteen

"That's the last one." Cali glanced sideways at Sam and Ian's mom then held her breath as the large crate wobbled in a sudden gust of cold wind. Momkay was on the ground crew at this end and Cali didn't want to think of what would happen to the people waiting patiently below the chopper's belly if the tether suddenly snapped. Lisa was dealing remarkably well with the demands of various muscle strains, two pulled tendons, and a broken toe from four solid days of lifting and lugging. The twenty woodstoves had been the worst and Mark would be using a crutch for a while, but the injuries from having a thousand-pound crate land on someone's head would be beyond her skills and well their nurse practitioner knew it.

The crate wobbled again and the chopper slid sideways. Lisa's fingers clamped down painfully on Cali's shoulder. "Good," the older woman sighed and Cali tried not to wince as they watched the ground crew scatter. "At least someone up there has some sense."

"That would be my mom," Wanda said proudly from Lisa's other side then long, black nailed fingers came up to shade her eyes. "Looks like Juno has everything under control again," Wanda said as the crate thumped down in the grass; a few minutes later, the clamps were removed and the chopper was on its way toward its temporary landing pad in front of the Quonsets.

Lisa grasped the handle of her wagon and took a step toward the ridge. "If I never see one of those oversized eggbeaters again, it'll be too soon," she mumbled.

Cali shared a knowing smile with Wanda then fell into step. Without the chopper, there would be no cozy village beside the lake and they both knew that Lisa wanted that as badly as they did.

"Momkay's coming," Wanda picked up the pace and passed Lisa at the bottom of the slope. "Hurry up, you guys," the goth yelled over her shoulder, "They're probably starving."

Cali grinned. Where food was concerned, her sister was becoming more and more like Grandma Maggie each day. Over the past week, Wanda had spent every spare moment dogging Jenna's heels as she mapped the areas around the camp where the most edible plants could be found and volunteered most nights to help Chloe make her flower soup or roasted tubers. Cali suspected that her sister's budding culinary interests stemmed from the fact that food and its future availability had become a subject of great concern among the grandmothers, and she sympathizes with Wanda's determination to never feel the gnawing ache of hunger that had plagued her early years, ever again.

"We have camomile tea and ham sandwiches for you," Wanda said as she stopped in front of Kaylyn. "Grandma Maggie said to enjoy the bread because this is the last of it, but she knew you'd be hungry and cold…"

"Well, she was right," Robert said as he scooted past Kaylyn and went to hug his wife. "No injuries this time, love."

"Not for want of trying." Lisa returned the hug then stepped away. "How could you just stand there…"

"It's been a long day." Robert shrugged; a sheepish grin twitched at the corner of his lips. Lisa scowled. "I guess we were all a bit tired and not thinking clearly. Won't happen again."

"Damn straight it won't." Lisa shook her head and turned away with a huff that would have put any one of the grandmothers to shame. Cali hid a giggle behind a cough. "Let's get this food up top. I'm sure that with all those boxes and crates, we should be able to find a place to sit down and share a bite."

"Chloe even gave me a thermos of hot water to wash up with." Wanda smiled at Lisa as she reached into her pocket then took a seat on a pile of tarp-covered bed frames. Basic hygiene was another thing that her Goth sister had taken an almost manic interest in lately, but Cali supposed that wasn't such a bad thing when Wanda spent so much time helping to prepare meals; from the pleased smile on Lisa's face, it was obvious that she agreed. "And I brought a piece of that eco-friendly soap Stephanie gave me." Wanda tossed the baggie that had appeared in her hand to Robert. "So we can do a proper job of it."

JoJo leaned her head in the open door of the helicopter and waved to catch Kim's eye. "Grandma Maggie says you're leaving."

Kim smiled as she approached. "We are. Juno and I have some things to pick up that we're definitely going to need out here. We're coming back first thing tomorrow."

JoJo nodded seriously, but couldn't quite hide the smile twitching at her lips. Grandpa Jake had shared a secret with her this morning, but he'd need Kim and Juno's help to make his plan work. Jo wasn't really certain why he'd chosen to tell her except that she was feeling kinda down and he'd obviously noticed; everyone seemed so happy traipsing around in the trees gathering wood and edible plants, but hard as she tried…she gave a mental shrug and pushed the thought away. "You want something to eat before you go?" She said trying to appear nonchalant. Grandpa Jake didn't want anyone but her and Grandpa Zeke to know what he was up to until it was necessary. She couldn't figure out why; it sounded like a great idea to her, but she was just a kid…what did she know. "Grandma Maggie says the soup is ready. It smells great. She also said you shouldn't be up there flying around on an empty stomach."

"Well, Maggie is a very wise woman," Juno said as she appeared at Kim's side. She turned to her partner and gave her a pleading look. "We still have plenty of daylight and I really am hungry." Then her look turned thoughtful. "Besides, you'll want to say goodbye to Lisa after the fright we must have given her…make certain she's okay."

A wrinkle appeared between Kim's pale eyebrows. "I suppose, but if I know my little sister, she was less frightened than angry."

"Something bad happened, didn't it?" Jo blurted before she could stop herself. "Is someone hurt? Momjay…"

"Everyone is fine." Juno squatted in the doorway and smiled reassuringly. "We just had a bit of a problem with the wind. It looked scarier than it was."

"Oh." Jo forced her lips into a smile. What more could she say? She was glad she hadn't been there, that she hadn't been forced to add one more fear to her seemingly endless list; that realization made her feel sad and embarrassed at the same time. Kim and Juno had been soldiers. They would have little sympathy for cowards.

"You okay?" Juno tilted her head to the side and her eyes narrowed.

Jo drew a deep breath and nodded, but she couldn't quite force herself to smile. "We'd better get going if you want to eat. Grandma Maggie said she'd save some for us, but that doesn't always work out the way she expects…especially if Trin and Billie decide to raid the pot when Gran isn't looking."

"Then lead on McDuff," Juno straightened, gave Kim's hand a squeeze, and took a step back. Jo didn't have time to move before the tall, dark-haired woman landed on the ground mere inches in front of her. Jo debated whether to tell Juno that 'lead on McDuff' was a misquote then decided against it; it's not like anyone would care what Shakespeare actually said when the world was falling apart all around them. Juno looked back at Kim still standing in the doorway. "Lisa won't bite, you know," Juno said then she turned on her heels and headed toward the camp.

Maggie passed almost full bowls of her special ham and white bean soup to Jo and the two pilots then settled herself carefully on an upturned log with a mug of rose-hip tea. Sophia, Billie, and Trin had spent most of the morning just beyond the tree line with Cerdwin and Jenna mapping the useful plants and learning rudimentary signs. Trin had been grinning from ear to ear when they'd returned loaded down with yellow dock, chickweed, burdock roots, and last fall's rose hips, enough to make a hearty soup for those staying the night and a delicious, healthy tea for the morning. It was a good start toward being able to eventually feed themselves, and she was glad to see her granddaughters taking an interest, but would it be enough?

"That was delicious, Maggie," Juno said as she scraped the bottom of her bowl. "Moving those crates was hungry work, especially when the wind came up."

"But no one was hurt, Grandmother," Jo hurried to add.

Maggie met Juno's eyes and saw nothing there to worry her. "Well, that's good to know."

"When do you expect the ground crew to be back?" Kim asked with a slight edge of concern in her voice. "I'd like to say goodbye to my sister before we head out."

"But you're not supposed to leave until Sunday. Grandpa Jake says the sau—" Ian's mouth clamped shut as he gave his brother a panicked look. Sam rolled his eyes.

Maggie tried not to smile; it was obvious that the grandfathers were keeping secrets again and doling them out like jellybeans. She'd seen Jake huddled with JoJo first thing this morning, talking in whispers, and now the boys knew something they weren't supposed to share. Not that she minded;

the 'grandfather secrets' as Grace called them, were always innocuous and most often shared as a distraction from issues too weighty for young minds.

"What kind of saw. A Chainsaw? A seesaw? Or maybe it's a jigsaw puzzle. You always liked those when you were little, didn't you, Ian?" Juno teased.

"You might as well tell her," Sam shook his head and smiled sideways at his aunt. Then he turned back to his brother. "You know she won't leave you alone until you do."

"But the sauna is supposed to be a surprise."

Maggie had a sudden image of sweaty, naked bodies rolling around in the snow and desperately hoped that that wasn't what the silly buggers had in mind. Billie's grin morphed into a snicker as Ian realized what he'd just done and ducked his head.

"Don't worry about it, kid," Kim said softly, "Your mom couldn't keep a secret if her life depended on it when she was your age. Besides, it's a good thing you told us."

Ian's head snapped up. "It is?"

"Uh-huh. We were planning on leaving the tethers behind when we came back, weren't we Juno?" Juno blinked then nodded her head vigorously, giving credence to the small lie that would allow their nephew to save face; Maggie smiled at the kindness.

"So the grandfathers have purchased a sauna," Maggie said into the moment of silence.

Ian nodded his head up and down a half-dozen times. He looked like he was enjoying letting the cat out of the bag now that he'd been vindicated. "Grandpa Jake showed us a picture if it. It's quite big and the stones are heated by a woodstove."

"A wood-heated sauna." Maggie tried to sound excited. "Sounds wonderful."

Ian grinned. "He said we'll be able to use it even in the winter."

"Is that what Jake told you, Jo?" Maggie asked hoping to catch her granddaughter off guard, but JoJo just looked surprised and shook her head. "Are you sure?" Maggie tilted her head to the side, but Jo was made of sterner stuff than Ian.

"Nobody told me anything about any sauna," Jo said calmly.

"Well, I think a sauna is a great idea." Kim stood up and headed for the plastic bin they used for a sink. She ruffled Ian's hair on the way by. "Why don't you and your brother go see if there's any sign of the ground crew. Even if they did stop for lunch, they should be almost back by now. If you find them, hurry them along. Okay. We have to be off soon."

"Okay, Auntie." Sam turned to JoJo and smiled. "Wanna come?"

Maggie held her breath as the old fears surfaced in her granddaughter's dark eyes. Jo looked at Juno then at Kim and squared her shoulders. "I'd love to come with you," she said with hardly a twinge.

"Are you guys staying out here now?" Sam asked as they waded through the tall grass, keeping their eyes open for wild critters. Jo had no desire to get up close and personal with another skunk or even one of the foxes that sometimes watched them from the trees. "Mom and Dad said we're going to close the house up this weekend." Sam continued. "Aunt Kim has this humongous tent with its own little woodstove; that's probably what they're bringing back with them tomorrow."

"Big enough for your whole family?"

Ian grinned over his shoulder. "Way bigger than that."

Jo looked up and swallowed hard; they were almost to the trees and still no sign of Momjay and the rest of the ground crew. "And it has a woodstove," she said in an attempt to distract herself from the inevitable. Wood burning stoves had suddenly become very important to her continued existence; maybe someday there wouldn't be any trees left to worry about.

"Yeh," Sam said thoughtfully, "They call it a prospector's tent. Aunt Kim thinks it would make a great washhouse when we get the yurts all up. You know. For laundry and bathing. I guess it has a kind of curtain…"

"There they are," Ian said as he took off at a run. "Come on you guys."

Jo stopped, wrapped her arms around her chest, and sat down. "I think I'll just wait here."

"You don't like the woods much, do you?" Sam lowered himself bonelessly to the ground and leaned back on his elbows.

Jo tried not to overreact. "What makes you say that?"

"Just a feeling." Sam shrugged. "I don't like them much either. Neither does my mom, to tell the truth. She says we'll eventually get used to it…"

"My mom died in the woods behind our house." *Was murdered. Stripped naked. Tied to a tree.* She wanted him to know that there were some things you just couldn't get used to, but she couldn't put those terrifying images in his head; he didn't deserve that any more than she did. "I was the one who found her."

"Whoa." She watched him from the corner of her eyes as he sat up and turned toward her; he looked almost as devastated as she felt. "That must have been terrible for you," he said softly.

A fleeting image of the old oak tree on the edge of the clearing just beyond the fire pit made her want to cry; she'd spent hours with that tree at Cerdwin's behest, touching it, talking to it, but it was still just a tree and the forest was still a cold and haunted place. A tear pooled in the corner of her eyes; she wiped it away with the back of her hand. "It was the worst day of my life."

"Maybe I can help," he said into the silence that had stretched between them. He waved toward the trees. "I can't make them go away, but I can promise to have your back so that you never have to go in there alone."

"You'd do that?" She turned and met his eyes. He had a kind and gentle face like his mom's and the look he gave her was full of wary sympathy…like he wasn't sure how his offer would be accepted. "But you said…"

"I know," He squared his shoulders. "I don't like peas either, but I still eat them."

She suppressed a sudden urge to giggle and saw his lips twitch. He'd be a good person to have at her back even if he couldn't make the nightmares go away. "Well, in that case," she said straight-faced and truly relieved. "I accept your offer."

"Well, that makes forty-two soup pots in various sizes, a dozen frying pans, a crate of cooking utensils, two trunks of material, a treadle sewing machine…"

"…that's Maggie's contribution." Kathleen smiled. "Apparently, it's a family heirloom."

"I suppose it could come in handy." Grace mused as she stared down at her clipboard; it just wasn't on the list. Then she cleared her throat and continued reviewing the completed inventory. It would take days to catalog the goods the members of Dragon's Flare continued to rescue from their soon to be abandoned homes; she was just glad that most of them stuck to the list they'd been given. She glanced at the sewing machine and shrugged. What could it hurt if a bit of useful contraband was thrown into the mix? "We also have eighteen snow-shovels, two dozen garden spades of varying lengths, four scythes, thirty pitchforks, and various other gardening tools…" She frowned at the next item. "Three locked metal boxes…"

"Those are the heritage seeds Hanna ordered," Megan said. "They just came in yesterday."

"In locked boxes?"

Megan shrugged. "Well, they are really valuable."

Grace shook her head and returned to her inventory. "We also have seventeen pairs of snowshoes, six pairs of cross-country skis, two dozen fishing poles plus tackle, two wooden bows…"

"…and a partridge in a pear tree."

Grace gave Megan a look that would have had any one of her grandchildren ducking for cover. Meg just grinned at her and took the clipboard from her hand. "We've been at this since first thing this morning, Gracey," the younger grandmother said, "and it's time for a break. Besides, it'll be supper time soon…"

"And Kaylyn's going to want to know that we only have two bows before they leave." Kathleen stood up from where she'd been sorting through boxes of canning jars; they might not be able to be used for their original purpose, but they'd be great for birch syrup or dried berries. "That's the priority right now. Apparently, Lee and her students have convinced one of the stores to give them a package deal…"

Grace frowned. "What do Lee's students know about hunting bows?"

"Quite a bit actually. Apparently, archery was one of the six noble arts way back when and many boys in China are still introduced to it at a young age." Kathleen grinned. "I guess the girls signed up for archery instruction as soon as they got here, not wanting to be outdone, and Lian actually made the school team this winter."

"Alright then," Grace said and closed the lid on a bench full of unused Hudson Bay blankets Megan had brought in.

Meg caught her eyes and smiled. "Steve would be glad to know his anniversary presents are finally going to be put to good use, Gracey."

"What I can't understand is why he kept giving them to you when you just put them away in the closet; especially since they've always been so expensive."

Megan shrugged. "He said I'd be glad of them someday. I guess he was right."

"Yeah, I guess he was." Grace turned and followed Megan out into the fading sunlight. They waited for Kathleen to join them before Grace locked the door. It had been a good day, all things considered; that thought made her smile. The list of essential equipment they still needed was getting smaller, the yurts had been safely delivered and, soon they wouldn't have to make the nightly trek into the city. Between all of the families, they'd managed to come up with enough tents to house almost everyone as comfortable as possible for the time being, and in a few weeks, they'd have the yurts up and the gardens started. At least that was the plan; whether it would come to fruition remained to be seen. Grace wasn't about to dwell on all of the unknowns that lay ahead of them; they had enough to take care of in the here and now…like axes and hunting bows.

"It looks like everyone is back from the lake," Meg said as they approached the makeshift kitchen. Then she glanced over her shoulder. "Feels strange not to have the chopper sitting out here. I wonder when Kim and Juno are coming back."

"Maggie says tomorrow," Kathleen fell into step beside Meg. "I guess they have some things they have to pick up and they needed the chopper to do it."

"Must be something big." Meg wrinkled her nose. "I wonder what it is."

"Tuck in, Ladies. We're calling this 'Forager's Surprise,'" Mae said as she passed around steaming bowls of soup. "Good for what ails you."

Grace stared at the green and yellow concoction then smiled to herself. Someone with a child's love of color had helped to make this soup. "Are those dandelion flowers?"

Trin giggled and nodded vigorously.

"Use your words," Cerdwin admonished gently.

Trin straightened her shoulders, raised her closed fist to eye level, and moved it up and down. Then she ducked her head and raised her spoon to her lips.

"So that's the sign for yes I take it."

Trin raised her head, smiled at Grace, and went through the motions one more time; Grace repeated it and Trin's smile broadened until it lit up her face.

"As soon as everyone has moved out here permanently, Trin and I will be offering signing classes to everyone," Chloe said.

Grace popped a flower into her mouth. "Well, sign me up." She smiled. "No pun intended."

"Glad to hear that, Grandmother," Kaylyn said as she put her bowl aside. "So how is the inventory coming?"

"About as well as can be expected considering the piles of stuff we have to go through. I suppose we should be grateful that we only included the basics when we redid the list." Grace chewed thoughtfully. "We've probably saved ourselves a pile doing it this way, but as far as the essential go, we have two bows, no axes except the one we've been using here, and no crosscut saws which we're definitely going to need with all of those downed trees scattered all over the place."

Kaylyn closed her eyes and groaned. "I was afraid of that."

"I take it that the money situation isn't good," Kathleen said gently. "I may be able to help with that depending on how long we have."

Jessie frowned. "What do you mean, Grandmother? You've already cleaned out your bank account for us."

"A lot of us have," Kathleen smiled. "But, in my case at least, the money just keeps coming in; since I won't be paying rent or insurance or utilities anymore, that money will just sit there until it disappears into the ether." Kathleen shrugged. "It's only a few thousand a month, but…"

"Why didn't I think of that?" Megan slapped her palm to her forehead. "I would have just let those pension checks go in and never come out and that would have been the stupidest thing I've ever done."

Grace couldn't help but smile. "Don't beat yourself up about it, Meg. That money may come in handy down the road, but the hunting gear needs to be brought in as soon as possible."

"Likewise the saws and the axes or it's going to be a cold, hungry winter," Kaylyn looked down at the inventory Grace had given her. "Why don't you let me take a look at the project accounts when we get home? Then we'll have a better idea of what we need to do." She raised her head to where her daughters were clustered together on the other side of the fire. Everyone else who wasn't staying for the night had already headed back to the city, anxious to get the last-minute details over and done with. "Time to go, girls." She ignored their groans and stood up. "We still have a lot of loose ends to tie up and sooner begun is sooner done. Right?"

"I guess," Wanda said. "I'll just be glad when we're out here permanently. There's a lot to learn about these woods and I can't do that if I'm not here."

"We'll keep that in mind," Jessie said as she winked at Grace then herded her children toward the car.

"I hope their social worker doesn't change her mind," Kathleen said as she watched them go.

Grace frowned. "About what?"

Kathleen shook her head. "It doesn't matter. I'm certain Jess and Kat will work it out."

Greg watched the five grandmothers climb into Hanna's SUV then closed the doors and wished them a goodnight and a safe journey. He'd made a point of walking them to their car in the evenings, not because he feared for their safety…he was an old man with wonky knees and would have sent one of the boys if that was the case…but he did enjoy their company and always sent a prayer to the source that this wouldn't be the last time he saw them.

"You coming back to camp any time soon, Old Man?" Tilly stepped onto the road at Greg's side and took his arm; he felt himself ease into the warmth of that gesture and suddenly realized that he was shivering. "Mae just made a pot of tea…the good stuff. It'll be well steeped by the time we get back."

Greg patted her hand but made no attempt to move. "Do you think she knows we're here, Til?"

"She?" Tilly's fingers tightened on his arm. "She, who?"

"The Source, Til. The All-mother. Do you think she understands that we're not quite ready to make the leap?"

"Of course, she understands, you old fool. Doesn't mean she wants to have anything to do with us in our present state." Tilly smiled to soften her words. "Don't worry. We'll get back to her someday, become what she intended us to be, but not if we don't survive what's coming." She smiled brightly. "Now come have some tea before it gets cold. It'll make you feel better."

Greg nodded and allowed her to guide him back onto the path. "What are we going to do if Kaylyn can't find the money in the budget for the things we still need?"

"She'll find the money," Tilly said through clenched teeth. "Now stop being so morose or I'll sic Jenna on you. I'm certain she's found some wild plant…"

Greg laughed; he couldn't help it. "I'm sure she has...and even if she hasn't found a cure for melancholia yet, she will eventually, especially with all those young men and women to help her." He gave her a cockeyed smile. "Maybe we should become vegetarians. Then we won't need to hunt."

"She'll find the money," Tilly snapped and pulled away.

But she can't find what isn't there. He choked back the desire to put that thought into words and nodded.

They continued their walk in silence after that and Greg was more than a little relieved as they approached the fire and Mae waved him to a seat. "The tea's still hot." She nodded toward the metal pot sitting on the grate at the edge of the fire. "But it'll be pretty strong by now."

"Just how I like it." Greg accepted a mug from Jenna a moment later and watched out of the corner of his eye as Tilly did the same. It was a small group tonight; Mark and Andrew were at the house with Cassie and Chloe battening down the hatches as best they could and preparing to extract Cassandra's sister and her niece from an abusive husband and father. There would be no going back after that; even if what they were doing wasn't technically kidnapping, Kenneth wasn't about to let his wife and daughter go without a fight.

"I wonder how the outhouses are coming along," Mae said into the silence and Jenna giggled. The cook shook her head at the younger woman. "It's not going to be so funny when we have sixty people living here day and night. As it is, that shallow hole the boys dug is starting to smell even with the ashes we've thrown in there and I'd like to get it covered soon."

"I went up to the ridge this morning," Greg put his mug aside and clasped his hands in his lap. "Jeb said the first hole would be passed the six-foot mark by this afternoon. Jake and Eric have already started on the frame and once Robert and Andrew get back tomorrow it should only be a matter of hours before the first toilet's ready to go."

"I hope you bought good, solid seats for them," Tilly said, "They're going to get a lot of use."

Greg swallowed hard and took a deep breath as his shoulders slumped.

"Don't tell me you forgot to order the seats." Tilly knew him too well not to recognize the signs.

"Okay. I won't tell you," he said trying to lighten the mood, but she would have none of it, and from the looks on their faces, neither would the rest of the women sitting around the fire. He pulled his cell phone from his pocket and dialed Robert's number.

"And tell whoever you're calling to buy good, solid, wooden ones…six of them," Tilly said thoughtfully, "It never hurts to have spares."

Even with four people scurrying around inside, the house felt deserted. Chloe had spent almost half her life living and working at Earth Song and a large part of her didn't want to leave despite the imminent danger. She ran her fingers lightly across the ancient table while her eyes scanned the kitchen. They'd packed everything they could find that was on the list and would be good to go come morning.

"We could take it with us you know." Mark stood in the doorway staring at her hand as it moved across the table. "The chairs too. I've already packed the paints and brushes along with Cerdwin's wheel and the carving tools in Greg's truck, but there's still room. We can put it all in the second Quonset until we find a place for it; there's tons of room in there."

"But none of that stuff is on the list."

Mark shrugged. "Well, it should be. We're artists, Chloe, even if everyone seems to have forgotten that lately; it makes me wonder who we'll be when we finally have a moment to breathe." He looked down at the table. "That's part of our history, Chlo…a shared memory. What can it hurt to take it with us?"

Chloe met his eyes and smiled. "Better be careful," she said softly, "People might begin to think you're all grown up."

Mark blinked then waved a dismissive hand at her. "Ain't going to happen." He pushed himself off the wall he was leaning against and winced just as the front door slammed; she wondered if his toe was bothering him. "So do we take the table or not?"

"It might give Greg a boost. He spent a lot of time sitting right here talking about the wonderful future we were going to create, but everything has been so hectic and he's been awfully down lately. Maybe between the paints and the table, we can put a smile back on his face." She closed her eyes and sighed. "Even if Tilly boxes both our ears, it'll be worth it."

Mark grinned. "So we take the table?"

"Yes."

"Everything's packed and ready to go." Andrew walked into the kitchen and paused in mid-stride as Chloe laughed. "Did I miss something?"

"Been a change of plans, Bro." Mark said, "Chloe and I have been talking…" He went on to explain the decision they'd made and the reasoning behind it.

Chloe watched as Andrew's initial frown morphed into a smile when Mark explained that having his paints and such a significant piece of Earth Song's history might lift Greg's spirits; it seemed that everyone had noticed that their elder didn't smile as often as he used to.

"Count me in, Bro." Mark pulled a crumpled piece of paper from his pocket and tossed it into the recycle bin by the door. "Be right back."

Chloe raised both eyebrows as she turned to Mark. "Was that the list?"

Mark crossed his arms and leaned against the doorframe; he looked cautiously pleased. "'fraid so."

"Grandma Lee just emailed me the estimate for the archery packages." Kaylyn sent the file to the Nan Cave printer and continued to scan the spreadsheet in her lap. "That last check Robert wrote should give us enough to outfit maybe forty people from what I just saw."

Jessie walked over to the desk and carried the freshly printed sheet over to Grandma Maggie. "Let's take a look," she said as she joined the older woman on the sofa.

The grandmother looked over at her and smiled. "My glasses have gone walkabout again," Maggie said, "So you read and I'll listen."

Jessie made a mental note to raid the drug stores for reading glasses before they left then nodded and looked down at the list of items. "Apparently, each package will include a recurve bow, a package of five strings, arm and finger guards, a simple sight, a carrying case, a quiver of twelve arrows, a skinning knife, and a hatchet."

"I don't know much about these kinds of things," Maggie said, "But that list sounds pretty comprehensive."

"I'd have to agree with you, Grandmother." Jessic continued to scan the page. "Lee says we're saving over a hundred dollars per person if we do it this way."

"But it still leaves us short."

"I don't need a bow, Kaylyn," Maggie said, "I'm too old to be trekking through the woods after deer and except for Lee…and maybe Grace, so are the rest of the grandmothers."

Jessie laughed. "Grandma Grace is as old as the rest of you."

"Don't tell her that." Maggie chuckled. "Besides it would be a point of pride with her, her being an ex-sergeant and all that entails…at least in Gracey's mind."

Kaylyn nodded thoughtfully. "I know what you mean, Grandmother, but that still leaves us fifteen packages short."

"Make that twenty." Jessie met Kaylyn's eyes and shrugged. "They've also put together five compound bow packages for winter hunting. I don't know what that means…"

"Compound bows have pulleys so they can shoot farther and pack a bigger punch." Cali grinned at them from the doorway. She held a tiny, burgundy book in her hand; Wanda peered over her right shoulder. "Can we come in?"

"Of course, you can, dear." Maggie waved them inside. "Maybe you can explain some of this stuff to us."

"I don't really know much, Grandmother. Just what I've gotten off the web." Cali sat down on the carpet and pulled Wanda down beside her. "Besides that's not why we're here." She frowned and shook her head. "Well, it is, but it isn't. Do you remember this?" She held up the tiny booklet pinched between her thumb and forefinger.

Kaylyn's eyes narrowed. "We already talked about this, Cali."

"I know we did, but you and I both know by now that university is no longer part of my future even if things don't get as bad as we think they will. I love Dragon's Flare, Momjay, and I want to spend the rest of my life learning all of the things it has to teach me." She shrugged. "Besides, once the flare hits, this money is going to be worthless; even if it still exists on some computer hard drive somewhere, no one will ever be able to find it."

"What she says is true, Kat. The banks will be forced to close, the economy will go bottom-up and, since it's plastic, we won't even be able to use our money as toilet paper." Cali giggled and Maggie winked at her. "Let me take a look at that." She reached for the book and Cali smiled as she placed it in the old woman's hand.

"And how do you feel about this, Wanda?" Kaylyn fixed her second daughter with a piercing stare.

"I think I've found where I belong, Momjay," Wanda said, and Kaylyn's eyes soften. "I didn't think I would at first, but I love the forest and all of the plants…it's amazing how many of them we can eat. It's like someone put them there just for us."

Maggie exchanged a look with Jessie. "That's a very interesting hypothesis," the grandmother said, "Have you talked to Jenna about it."

Wanda blushed. "Of course not, Grandmother. She'd think I was crazy." Then her gaze caught on Kaylyn's t-shirt and her eyes widened. "Or maybe not."

"Why don't you talk to her and find out." Kaylyn smiled. "Now, back to your money…"

"Is it enough to make up the difference, Grandmother?"

Maggie nodded. "It's more than enough, Cali."

"Then we should go and buy the bows tomorrow, so everyone can start practicing with them,"

Wanda stood up. "I'll go up and tell JoJo and Billie…"

"Tell them what?" Kaylyn tilted her head to the side and met Wanda's stare.

"That you agree." Wanda's face fell. "You do, don't you?"

"On one condition," Kaylyn said, and both girls held their breath. "I want each of you, including Jo and Billie, to make a list of five things that would help to make your life better in the years to come. Things you presently don't have in your possession. When you're done, we'll talk about this again."

"But I don't…"

Cali grabbed Wanda's arm and dragged her toward the door before she could finish. Jessie tried not to smile; Cali had always known that discretion was the better part of valor…especially when Kaylyn was involved. "Thanks, Momjay," Cali said over her shoulder. "We'll get right on that."

Jessie waited for the sound of footsteps on the stairs then turned to Kaylyn. "Mind telling me what that was all about."

"Our girls have big hearts and a strong sense of what is right, but they're still children." Kaylyn sighed and her eyes glistened in the firelight. "Cali has dreamed of going to university almost since the moment she started taking lessons from the grandmothers. Wanda wanted to be a game designer."

"I know, love, but…"

Kaylyn shook her head. "Let me finish," she said and Jessie nodded. "We put that money away for them so that those dreams could come true someday, but you were right, Maggie, we all know that isn't going to happen." She sighed and ran her fingers through her hair. "But luckily they have other dreams now." She threw her hands up and brought them down loudly on her knees; Jessie winced. "Of course, we can't leave the money in the bank, but before they empty out their bank accounts to ensure that our new family can feed and protect itself, I think they deserve to spend some of that money on themselves and their dreams without feeling guilty about it."

"So you will make that a condition of releasing the funds for other purposes." Maggie grinned and patted Jessie's hand. "See, I told you she was the brains of this outfit."

Jessie met Kaylyn's eyes and smiled. "I never doubted that for a moment, Grandmother."

"Good." Maggie leaned back and folded her arms across her narrow chest. "Because I can hardly wait to see those lists."

Chapter Twenty

"Andy. You're early." Jessie surreptitiously wiped the sleep from her eyes as she took off the Trin-proof chain and pulled the door open. "You said ten o'clock."

"I know I did, Jess." Andy glanced over her shoulder toward her car. A child's face was pressed against the passenger side window and there were signs of movement in the back seat through the tinted glass. "But I kinda have a bit of a situation here and I could use your help." She shrugged and turned pleading eyes back to Jessie. "I have six children in my car from a now-defunct group home and it's going to take some time to find them temporary placements for tonight…"

"Okay, I get it. Bring them in." Jessie stepped back from the door and smiled; Andy's whole body relaxed against the door frame. Jessie wouldn't have even considered sending the children packing when they had nowhere else to go and Andy had obviously been banking on that fact. Despite the damper, this put on the family's plans for the afternoon, those children very obviously needed out of that car, and selfish as it may be, she needed Andy relaxed enough to okay her and Kaylyn's plans, ostensibly for the summer. "Take them into the kitchen. You know where it is. I'll rally the troops."

"Thanks, Jess," Andy said as she turned away, "I owe you big time."

Jessie closed the door and leaned against it. *Just keep yourself alive, Andy. That'll be payment enough.* She drew a deep breath to steady herself, checked that the door was unlocked, and dashed up the stairs just as Maggie came out of the Nan Cave. "Visitors for breakfast, Gran." Jessie called over her shoulder as she hit the landing, "I'll be right down."

She knocked three times on each door as she headed toward the room she and Kaylyn shared.

"What's going on, Momjay?" Cali asked as she stuck her head out into the hallway. "It's not even eight o'clock."

"Andy's here…"

"Already?"

Jessie stopped and turned on her heels. "She has a bit of a situation and needs our help. You'll see what I'm talking about when you get downstairs. Now round up your sisters, please, remind them what we talked about last night and go down and say hi. I'll get Momjay…"

Just then their bedroom door opened and Kaylyn stepped into the hall fully dressed. "Well, what are we waiting for?" she said as all eyes turned toward her. "Let's not keep our company waiting."

"But we're still in our pajamas," JoJo whined and tugged at the belt on her bathrobe.

"You look fine," Jessie said as she led the way downstairs though she could fully sympathize with Jo's dilemma; no one wanted to meet strangers in their bathrobe. "Besides, our visitors look to be around Trin's age, so they probably won't even notice."

"Did you hear that, Trin?" Cali looked down at the little girl holding her hand. "Maybe you can make some new friends."

Trin made the sign for a friend that Chloe had taught her then pulled her hand free and skipped ahead. The smell of eggs and bacon wafted into the hallway as she pushed the kitchen door open.

"You've got to be kidding. That's…that's despicable." Kaylyn drew her deck chair closer to Andy's. The young social worker had just finished explaining how she'd ended up on their doorstep at eight o'clock in the morning with five children in tow. At the moment, those children were playing a noisy game of soccer on the back lawn with Trin while the rest of the girls showered and dressed. "The house manager actually absconded with all the funds…and the staff walked out because they hadn't been paid."

Andy nodded. "All except for Mildred. She phoned me and waited until I got there. She showed me a note from the landlord to the manager saying the lease was up and since they were in arrears, it wouldn't be renewed." Andy shrugged, "I think Mildred might have stayed and taken over the house except for that."

"So what are you going to do now?"

Andy shrugged. "I have a call into my supervisor. We'll probably end up putting them in a hotel until we find placements for them. It's a shame though…" Her watery eyes scanned the activity taking place on the lawn. "These kids have been together long enough to have formed a bond; now they're going to lose yet another family."

Kaylyn clenched her jaw against the sadness in Andy's voice; if Kaylyn could, she'd take Andy and the children back with them to Dragon's Flare, but they didn't have the room or the resources even if there was some way to pull it off. *We can't save everyone.* That had become her mantra every time her heart ached to steal someone away from what the fates had in store for them. She tried to tell herself that it might not be so bad for those left behind in the city, that people would band together to share their resources, plant gardens, set up systems to clean water and stay warm; maybe some would actually manage to do that at first, but in the end, would it matter? She knew the darker side of human nature all too well and there would always be some bully to come along and take it all away when there was no one bigger around to stop them.

"That's great isn't it, Kat?"

Kaylyn blinked. What could be great about children losing their homes, and possibly, their lives? "Sorry, Jessie, I think I lost the thread of the conversation there for a moment."

Jessie gave her a lopsided smile. "Andy says we've been given the okay to take the girls away for the summer."

"Hey, that's great. The girls will be so pleased." Kaylyn swallowed against the lump in her throat and put all of the enthusiasm she could muster into those words. Then she stood up and retrieved her cup from the arm of the chair. "I'm going to spread the good word and make certain everyone's ready to go."

"Go?" Andy blinked over the rim of her mug.

Jessie hurried to reassure the younger woman. "Maggie will stay here with you until you get things sorted, so don't worry. We won't be gone too long, but we promised the girls that we'd take them shopping for new camping gear and since we'll be leaving soon for Grandma Meg's cabin we really don't want to put it off."

"Cabin?"

Jessie nodded. "The cabin will be the first stop on our journey. It'll give the girls a chance to acclimatize before the real outdoorsy stuff begins."

Kaylyn choked back a laugh as Andy nodded sagely; if the young social worker only knew that there was no cabin, no family vacation, no time to get acclimated to their new lives. What they had instead of that idyllic future was the enigmatic words of an elderly woman, a section of old forest, and a ton of hard work that may…or may not preserve their lives in the times to come, but Andy would never know that. A thread of guilt twisted around Kaylyn's gut as the younger woman settled back in her chair and smiled. They were leaving Andy to a future she couldn't even begin to imagine; she definitely didn't deserve to be ridiculed for her ignorance. *Dammit. What's come over me?*

"You okay, Kat?"

"I'm fine." She could feel Jessie's eyes on her back as she pulled the door open and stepped inside. *Liar. Liar. Pants on fire.*

"We have to go right now," Jenny yelled hysterically into the phone. "Kenneth called. He's at the airport."

Mark pulled his cell away from his ear and put it on speaker. "Calm down, Jen. Are you all packed?"

"Of course, we are. Most of our things are already at the camp. All we have are two bags."

"Good," Mark said firmly. "You know that little coffee shop down the street…the one that sells the really good sticky buns?"

"Yes." He could hear all the tension she was feeling focused on that single word.

"I'll meet you there in twenty minutes."

"We'll be there." The phone went dead.

"What's going on, Mark?" Cassandra poured herself a coffee and leaned against the cupboard to drink it. "I thought I heard yelling."

"That was your sister. Kenneth is at the airport."

"Damn his hide," Cassandra spluttered. "He wasn't supposed to be back until tomorrow."

Mark pulled his jacket from the hook by the door. "The best-laid plans," he said as he shoved his arms into the sleeves. "I told her to meet me at that little café you like. You need to get everybody up and ready to go as soon as I get back. We don't want to be here when he realizes that his wife isn't at home. This is the first place he'll look."

"Thanks, Mark." Cassandra drained her cup then set it in the sink; Mark wondered if she was going to wash it before they left. Would it really matter if she didn't? "We'll be ready when you get back."

Mark nodded and headed for Cassandra's car. It was only a short drive to the café and traffic was good; he made it to the tiny strip mall in less than ten minutes. Jenny and Britney were huddled just inside the door of the café when he pulled up.

"Lookin' good, Brit. Like the new 'do.'" Britney wrinkled her nose as she climbed into the back seat. Her mother slid into the front.

"Her father demanded she has it cut," Jenny hurried to explain. "He thinks short hair is more practical for young girls. He did it himself."

Mark winked over the back seat. "It'll grow back, but in the meantime, you look great, Brit. Now buckle up so we can get out of here." He gave her his warmest big brother smile then turned and hit the gas. A bad haircut was far from the worst abuse Kenneth had perpetrated on his wife and daughter and Mark was glad that their nightmare was over.

"Are you sad, Mom?"

Lisa nodded as she tucked the house keys under the mat for the last time. "A little, but it's just a house now, Sam; we're taking the parts that made it a home with us and that's what really matters…you and your brother and your dad…"

"…and you."

"And me." She gave him a hug then led the way toward the car. They had one more stop to make before they started the trek north for the last time. Everything they would need from the house over the coming years was safely stowed in the Quonset hut along with a few items that weren't on the list, but simply couldn't be left behind. They had signed the boys out of school this morning, emptied their bank accounts, and turned off the utilities; now all they had to do was buy the warmest gear they could still afford for the coming winter and they would be good to go.

"Mrs. Black is watching us," Sam said as Lisa opened the back door and waved him inside.

Ian peeked his head out. "She's always watching us. It's like we're her favorite reality show. Now, will you get in here before she decides to pay us a visit?"

Lisa smiled to herself as Sam gasped at the thought and scrambled inside. She wondered how long it would take for Mrs. Black to realize that her favorite reality show had just gone off the air for good. "Buckle those seat belts, boys," she said then closed the door and climbed into the front seat with Robert.

"All set?" Even though he was smiling, his eyes were sad when he turned to look at her; they'd lived in this house since the day they were married and, as much as she knew he was tentatively looking forward to the years ahead, she also knew how hard it was for him to just let it all go.

She nodded and pulled the belt across her hips. "Where to now?"

"There's a hunting and camping goods store that Kim recommended. She said we should be able to find everything we need there…good quality, but expensive." Robert grinned as he turned the key in the ignition. "Good thing my severance package came in when it did. I've always wanted a down jacket and that's what Kim said we need to buy."

Lisa squeezed his thigh. "No regrets?"

"You mean because our whole life has been turned upside down." He smiled as he pulled into traffic. "Nope. Nada. Not a one."

She didn't quite believe him, but she'd let him have this one. "Good. So it doesn't bother you that we may be sleeping under the stars until everything gets sorted out."

Robert grinned. "Sounds tempting, but the boys and I have decided that having a tent of our own would be a good thing since it's going to be a long time before we get to move into the yurts."

"But can we afford it?"

Robert nodded. "Sam looked up the store's website. After we buy the winter gear, we'll have enough left over for a tent and four camp cots." He looked in the review mirror. "Right boys?"

"Ya, Dad," Sam called back. "It'll be our home away from home."

"Make sure you have your lists girls," Kaylyn called up the stairs. "We're leaving in ten minutes."

Cali appeared on the landing. She was wearing a pair of her new blue jeans and a red t-shirt with the words "bring it on" emblazoned across the front. Kaylyn couldn't help but smile at how appropriate the sentiment was. "But don't you want to look at them?" she asked as she moved down a step and held out a folded piece of paper.

Kaylyn smiled up at her eldest daughter. "Did you list five things that will be important to you in the future?"

"Of course, but..."

"Did you list anything that Momjay and I wouldn't approve of?"

"Of course not." Cali sighed. "So you don't want to see our lists."

"No, love, I don't. Now round up your sisters, please, and get them down here before Momjay leaves without us. We're supposed to meet Grandma Lee at the store in two hours and we still have to go to the bank."

"Okay. Be right back," Cali said over her shoulder. Then she was gone.

"You're really not going to check those lists," Jessie said as she came to stand at Kaylyn's side. "What if they blew the whole wad?"

"You know that's not going to happen." Kaylyn squeezed the hand resting comfortably on her shoulder. "I'm more worried about how we're going to get all of that money from the bank to the store."

"I'm sure the bank manager will know." Jessie smiled. "That is their job after all."

"We're ready, Momkay." Billie leaped down the stairs followed by her sisters. They were all wearing jeans...not all of them blue...and multi-colored t-shirts; a fitting uniform for the days to come.

Kaylyn stuck out her hand before Billie barreled past her. "Go tell Grandma Maggie we're leaving." She redirected Billie's momentum toward the kitchen. "The rest of you get your jackets on and head out to the van. Momjay and I will be out in a minute." With that, she took Jessie's hand, led her into the Nan Cave, and closed the door. She needed something...anything that would help ease the lingering ache in her chest.

"Kat, what's going on?" Jessie moved closer; the concern was written all over her face. "You've been acting strange since Andy showed up."

"Survivor's guilt." A tear trickled down Kaylyn's cheek.

Jessie frowned then recognition flared in her eyes.

Kaylyn nodded. "Grandma Kate said it could happen to any of us..."

"...and probably would considering that most of us wear our hearts on our sleeve." Jessie drew Kaylyn into a tight hug and rested her chin on the top of her head. "I don't know what to say, Kat. I've been trying not to think about the future while Andy and the children are here..."

"Has it worked?"

"Some." Jessie released Kaylyn and stepped back. "I know it's selfish, but I just keep telling myself that our resources are limited and I refuse to put our daughters' lives in jeopardy for the sake of anyone else." Her tone became plaintive. "It's the only way I can deal with it."

"I should have realized…" She met Jessie's eyes then reached out and took her hand; Jessie considered Andy to be both a colleague and a friend; of course, this would be hard for her. "We'll get through this. Right?" she said softly, "And in a couple of days we'll be so busy we won't have time to think about anything else."

"We can only hope." Jessie forced a smile and nodded. "We'd better go before Cali sends in a search party."

Kaylyn closed her eyes as a sudden shiver of dread ran down her spine. Her girls weren't strangers to the need to save those they cared about; would they feel the same way about the social worker who had found them the family they deserved and the six children they'd spent the morning with. *It's time to put all this world behind us while we still can.*

Kenneth Black hadn't phoned his wife from the airport; he'd phoned her from the big box mall down the street where the background noise was sufficient to create the illusion of a bustling concourse. He'd been quite proud of his subterfuge, especially since it was only a two-minute drive from the mall parking lot to the corner by his house; anyone trying to flee the premises would have had insufficient time to make their escape before he arrived. It was a great plan; he just never imagined that it would be his wife and daughter running away from everything he worked so hard to provide for them, suitcases in hand.

"Damn her." His fist came down on the steering wheel causing the car to swerve slightly. He braked and stared at the café four doors down waiting for his wife and daughter to make their next move. He'd been convinced that Jenifer was seeing another man and his daughter was covering for her out of misguided loyalty. For weeks, the two of them had been skulking around the house, whispering behind their hands and avoiding being in his presence like the plague; what else was he to think.

"So where are you going, my dear?" He'd watched as Jenny and his daughter had climbed into Cassandra's car. He'd very calmly decided to follow them to Earth Song when he recognized the car instead of trying to confront them in front of their neighbors, but any idea he had of storming into that godforsaken house and dragging his wife out by her hair had been dashed when the car rolled passed Earth Song and two fully laden trucks fell in behind it.

Kenneth cracked open a bottle of water, took a long drink then eased his way into traffic three cars behind the motley convoy. He wondered if his wife had found another place to live and the junk loaded on those trucks was intended to furnish it. He recognized the table from the few times he'd been invited to an Earth Song family dinner, but he couldn't imagine what would be in the rest of those boxes.

The trucks led him from one end of Winnipeg to the other and just when he was certain that they must be near their destination, they turned north and headed out of the city. That was almost two hours ago, the last half hour of which had been spent skulking down dirt roads trying not to be seen. He supposed all the dust had helped to mask his presence, but it had also made it difficult to see exactly where he was going. It hadn't taken much more than a second's miscalculation as he turned down yet another narrow lane for his front wheel to catch the ditch and drag him in.

"Goddamned son of a bitch." Water sloshed in his shoes as he climbed up the bank. He clenched his teeth, kicked off his very expensive loafers, and sat down. He'd lost his prey, and if that wasn't enough to make his blood boil, he had no idea where he was, and the GPS on his very expensive cell phone was sitting in two feet of water.

He starred at the underbelly of the car and wondered how far it was to the nearest phone. He couldn't just sit here and wait for someone to come along; they hadn't met another vehicle once they'd left the highway and he certainly didn't want to be caught out here after dark.

He pushed himself to a standing position, shoved his feet into his wet shoes and stared down the empty road. "Don't you worry, Jennifer, I'll find you and when I do…" He shook his head and turned on his heels. "There'd be hell to pay…and much, much more."

"Sam! Ian!" Wanda darted across the store parking lot. "What are you guys doing here?"

Ian gave her a lopsided grin as he pulled open the door and held it for his mom and dad. "Probably the same thing you are. We're picking up winter gear and a tent then it's *hasta la vista* Winnipeg."

"Really?" Wanda glanced over her shoulder as her family approached. "You're so lucky. Sometimes I think we'll never get out of here for good."

"Thank you, Ian," Momjay said as she smiled at the two of them then stepped inside. "Come along Wanda, we have a lot to do and I'm hoping Grandma Lee is already here."

Wanda shrugged as her sisters greeted Ian then followed their mom into the store. "Guess I'd better go. We're picking up the bows today. I'll see you later."

"I'll come find you," he called after her. Wanda smiled and then her smile became an ear-to-ear grin as she stepped across the threshold. If someone had told her a few months ago that the inside of a store that sold nothing but hunting and camping gear could make her feel so excited, she would have told them that they were crazy, but not anymore. "This place is so awesome," she said and meant every word of it.

Billie appeared at her side, her finger extended toward a row of clothing racks. "Those jackets look like the kind soldiers wear," she exclaimed. "Maybe I can get one."

"Maybe later. Now come on before we get lost." Wanda wrapped her arm around her younger sister's shoulder and steered her toward the back of the store. "Once the bows are paid for, we can go shopping. I want to look at the tents," she said thoughtfully. The only tent they had was an old, orange pup tent that they'd played in in the back yard and she suspected that was one of the reasons they weren't leaving right away. She would have gladly bunked in the Quonset if it got them back to Dragon's Flare any sooner, but the moms wouldn't have it for some reason.

"Maybe we could get two tents, one for the family and one for the grandmothers." Billie's face lit up. "Maybe we could buy them each a cot as well…like the one Chloe has; then they won't have to sleep on the deck boxes in the Quonset to be up off the ground. That's an awfully long way for them to walk every day to be with the rest of us."

Wanda squeezed Billie tighter. "When did you get to be such a thoughtful person?"

Billie shrugged; she looked truly puzzled. "I don't know."

"Well, don't worry about it, kid; it's a good thing." Wanda guided them around display shelves of knives and binoculars and ammunition to a window marked 'orders.' Grandma Lee was talking to a man in a camouflaged vest; Momjay stood beside her. Robert and Lisa were talking to Momkay beside a wall display of knapsacks.

"What's going on?" Wanda asked as she came up behind Cali.

Cali looked over her shoulder. "Grandpa Eric was supposed to pick up the bows, but his truck is in the garage and won't be fixed for a couple of days and all of the Earth Song vehicles are already at the camp."

"Maybe Robert could rent a truck again."

Cali shrugged. "I don't think Robert will have any extra money after they buy the things they need, from what Sam said, but maybe 'we' could rent the truck…well our moms could and we could pay for it."

"That's a great idea, Cal. Let's go tell them." Wanda grabbed Cali's hand before she could protest and dragged her toward the adults. "Cali has something to tell you," she said as they stopped in front of Momkay.

Kaylyn frowned at her daughters, but didn't otherwise chastise them for their rudeness; Wanda knew that would come later. But this was important. "Yes, Cali?"

Cali glared at Wanda then straightened her shoulders. "We were just thinking that, since Grandpa Eric's truck isn't working, maybe you and Momjay could rent a truck and drive it up tomorrow. Wanda and I could pay for it."

"You'd need a credit card," Robert said.

"Got one right here." Wanda grinned as she pulled the little plastic wallet the bank manager had given her out of her zippered pocket and flipped it open. "Prepaid."

Robert raised an eyebrow in Kaylyn's direction. "It's a long story," she said, "But the card is perfectly legitimate."

Sam peeked around his father and grinned at Wanda. "Does that mean you're rich?"

Wanda grinned. "I wish. But I could probably spring for lunch at one of those fast-food restaurants you like so much when we get back with the truck." She wiggled her beringed eyebrows at him. "It'll be our last chance."

"Ah. I don't know…"

"I think we'll take you up on that offer." Lisa grinned at her son. "It'll be the last time we'll get to eat greasy food in a cheesy restaurant."

"Gee thanks, Mom," Sam made no attempt to hide his grin. "I think I just lost my appetite."

"That's the last bundle of bum wipes," Grace chuckled as she closed the lid on her military trunk. She set a partially used bolt of white flannel on top and tied it closed with a strip of the same material. "An even fifty dozen and forty dozen menstrual pads, so we should be good to go."

"Only if everyone takes care with them." Matibi turned off her sewing machine and pushed herself back from the table. "It's going to take a while for some people to get used to cleaning shitty rags instead of throwing them down the toilet."

"My mom had to deal with shitty diapers every time she had a baby and so did I," Hanna said. "As a matter of fact, everyone used cloth diapers before they came out with those throwaway things. We'll adapt. Besides, our bum wipes are far superior to the Eaton's catalog."

Matibi giggled. "I certainly hope so."

"Now that we've got the necessaries all done," Grace said as she sat down on the couch beside Meg. "Has anybody given any thought to when we're going to make the transition? Greg says we shouldn't wait too long just in case and I agree with him. It would be a real shame if we put out all this effort and ended up stuck in the city."

Kathleen nodded. "I talked to Maggie this morning and she said they'll be leaving either tomorrow or the next day."

"Ingrid and Harold bought a tent yesterday along with some dried foods and left this morning with the kids." Hanna smiled. "I'm going to buy the children new winter boots and snowsuits from my last pension check. They love being outdoors, and I don't want anyone getting frostbit."

"Make certain you buy them a couple of sizes too big then they can grow into them." Meg shook her head. "Heaven only knows what any of us are going to be wearing in a few years. It's scary to think about actually."

"Then let's not think about it. At least not right now."

Meg shrugged. "It's not all that easy, Gracey."

"Maybe not." Kathleen said, "But right now we have other, more immediate, things to consider. Like when do we leave and what are we going to do when we get there? I don't have my big tent anymore so that's not an option."

Megan shrugged. "Then I guess we either stay here…which isn't an option either…or we set up house in the Quonset and bribe someone to bring us water."

"Or..." Grace said, "We could get our heads out of our butts, pool our resources, and buy a tent so we can be a part of what's happening; it's not like we haven't done it before. I have pension money in my account that needs to be spent since I've already earned it."

"Nadir got her final paycheck this week so my grandsons now have everything they need,"

Kathleen smiled. She even bought a tent with room for me if I need it. So my money is free. "I'd like to make a suggestion though."

Grace shrugged. "Okay with me."

"I'd like to get Stephanie involved in this. The last time I spoke to her she seemed a little lost. She'd just signed the DNR order for her daughter and made the arrangements for her internment." Kathleen shook her head. "It was probably the hardest thing she ever had to do and I'd like her to know that she isn't alone."

"You're right. I don't have her number, but I'll ask Maggie to give her a call." Megan tilted her head to the side and frowned. "Seems strange not having Maggie here. Maybe we should drop in. Let her know what's happening. Her guests should be gone by now...don't you think?"

Matibi nodded. "Sounds good to me. Maybe we can even scrounge up a meal for old time's sake."

"Hold that thought." Grace stood up and walked toward the kitchen she and Kathleen now shared. "I think we have some stew meat in the freezer. Meg, why don't you make that call; let her know we're coming by and ask her to invite Steph."

"I'll do that." Meg started to dial Maggie's number then paused halfway through. "Someone will need to pick Steph up."

"Tell Maggie I'll do it." Matibi grinned. "The rust bucket still has a few miles left in her."

"So, here's what's going to happen." Kaylyn wadded her empty sandwich wrapper into a ball, tossed it onto her tray, and brushed the crumbs from her fingertips, grateful that her stomach hadn't decided to rebel against the amount of grease and salt she'd just consumed. "Robert is going to drive the truck to Dragon's Flare this afternoon after it's all loaded. In the meantime..." She exchanged a look with Lisa. "...we're all going to do some shopping.

Apparently, Kim and Juno have advised that we should all be wearing down this winter…"

"But you just bought us new winter coats last year." Wanda protested.

"And those are great for going from the house to the bus stop or even for short walks on plowed streets." Kaylyn locked eyes with her goth daughter, "But you're going to be spending a lot of time outside, aren't you? At least that's what it sounded like when you were talking about winter forage."

Wanda sighed; no one else at the table made a sound.

"Why don't you want new winter clothing?" Jessie asked into the silence. "You should still be able to buy all the things on your list, right?"

"It's not that, Momjay. It's just…"

"…we want to buy tents." Billie huffed as every eye turned in her direction. "…and camp cots for the grandmothers and Stephanie because we don't want to be stuck in the city any longer and the grandmothers shouldn't have to sleep so far away from everyone in the Quonset hut."

"Maybe the grandmothers have found their own tent," JoJo said helpfully.

Billie glared at her. "And what if they haven't?"

"Okay. Change of plans." Kaylyn gave Lisa an apologetic shrug. "I guess we won't be looking for winter clothes today." Jo opened her mouth to protest, and Kaylyn put up her hand to stop her. Of all her daughters, Jo was the least likely to put someone else's needs ahead of her own at this point in time. It was a disturbing change and though she knew the cause, Kaylyn was still unable to come up with a solution to her daughter's very real and painful problem. "We will take the rest of the afternoon to complete the lists each of you girls has made then we'll talk to the grandmothers and find out if they have a tent…"

"…and camp cots," Billie chimed in.

Kaylyn couldn't help but smile. "And camp cots. Then we'll go from there." She turned to Lisa. "Sorry about this."

"Hey, no problem." Lisa turned to Wanda and Billie. "The grandmothers are lucky to have you in their corner."

"What about Mel and Caroline?" Sam met Wanda's eyes; he looked slightly guilty. "Have you heard anything from them?"

"Not since they left last week to pack up the store. Caroline said she'd have a truck full of useful books for us the next time we saw her." Wanda sighed and shook her head. "I'll phone her; make certain they're okay and whether they need anything."

Sam smiled. "Thanks, Wanda. You're the best."

"Hip waders. Five pairs of binoculars." Jessica looked sideways at Cali. They were sitting in the front seat of the van waiting for the others to finish up inside the restaurant. "Five?"

"Trin made a list too. She gave it to me when she decided to stay at the house with her new friends." Cali held up a page with pictures glued to it. "We let her loose on the catalog Grandma Maggie ran off for us after we were done with it. We're all going to pitch in since she doesn't have an account of her own."

"Of course, you are." Jessie shook her head and smiled. "So what's next?"

"We're each going to need a sturdy pair of boots. Our sneakers aren't going to last very long scrambling around in the woods."

Jessie added boots to her comprehensive list. So far they had binoculars, boots, hip waders, compasses, and backpacks; nothing very spectacular. "Okay. What else?"

"Trin wants a tree stand and a ladder." Cali shrugged. "To find friends…at least that's what I think she said."

"Oh." A sudden image of her youngest daughter sitting in a tree with her binoculars grinning down at the world made Jessie smile. Trin would be safer up there than she would be chasing little critters through the forest…and she climbed like a monkey. What could possibly go wrong? She added the ladder and tree stand to her list. "Okay. What's next?"

"I need…" Cali drew a deep breath and swallowed hard. "Juno and Kim have asked me to go exploring with them once the yurts are set up. They made kind of an air photo map of the area and it needs to be verified from the ground, but…"

"But…" Jessie chucked Cali under the chin and drew her head around so that their eyes met. "Is there something special you need to make this happen…that is if you even want to go?"

"Of course, I want to go, Momjay. I can learn so much from Kim and Juno." She sighed deeply. "But they won't take me unless I have the proper gear. There are a lot of things I'll need if I go with them…Juno made me a list…"

Jessie smiled. "And that list has more than five items on it."

Cali rolled her eyes. "Way more…and some of it is really expensive. Just the medical kit is eighty dollars…"

"…but it could save your life," Jessie raised both eyebrows. "If I was to hazard a guess, everything on that list is essential to you coming back in one piece."

"That's what Juno said."

"Then I don't see any alternative." Cali tensed and Jessie smile reassuringly. "We're going to need to know as much as we can about our environment if we're going to survive there and it sounds like you're committed to helping with that. So…you and I will put your pack together today while Momjay helps your sisters with their purchases."

Cali sighed. "But the tents…"

"You let me worry about that." Jessie patted Cali's knee and smiled. It was painfully obvious, even to a doting mom, that her eldest daughter was no longer a child. She was a young woman determined to help her community and Jessie would damn well find the where-with-all to make that happen and keep her safe in the process.

Cali grinned and flung her arms around Jessie's neck…a little girl again…at least for a moment. "Thanks, Momjay."

"I don't see any sign of Andy's car, but it looks like the grandmothers are all here." Jessie pulled the van up to the curb in front of the house. "And doesn't that truck with 'Second Time Around' on it belong to Caroline?"

Wanda peered over Jessie's shoulder. "I guess she got my message."

"Message?" Jessie met Wanda's calm eyes in the rear-view mirror. "What message?"

Wanda gave her a cockeyed grin. "You were sitting right there Momjay when I promised Sam that I'd check up on Mel and Caroline since we haven't seen them or heard from them in a few days." She shrugged. "So when they didn't answer, I left a message inviting them over. I figured that if they didn't show up, we could go look for them."

"Well then, I guess we should get inside." Kaylyn squeezed Jessie's knee effectively quelling any comment she might have made. "Take your purchases up to your rooms, girls, then meet us in the kitchen. I assume that's where everyone will be."

"I hope there's something to eat," Billie said as she climbed out of the van behind Wanda. "I'm starving."

"You're always starving," JoJo grumbled. "Better get used to it, Chubby Butt."

Jessie bit down on her initial reaction to illicit an apology on Billie's behalf; there had been more behind Jo's words than the simple desire to irritate her sister. Jessie placed a hand on JoJo's shoulder and gently turned her around; she didn't resist. "Why did you say that, Jo?" Jessie asked as their eyes met.

"Because it's true." Jo's eyes narrowed. "I know what the prophecy says about seizing the day and fleeing to the forest; it's supposed to give us hope, make us think that if we're stout-hearted enough, we'll find a way to survive, but you don't really believe that, do you?" She spat the question out like an accusation.

Jessie dropped her hands and took a step back.

"Thought not." Jo spun on her heels and ran toward the house before anyone could make a move to stop her.

A hand came down on Jessie's shoulder. "You get the girls inside, I'll talk to Jo."

Jessie nodded and turned to find three pairs of eyes staring at her expectantly; it was then that she realized she hadn't answered Jo's question. "You want to know whether I still think it's possible for us to save ourselves." None of them moved. She sighed and plastered a smile on her face. "Wanda, how many edible plants have you learned to identify in the past two weeks?"

"Momjay, I…"

"Rough estimate."

"A dozen."

"And, Billie, those snares you and Sophia helped Grandpa Jake set…"

"How—"

"—did I find out?" She shrugged unwilling to rat out Stephanie as her source. "How many rabbits did you snare?"

A smile twitched at the corner of Billie's lip. "Two rabbits and a squirrel. Grandpa Jake said he'd clean them and give them to Mae for the stew."

Wanda looked slightly ill. "We ate a squirrel."

Billie grinned. "It didn't kill you, did it?"

"And you, Cali." Jessie turned to her eldest daughter choosing to ignore that last comment. "Didn't you say that part of your exploring will be dedicated to mapping the deer trails and locating the grazing areas? Why is that?"

Cali gave her a questioning look then took a deep breath. "So the hunters will know the best places to go to find the herds."

"Exactly. Which means more meat for the pot, right?" Jessie watched them share a look before they turned to her and nodded. She smiled at each of them. "I have to admit that, until those yurts were on the ground, I had some doubts about the future, but the way everyone came together to get the work done was phenomenal. Now we'll have warm and cozy homes this winter, fresh, clean air to breathe and the beauty of nature all around us…and we have young people like you dedicated to filling our bellies and learning everything they can about our new home…"

"So is that a yes, Momjay?" Wanda asked softly, "Because I really want it to be a yes."

Jessie nodded. "It's a yes."

"Good." Wanda hefted her bag over her shoulder with grim determination. "Then I'll go tell JoJo that. I think she needs to hear it."

Jessie was halfway through her second bowl of stew when Kaylyn entered the kitchen, followed by Wanda and Jo. Her middle daughter looked calmer and, perhaps, a bit embarrassed as she took her seat and stared down at the table. Wanda dished out bowls of stew for the three of them and Kaylyn poured tea as looks were exchanged around the table.

"All sorted," Kaylyn said giving Jessie's knee a reassuring squeeze as she took her seat. "So what did we miss?"

Jessie cleared her throat and smiled in Jo's direction; the look her middle daughter gave her in return was more apologetic than hostile though she sensed something lurking behind that dark gaze that told her everything might not be as sorted as Kaylyn thought. "We were just discussing what Lisa told us about the winter gear we're going to need," Jessie said.

"And Kim and Juno are right," Grace commented from across the table. "Down is best with the weather we're going to be facing. It's also something we'll be able to maintain since there should be lots of geese landing on that little lake of ours."

"Geese?" Billie blinked up at Grace.

Grace smiled and nodded. "That's where down comes from. My grandmother used to stuff our mittens with it after the hunt. Waste not. Want not. She'd say."

Kathleen frowned into her mug. "But down clothing is very expensive these days."

"Isn't everything?" Matibi pushed her bowl away and leaned back. "I'm still trying to wrap my mind around how costly this whole endeavor has been when what we're aiming for is a simpler life."

Kathleen nodded. "Is it any wonder that people struggle along in the city no matter how much they may hate it? Just that piece of land would be beyond most people's pocketbooks...but I digress." She returned her attention to Kaylyn. "As far as I know, our budget is pretty much maxed out now that we've bought the medical supplies and the bows, so where is the money going to come from for this little venture. If we'd thought of it ahead of time..."

"Can I tell them, Momjay?" Billie looked up from her bowl and grinned across the table. The image of the Cheshire cat came suddenly to mind as Jessie nodded her consent and sat back to listen.

"If you're referring to your school fund, we already know about that, dear." Kathleen smiled, "But you already paid the balance on the bow packages..."

"...and we still have tons of money left."

"Well, maybe not tons, Billie." Cali smiled at her moms. "But a lot of money went into those accounts every month...maybe more than our moms could truly afford sometimes with all the added expense of raising four girls, but there is still quite a bit left and we need to spend it before the money isn't any good anymore."

Billie nodded vigorously. "That's why we're glad you're all here, so we can figure out what we still need...like tents and camp cots and all the clothes Kim and Juno said we should buy to stay warm..."

"...and dry." Jo lowered her spoon looking a little shaky but determined. "I hate the idea of spending the rest of my life surrounded by forest and you all know why that is..."

"Jo..." Grace squeezed Billie's hand then subtly shook her head. Jessie was glad to see that Billie understood. JoJo had something to get off her chest and they needed to give her the space to do that.

Jo glanced at Billie then looked down at the table. "I don't know if I'll ever get over my mom's death, but I can't just curl up in a little ball and let the world go by either. I may not like the forest, but Momjay reminded me how much I love the water and there's a whole lake out there with lots of useful things in and around it. I can gather plants from the swamp or build a raft and fish like my grandpa taught me; I'll be able to pull my weight…" A genuine smile lit up her face and Jessie felt some of the pressure on her shoulders ease. *That's my girl.* "My grandpa told me that the best time to fish is when it's raining, but that there's nothing worse than being wet while you're waiting for the fish to bite."

"So we need to add rain gear to our list." Kaylyn smiled proudly at her middle daughter and pushed her bowl aside. "I guess what we need to know is what 'appropriate' outdoor clothing each of us already has and what's still needed."

"Well, we should go, Soph." Stephanie stood up and reached for her coat.

"So you have everything you need?" Grace rested her hand on Billie's shoulder. "Because we can't afford to have our people getting frostbit or coming down with pneumonia because they're not dressed properly. Right, Billie."

Billie grinned at Sophia. "That's right, Sarge."

Maggie patted Stephanie's arm. "Sit down, Steph. You and Sophia and Caroline and Mel are family now, so this involves you too."

"Thanks for that, Maggie." Caroline pulled Melanie into a one-arm hug as Stephanie sat down. "From both of us. I tried to sell some of my books, but…" She shrugged.

"So, if you will all list what you have," Kaylyn sighed. She looked as tired as Jessie felt. "I'll run some numbers tomorrow and then we can go down to the store on Friday…"

"That won't work."

Kaylyn frowned at Meg. "And why not?"

Megan narrowed her eyes in Maggie's direction. "Are you going to tell them…or should I?"

"I think you did the right thing Grandmother."

"Thank you, Cali." Maggie smiled at the little girl munching her way through a biscuit at Cali's side; Trin licked strawberry jam from the corner of her lips and smiled back. "But it wasn't my idea…at least not at first."

Jessie followed Maggie's almost imperceptible nod. "Trin?"

Maggie shrugged. "She overheard Andy say she needed a house for the children so she could keep them together. We talked for quite a while then Andy went out to check on the children and Trin made it quite apparent that her new friends should come and live here." Maggie made the signs for friend and home then pointed rather emphatically at the floor. "Though I must admit that it took a few goes before I understood what she was actually saying."

"It'll be interesting to see what mischief she'll be getting into once she starts her lessons with Chloe in earnest," Megan mused. "She'll probably have everyone wrapped around her little finger. Isn't that right, Trin?"

Trin shoved the rest of her biscuit into her mouth and grinned.

"I didn't say anything to Andy at first." Maggie kept her eyes focused on a spot above Trin's chair; she wasn't ready to face the rest of her grandchildren head-on…not yet. "This house has been in my family for almost a hundred years. I was born in the master bedroom upstairs and my Samuel breathed his last in the room we now call the Nan Cave, so it wasn't easy for me to think about strangers living here."

"I can understand that." Grace's voice was gruff and tinged with sadness. "But sometimes you just have to suck it up and do what you have to do."

Maggie gave Gracey a grateful nod; she'd known all along how difficult it had been for her friend to part with her home no matter how hard Grace had tried to hide it. Maggie lowered her eyes to the silent faces around her; what she saw were a few tears, a little confusion, and a lot of love. "Then I realized that Andy isn't a stranger and it would be disrespectful to leave this beautiful, old house empty when it still has a purpose to fulfill." She met Jo's tear-filled eyes and smiled. "You're probably the bravest of us all, Josephine; I wouldn't have done this if I didn't think that that was true."

Jo dried her eyes on her sleeve. "And why's that, Grandmother?"

"Because now we have no choice. Come tomorrow we'll be living in the forests of Dragon's Flare full time…no more excuses. No more coming home at night to hot showers and flush toilets."

"I can handle it, Grandmother." Jo swiped at her eyes again.

Billie sat up straighter. "Me too, Grandmother."

"Does this mean we'll be leaving tomorrow for good?" Wanda asked. There was a brightness in her eyes that left no doubt as to the answer she wanted.

Maggie nodded and gave Kaylyn an apologetic shrug. "Andy and Mildred will be bringing the children over at one o'clock. I gave Andy my key and told her they could have the use of the place for the five months we'll be gone or until they find another house; whichever comes first."

Jessie sighed with relief; it was the first sound she'd made since Maggie started her explanation. "So she still thinks we're coming back."

"Very much so. She's really looking forward to hearing about the girls' adventures."

"But how are we supposed to…" Wanda stopped and leaned back in her chair as though something in Maggie's eyes had told her everything she needed to know.

"Cali, can we talk to you for a moment?"

Cali looked up from the book cradled in her lap. Her moms stood in the bedroom doorway carrying a large shopping bag each and a small box. "Sure, Momjay. Come on in."

"Wanda told us that you're worried about taking Mouser with you when we go. Why didn't you come to us?" Kaylyn sat down on the end of Cali's bed and glanced around. "Where is the little fur ball anyway?"

Cali nodded toward the opposite side of the room as Trin emerged from her blankets with Mouser cradled in her arms. "Trin and Mouser really like each other. Maybe Mouser was meant for Trin. Maybe that's why Mouser showed up when she did." Cali shrugged. "And that's okay with me, but she's still my responsibility. Trin's too little to take care of her yet." she said softly, "So I dug out that rabbit cage Grandma Maggie had in the basement and cleaned it up; it doesn't look like much, but it'll keep her safe and Grandma Maggie solved my litter tray problem." She nodded to the spot beside the door.

Kaylyn chuckled. "A cake pan. How appropriate."

"But you can't keep her caged all the time," Jessie said.

Cali looked down at her hands. "I know. I thought about carrying her in a knapsack, but she didn't like it and I can't blame her. She couldn't see anything…" A tear trickled down her cheek. "But I don't know what else to do. Maybe she'll get used to it…"

"…or maybe she won't have to." Jessie pulled the desk chair out and sat down. She held out a bag and the box.

"What is it?" Cali watched Trin ease her way toward the bed; she had toothpaste on her chin. Cali patted the bed beside her. "Pass Mouser to Momkay, Trin, and you can help me."

Trin climbed up onto the bed, kissed Mouser on the top of her head, and handed her to Kaylyn. Cali reached into the bag and pulled out what looked like a cloth purse.

"It a cat carrier…well, a kitten carrier actually." Jessie said, "You sling it over your shoulder and there's a place in the top where she can look out."

Cali hugged the bag to her chest. "It's wonderful. Now we can take her everywhere with us. But how…"

"Grandma Kate picked everything up for us. She was smiling when she gave them to us, so I think she enjoyed doing it." Kaylyn scratched under Mouser's chin. "You may not realize this, Cali, but Katie thinks very highly of this little girl."

"I'm glad to hear that." Cali handed the cat carrier to Trin and stuck her hand into the bag. Over the next ten minutes, she unearthed a small harness and a leash, a cat water bottle and playpen, and a box of Mouser's favorite food. Cali could hardly contain herself she was so happy.

"The next time you have a problem, come to us right away. Okay?" Kaylyn said as she returned Cali's hug, "If we can help, we will. You should know that."

"I do, Momjay." Cali's shoulders slumped, "But I promised that I would take care of her."

"And you have," Jessie said. She smiled at Trin still sitting with the cat bag tucked to her chest. "Just like you take such good care of your sister, but we all need help sometimes Cali." Jessie patted Cali's knee and stood up. "Just remember that. Okay?"

Cali nodded. "I will. And thanks again."

Chapter Twenty-One

Robert said, "You'd be coming in today with some tents and other things to go down to the beach, so we decided to wait until you got here to make the last trip." Juno took a step back as Kaylyn crawled out of the van.

"Much appreciated," Kaylyn said as she helped Maggie and Trin climb down. "I really had no idea how we were going to get the tents down to the lake and set up before tonight. The rest of it can probably wait until tomorrow."

Juno looked over Kaylyn's shoulder as two trucks pulled in behind her. "I see what you mean."

"Who took the rental truck back?" Kaylyn rolled up the window and closed the door. "I thought I was going to have to do that tomorrow."

Juno smiled. "With everyone trickling in, we have lots of strong arms to help move things around. It took less than two hours to get the bows under cover, so Robert decided to take the truck straight back. Mark followed him in."

"I'll have to remember to thank them."

Juno nodded. "Ah, here they are." Two young men with ebony skin and curly black hair stepped onto the road followed by Grandma Lee and her students. "They're going to move your tents and anything else that needs to go to the beach into the chopper."

"Lee did say that they were coming out early," Maggie moved around Kaylyn and went to greet her friend as Lee stepped onto the road. Matibi scurried past waving to the two boys she'd agreed to sponsor last summer; they looked genuinely happy to see her.

"I guess we should get this show on the road then." Kaylyn turned toward the back of the van.

Juno gripped her elbow. "Why don't you let the youngsters taken care of it?" She smiled as Kaylyn frowned over her shoulder. "If Jessie looks anything like you, you could both use some downtime. Chloe has tea waiting. Go ahead. I'll send the grandmothers after you."

Kaylyn tried to smile but her eyes were moist and her jaw trembled. She hadn't realized how exhausted she was until this moment. "That sounds great."

Juno grinned. "And don't worry about Cagney and Lacy; they're as gentle as newborn lambs."

Kaylyn held tight to Trin's hand as they took the path toward the meadow. Somewhere out there were two highly trained German Shepherds who had been released from the military at the same time as their handlers. She didn't know what to think about that despite Juno's reassurance.

Kim and the two dogs met them as they exited the trees. "Glad you made it," the tall blond said with an easy smile. Cagney and Lacy sat quietly at her side.

Kaylyn tightened her grip on Trin's hand and dug in her heels bringing them to a halt just out of arms reach of Trin's intended targets.

"They're good girls. They won't hurt her...or you," Kim said squatting between the two dogs and looping her arms around each of their necks.

Kaylyn swallowed hard and took a step forward. Big dogs had always made her feel uneasy, but she had come to trust Lisa's sister. "I suppose you should introduce us," she said with a wry smile, "since we're going to be neighbors."

"Pack-mates is probably a more accurate term in this case," Kim said as she reached for Trin's outstretched hand. She looked up and met Kaylyn's eyes. "It's okay. You can let her go."

"Of course." Kaylyn forced her finger opened and tried not to wince as Trin let the dogs sniff her hand and gave each of them a hug. A dearth of pets of any kind as a child had left Kaylyn ill-prepared for the sudden intrusion of two very large and potentially dangerous animals into her life. *Not your decision, KitKat, so deal with it.*

"Now it's your turn." Kim stood up and brushed the grass from the knees of her pants.

Kaylyn nodded and joined Trin. She held out a tentative hand as her youngest daughter hugged the two dogs; they returned the favor with enthusiastic and very wet kisses.

"Aren't they beautiful…and so gentle," Grandma Maggie said over Kaylyn's shoulder a few moments later. "The camp will be safer with them around."

"You think so?"

Maggie smiled. "My father's parents had two of them on their farm; I practically grew up with them. They kept the chickens safe, the cows from straying and me out of trouble…and they weren't nearly as well-trained as I imagine these two are." Maggie let each dog sniff her hand then stepped away. "Time for tea."

Kaylyn lowered herself to the ground and accepted a cup of pine needle tea from Chloe. Only one tent, the fire pit, and a scaled-down kitchen remained of what had been a fairly large camp the last time she'd been here. She felt a little guilty as she watched the steady stream of bags and boxes being loaded into the chopper, but not enough so to make her move her weary butt to help out. Hopefully, tonight, she'd be able to get more than a few hours of sleep.

"We moved all of our tents to the beach yesterday. We have quite a nice little camp set up down there." Chloe smiled over Kaylyn's shoulder to where Trin was playing with her new friends. "And with the dogs on guard duty, we had a very restful sleep. They're also excellent baby sitters in a pinch."

"So Maggie was right, they'll make a good addition to the community." Kaylyn eyed Chloe over the rim of her cup.

"Most definitely, along with the two canoes and that huge white tent Kim and Juno brought. It has its own portable stove and we're going to use it as a kitchen for the duration."

"Did I hear you mention a canoe?" Jessie nodded to Chloe then sat down beside Kaylyn's cup in hand. She looked as weary as Kaylyn felt. They'd spent long hours last night checking and rechecking their preparations for their move and comparing notes on any apprehensions concerning their daughters, foremost of which was Jo's crush on Sam. His comment at the restaurant about Wanda being "the best" had turned out to be the actual trigger for Jo's anger that afternoon. Thankfully, Wanda had set Jo straight about her definitely non-romantic friendship with the two brothers, but Jessie hadn't been certain that would be the end of it since Jo already had so much on her plate.

"I did." Chloe smiled. "And it's just what we needed. Jenna thinks there's wild rice in the lake that we'll be able to harvest now we have the means to do so, and if there are any fish in that lake, a canoe will certainly make it easier to catch them."

"Jo will be so excited." Kaylyn grinned. She couldn't wait to see the look on her middle daughter's face when she realized that she didn't have to build a raft after all. "If there are any fish in there, our JoJo will find them; I'm certain of that."

Jessie nodded vigorously. "She used to spend the summers at her grandparent's cottage before they died. Her grandpa taught her to fish as soon as she could hold a rod from what Jo says."

"Well, if she can bring the fish in, we'll soon have a smokehouse to help us preserve them, thanks to Jake. He had Juno and Kim fly the materials in yesterday." Chloe shrugged. "Maybe he knows Jo likes to fish; he was certainly disappointed that she wasn't here."

Jessie shared a grin with Kaylyn. "Grandfather Secret."

Chloe looked puzzled for a moment then she smiled. "Like the sauna. It came in yesterday too."

"Sounds like Kim and Juno have had a lot on their plates." Kaylyn raised her cup and took a long drink.

"They have." Chloe nodded toward the activity around the chopper. "But this is their last trip. They'll be staying for the bonfire tonight then they're flying to Winnipeg in the morning. They'll be back here permanently in a few days."

Kaylyn grinned. "A bonfire sounds like a really great idea after all the hard work everyone has put in to get us this far." She watched out of the corner of her eyes as Maggie stood up suddenly, said something to Katie and scurried away; she had a pleased smile on her face.

"Be back in a few minutes," the elder tossed over her shoulder. "Need to check on my drums."

"So that's what was in those bags." Jessie grinned then turned to Chloe. "The drums belonged to Maggie's mother. I guess Great-Grandmother Nettie hosted a drumming circle at the house every week until she died. Maggie taught me some of the patterns when I was younger, but I never really got the hang of it. I'm much better with the penny whistle." She shrugged. "No sense of rhythm."

Chloe watched Maggie's progress with a thoughtful glint in her eyes. "How could we have been so mistaken?" She frowned and shook her head.

"After all those years of planning and anticipation, I don't think we ever truly understood what we were seeking."

Kaylyn frowned at the deep sadness behind those words. "But we're getting there, aren't we?" She leaned forward as Chloe stared down at her hands; the sudden change in the older woman's demeanor was as disturbing as the words she had just spoken. Kaylyn grasped at the only straw she could find. "Are you worried about the drums?"

"Worried?" Chloe blinked up at her. "Goddess no! We've been so busy worrying about all the things we'll need to preserve our bodies and even our minds that everyone seems to have forgotten the things that touch our hearts and our souls."

Jessie smiled proudly. "Not Maggie."

"Or Mark and Andrew." Chloe breathed deeply as she sat up and squared her shoulders. "I didn't think much about it when the two boys decided to bring everything they could carry from the studio; I was too busy being angry over the space they were taking up to think about their motives…even when Mark tried to explain them to me." Chloe sighed. "Besides, not everyone paints or carves or throws pots. But music is universal, isn't it? It's in our blood." She smiled as her eyes grew distant. "It makes us sway and dance and hum along and at times we don't even know that we're doing it." A sad smile twitched at the corners of her lips. "You'll have to forgive an old woman; I've just realized how important music is to me and that I don't want to spend the rest of my life without it…silence or no silence," she said emphatically, "and Maggie's drums may just be our saving grace."

Kaylyn shivered. "There must be other musicians among us," she said as she sipped her tea; trying to remain calm. Chloe was right; music was a constant background to Kaylyn's world and the sudden realization that the silence would take much of that away threatened to bring tears to her eyes. "Surely they would have brought their instruments."

"I hope so," Chloe shrugged. "But they weren't on that damn, short-sighted *this is all we need to survive*, the list we all agreed to, and I haven't seen any evidence of them."

Jessie laughed. "You wouldn't for just that reason. I know everyone agreed that with the limited time and space we have, we needed to target just the essentials, but I'll bet those instruments magically appear as soon as Maggie brings out her drums."

"Wouldn't that be lovely?" Chloe closed her eyes and sighed. "I always did enjoy a good jam session."

"Thank you for that, love," Kaylyn slipped her arm into Jessie's as they watched their middle daughter scramble onto the helicopter.

"Kim was happy to do it after I explained why." Jessie shrugged. "Jo's had enough traumas in her life lately; it was nice to be able to spare her this one. She even gets to co-pilot since Juno's walking the dogs down…with Trin and Billie's help."

Kaylyn smiled. "Thought of everything didn't you."

"That wasn't my idea, it was Juno's. She made it sound like they'd be doing her a big favor." Jessie waved to JoJo and turned toward the line of people heading for the forest. Billie and Trin led the parade sandwiched between the two dogs with Juno walking easily behind them. "Billie wasn't really happy about it at first, but she appears to have gotten over it."

"And Trin has fallen in love with her new, furry friends, so she wouldn't mind at all."

"I doubt she even noticed." Jessie took Kaylyn's hand as the chopper lifted off. "We'd better get going before we get left behind. According to Greg we only have four hours of daylight left and we're going to need all of it to get there and get our tents set up." They moved into line in front of the grandmothers.

"You know, I have to admit that I'm still a bit overwhelmed by what our girls have done," Kaylyn said as they moved forward. "They could have bought themselves anything with that money…like ten years' worth of those gummy bears Billie likes or that boat JoJo had her eye on…"

"…or a whole Quonset hut full of scribblers, sketchbooks, and D&D paraphernalia."

"Exactly. But instead, they put most of it into buying tents and winter outfits for over half of the community." Kaylyn squeezed Jessie's hand. "I always knew our girls were special, but now I'm certain of it."

"I couldn't agree more" Jessie smiled. "I'm not saying that they're perfect…not by any stretch of the imagination, but they're kind and caring and amazingly perceptive at times. What more could a mother want?"

"Not to sound like a whiny child, but are we there yet?" Maggie moved up behind them and put her hand on Jessie's shoulder.

"That's right, you've never been to the lake have you, Grandmother?" Jessie looked over her shoulder and immediately slowed her pace. "Are you alright, Grandmother? Maybe we should take a break."

Kaylyn saw Maggie wince and shake her head. "I'm fine, but I must admit, this isn't the easiest walk I've ever taken; the footing is atrocious. Now I understand why our water carriers were so tired when they got back to the old camp."

"Makes me wonder how anyone could have imagined dragging those yurts through this mess…" Grace growled and a branch snapped as she moved closer. "…let alone everything else that was too heavy or awkward to be carried down here on our backs. It would have been a disaster from start to finish."

"I think…" Kaylyn caught her toe on an exposed root and grabbed a nearby branch to keep herself from falling. "I think we're lucky Kim and Juno came along when they did," she said over her shoulder.

"It wasn't luck," Grace muttered.

Maggie chuckled. "Then what was it, Gracey?"

"I don't know exactly, but it wasn't luck. I'd know if it was," The Sargent growled, "And before you ask, it wasn't that damned prophecy either or it would have said something about whirlybirds or deliverance from on high."

Kaylyn muffled the sudden urge to laugh behind an open hand. It was startling to realize that the 'eyes front, boots on the ground' Grandmother had just admitted to believing in the existence of something she couldn't see, hear, taste or touch. A fleeting image of Kaylyn's Goth daughter grinning over the possibility of a benevolent Mother planting a wild garden for her children to find sent a shiver of hope and anticipation down Kaylyn's spine. Maybe Grace was right; maybe it wasn't luck or the prophecy that brought Kim and Juno to them. Maybe it was something more and maybe, just maybe, she should talk to Chloe…let her know that they might not have gotten it all wrong.

"Well, whatever it was that brought those two here, I'm grateful to it," Maggie said. "Once down this path is good enough for me."

"Almost there, Grandmother," Jessie said as they made their way around the slight bend in the trail and their new home came into view. "Welcome to Dragon's Flare."

"So what do you think, Grandmother?"

Maggie didn't know whether Cali's question pertained to the awe-inspiring beauty of their surroundings or the tent her granddaughters had erected after only three tries; she decided to err on the side of caution. "The tents are lovely, so big, and that shade of blue fits in quite well with our beautiful surroundings. It'll be a treat to sleep in them."

Cali looked pleased. "Juno figured out how to zip them all together to make a big tent with different rooms." She stood back and surveyed the area around her. "Momjay invited Kim and Juno to share with us since we have oodles of room and their big tent is going to be used as a kitchen while we're putting up the yurts."

Maggie frowned, remembering Kaylyn's timidity around the dogs. "And where are Cagney and Lacey going to sleep."

"Outside, I guess." Cali's instinctively cradled the bag hanging from her shoulder. Maggie wondered if she'd introduced Mouser to the dogs yet. "Apparently, they like to keep an eye on things at night."

"Well, that's handy."

Cali nodded. "That's what Momkay said." She shrugged. "I guess there's a lot more than a few skunks to worry about. Jenna said they've heard coyotes every night since they set up camp and Andrew thinks he found bear spoor…that means the tracks in this case since he's not a dog and can't smell them."

"So you found a new word," Maggie smiled despite her sudden concern. "Were the tracks recent?"

"Grandpa Zeke said they were probably made before the ground froze last winter."

Maggie hugged Cali to her side. "Then I guess it's fortunate that we have the dogs to protect us."

"Sure is, and Lacey's pregnant." Wanda appeared from inside the tent. She glared at Cali. "So we won't run out of protectors. Now, will you please go find Grandma Lee, Cali? We're ready for the next tent."

"Be right back, Grandmother," Cali said as she turned and sped away.

Maggie watched as the young women veered toward the distant chopper. At first, Maggie had wondered why they'd placed the landing pad so far from the camp, but on further inspection, she'd realized that the landing site was right beside the area with the most prints leading down to the water leaving the opposite end of the verge available to the tents; a smart move even if it did mean carrying the load a little farther.

"Would you like to come inside, Grandmother?" Wanda held the door flap open. "I think you'll love the camp cots; they've even got pockets and a cup holder."

Maggie grinned as she stepped inside. "And I have just the cup to go in it." She raised her half-empty travel mug. "A present from Grandma Kate. She knows how I hate bugs in my tea."

"Ew."

Billie grinned at Wanda as she approached the door. "Lots of protein in bugs."

"Don't start that again." Wanda turned mournful eyes toward Maggie. "I had nightmares for a week after Billie and Grandma Grace got through telling us how good bugs were to eat."

"You weren't the only one, I'm certain." Maggie fixed Billie with her most grandmotherly stare and was pleased to see that, even in the wilds, it still worked.

Billie shifted from one foot to the other and her shoulders slumped forward. "Sorry, Grandmother. I won't talk about it again."

"Thank you." Maggie smiled when Billie looked up. "Now why don't you show me these lovely cup holders?"

A faint aura of vibrant pink capped the trees on the west side of the lake by the time the tents were up and ready to receive their occupants; a slight chill had begun to permeate the air. "Put a sweater and your hoodie's on girls, it going to be a cool one," Kaylyn said as she helped Trin tie her new boots.

Maggie handed Jessie a canvas drum bag, not taking no for an answer then gave the same to each of her four oldest granddaughters. Billie stared at the bag wide-eyed. "What is this?"

"It's a drum," Maggie said as she reached into her own bag and pulled out a miniature replica of the larger drums and a tambourine. She handed the small drum to Trin who immediately hugged it possessively to her chest.

"I'll take that." Jessie reached for the tambourine and passed her drum to Kaylyn in one, smooth motion. She gave Maggie a sheepish grin. "Chloe's really looking forward to hearing some music tonight and I wouldn't want her to be disappointed." She winked at her partner. "Kat has oodles of rhythm…"

"We're supposed to play these…" Cali peered into her bag. "…in front of everyone…by ourselves."

Maggie smiled. "No, dear. Not by yourselves." She moved to the inner door flap and held it open. "Juno. Kim. Could you come in here, please, and bring your instruments."

Kaylyn nudged Jessie with her elbow. "You were right."

Juno and Kim ducked into the tent each toting a black case. Neither of them looked guilty about possessing contraband. Juno set her case on the nearest cot and opened it.

"A violin," Cali said as she took a step closer.

"Actually, I like to call it a fiddle." Juno grinned. "Violin is too classy for the music Juno and I like to play."

"Is that a guitar," Jo asked pointing to Kim's bag. "It's a funny shape."

Kim smiled and opened her case. "That's because it's a mandolin. It was my mother's. Lisa was never interested in playing it, so Mom gave it to me when I enlisted, along with her music books."

Jo ran her fingers gently over the strings. "It sounds pretty. Are you going to play it tonight?"

"Of course, she is," Maggie said with a grin, "Bonfire nights are about celebrating with your friends and family and you can't celebrate properly without music. Now come on before all the food is gone."

Kat exchanged a smile with Kim then slung her bag over her shoulder; she hadn't seen Maggie this excited in a long time. "Let's go girls and don't drop those bags."

Cali caught up to Kaylyn as she stepped out into the cool, night air. "Do you think Grandma Maggie would let me play my penny whistle instead," she whispered, "I've never played drum before…and I don't think Mouser would like it…too loud."

Kaylyn gave her daughter what she hoped was a reassuring hug. "This is important to Maggie for some reason, so let's not disappoint her. Okay? If you're worried about Mouser, I'm sure Grandma Kate would be happy to hold her."

Cali nodded, but she didn't look happy.

"Food," Billie said as she dashed past them. "Smells like beef stew."

Cali giggled. "Actually, it's black bean and 'wiener' stew. I saw Cerdwin cutting up the wieners when I went to get some water. I guess Robert and Lisa brought them with them; they were in their freezer." She shrugged. "We might have had hotdogs, but there wasn't enough for everyone."

"Black bean and wiener stew sound fine to me," Kaylyn said. She spied Katherine and the other grandmothers sitting on a tarp not far from the fire pit and felt a twinge of guilt that she hadn't yet found a way to provide them each with a chair. She pointed toward the tight, little cluster. "How be we put these drums over by the grandmothers and you can talk to Grandma Kate about Mouser while I get us each a plate. It looks like they're almost ready to light the fire."

"We did it!" Mark stood with his fist in the air. "We beat the flare."

A cheer went up and Jo stopped in the doorway of the cookhouse as flames burst into the sky; firelight illuminated the smiling faces of her new extended family as tears welled in her eyes. Despite everything, she belonged here; she knew that now. Kim had told her about the canoes waiting beneath a tarp in the second Quonset hut…waiting for her. While they were flying toward the lake, the older woman had joked about asking forgiveness instead of permission and how she preferred to do her fishing with her feet on dry land. Jo couldn't imagine being afraid of the water, but fear was fear no matter its source, and Jo felt that perhaps she'd found a kindred spirit in the tall, blond pilot. She spotted Kim and Juno sitting with the grandmothers and headed that way; Billie would be somewhere nearby and Jo had something she needed to say.

Jo found her sisters sitting on their emergency blankets in front of her moms. She dropped into the space between Billie and Wanda and handed Billie the second plate of stew Cerdwin had given her in exchange for a promise to do dishes later on. Billie eyed it suspiciously. "I didn't ask for that."

"I think it's a peace offering," Momjay leaned forward; her voice was barely audible over the noise. "Am I right, Jo?"

JoJo nodded as she watched Billie's fists unclench. Since her sisters had been avoiding her for the past few days, Jo had had a lot of time to think about the hurtful things she'd said and how lonely it was without her sisters to talk to. "I'm really sorry, Billie." She nudged the plate toward Billie's hand. "I had no right to say what I did."

"Ah, you were just mad." Billie eased the plate from between Jo's fingers. "I know what that's like…but don't do it again. Okay?"

Jo breathed a sigh of relief. "Okay."

"Inhabitants of Dragon's Flare," Mark continued as the sound of excited chatter died away. "We have a real treat for you tonight, but before we bring Maggie and her Musical Misfits up here to entertain you." He blew a kiss in Maggie's direction as everyone laughed then lifted a black, vaguely triangular bag from the ground. "Would Chloe please come up here? Andrew has a little gift for you."

"My harp!" Jo turned to where Chloe sat beside Momjay. Tears rolled down the older woman's cheeks. "I thought…I thought I'd never see it again."

"I have something I would like to say." Chloe looked down at the harp case as though she still couldn't believe that she was holding it. In all the years that Kaylyn had known Chloe, she had never heard her play; someday she would ask the older woman why that was so, but not tonight. Tonight Kat would play Maggie's drum and hope she didn't make a fool of herself.

Chloe raised her head and smiled at the people gathered around the fire. "Tonight we celebrate our successes and there have been many of them, but tomorrow the really hard work begins…" There were a few groans as people glanced toward the ridge. "…and I'm not talking about putting up a few yurts; we've already proven that we can do the grunt work. I'm talking about the need to define ourselves as a people, to determine who we will become in relation to this beautiful place we now call home."

Chloe smiled over her shoulder. "I have been given two gifts tonight: my lovely harp and the realization that we, as a people, are unique. We are not those ancient hunters who roamed these forests and survived here by the strength of their arms and the sweat of their brow. Nor can we ever be those people; though we can learn a great deal from the knowledge they passed on, we have learned too much about this world and the human condition to ever truly go back. Neither are we so engrossed in the machinations of the present that we couldn't give them up at a moment's notice. We have cleaned out our bank accounts and literally walked away from our jobs and our homes; not simply because a prophecy has urged us to do so, but because we are uniquely suited for what lays ahead." Chloe drew a deep breath and squared her shoulders. "We have been chosen, my friends, and tomorrow we must begin to determine what that means."

A ripple went through the people crowded around the fire, part sound, part something else as Chloe turned abruptly and disappeared toward the tents. Kaylyn smiled. She had no idea where Chloe's words had come from, but she'd felt the gentle touch of an unseen presence urging Chloe on…or maybe that was just Kaylyn's own desire speaking to her; her need to believe that they weren't alone out here.

The soft refrains of a waltz Kaylyn didn't recognize filled the void Chloe left behind. Juno winked at her as Maggie picked up the beat. Grandma Matibi along with Kwasi and Ebo and the rest of the grandmothers were quietly urging everyone to form a circle around the fire. Kaylyn watched Maggie's hands and tried to follow along.

"Join hands and listen to the beat." Matibi grabbed Kwasi's hand and demonstrated from inside the circle. "Step right, feet together, bob, bob. Step right, feet together, bob, bob. Now you try. Step right…"

Chapter Twenty-Two

Wanda smiled to herself as she entered the cook tent and took her place at the end of the line. Last night had been amazing and there had been promises made of more such nights to come; she hoped that was true. She'd really enjoyed the drumming and the dancing and the good feeling it had given her inside.

She stepped forward and a beige and green glop landed on her plate. "Tastes better than it looks," Cerdwin said as she held out a mug of black tea. "And you can wash it down with this. Maggie thought everyone would probably need a pick-me-up after the late night we had, but so far everyone seems fine; some more so than others." She drew Wanda's gaze to the back corner of the tent. Seated around an ornately carved table on equally ornate chairs, her seven grandmothers were engaged in an obviously heated conversation with Tilly.

Wanda blinked twice but the image didn't disappear. "Where…"

"Mark and Andrew snuck the table and chairs in a few days ago," Cerdwin said in anticipation of Wanda's question; tables and chairs certainly hadn't been on the list. "They hid them with the stuff up top and brought them down last night before they went to bed. The boys thought it would be nice to preserve some of Earth Songs history…especially for Tilly." Cerdwin sighed. "She almost blew a gasket when she saw it."

"Are you going to stand there all day?"

"Hold your horses, Ian. Can't you see we're talking here?" Wanda gave Cerdwin an apologetic smile and stepped out of line.

"Am I supposed to eat this?" Ian sounded genuinely puzzled as she moved past him. "Really?"

Wanda smiled to herself on her way to the door. She imagined there would be a lot of rude awakenings in their foreseeable future; wild greens and oatmeal for breakfast might not be the worst of them. She was glad her moms had sat her and her sisters down and explained some of those changes so they wouldn't come as such a shock. They'd talked about the limited choices of food and how important it would be to eat everything on their plate whether they liked it or not. Then they'd gotten into things like cloth bum wipes and menstrual pads; how they would need to be carefully washed and how difficult that might be when or if the soap ran out. Wanda had decided right there and then that soap making would be a priority for her; she'd already consulted the DIY manual she and Cali had put together for instructions. Maybe Mel would like to help; she was good at crafty things and it might get her over some of her shyness.

A light breeze ruffled Wanda's hair as she stepped from the cook tent and looked around. She had a twinge of nostalgia for Grandma Maggie's kitchen as she spied Jenna sitting on her emergency blanket beside a scrawny birch tree methodically spooning porridge into her mouth; her eyes were unfocused and she seemed to be deep in thought. Wanda sat down on the corner of the blanket and set her cup on the ground beside her. "Hey, Jen," she said softly, "You okay?"

Jenna shook herself and offered Wanda a weak smile. "Yeah, I'm fine. Just thinking."

"About what?" Wanda took a mouthful of porridge and let it slide down her throat. The flavor was…interesting.

"The speech Chloe made last night. Tilly's really angry at her about it." Jenna sighed as Wanda took another mouthful and chewed it this time. "She said that Chloe had no right taking all the years of research and preparation that's gone into finding our way back to the source and throwing it out the window like it meant nothing."

Wanda swallowed the soggy mouthful and frowned. "This is connected to the t-shirt Momkay wears all the time…the earth mother one. Isn't it?"

Jenna laughed. "Tilly hates that shirt. She says it's sixties jargon and trivializes everything we're searching for."

"But Momkay really believes that there is an Earth Mother. She's never really talked about it. I guess she thought we'd ask when we were ready. I guess she thought wrong." Wanda put her plate down and picked up her mug; Jenna sat quietly with her empty bowl in her lap. "When I was little," Wanda said after taking a drink of the cool tea, "I used to sneak out to the garden at night and listen to Momjay carry on long conversations with someone who wasn't there. I told Grandma Maggie about it because I thought it was kinda strange; she said that the garden was like Momjay's church and I shouldn't worry about it. So I didn't." She shrugged. "Maybe I should have…at least enough to ask her about it."

"Tilly would probably say that Kaylyn was wasting her time; anyway, that the source won't make herself know to us until we've become truly human…like our most ancient ancestors." Jenna shrugged. "That was Helka's theory anyway. I guess when Helka got sick, Tilly promised that she and the members of Earth Song would carry on her work; she takes that promise very seriously."

"So that's why she fought so hard to keep the items on that list to a bare minimum."

Jenna nodded; her eyes were sad. "The less we have, the less we need to get rid of when the time comes, but I guess something happened yesterday to make Chloe rethink that decision. I heard her trying to explain to Tilly that we don't need to give up the things that make us happy, like music and a good chair, to find the source because she's already here just waiting for us to acknowledge her."

Wanda nodded then took a deep breath. It was now or never. "I think Chloe's right," she said watching Jenna's eyes. Maybe her new friend wouldn't think she was crazy after all. "Every time we find a new plant that we can use, it feels like someone put it there just for us…like there's someone looking out for us. Maybe this sounds silly, but sometimes it's like I can feel her smile…like she's happy we're here."

Jenna's eyes widened. "You're serious, aren't you? Please, tell me that you're serious."

"I've never been so serious about anything in my life." It felt like the right answer…maybe the only answer.

Jenna drew a relieved breath then she smiled. "Too bad there isn't a t-shirt shop around."

Wanda found Kaylyn at what was basically the center of their new camp watching as Trin played her drum for a circle of dancing children. Wanda grinned at the look of pure bliss on her youngest sister's face. "She's really good at that."

Kaylyn looked up and held out her hand; Wanda took it and allowed herself to be pulled down to Kaylyn's side. "She is. It's almost like she's found her voice. Now, what can I do for you?"

Wanda wanted to say that she was just there for the company, but Momjay seemed to have a sixth sense about these things and would know that was a lie. "I talked to Jenna about what happened with Chloe last night…among other things; she seemed more confused than upset." Wanda went on to describe Tilly's reaction to Chloe's speech and the arrival of the Earth Song dining table and Jenna's subsequent relief when she found out that Wanda shared her sense of a benevolent presence watching over them. "But she didn't think she should say anything in case she was wrong." Wanda didn't mention the t-shirt.

"Sounds like the two of you have a lot in common."

Wanda smiled at the gentle rebuke. "I really like her mom; maybe that's why…we're both idiots when it comes to sharing the important things." Then her smile faded. "But she did say that she was worried about what Tilly will do next."

Kaylyn nodded thoughtfully. "I've been wondering that myself." She gave Wanda's hand a squeeze. "Tilly never had much patience for anyone who questioned Helka's premise…and Chloe's not the first."

"Were you one of them?" The question was out before Wanda could call it back.

Kaylyn smiled at her. "No more than most teenagers question their parental authority. For the most part, I just took out the things that I found intriguing and ignored the rest. When I moved in with Jessie and Cali came along, I was too busy being a mom to worry about a theory that may or may not be proven." She shrugged. "I guess it just became irrelevant."

"But you still believe in some of it." Wanda pointed at the faded t-shirt half-hidden by Kaylyn's favorite denim jacket.

Kaylyn grinned and gave her daughter a one-arm hug. "How could I not when she's supplying us with such lovely vegetables?"

"You used to talk to her…in the garden," Wanda said.

"And you used to watch me." Kaylyn smiled. "I knew you were there even before Grandma Maggie told me."

"She said it was your church."

"More like an open-air temple." Kaylyn waved her free arm around. "Like we have here…if that's how you choose to think about this amazing place. As for what Chloe said, I believe she has the right of it; we are unique, each and every one of us, a solitary expression of our mother's love and just by being here we are celebrating that uniqueness in her name." She drew a deep breath and a touch of regret crept into her voice. "But you'll have to make up your own mind about that too, eventually…and don't let anyone tell you otherwise."

Wanda snuggled a little closer. "I understand. Thanks, Momjay."

"No problem, love."

Matibi took the freshly washed plate Maggie held out to her and dried it with an oversized tea towel. "If I remember correctly, there were seven, intelligent and highly educated women sitting around your table the day Tilly paid us that visit," the social anthropologist said, "You'd think that at least one of us would have realized that something like this could happen."

"Perhaps some of us did." Maggie plunged another plate into the bucket of soapy water. "But were so stressed out at the time by our lack of wilderness relevant skills that it seemed like an acceptable trade-off."

"Are you saying you had doubts and didn't say anything?" Matibi didn't wait for an answer. "That's not like you, Maggie."

"Would it have made a difference if I had? We needed their expertise, Mat." She gave the plate a final scrub and passed it on. "And you have to admit that their assistance has been invaluable."

"That doesn't change the fact that Tilly has become completely unreasonable."

"If you're talking about the fact that she blames us for the boys' perceived betrayal and Chloe's sudden change of heart, I couldn't agree with you more." Maggie moved to wipe down the multipurpose folding table that had apparently come in with the tent. "But I can't blame her for being upset. I'm certain that when we agreed to whittle down our list of necessities to just the bare essentials, she must have believed that she was one giant step closer to proving Helka's theory."

Matibi snorted. "And once again, we let our anxieties overrule our common sense. I left a lovely set of ebony-wood stacking tables behind because they'd been deemed non-essential; now I have nowhere to put my teeth at night."

"At least some of us know when to seek forgiveness instead of permission," Maggie smirked, and Matibi rolled her eyes. "The music last night was lovely, wasn't it?" Maggie continued. "And such a range of contraband instruments. Not that I think Tilly will ever find it in her heart to forgive any of us for that."

Matibi swiped her fingers through her hair. "And that's the problem, isn't it. We didn't invite these people here to become Tilly's experimental test subjects, but I doubt that anything is going to stop her from trying to make that happen."

"Then we'll have to make certain that everyone is aware of that possibility and can make an informed decision for themselves." Maggie shrugged. "I have no desire to follow Tilly down her rabbit hole, but there may be others who would be interested."

Matibi frowned. "Just what we need…our own little cult."

"I doubt that'll happen." Maggie flashed back to the conversation she'd overheard while reading in her tent this morning. "I happen to know that Wanda and her new friend Jenna have taken Chloe's words to heart. Apparently, collecting wild plants gives you a unique perspective on the source/Earth Mother debate."

"Jenna. From Earth Song? Now isn't that interesting."

Maggie nodded. "But I'll ask Kaylyn to keep an eye on the youngsters; she'll know what to look for if things get out of hand. Right now, however, we have more pressing concerns. Having a day free to relax and explore was a good idea, but starting tomorrow we're going to need something in place to make certain that everything gets done in a timely fashion."

"Like putting up the yurts."

"Or emptying the chamber pots." Maggie shrugged. "There are dozens of small chores like that we probably haven't even thought about and they're going to need taking care of on a daily basis or we're going to be…"

"…up shit creek without a paddle." Matibi laughed at Maggie scowl and shook her head. "Don't tell me that wasn't what you were thinking."

Maggie allowed herself a small smile. "Perhaps. But seriously, Mat, we haven't even started to get a grip on what this new life is going to require of us and if we don't do that sooner rather than later, Tilly's little tantrum is going to be the least of our worries."

Matibi nodded. "I guess we should talk to Kate and the others…get their opinion on all this before we take it to the next level. It might be a good idea to bring everyone together for a campfire tonight…clear the air."

"I think you're right; nip any problems in the bud. Maybe we can meet with the grandmothers over lunch to set up an agenda." Maggie sighed and offered Matibi a wry smile. "Think Tilly would mind if we used her table?"

Greg puffed his way up the incline leading to their building site, a thermos of black tea and a half-dozen energy bars from his private stash tucked into the knapsack slung over his shoulder. The boys had fled Tilly's wrath before breakfast was ready and the food was as much a peace offering as it was a simple act of caring.

He stopped as the land flattened out before him and waited for his breathing to slow. He'd been a struggling artist with a middle management day job when he'd been drawn into Helka's circle. Living on the outskirts of a small rural community as a child, he'd cultivated a love for the wild spaces that had never disappeared; the promise that he could someday return to that idyllic setting in the company of fellow artists was more than enough reason for him to become part of the Earth Song Artist Collective. He wasn't certain that he had ever truly believed in their quest to find the source; the thought of spending the rest of his life creating art in a place like this had been enough for him…that and a deep sense of devotion to the welfare of his chosen family.

"What are you doing here, Old Man?" Mark stepped from behind a pile of boxes wrapped in plastic sleeves, couched his fists on his hips, and tilted his head; suspicion was written all over his face.

Greg forced a smile and held out the bag. "I come bearing food and drink…nothing else. You can frisk me if you must."

Mark's lips twitched at the reference to a game they'd played when Mark was a child and Greg was a much younger man; he took the bag from Greg's outstretched hand and spun on his heels. "Come on, Old Man. Andrew needs to talk to you."

They wound their way through orange and blue mounds of rain-proofed odds and ends to the area in front of the third outhouse where a stack of leftover lumber served as a windbreak and seating area. Andrew sat on the far end of the makeshift bench staring into a tiny fire surrounded by rocks they'd dug out of the ground; Greg walked over and sat down beside him. "You hungry?"

"Of course, he is." Mark sat down on Greg's left. "But it's hard to think about eating when your stomach's all tied up in knots. Isn't that right, Bro?" Mark leaned forward. "Go ahead. Tell him what you told me. Maybe he can help."

Andrew's jaw clenched and for a moment Greg feared that the young man would keep his thoughts to himself, push them way down where they would fester and cause more pain; obviously, Tilly's scathing rebuke had cut him badly. Then the floodgates opened and it all came pouring out. "Do you know where I found Clo's harp?" Andrew blurted. "In the back of Tilly's closet in that little room under the eaves. Why would Tilly do that, Greg? Chloe loved that harp. It broke her heart when it went missing."

"Maybe she loved it too much," Mark's voice held a sharp edge of angry sarcasm and something more that Greg couldn't quite place, yet he couldn't keep himself from feeling that the young man's emotions were justified. "Maybe Tilly thought that if she took it away," Mark continued, "Clo wouldn't have to struggle with giving it up when the time came."

Andrew laughed hysterically. "You mean when we strip ourselves naked and give up all our little comforts so the source realizes we're here. Come on, man, you haven't believed that since you were twelve."

Greg frowned and turned to Mark. This whole thing was starting to make him feel slightly nauseous. "Is that true?"

Mark drew a deep breath and nodded. "Blame it on Kat." He shrugged and looked away, but not before Greg saw the glimmer of tears in the young man's eyes. "I found her journal in the studio the night she left. I was going to give it back, but…"

"You decided to read it instead."

Mark nodded. "I knew it was wrong, but I was glad that I did it…still am. Kat had it all figured out, Greg…made all the scary stuff Tilly was always talking about going away. Apparently, Kat decided a long time before she left Earth Song, that Helka's theory was flawed. She said the source, or the Earth Mother as she called her, created her human children with the potential to grow and evolve; that trying to go backward may ultimately destroy the essence of what we are. She said that no true mother would demand such a sacrifice from her children no matter how many mistakes they've made; especially when all we really needed to do to reconnect with the source was to open our minds and our hearts to her and she would show us the way." Mark grinned. "Kat did agree that finding that connection would probably be easier in the uncluttered peace and quiet of the forest, but not if we've made our existence so uncomfortable that our minds are focused on merely surviving and nothing else."

Greg stared into the fire as Mark's words pried opened a floodgate of long-repressed thoughts and emotions. Earth Song had given his life a purpose and a direction, but not in the way Tilly expected; he could admit that now. His art had always been his focus and he'd been guiltily ecstatic when the boys had brought him his paints; it was then that he realized that he had never truly believed in Earth Song's theoretical underpinnings, that giving up the thing that was most important to him wasn't something he was able to do no matter how many lies he told himself. "I think Kat has the right of it," he said with a sudden sense of release, "And Helka might even have agreed with her if she was still around."

Mark laughed. "But will Tilly?"

"Doesn't matter," Andrew said, "this isn't Earth Song and Tilly's not in charge anymore." He stood up and poured water over the fire. He raised an eyebrow in Mark's direction. "You coming?"

"Where?"

"To find Kat." Andrew grinned. "Time you gave her back her journal."

"JoJo, come on. You have to see this." Jo looked up from the book she was reading just as Billie and Sophia skidded to halt outside the tent. Billie pulled the flap aside and stuck her head in through the opening. "Kim and Juno left you a gift. I have the note right here."

Jo swung her legs over the side of her cot and sat up. She squinted toward the open door hardly daring to hope. "Where did you find it?"

Billie grinned and shook her head. "That would spoil the surprise. So, are you coming or what?"

Jo opened her mouth to tell her bratty, little sister that she already knew about the canoes then snapped it shut. She'd promised Momjay that she'd try to find her way back to her former self somehow. There was a time when she would have played along just to see Billie smile; maybe a simple act of kindness like that was a good place to start. "I'm coming," she said as she shoved her feet into her boots and stood up. "But this better be good."

"Oh, it is." Sophia stepped back as Jo zipped the flap closed and bent to tie her laces. "Grandma Steph saw the chopper leave and come back really early this morning. She sent me and Billie down to see what they'd left behind after we finished breakfast."

"It took us a while though." Billie chuckled. "Kim and Juno hid them really good. Come on. We'll show you." She waved the plastic bag with the crumpled note inside in Jo's direction. "Then I'll give you this."

Jo clenched her teeth, holding the words back as Billie turned away and headed for the beach.

Small fingers clasped her hand.

"Don't be angry at her," Sophia said as their eyes met. "Whether you believe it or not, she loves you very much. It was so exciting for her when she found out that the gift Kim and Juno left was for you; she knows how much it will mean to you."

Jo drew a deep breath and nodded. "I love her too." Jo smiled as Sophia's eyes twinkled. "So I suppose we should get going before she thinks we got lost." She felt Sophia's grip tighten, giving her no choice but to follow as they veered toward the edge of the swamp.

"They used one of those camouflage things to hide them." Sophia smiled over her shoulder. "Thanks for not telling her."

Jo frowned. "Telling her what?"

"That you already knew what the surprise was."

"How…"

"There you are." Billie appeared where the cattails touched the verge as if by magic: a wisp of mottled green fabric piled at her feet. Sophia giggled. "Pretty neat, eh?" Billie said as she grabbed the edge of the cloth and started to pull it away from the water.

Sophia stepped in to help and Jo followed her; a minute later, two large canoes raised above the ground on log ends sat proudly on the verge. "The blue one is yours." Sophia giggled, "It says so in the note."

Jo let out the breath she wasn't aware she was holding; in her whole, entire life she had never seen anything so beautiful. "They're perfect. Thank you."

"So you're not angry." Billie took a tentative step forward, the plastic bag held in front of her like a shield. "That we read the note."

Jo sighed and shook her head. "I probably should be, but I'm not. I would never have found them without you and…" The look she gave Billie's strange friend was full of questions. "…Sophia."

Juno stared at the wad of hundred dollar bills her business partner slapped down on the counter in front of her. "What's this for?"

Dan leaned his elbows on the polished surface and grinned. "Damnedest thing," he said, "This short, bald guy walks in here this morning and hires us to help him find his wife. Said she disappeared somewhere up near that big game preserve north of Gimli."

"You're kidding. Right?" Juno felt the cold fingers of premonition tighten around her gut.

"Nope. Said he followed her when she took his daughter and ran, but he lost them when his car went off the road. Offered us triple our usual fare if we'd take him up first thing this morning. Just got back a half-hour ago." He gestured toward the money. "That's your share."

"And did he find what he was looking for?"

Dan shrugged. "That area is pretty sparsely populated. We did spot a group of campers tucked in beside a lake. He got really excited about that. Wanted us to land until we told him that we'd need permission since it was private property. Then there were some vehicles on the side of the road that he thought he recognized. He demanded that I put down beside them…said the roads were public domain and no one would make a fuss." Dan sighed and shook his head. "By then I was beginning to think that his wife may have had a good reason to run. I know you think Bill has a foul mouth, but he has nothing on this guy. When I told him no, those landings weren't in our contract he cursed me six ways to Sunday. So I just turned around and came home. Sounded like he'd be heading back up there with his buddies on the weekend." He grinned. "Good thing he paid up front."

Juno let out the breath she hadn't known she was holding and shoved the cash into her pocket. "Thanks, Dan. The Snow Eater's been cleaned and refueled. Gotta go." she said as she turned toward the hangar.

"When will you be back?" He yelled as the doors swung closed behind her.

When hell freezes over. She patted Snow Eaters nose as she hurried past; she was going to miss the old girl. She found Kim stowing their duffle bags in the back of their jeep just outside the landing bay doors. "We need to go…now," she said as she slid into the driver's seat.

Kim frowned as she stepped into view. "But I haven't said my goodbyes yet."

"Maybe later." Juno reached over and opened the passenger side door. "Come on. I'll explain on the way."

"Walk with me Grand Daughter; there's something I want you to see."

Jessie opened her eyes and rolled onto her side; the cot protested the shift in weight. "I don't feel much like walking right now." In truth, she didn't feel much like doing anything.

"You feel responsible, don't you?" Kathleen lowered herself to the empty cot across from Jessie's. "I know you were there when Tilly had her tantrum. Cerdwin told me how quickly you left." The elder sighed and shook her head. "I figured you might need someone to talk you out of that notion."

Jessie frowned. "You think that it was just a tantrum?"

"I do." Kathleen tilted her head. "What else could it have been?"

"A promise of worse things to come." Jessie sagged against her pillow. "You weren't there, Grandmother. You didn't hear the things she said. And all I could think was that it was my fault. I was the one who urged Kat to bring them on board." She wiped her eyes with her sleeve. "I knew they had their own agenda, but I never once thought that they would turn it against us."

"They?" Katie frowned. "I thought we were talking about Tilly."

"But."

Kathleen stood up and nodded toward the door. "Walk with me."

Jessie blinked as she gave in and followed the grandmother into the sunlight. "Your partner is a very wise woman. I found that out when she came to me for advice on raising an abused child," the old women said, "We talked about a lot of things from her past. She told me that she was well aware of the flaws in Earth Song's proposed experiment; figured that out for herself when she was barely JoJo's age. Her Earth Mother is not the harsh, unforgiving entity of Helka's theory and I know of at least two other members of Earth Song among others, who have come to share Kaylyn's views. You can't walk these woods without sensing a benign and watchful presence waiting patiently to be acknowledged." Kathleen's smile lit up her face. "If an unrepentant agnostic such as myself can feel her existence, soon there will be others."

"But…"

"Such a beautiful place," Kathleen said as they topped the rise and entered the forest, "Peaceful too. Can you feel it? Like being cradled in your grandmother's arms. No one can take that away from us, Jessie, and certainly not an angry, old woman who is about to find out that she's been living a lie for a good part of her life."

"That's rather harsh, Grandmother." Jessie paused as her muscles relaxed and the peace Kathleen spoke of seemed to seep into her bones; it was a startling sensation though it seemed to warm her from the inside out. She smiled. "Especially for you."

"Sometimes it's necessary to pull back the curtain and expose the pretender. There is too much potential here for a peaceful, uncomplicated life to let Tilly's rage destroy it. Come. I have something important to show you." Kathleen took Jessie's hand and pulled her off the game trail and into the trees. "I hope we're not too late," was all the old woman said as she pressed a finger to her lips and moved quietly forward.

"Well, I'm glad you decided that you aren't going to be part of that." Sam's voice. Close ahead. "It sounds really creepy. We're already human. Right? How's that going to change even if we give everything up?"

"I think you're missing the point, Bro. We don't have to give up everything to be part of all this. All we have to do is become a better version of ourselves...like a real cool avatar."

Wanda's groan. "For a second there, I really thought you were being serious, Ian."

"But I was...I am. It's just a lot to take in all at once, you know. I'm okay with the idea of an Earth Mother who just wants the best for her children; she sounds like my mom in that way. And Ibo and Kwasi's people have believed in her forever. Right, Bro? Isn't that what you said?"

"That is correct. Asase Yaa provides my people with everything we need to help us sustain our lives," Kwasi the soft-spoken, gentle giant. "And she will continue to do this in our new home."

"And I guess I can believe it when you say she's all around us because I can feel her sometimes...at least I think I can. I told my mom about how good it made me feel to be in the woods. She said that the Japanese believe that the forest is a place of healing. She called what they do there Shinny Rinny...or something like that."

Sam giggled. "Shinrin-Yoku, dummy. It means 'forest bathing.'"

"Yeah. Whatever." There was a touch of hurt pride behind those words. "But I think it's more than that...more than just the trees."

"Don't think about it so much, Ian" Cali's voice was soft and gentle. "Just let the feelings find their own path. Just close your eyes and let her in. That's what Momkay does when she thinks no one is watching and the look on her face...well, it's so peaceful, so full of joy. I'm not quite there yet, but I...we have lots of time."

"You've been watching her?" Wanda's voice. "Why?"

"Because I needed to know. Cerdwin told me about Helka's theory; it didn't sound like something Momjay would condone, but I needed to be certain." There was a smile in Cali's voice. "And I was right."

"I also feel her presence." A different voice, soft and sibilant. Hua…one of Lee's s students. "My mother calls her Hantu of the Deep Earth…the Earth Mother is definitely here…in this place."

Jessie sank to her knees then to her belly where the bushes thinned just enough for her to see her daughters and their circle of friends.

"They call themselves 'the gatherers' now." Kathleen's voice was soft in Jessie's ear. "They know what's in these woods better than anyone else. You could learn a lot from them."

Jessie smiled. "I already have."

Jessie squeezed Wanda's hand as they waited for the members of Earth Song to follow their guides into the clearing. Not all of them had responded to the invitation, but that was to be expected. The gatherers waited until all of their guests were seated then took their places at Jessie's side; the young people seemed nervous, but confident, and that's all she could ask for.

"I think that's everyone who's coming," Chloe said as she wrapped her arms around her raised knees. "So what's this all about?"

Jenna rolled her eyes at Wanda, but neither of them said anything. Jessie cleared her throat. "I was the one who asked Kaylyn to invite the members of Earth Song to be part of this project. I was confident that we could all work together to build a community that would not only survive but would also thrive in this place." She drew a deep breath and let it out slowly. "But after I heard what Tilly said in the cook tent this morning, I've been afraid that I may have made a huge mistake."

Mark straightened and looked around. "Tilly doesn't speak for all of us," he said into the silence.

"Mark!"

"He's right, Mae." Greg ran his fingers through his thinning hair. "Tilly has taken things too far this time. I know she made a promise, but it wasn't really her promise to make…not for the rest of us. This morning, I stood beneath these trees and opened myself to the world around me. I needed to know the right of it, so I closed my eyes sent my heart out to the source and she answered me. I was touched by the all-mother's hand...she noticed me and I didn't have to give up everything that makes me for it to happen."

"Good for you, Greg." Jenna smiled at the old man. "Now we're getting somewhere. Who else wants to share?"

Andrew raised his hand. "I would."

"This is ridiculous." Mae stood up. "I don't need an intervention to tell me what I think."

"Mae, sit down, please." Chloe reached out her hand. "I know you're upset and confused, but this may be our only chance to salvage something of what we had and move forward. Can you honestly say that you would follow the path Helka laid out for us if there was another way to touch the source?"

"And that's why we're here," Wanda gestured toward her friends. "To show you another way."

"You're just children. What do you know?" Mae closed her eyes and sighed. "I'm sorry. I didn't mean that."

"That's good," Jenna said, "because you all know how I feel about being called a child."

Mark stifled a laugh with his hand. "And I've got the scars to prove it."

Andrew patted the empty space beside him. "Please sit down, Mae. I really do have something to say and I'd like you to hear it."

Mae sighed then nodded and took her seat. "Get on with it then."

"I was only ten years old when Tilly decided to tell me all the dark and frightening details of Helka's theory. I didn't understand a lot of what she said, but what I did understand gave me nightmares for months. I've often wondered why she couldn't have waited to tell me such things until I was older, but I never asked her, and then it became irrelevant." Andrew smiled at Mark. "A while after my talk with Tilly, Mark came to me with a little red leather diary in hand and read me these words. *The Earth Mother created all of her children with the potential to grow and evolve; to try and reverse this process could ultimately destroy the essence of who we are meant to become. No true mother would demand such a sacrifice from her children no matter how many mistakes they have made. All we need to do to reconnect with the 'earth our mother' is to open our minds and our hearts and let her in; she'll be there to guide us.*" Andrew raised his chin and looked Mae square in the eye. "The nightmares stopped that day and, since then, I've come to realize that what was written in that little book is true…every word of it. She's here Mae; all you have to do is reach out to her."

"I can't believe you remembered all that…almost word for word." Mark grinned in Andrew's direction. "Wow, Bro. I'm impressed."

"Whose words are they?" Chloe took a deep breath. "I'd really like to know."

"They're my mom's. Aren't they?" Wanda leaned forward and Mark nodded. Jessie felt her daughters' fingers tighten around her own. "Good. Now I won't have to explain why when I ask you to close your eyes and open your minds to the wonder of this place."

"Do you mind if we join you?" Kaylyn stepped into the grove as Trin gave one more tug then let go of her mom's hand; a gaggle of children followed close on her heels. "Trin seems to think it's important that we be here."

Mae scowled at Kaylyn but refrained from saying anything. Jessie smiled at her partner. Kat had been adamant that her presence during this gathering would be more of a hindrance than a help and that she had perfect faith in Wanda and her friends to pry open peoples' minds…at least enough to understand the gift they were being given; apparently, Trin had another idea. Her youngest daughter grinned and sat down between Cerdwin and Mae.

"Of course, we don't mind," Wanda said sincerely. She smiled as Kat and the children found places to sit then she sat up straighter and took Jenna's hand. "Close your eyes. Take a deep breath in and let it out. In and out. Open your mind and your heart to the spirit of this place and let her in."

Chapter Twenty-Three

Cagney scented the air and whined as Juno moved onto the verge. "She smells hints of rabbit stew, I bet." She smiled at Kim then gave the hand signal that would allow the dogs to roam freely. "Off you go, girls. Find Sam. Just save some stew for us." Lacy chuffed in agreement then took off toward the fire with Cagney at her side.

"Not nice, Junie. You know how Sam feels about dog spit." Kim said as they followed in the dogs' wake.

"Kim you're back." They'd almost made it past the swamp when Jo appeared as if out of nowhere; she launched herself at Kim and hung on tight. Kim staggered backward until Juno grabbed her arm and drew her to a halt. "I was just checking the canoes. Thank you. Thank you. Thank you." Jo grinned. "They're beautiful. Billie and Sophia found them. Thank you so much."

"You're welcome." Kim turned pleading eyes to Juno as the child continued to cling to her. Her partner was always better with kids than she was.

Juno grinned then held out her arms. "Hey. What about me?"

"Oh, yeah. Sorry." Jo let go of Kim, gave Juno a hug then stepped back. "Thanks, Juno."

"You're most welcome." Juno winked at Kim then nodded toward the people seated around the fire. "I don't see any kids?"

"The little ones are having a sleepover in the dining tent. Grandma Hanna snuck in a box of toys and games so they're all happy and the adults…" She smiled proudly. "…are having a supper meeting. You got here just in time; it hasn't started yet."

"You sent the dogs to find me, didn't you, Aunt Juno?" Sam said accusingly as they approached the fire. "They got spit all over me."

Juno grinned. "Now you won't have to wash your face." Sam groaned and turned his back to her. Cagney and Lacey sat on either side of Maggie happily licking the bottom of their bowls. "Think we could get some of that stew," Juno approached the pot Chloe was stirring. "It sure smells good."

"You're back early, aren't you?" Chloe said as she handed Juno a bowl and dipped out a second one for Kim. "Probably a good thing though. Lots of things to be discussed tonight."

You have no idea. Juno took the two bowls and carried them over to where Kim had taken a seat beside Kat and Jessie. "Have you told them?" She asked as she handed Kim her bowl.

Kaylyn lowered her mug. "Told us what?" Kim just shrugged.

Juno sighed and lowered herself to the ground. "What Kim doesn't want to tell you is that we're going to be having some very unwanted visitors." She went on to give them the abbreviated version of what Dan had told her earlier in the day. "So we picked up the things we needed and headed back right away."

"I don't believe this," Jessie shook her head as Juno stopped talking and picked up her spoon. "One crisis after another."

Juno frowned but didn't comment; she didn't know what other crisis they were facing, but this one could definitely make a mess of things. "Kim and I have some ideas on how to get ahead of this one, but it's going to take all of us to pull it off."

"I'll go tell the grandmothers what you just told us." Kaylyn stood up and brushed the wrinkles from the knees of her jeans. "They called this meeting, so they'll have to decide where to put it on the agenda."

"Sooner would be better than later." Juno glanced at her partner for confirmation; Kim nodded. "If our plan is to work, we'll need to get the details hammered out tonight."

Kaylyn nodded. "I'll be back in a few minutes."

Juno watched Kaylyn walk away then turned to Jessie. "So this other crisis…" She let the words hang in the air between them as she took a mouthful of stew and chewed it slowly.

"Hey. No judgment here. When you're grounded in enemy territory, you use the tools at hand," Kim said as Jessie finished describing the events of the past day. "Let me ask you this; if you hadn't invited Earth Song on board, what would the future look like for the rest of us right now? Remember, it was Greg who spearheaded the purchase of the yurts and it was Chloe and Jenna who taught the kids how to find the wild greens that are supplementing our food supply."

"And wasn't it Mark and Jeb and Andrew who helped Robert put up the toilets?" Juno added.

"We'd be living in a soup can, hauling water through the woods and eating beans and rice until the food runs out." Jessie shook herself and sighed. "I know all that and I'm hoping that something positive came out of our gathering in the grove so we can continue to move forward, but…"

"No time for that right now, love." Kaylyn slid in beside Jessie and nodded to Juno. "The grandmothers have moved you to the top of the agenda and they sent JoJo to find Tilly…"

"Tilly's not here." Jessie frowned. "Anyone else?"

"Jake and Zeke, but no one seems too worried about that." Kaylyn shrugged. "Apparently, they have another secret they're keeping and no one has caught more than a glimpse of them in days."

Kim laughed. "Like the Secret Sauna. Apparently, our nephews have taken on the responsibility of keeping it in working order once it's built. Sam thinks it's great since he's such a clean freak."

"That's what the grandfathers do," Kaylyn laughed. "I've never been able to figure out which comes first, the secret or the child, but the connection is always meaningful and involves some sort of responsibility that is always willingly accepted." She turned to Jessie. "So who is the designated holder of this secret?"

"Kathleen asked, but neither of the grandfathers was forthcoming."

"You…" Kim met Juno's eyes and smiled. "… 'we' have a very interesting family."

Jessie huffed. "That's one way to look at it. So did Jo find Tilly?" As one they turned their attention to the people seated around the fire.

Juno pointed. "Isn't that Tilly with…"

"Trin," Kaylyn laughed. "I wondered how long it would take her to find her way out here." Her eyes followed her youngest daughter as she proudly took a seat between Billie and Sophia. "I suppose it'll be okay."

"Can I have your attention, please?" Maggie waited for the murmur of voices to die down. "We've just received some disturbing news that needs to be shared before we continue with the rest of the meeting." She peered around the circle. "Juno? Kim?"

Juno waved her hand then stood up. "Right here, Maggie."

"You and Kim have the floor."

"Thank you, Grandmother," Juno said as Kim came to stand beside her. "A man looking for his runaway wife and daughter paid one of my partners a large sum of money to fly him up here this morning…probably not long after Kim and I left." There was a sharp intake of breath and a muffled sob from the other side of the fire; the only other sound was the snap/crackle of burning wood.

"Even if it's Kenneth, how could he know where we are?" Tilly demanded into the silence. She glared around the circle. "Unless someone told him."

"Apparently, he followed Jenny when you're people left the city the last time, but his car went off the road…"

"That must have been the one we saw being towed the next morning," Caroline said, "That was miles down the road though."

"Close enough to give him a general area," Kim said, "When they flew over this morning, they found the camp. He also recognized some of the vehicles…"

"But nobody saw them." Britney sobbed.

"They would have been quite high up. If you weren't looking for them…" Juno shrugged. "I'm sorry; I don't know what else to tell you except that he said he and his buddies would be coming back this weekend…and it won't be by chopper."

Britney shot to her feet and turned to her mother. "We have to leave." Her voice rose hysterically. "He'll kill us this time, Mom. You know he will."

"We won't let him hurt you," Juno said as she caught and held Britney's eyes. She'd seen this kind of fear often enough times on the battlefield; it needed a firm hand and a clear direction. "Now sit down. And listen up. Kim and I have a plan and we're going to need everyone's help…including yours."

"Mom?"

"Do what she says, Brit." Jenny leaned her chin on her upraised knees. She looked utterly defeated. "We're all out of options. Besides, I thought you liked it here."

"I do, but…"

"Then sit down and let Juno speak."

"So, first thing tomorrow we'll unload the Jeep and take all of the vehicles into town…scatter them around. Gimli has free parking everywhere, so no one should notice for a while." Kim smiled at Kaylyn. "We'll all come back in the 'soccer mom' van; we'll hide it in that little alcove down the road and cover it with the camouflage net. Any questions so far?"

Mark's hand went up. "Just because we move the cars, it still doesn't guarantee that they won't find the road. So how are we going to keep them off the property?"

"We don't." Kim paused as a ripple of confused disbelief worked its way through the crowd. "Moving the cars gives us plausible deniability…they were here but they left. Then we find you a suitable place to hide until we're certain they're not coming back."

"And just where would that be?" Tilly stared at Kim as though defying her to answer.

"Trin knows." Sophia stood up and dragged Trin up with her.

Billie scrambled to her feet. "Soph, you don't have to…"

"Yes, I do, Billie. Otherwise, how is Trin going to tell about her secret?"

"Of course." Kathleen smiled at Sophia. "Jake said no one would hear about this secret until it was ready to be revealed. I guess he didn't know that Trin has a special friend. So where is this safe place, dear?"

"This is ridiculous," Tilly growled. "We all know Trin can't talk."

"Except inside my granddaughter's head." Stephanie raised her chin and stared at Tilly defiantly. "Now shut up and listen unless you want that child…" She waved a hand toward Britney. "…and her mother to end up back where they started."

"Ain't going to happen." Cassandra glared at Tilly then turned to Sophia. "Go ahead, Child."

Sophia nodded. "Trin says that Grandpa Zeke and Grandpa Jake have built a little house…no, a barn…with the wood Juno and Kim delivered to the tiny meadow…the one with the pond. It's…"

"It's north and west of here…about half a mile."

"So, you knew about this…this barn." Tilly shook her finger at Kim. "And just what need do we have for a barn anyway?"

Kim gave her an easy smile. "I don't know, Ma'am. Juno and I just delivered the wood and you should be glad we did. At least you won't be sleeping under the stars somewhere tomorrow night."

Tilly opened her mouth to respond and Chloe stood up. "Don't say anything else, Til. I know you're angry at the world right now, but Britney and

Jenny need help and Juno and Kim have come up with a way that we can do that...as a community. The least we can do is offer them our support."

"That was very brave of you, Sophia," Maggie said as Sophia and Billie helped her carry the dishes back to the cook tent. "I know some people have reacted badly when they've found out that you can hear people's thoughts."

"My Grandmother says it's called telepathy. I used to wish that I didn't have all those thoughts in my head; some of them weren't very nice." She raised her head to Maggie and smiled. "But since we came here, I've been able to keep the voices out unless I want to hear them. I like talking with Trin. She's really funny sometimes and..." She pursed her lips and nodded to herself. "...well, she really loves her new family. I just thought you should know that."

Maggie nodded thoughtfully. "Maybe you and I and Trin could sit down someday and have a chat. Do you think that's possible?"

Sophia grinned. "I think Trin would like that. Maybe you should ask her."

"I'll do that as soon as we get the Earth Song people squared away."

Sophia tilted her head to the side and frowned. "I think you should stop calling them that. They're Dragon's Flare people now. Aren't they? At least that's what Andrew said and Mark agreed with him."

Maggie frowned. "Did you..."

"No, Grandmother," Billie piped up. "I heard it too."

"I'm sorry." Maggie shook her head. "You'll have to forgive an old woman for leaping to conclusions."

Sophia smiled. "It's okay. I know you didn't mean anything by it. But Andrew was really serious and he said there were others who felt the same way."

"And when did you hear this?"

"While we were waiting for supper," Billie said, "They just sat down behind us and started talking."

Maggie sighed as they pulled back the flap and stepped into the strangely silent tent. A battery-powered lantern cast a soft glow as she wove her way between the sleeping bundles. She wondered what impact Sophia's revelation would have on tomorrow's proceedings. Would the barn be big enough to hold such dissension or would it bring the members of Earth Song closer together with a new purpose to guide them; she supposed that only time would tell.

"I'll take those, Maggie," Hanna said as stood up from the table and held out her hands.

"I'm impressed," Maggie said as she unburdened herself of her armful of plates. She nodded toward the sleeping children. "I thought they'd still be awake and raring to go."

"Most of them are my grandkids, so that makes it easier." Hanna smiled as Casey raised her head, looked around, and settled back down. "And the dogs helped."

"Are you going to be here all night? Do you need anything?"

Hanna smiled and shook her head. "Ingrid and Harold will be back soon. They'll fill me in on the meeting then take over for the night."

Maggie almost offered to stay, but it was dark out and she needed to make certain the girls got back to their tent in a timely fashion. "Then I'll see you tomorrow." She turned to where Billie and Sophia had just put their load of dishes away. "Come on, girls. We need to get back before they send out a search party for us."

Billie giggled. "They won't do that, Grandmother. We're with you."

An old woman with a wonky hip and no sense of direction. "Well, then crank up that flashlight of yours, Billie, and let's hope that your light and my reputation is all it takes to get us safely home."

"Look at the sky, Brit." Cassandra shifted her weigh forward on the log she and Jenny had placed in front of their tent. "Have you ever seen so many stars?"

Britney glanced up and shook her head, but it was obvious that her mind was elsewhere. "Do you think he'll just go away and leave us alone, Auntie Cass?" A tear slid down the young woman's cheek. "Cuz I won't go back with him. He's…he's a pig. And he thinks he owns us."

"Hey." Cassandra pulled her niece in for a hug. "It's a good plan and everyone is willing to do their part. And when Wanda sends him into the wilderness at Riding Mountain, I'm certain he won't be coming back any time soon."

"Then Mom and I will go to the police and file for a restraining order." Britney's shoulders slumped. "We should have done that a long time ago. Right?"

"Your mom should have, yes. But fear does strange things to people." Cassandra chuckled. "Just look at us. Scrambling for a way to survive out here because we're afraid the world's going to end."

Britney snuggled in closer. "But that's okay; it's nice out here...and the other kids don't make me feel like I don't belong."

"Well, I'm glad to hear that." Fabric rustled and Cass looked over her shoulder.

"Time for bed you two," Jenny walked out of the tent and extended her hand to Cassandra. "Need a boost."

Cassandra smiled and took her sister's hand, but made no move to get up. "You okay with all of this?"

Jenny nodded. "Better late than never right? Don't worry." She glanced at her daughter. "As soon as he's gone, we'll tell our story to the police and get him out of our lives once and for all. Okay?"

Britney stared at her mother for a moment and Cassandra didn't have to guess what thoughts were going through her head; Jenny had let her daughter down numerous times in the past. "Okay, Mom," Britney said and stood up. Between the two of them, they got Cassandra to her feet and moving toward the tent.

Billie unzipped the door to the tent she shared with her sisters and Sophia then gave Maggie a hug and slipped inside. "Thank you, Grandmother." Sophia gave Maggie a shy smile. "For everything."

"You're very welcome, Child."

Sophia sighed then wrapped her arms around Maggie's waist. "There's another voice I hear sometimes, Grandmother. It's a kind voice, very gentle but very strong. I thought it was you, but it's not."

Maggie pulled the tiny body closer. "And what does this voice tell you?"

"That all will be well." Sophia took a step back and raised her eyes to meet Maggie's. "Who do you think she is, Grandmother? I'd like to talk to her in person."

Maggie looked into those clear blue depths so full of joy and promise...like sunlit skies. Gentle fingers probed at her mind; coaxing her to understand. *Flee to the forest and the fen. It's here the child of light will ken.* "Maybe you and I can look for her together," she said and was rewarded with a huge grin and another hug. "Now off to bed with you. We'll talk again tomorrow."

Sophia nodded. "Goodnight, Grandmother," she said and ducked inside.

Maggie waited for the flap to be secured then followed the faint path around the cluster of tents. After listening to Kat and Wanda this morning, Maggie had a strong suspicion about who Sophia's mystery voice belonged to, but to actually test the veracity of those thoughts would require her to peel back the layers of the skepticism she'd built up over the years and expose the kernel of hope that had lain dormant, perhaps for far too long. *I danced in your honor. Do you remember? Before my heart broke and silence filled the gap between.*

"Are you okay, Maggie?" Kathleen closed the book she'd been reading by flashlight as Maggie stepped inside. "You look like you've met a ghost."

Maybe I have. "I look that bad, do I?" Maggie said hoping to deflect the conversation away from things she didn't want to deal with at the moment. Sophia's mystery voice had promised that all would be well; she'd take that on face value for now and see where it led her. "Too much talk and too little sleep will do that." Kathleen nodded. "So where's everyone else?"

"Pee parade." Kathleen laughed as Maggie closed her eyes and shook her head. "Juno and Kim offered to escort everyone up to the toilets before bed."

"And you didn't take them up on it."

"Didn't want you to come back and find the whole place deserted." Kathleen patted the space beside her on the cot and Maggie accepted the offer. "I've been thinking about Jake and Zeke while I've been waiting…"

"I wouldn't worry about those two…"

"Unless they show up before…" Kathleen frowned. "What's the husband's name again?"

"Kenneth."

Kathleen nodded. "Right. So what happens if our silly-buggers show up before Kenneth has come and gone? Especially since Earth Song's people are sleeping in their barn."

"A very wise little girl just told me that we needed to stop calling them Earth Song's people." Maggie smiled and shrugged. "Apparently, some of them don't want that association any longer. But you're right to worry about Jake and Zeke turning up at the most inopportune moment; they seem to have a knack for doing that sort of thing."

"Whoa. Take a step back there for a moment, Maggie." Kathleen scowled down at the book in her hand. "Are these Earth Song defectors going to cause a problem tomorrow? That whole contingent is going to be living in pretty close quarters for a while with nothing to do except get on each other's nerves."

"Well, hopefully, Kat can talk some sense into them if that happens." Maggie smiled at the shocked look on Kathleen's face. "I guess she was at one of the suppers Kenneth attended."

"But that would have been years ago."

Maggie shrugged. "She doesn't want to take any chances that he'll recognize her."

"Knowing Kat will be at the barn makes me feel a bit better, but that still doesn't solve the problem with Jake and Zeke." Kathleen sighed. "Do you think Jake remembered to take the phone Jess gave him? Maybe Jess could give him a call when she gets back…tell him to stay away until they get the all clear." She frowned. "Don't those phones need to be charged?"

Maggie chuckled. "Cali took care of that problem as soon as she figured out that we'd be moving out here sooner rather than later. She bought two little solar chargers with her allowance and sets them up on that empty crate behind her tent every morning so that anyone who needs to can use them."

"And do you actually think Jake would remember to do that?" Kathleen shook her head. "Because I don't."

Chapter Twenty-Four

"Those four boxes go back to the camp." Juno pointed to the green crates sitting beside the Jeep. "They're full of ration packs for the people going into hiding. The rest can go into the quonsies for now, but be gentle; some of the contents are fragile."

"You seem to have thought of everything," Jessie said as she helped Cali load her wagon. "So what's in the trailer?"

Juno smiled at Kaylyn over Jessie's head. "Should I tell her?"

"You…you got them, but how…" Kaylyn shook her head and grinned. "Doesn't matter. The grandmothers will be so happy."

Jessie tucked one last box into the wagon and stood up as Cali headed toward the path into the meadow. "Would someone like to tell me what's going on?"

"The lawn chairs for the elders, Jessie." Kaylyn grinned. "I asked Kim and Juno to pick them up if they had time and…well…"

"It was our pleasure," Juno said, "And it didn't take long since the store is only a few blocks from the hangar. Wanna see?"

"Of course, they do," Kim said as she pulled her key ring from her jacket pocket and moved to the back of the trailer. Kaylyn and Jessie followed her.

The door rolled up on an explosion of color. "They're…they're beautiful." Kaylyn gasped as she peered inside. Each chair had smooth, redwood arms, a sturdy metal frame, and a brightly woven cover in one of four different designs. "I was expecting those mesh things the grandmothers always buy."

"Well, these are sturdier. And they don't weigh much," Kim said. "We should be able to walk them back to the camp two at a time. There are eight youngsters and only two wagons that need to go back right now, so the kids should be able to take half of them. We'll leave the rest at the end of the path and carry them in ourselves once we get back."

"The rest of the drivers are on their way," Wanda said as she dragged her empty wagon on to the road. "So what's next?"

Juno waited until all of the young people made their way back to the vehicles then explained what needed to be done.

"The grandmothers are going to love these," Mel said as she pulled two of the chairs from the trailer; there was a tinge of wistfulness in her voice.

Kaylyn smiled. "There's one for Caroline too."

"Really?" Mel grinned. "She's going to be so happy. She says that sitting on the ground makes her bones ache and that makes her cranky. I think she'll really like the one with the red, black and gold. It'll match her favorite shirt."

"Wow." Ian chuckled. "I think that's the most words I've heard you say at one time since…since forever."

"Ian!"

"It's okay, Wanda," Mel said, "He's right, but you know what, I have a home and a family now and I don't have to worry anymore about what will happen to me if I say the wrong thing. So…" She turned to Ian and grinned. "You're going to hear a lot more from me. Hope you can handle it."

"You asked for that, Bro," Sam said as Ian groaned and Wanda giggled.

"Okay, guys and gals, let's get the rest of the chairs out so we can get going," Kaylyn said with a hint of a smile in her voice. "Don't forget to lock the quonsies. And Wanda, make certain Tilly, Chloe, Mae, and Greg each get a chair to take with them. We'll be back as soon as we can."

"Will do, Momkay. See you in a little while."

"And Cali."

"Yes, Momjay?"

"Keep trying to get ahold of Grandpa Jake. We really need to talk to him. Put Grandma Maggie on the line if you do make contact."

Cali smiled and rolled her eye. "Oh, he'll love that."

Wanda looked over her shoulder and waved to the grandmothers as she followed her moms toward the northern side of the lake and the pine forest beyond. A canopy of thick bows cast dark shadows on the ground below, blocking out most of the sun's nourishing rays and keeping the ground clear of grasping vegetation. "This should be an easy walk even with the wagons," she heard Kim say, "But keep your eyes open and shout out if you see anything."

Wanda adjusted the pack she'd volunteered to carry and glanced sideways at Jenna; her friend was sniffing the air and smiling. "I smell cedar," she said reverently. "Do you know what that means?"

Wanda shook her head and smiled. "No, but I imagine you're going to tell me."

"Of course." Jenna sighed and gave her wagon a tug; it bounced over an exposed root then slid forward. "But not right now." She grinned mischievously. "Look it up when you get back to camp; it'll give you something to think about until I get back."

"And what will 'you' be thinking about?"

A cloud seemed to pass across Jenna's face; her smile disappeared, and for an instant, Wanda wished she could take the question back. "I'm sorry, Jen."

"Don't be. It's not your fault Kenneth found us just when I thought I'd finally got my life sorted out." Jenna gave the wagon another tug. "I know everyone believes this plan will work and eventually Kenneth will be out of Britney's life forever, but a restraining order is just a piece of paper. How's it supposed to keep Kenneth…and his friends…from coming back here because, once he finds us, this place won't be a secret anymore."

Wanda took a deep breath of cedar and pine and damp earth; salty moisture damped her lashes. "I don't know, Jen. Maybe we just have to believe that that won't happen. Momjay says that living in fear makes you a victim and I have no intention of being another one of Kenneth's casualties…and neither should you."

Jenna nodded thoughtfully then quickened her pace. Wanda looked up to see her moms waiting for them to catch up. "This is not the time to get distracted, girls," Jessie said as Wanda and Jen hurried to close the gap between them. "You, of all people, know you have to stay alert when you're beneath the trees."

Wanda felt embarrassment warm her cheeks. "You're right, Momjay," she said as she met Jessie's eyes. She wanted to tell her mom what Jen had said, but this wasn't the time or the place. "Won't happen again," she said as she glanced sideways at Jen; her friend nodded her agreement.

Jessie smiled, took Kaylyn's hand, and waved the girls forward. "That's good. Now let's get a move on. I'm really looking forward to exposing the grandfather's most recent secret."

Kaylyn laughed. "Unless someone knows what's going in that barn, I think the better part of their secret is still intact."

Jessie sighed. "I suppose you right."

"Welcome to your home away from home," Juno said as she led the way out of the trees and into a tiny glade surrounded by tall, fragrant pines. A miniature barn with only half of a roof stood proudly beside the pond. "Nice, huh?"

"It's lovely." Kaylyn took a deep breath and squeezed Jessie's hand. She would have much preferred to return to the camp with Jess and the children, but she had no desire to make herself a target for Willian's rage if he recognized her. "We'll be just fine here for a few days."

"But the roof's not finished." Tilly stepped up to face Juno. The younger woman pursed her lips and held her ground. "I told you we should have brought the tents."

"Then go back and get them," Kim said stepping forward and giving Tilly her easy smile. "The rest of us will wait right here while Kwasi and his crew make the barn shipshape."

"We finish it today," Kwasi stepped forward and lowered his end of the cot he and Ibo had carried through the woods. Mathew, Keven, and Bao moved to join them. "Grandfather Jake said."

"So you five have been building the barn for him and Zeke." Juno laughed. "I wondered how they were going to manage on their own."

"Jake figured Keven and I needed something to keep us occupied until we start putting up the yurts." Mathew smiled at Jenna. "And since we're not really into plants, he asked us to help out."

Jenna grinned back. "So you must know what they're going to keep in there."

"Nope."

"Aw. Come on Matt."

Mathew shrugged. "I'd tell you if I could, Sis, but they never said…"

"…and we never asked." Kevin grinned at his half-sister then turned to Juno. "We should get to work if we're to be done by this evening."

Mark stepped around Tilly. The old woman closed her eyes and sighed as he cocked his head at her then turned to Kwasi. "I'm good with heights. I'd like to help."

"Me too." Andrew chimed in. "We helped Greg reshingle the garage, so we won't be in the way. Right, Greg."

"That's right." Greg met Tilly's glare and shrugged. "They're quite good at it actually."

Kwasi nodded. "Then we should get started as Keven said."

"And what are the rest of us to do?" Tilly demanded as the building crew headed off toward the barn.

Juno whistled for the dogs then took Kim's hand and smiled at Tilly. "We're going to do some exploring. You're welcome to join us. Maybe you'll find what you're looking for out there."

Jenna giggled behind her hand as Tilly spluttered a retort and turned away. "Can I come?" The young woman asked. "I'd like to see what plants are available around here."

Wanda stepped forward. "Me too."

"And me." Britney gave her mother a wistful smile as Jenny frowned. "I'll be fine, Mom."

"Anyone else?" Juno smiled at Britney as she moved to Wanda's side.

"I think I'll just stay right here and enjoy the sunshine." Kaylyn pulled Jessie down to sit beside her on the grass.

"Sounds good to me." Chloe opened her new chair, sat down, and leaned her head back. "I could get used to this," she said as she closed her eyes.

"So, we're just going to sit here?" Tilly demanded.

"Looks like." Kaylyn smiled at the look of bliss on Greg's craggy face as he eased his chair open and sat down. "Take a load off, Tilly," he said as he leaned back and closed his eyes. "Enjoy what the source has given us."

Tilly stared at the people around her as they made themselves comfortable then dropped her unwanted chair to the ground and trudged off toward the forest. "She'll be okay. She has her bear spray with her," Cerdwin said as Kaylyn started to get up. "Maybe some time alone beneath the trees will help her understand." Then Cerdwin smiled. "Of course, no one is ever alone here, are they?"

"Time for lunch," Juno called as she stepped out from beneath the trees an hour later carrying a cloth Gatherer's sac. She stopped beside the wagons as Cagney and Lacy came to sit beside her.

Kaylyn blinked up at Juno and pointed at the cloth bag. "Raw greens for lunch. Can't wait."

"These are to take back to camp," Juno said as she shook the sac then deposited it on top of the wagon with the green crate. "Now come on. The work crew is probably starving and you wouldn't want to miss out on something really yummy."

Kaylyn blinked and turned to Jessie. "Did she say 'yummy'?"

"That's what she said." Jessie stood up and helped Kaylyn to her feet. "Guess we better go and find out what she's talking about."

"Wait a minute," Greg said as he stood up and folded his chair. He wiped the sleep from his eyes and glanced at the people around him. "Tilly's not back yet. Shouldn't we go look for her? It's been quite a while."

Juno ran her fingers through her hair and sighed. Kaylyn could sense the pilot's frustration; Tilly seemed to fight her every step of the way and this was just another example of that. "There's a lot of woods out there…"

"Isn't this Tilly's jacket," Kim said, picking up a black windbreaker from the second wagon.

Juno gave her partner a grateful smile. She took the jacket and sank to her heels between the dogs. "Scent," she said as Cagney moved in to sniff the material. The shepherd chuffed then sat back expectantly.

"What's she doing?" Britney asked as Juno scratched behind Cagney's ear then repeated the process with Lacy.

"Finding Tilly." Kim smiled and took a step forward as Juno stood up. "I'll go with them," the tall blond said, "I could use a good run. You go ahead and get everyone fed. We won't be long."

"You're sure." Kim cocked a pale eyebrow and Juno smiled as she gave each dog a final sniff of the garment. "Of course, you are."

Kim smiled back, called the dogs to her side then pointed in the direction Tilly had taken. "Find."

"Let's go," Juno said. She grasped the handle of the closest wagon as Cagney picked up the scent and headed toward the distant trees with Kim and Lacy close behind. "Time for lunch."

Greg picked up his chair and Tilly's. "Can someone bring the other wagons?" The old man said. He watched Juno head relentlessly toward the barn and decided that he should apologize to her for Tilly's stubborn foolishness…but not right now.

"We've got them," Wanda said. She and Jenna appeared at Greg's side; picked up the handles and moved into line. Wanda grinned at Jessie. "Lead on McDuff."

Jessie laughed, took one of the chairs from Greg, and led the way toward the cluster of people huddled beside the barn. She wasn't falling for that one again.

"Good. You're just in time for the demonstration," Kaylyn said as she moved aside to make room for the late-comers.

Juno was seated on the ground with the contents of a brown bag spread out around her. "The chipotle chicken is my favorite," she said, "But we also have spaghetti and meatballs, poutine, and beef macaroni."

"In those pouches," Keven said. "Unbelievable. So how do we cook them?"

"With this." Juno opened the larger white pouch and slid the one marked 'chipotle chicken' inside. Then she held the white pouch up. "Will you do the honors, Kat? Just a few drops from your canteen."

"With pleasure." Kim smiled, unhooked her canteen from her belt then nodded toward the white pouch. "I just pour it in there. Just a bit. Right?"

Juno nodded. "Ta da. One hot meal coming up," she said as Kaylyn dripped a small amount of water into the bag. Juno immediately lowered her arms and set the steaming pouch on the ground. "It'll be cooked in about twelve minutes." She grinned. "And if you don't have water you can always use urine."

"Ew. Another potty joke." Wanda wrinkled her nose. "Good thing we brought lots of drinking water with us. So do we get to choose whatever meal we want?"

"Just a sec, guys." Jessie held up her hand as the young people gravitate toward the open crate. "If we each have one, will there still be enough for the people who are staying here?" Jessie asked. "We wouldn't want to leave them short."

"That crate contains a week's rations for twelve people," Juno said, "So I think we're fine."

"I want poutine," Kevin said with a whoop. "Hope it has lots of gravy."

"Make mine beef and macaroni."

"I want chicken."

Kaylyn smiled and shook her head at Juno. "You realize you've just ruined them for rabbit stew…maybe forever."

Juno returned the smile and shrugged. "Would you have preferred raw greens for lunch?"

"Hell, no." Jessie brushed past Kaylyn and headed toward the wagon. "Make mine spaghetti and meatballs."

Halfway through the meal, Tilly stumbled into the glade wide-eyed and disheveled with Kim and the dogs at her side. Greg guided Tilly gently toward her chair and offered her a drink of water. "You all right, Til? What happened?"

Tilly looked up at him and shook her head. "I…I don't know. I must have bumped my head. Everything's just really fuzzy."

Greg looked over his shoulder at Kim. "Thanks for finding her."

Kim nodded. "Just keep her quiet for a while. Okay? At least until Lisa can have a look at her."

"I don't need any doctoring. All I need is a few hours rest and I'll be right as rain." Tilly raised her chin in Kim's direction then reached for Greg's hand and struggled to her feet. "Help me to my cot. I need to take a nap."

"You didn't expect her to say thank you. Did you, Love?" Kim felt Juno's hand come down on her shoulder as she watched Tilly stagger toward the barn. "Why don't you come and get something to eat?"

"She didn't hit her head," Kim said as she covered Juno's hand with her own. "I checked. She was just lying on the ground staring up at the trees when the girls found her. I think she'd been crying."

"Well, you've done everything you can. Greg will take care of her now." Juno slid her hand down Kim's arm until their fingers touched. "The girls are waiting. I promised Cagney I'd make beef and macaroni."

Kim laughed and turned to face her partner. "Now there's an offer I can't refuse." She followed Juno toward the food wagon. "I see that the roof's finished."

"Kwasi said that having two extra pairs of hands made everything go faster. I guess Mark and Andrew are going to do the painting while they're here."

"Let me guess. They're painting it red."

Juno chuckled. "Purple…well, mauve actually. I guess the paint was on sale."

Kim choked back a laugh. "You're kidding, right."

"Nope."

"Kim. Glad you're back." Jenna said as she pointed to two steaming, white pouches sitting beside the food wagon. "Juno said both you and the dogs like the beef and macaroni best, so we got two of them started. We thought you'd be really hungry after all that running around."

"Well, you thought right," Kim called the dogs to her and sat down beside Juno. A few minutes later a pouch and a spoon were pressed into her hands.

"Eat up," Wanda said. "We'll take care of the girls."

"Gather around, please." Juno let out a shrill, two-finger whistle to get everyone's attention. In the past few hours, they'd managed to sweep up the stray nails and the sawdust from the main room of the barn, cordon off a latrine, and set up the cots apparently without waking Tilly, though Juno had her suspicions. Now it was time to go. "Please. Everyone. Gather around." She waited while a circle formed around her on the grass then sat down. The others followed suit. "Just a few loose ends before some of us head back. First of all, I need to ask those of you who are staying to turn off your cell phones."

"My mom and I already threw ours away in town," Britney said from her seat beside Jenna. "They didn't belong to us anyway…not really."

Juno nodded. "Smart move. Now for the rest of you…"

Greg frowned. "Why?"

"Because we don't want Kenneth to have any means of tracking you. You're supposed to be on your way to Riding Mountain. Right? It'd be kinda hard to pull that off if your GPS says your sitting right here." She reached into her pants pocket, pulled out a pay-as-you-go phone, and handed it to Kaylyn. "Just in case you have an emergency, you can use this to reach me."

"You heard the lady," Greg said as he pulled out his cell phone, turned it off then raised his head and met Juno's eyes. "Anything else?"

Juno nodded. "Kwasi's crew has set up a washroom for you in the storage area. Your little bucket seat is in there, but you'll need to dig a trench for the waste and find some way to keep the pit covered. Deer graze in this meadow and we don't want to cause them any harm." She pointed behind her. "There are two lanterns in one of the wagons; use them sparingly. And, please, stay close to the barn. We wouldn't want anyone else to get lost."

Greg took a deep breath and glanced toward the barn where Tilly still slept. "You can say that again."

Juno looked at the tired, anxious faces around her and put on her best smile. "It will only be a few days before you're back at the camp and hard at work again, so treat this as a bit of a holiday. Okay."

"Juno. Kim." Britney stood up and worked her way closer to where the two pilots sat with the dogs between them. She stopped and stuck out her hand. "I just wanted to let you know that, although it might not seem that way, most of us are grateful for what you've done. I know I am and my mom and my Aunt Cass…"

"And me," Mark said. He waved his arm to take in the entire circle. "And everyone else sitting here. Isn't that right?"

"That's right, boy," Greg said with a wistful smile.

"I just thought you needed to know that." Britney took another small step forward, her arm still extended. "That your help is appreciated."

Juno stood up and took the outstretched hand in her own. There was a tightness in her throat as their fingers entwined. "That's good to hear." She said softly. "Thank you." She pulled the youngster in for a quick hug then stepped away. "Take care of yourself while we're gone."

"I'll make certain she does," Cassandra said then turned and shook Kim's hand. "Thanks for bringing Tilly back. As crotchety as she is right now, we'd miss her."

Kim pursed her lips and nodded then turned to Juno. "We should get going. We need to get back to camp before dark."

Jessie stood up and pulled Kaylyn to her feet. "I guess we're leaving." Her voice held a tinge of sadness as she drew Kaylyn into a hug. Then she turned to gather up her daughter and the work crew.

Juno said her goodbyes then headed toward the trees. "Let's move it, people. Time waits for no one…and neither does rabbit stew." She smiled at the muted groans behind her.

Kaylyn counted heads then kicked off her boots and lay down on her cot. It felt strange not having Jess and the children close at hand; especially since she no longer knew where she stood with these people who had been the only family she'd known for a good part of her life.

Supper had been a quiet affair…too quiet for her liking…and the need to conserve the lights had sent everyone to bed with barely a word spoken between them. The fact that Tilly had refused the offer of food and had gone right back to bed after using the makeshift washroom had done little to ease the strain of the evening. It was as if everyone had something they desperately wanted to say but lacked the courage to say it.

She sighed and stared up at the ceiling listening to the sounds of the night. Four species of frogs raised their unique voices in song, and somewhere in the distance, a coyote called to his mate. A soft snore from the direction of Greg's cot made her smile; the old man was holding up well…all things considered.

Her eyes drifted shut and opened again as a shaft of moonlight skittered across the floor then disappeared as the doors snicked closed. She didn't have to look to know which cot was empty. She sat up, shoved her feet into her boots, and followed Tilly out into the moonlight.

"Mind if I join you?" Kaylyn asked as she plunked Greg's chair down beside Tilly's; perhaps the gift was appreciated after all.

Tilly raised an eyebrow in Kaylyn's direction. "Would it matter if I said no?"

"Probably not." Kaylyn leaned back, rested her elbows on the chair arm, and folded her hands in her lap; Tilly shook her head and went back to staring at the forest. "So what really happened out there, Tilly?" Kaylyn asked into the silence.

Tilly stiffened. "I told you. I bumped my head."

"Kim said you were crying."

"Does it matter?"

"I think something happened out there that frightened you; something that made you doubt everything you've believed in for the past twenty years."

Tilly wrapped her arms around her stomach; her breath came in short gasps. "You don't know what…what you're talking about. Now go away."

"Okay. I'll go, but before I do, I have something to say to you." Kaylyn leaned forward and propped her elbows on her knees. "I think you found the source today…out there…waiting for you and I think that's what frightened you. You've spent years clinging to a promise you made to someone who is dead and beyond caring and you've been clinging to it so hard these past weeks that you've forgotten what's really important." Kaylyn stood and pointed toward the barn. "Whether they're able to share your dream any longer or not, the people in there love you…I love you…don't just throw that all away." She took a deep breath. "That's the last thing Helka would want you to do and I think that buried somewhere deep inside, you know that."

Chapter Twenty-Five

Jessie woke her two eldest daughters just as the sun came up over the lake. "Rise and shine, girls. Juno's making the watchers breakfast and then we'll head down to the meadow."

Cali blinked sleep from her eyes. "I didn't know Juno could cook."

"Oh, are you in for a treat?" Wanda giggled as she rolled out of bed and reached for her clothes. "I hope there're bacon and eggs." Her goth daughter grinned as she pulled on her black jeans; her sister stared up at her as though she had just grown a second head.

"I take it we're having MREs for breakfast." Jessie smiled at Cali's look of confusion as Wanda nodded. "You must have heard about the magic meals in a bag Kim and Juno brought in with them."

Cali frowned. "But I thought they were for the people in hiding…so they didn't need to make a fire."

"Nope. Not just for them." Wanda shoved her feet into her boots, pulled the laces tight, and stood up. "Hurry up, Cal," she said as she picked her jacket off the floor. "I'll meet you at the fire pit."

Cali sighed and reached for her t-shirt. "You go ahead, Momjay. I'll be along in a minute."

"Is everything alright, Cali? You look like you have something on your mind." Jessie sat down on Wanda's cot as Cali pulled the red shirt over her head then dug through her knapsack for a brush. The two girls had packed the necessities and moved to one of the smaller of the Earth Song tents when those who remained behind spread out around the camp; it wasn't a comfortable arrangement for anyone, but empty tents would have been a clear giveaway that something was up. "Did you sleep okay?"

"I slept fine, Momjay. So did Wanda." The corners of Cali's mouth quirked up. "She seems to have adjusted to the sleeping arrangements pretty well…all things considered."

"So.no nightmares."

Cali shook her head thoughtfully. "Even Trin sleeps through the night…now that Momjay found her dragon in that bag of blankets."

"Thanks for keeping an ear out for them." Jessie smiled then tilted her head to the side. "So what 'does' have you looking so world-weary?"

Cali laughed. "That's a good word…weary. But not with the world; just a small part of it." She tilted her head to the side and her eyes grew distant. "When Wanda first invited me to join the gatherers, I thought it would be good practice for when I go with Kim and Juno to complete the mapping." She ran her fingers through her sleep tousled hair. "But it became more than that," she said softly. "I didn't want to believe what I was sensing at first. Wanda kept talking about how the Earth Song theory was bogus because she and Jenna and some of the other gatherers had already found the Earth Mother; it all sounded like a scenario from that fantasy game Wanda and Momkay used to play, but the more time I spent under the trees exploring that sensation, the more I came to believe that there's something to it; that there really is a presence here that will guide us if we open ourselves to it."

"But that sounds like a good thing," Jessie remembered the passion in her oldest daughter's voice as she talked about the peace and joy she saw in Kaylyn's eyes when her mom opened herself to the Earth Mother.

"It is Momjay, but now all this upheaval around Britney's father has brought back bad memories; it's starting to make me doubt things again and I'm afraid that I might lose everything I've gained." Cali closed her eyes and sighed. "And I don't want that to happen."

Jessie leaned forward and shook her head; she wished Kaylyn was there. "It won't and do you know why…"

"Hey, you two." Wanda pulled back the door flap and peered inside. Cali swallowed hard as her eyes locked with Jessie's for a moment then slid away; regret and resignation were obvious in the tight set of her jaw. "There's hash browns and bacon out here." Wanda said, "Come get it while it's hot. Juno says we're leaving in ten minutes."

"Tell her we'll be right there." Jessie saw her second daughter nod before she disappeared; she leaned forward and squeezed Cali's knee. "We need to go, but we'll talk about this later. Okay?"

"Sure, Momjay." Cali gave Jessie a wistful smile then knelt beside her bed. "Come on, Mouser, breakfast time."

"Kat. Kat, wake up." The call came soft and pleading; barely more than a whisper. "Please, Kat, I need your help."

Kaylyn felt an insistent hand grasp her shoulder. She opened her eyes and took a deep breath. "Jenna?"

The young woman straightened; relief softened the edges of her fear as she took a step back. "It's Tilly. Come," was all she said as she hurried toward the door.

Kaylyn swung her legs over the side of the cot and shoved her feet into her boots. No one around her stirred. She walked softly toward the door and followed Jenna outside. Tilly sat rigid in her chair staring toward the woods just as she had been when Kaylyn left last night.

Kat swallowed hard as she approached the young woman hovering above the chair. "Let me take a look," she said, trying to sound more confident than she felt. She leaned in and pressed two fingers to Tilly's jugular; the skin was cold to the touch.

"Is she...Is she..."

"Dead?" Jenna nodded wide-eyed. "No. Her heartbeat is strong," Kaylyn said as she straightened; the younger woman's shoulders sagged with obvious relief. "But she's cold and her breathing is shallow. We need to get her warmed up."

"Should we take her inside?" Jenna took a step toward the door. "I could get Mark and Andrew to help."

"No." Kaylyn stared down at the woman who had been a second mother to her when she'd most needed one; she couldn't take the old woman's last vestiges of pride from her unless it was necessary. Jenna watched her with puzzled eyes. "Moving her may cause her harm. What we need are blankets, warm clothes, and a hot drink to heat her core."

"But we can't build a fire." There was panic in the young woman's voice. "How are we supposed to heat the water?"

Kaylyn took a deep breath and searched her mind for an answer; thanks to Juno, they didn't need fire to make things hot. "We'll use the ration packs."

"But how..."

"Please, Jenna, I don't have time to explain right now. Just go inside and get our blankets, a canteen of water, three ration packs and...three of your gathering sacs." Jenna opened her mouth then slammed it shut, nodded uncertainly, and backed away. "And try not to wake anyone," Kaylyn whispered as the younger woman turned and fled.

Kaylyn squatted beside Tilly's chair, fear and anger struggling for supremacy as she stared into the old woman's eyes. "Look what you've done to yourself?" She shook her head. "I hope it was worth it."

"I've got it...everything you asked for."

Kaylyn looked up to find Jenna hovering at her side, two bulging pillowcases clutched in her hands. Chloe peered over the young woman's shoulder. "How can I help?"

"I...I didn't..." Jenna stammered as she held out the bags.

Kaylyn forced a smile. "No harm done." She stood up and nodded to Chloe who stepped forward to take Kaylyn's place for a moment.

"She's hypothermic," Chloe said as she straightened. "We need to bring her body temperature up...quickly."

Kaylyn nodded. "And here's what we're going to do..."

"There, that should do it," Chloe said as she slipped a heated ration pack wrapped in a gatherers sack down the front of Tilly's sweater a dozen minutes later. A second pack rested in Tilly's lap; Chloe gently placed Tilly's hands on top of it and sealed everything inside a double layer of blankets. She smiled at Kat. "A spaghetti and meatball heating pad...who would have thought?"

Jenna giggled a bit hysterically and held up the third meal pack. "So what do we do with this?" She asked as she handed it to Kat.

"We need to warm up her insides as well as her outsides." Kaylyn tore open the pouch, dumped half of the contents on a discarded brown wrapper then refilled it with water. Jenna frowned as she watched Kaylyn stir the contents with a stick. "So we'll just make her a little beef broth," she said as she drained the liquid portion into a mug and held it out to Chloe. "Do you think you can get some of this into her?"

Chloe nodded. "I can certainly try. Jenna, come help me."

Kaylyn sank to the ground to watch as Jenna supported Tilly's head while Chloe dribbled steaming, brown liquid into the elder's open mouth. "That should about do it for now," Chloe said as she gently wiped Tilly's mouth and chin. "Now all we can do is wait."

"The sun will be up soon." Jenna sat down beside Kaylyn. "That'll help, won't it?"

"I'm sure it will," Chloe said as she adjusted Tilly's blankets and joined Kat and Jenna on the ground. Then she turned to Kaylyn. "How do you think this happened? She must have been out here most of the night."

Kaylyn swallowed hard. "I…"

"It is done," Tilly said in a voice that wasn't quite her own. Chloe leaped to her feet as the old woman's eyes closed and her head fell forward; she pressed two fingers to Tilly's neck and smiled. "I think she's asleep."

Jessie took a deep cleansing breath of the cool morning air then fell into line beside Juno. "So you know what you're supposed to do?" The dark-haired pilot asked as they left the sunlight for the shadows and the meadow beyond.

"I huff and I puff then I let the big, bad wolf in." Jessie let her smile slip, but only for an instant. Kenneth and his friends weren't welcome here and it was up to her to tell them that.

"Well, that's one way of putting it." There was a hint of laughter behind those words. "But, yes. We're going to let Kenneth in. We're going to use his ego against him…make him feel like a big man so he goes away thinking that he's won and there's no reason to come back here."

Jessie chewed at the corner of her lip. "I certainly hope so." Juno's hand came down on Jessie's shoulder. "Don't forget, Kim and I and our girls will be close by if anything goes wrong and all of the watchers have the RCMP on speed dial."

Jessie snorted then followed it with a laugh. "Do you know how absurd that sounds?" Then the laughter died. "Maybe Tilly's right; maybe we did bring too much of our old lives with us."

"Don't even go there, my friend," Juno said seriously, "Right now those phones are useful and that's all that matters."

"Speaking of phones," Jessie said as she looked up in time to see her oldest daughter running back down the trail waving her bright red cell phone in the air.

"I got him, Momjay," Cali said as she skidded to a halt. "I got ahold of Grandpa Jake. I told him what's happening. He said he wants to talk to you."

Jessie grimaced then took the phone. "Hi, Jake…yes it's true…I understand that…Can you give us until tonight at least? Okay…Goodbye."

"Tonight," Cali said in disbelief. "But what if…"

"It'll be okay, Cali," Jessie said handing back the phone. *At least, I hope it will.* "You did a good job getting ahold of them. He said that the animals will be fine until tonight if they pull off the road, but then he'll have to bring them in." She forced a smile. "He also said that he and Jake were bringing their ripples with them."

Cali frowned. "Their ripples?"

"And I thought you found my little speech inspiring." Jessie raised her eyebrows and saw understanding dawn.

"Their ripples…you've got to be kidding." Cali looked like she didn't know whether to laugh or cry. "I don't want to be around when the grandmothers hear about this. Where will they sleep? We don't have enough beds."

"We'll figure something out," Jessie said trying to sound more confident than she felt. "I just hope the ripples know how to care for the animals…and before you ask, no he didn't tell me what they are."

"I hope they're goats," Juno mused; then she looked up and blushed. "I just love goat cheese that's all. Now let's get a move on," she said, picking up the pace. "If I don't miss my bet, we won't have long to wait."

Jessie unclipped her canteen from her makeshift belt and sank into the chair she'd borrowed from Grandma Maggie last night. The older watchers had set up their little ruse around the old fire pit, hoping to give the impression of an extended family enjoying a day in the sun, totally oblivious to the fact that all was not right with their world.

"Well, this isn't what I expected to be doing this morning," Megan leaned back in her chair, closed her eyes, and immediately opened them again.

"What did you expect to be doing, Grandmother?" Jessie heard a sharp intake of breath from the other side of the circle; Grandma Grace looked down at her lap and shook her head as Jessie sought the source of that unspoken comment.

Lisa muffled a laugh with her hand and Megan sat up straighter. Her eyes darted around the circle. "I…I can't say."

"I think Meg is a lot like my Ian; can't keep a secret even if her life depended on it," Lisa said, not unkindly then turned to Jessie. "So I'm going to rescue her." She winked at Meg. "Robert and I and some of the grandmothers have been working on the inventory the past few days."

Jessie glanced at the people around her. "So this is where you've been disappearing to. Why didn't you say anything?"

"We figured that you and Kat had enough on your plates," Grace said with a sideways scowl at Meg. "Besides, we needed something to do and figure out what we have and what we still need...the previous list notwithstanding...seemed like a good use of our time."

"So you've changed the list." Jessie glanced at Lisa for confirmation.

"We didn't change it so much as add to it," Robert said from beside his wife. "Our boys told us some of what was going on and the actual reason the list ended up being so minimal. We'd had second thoughts about the things we left behind at the time, but we could understand the need to ensure that the essentials were covered. Even so, we did bring a few things..." He smiled sheepishly. "But that's not important right now."

"What is important, is that we don't need to struggle from the get-go." Grace adjusted her blue beret and leaned forward. "So we've been adding things like extra candles and soap and washbasins and water pitchers to the list..."

"...and tables to set them on," Meg added.

Lisa nodded. "And it would be nice to have privacy screens and washtubs for bathing and laundry. It's going to be important that we keep ourselves clean and not everyone can tolerate a sauna." She shrugged and sat back. "Anyway, the elders all have money going into their accounts in two days and we thought that, if we're lucky, we should be able to find what we need in Gimli before the flare hits."

"They even have a second-hand store." Megan grinned. "Never know what you'll find in one of those places."

Jessie nodded then smiled at Megan. "I can certainly understand why sitting here trying to look like you're enjoying yourselves would seem counterproductive, but we need a presence out here so Kenneth and his buddies can't just stroll right in and make themselves at home."

Meg shrugged. "I was just saying."

Jessie nodded then glanced over to where the majority of the young people were involved in a game of soccer. "Well, at least the kids are enjoying the downtime."

"They deserve it," Lisa said, "I don't think my boys have ever been so diligent about anything as they are about gathering plants...among other things." Her brow wrinkled into a frown as she turned to Jessie. "I think you and I and Kaylyn should have a little talk. Just so I'm clear about what my boys have gotten into."

"Well, speak of the devils." Robert laughed as Ian pelted toward the circle. "One of them at least."

Lisa stood up and watched her son's progress with concerned eyes. "Kenneth and his men must be here."

Ian skidded to a halt beside Jessie. "Juno says you should come. Something strange is going on."

Jo followed Sophia and Billie into the cook tent and veered toward the ornate table in the back corner where Grandma Maggie and Grandma Lee sat behind a pile of slightly wilted greens. With most of the gatherers occupied with other pursuits for the foreseeable future, Juno's offering from yesterday would be greatly appreciated by those left behind.

"You two go ask Grandma Hanna if you can get something to eat," Jo nodded toward the woodstove where a tall figure in a long, black, wool dress bent over one of the larger soup pots. "She said she was making rice and beans today and we won't be here at lunchtime."

"You hope," Billie said. "What if Grandma Maggie says no?"

Jo pursed her lips and shrugged. She'd been asking herself the same question all the way here.

"We'll cross that bridge when we come to it," she said, trying to sound more confident than she felt. "Now go eat."

"Aye. Aye. Captain." Billie grinned and gave her a three-finger salute before Sophia grabbed her friend's hand and pulled her away.

Jo smiled and continued toward the back table. She'd thought that she might feel guilty about staying behind when the watchers left, but she didn't. This was the perfect time for her to check out her new craft; she just hoped Grandma Maggie agreed.

"JoJo." Maggie looked up and smiled. "How can I help you? Are you hungry?"

"I'm fine," Jo said as she nodded to Grandma Lee and took a seat. She folded her hands on the table and drew a deep breath. "I think it's time for me to drop my line and see what bites."

If her grandfather's teachings were right, these unharvested waters should be teeming with life; it may even be enough to tip the balance in their favor in the food department if they managed it carefully. "A good fish stew would be a welcome change from rabbit, don't you think, and it would go well with the rice."

Maggie nodded. Her eyes were grave, but there was a hint of a smile in her voice. "So you want to take your canoe out. And Billie and Sophia?"

Jo glanced over her shoulder to where the two girls were busily eating. "I'd like them to come with me. Three lines in the water are better than one," she said as she turned back around. "Kim gave me four collapsible fishing rods and a tackle box when they got back last night and there are life jackets in each boat. We'll stay close to shore…"

"Well, come on then." Jo gaped at the grandmother as she stood up and pushed in her chair. She scooped the greens into a bowl and turned to Lee. "Want to do some fishing?"

Jo sagged against her chair; this wasn't what she'd expected. "You're…you're coming with us?"

Lee frowned then stood up and took the bowl from Maggie's hands. "Looks like."

"But Grandmother…"

"Four lines are better than three." Maggie smiled as she worked her way around the table. Then the smile disappeared and her eyes narrowed. Jo knew that look; there was no getting around it. "And when your moms get back, I'll be able to tell them that they won't need to worry when you're out on the water because you know exactly what you're doing and will keep yourself and anyone with you safe from harm." She held out her hand and the smile was back. "Besides, chopping greens is getting boring."

JoJo gulped and stared at the offered hand for a moment then wrapped her fingers around it and stood up as all her protests went unspoken. The grandmothers were just trying to make certain she knew what she was doing out there and their assurances would go a long way with the moms when Jo starting fishing in earnest. She returned Maggie's smile then stepped in for a hug. "Thanks, Grandmother."

"I'll go tell Hanna we're leaving and send Billie and Sophia after you." Grandma Lee headed toward the opposite end of the tent. "We'll meet you outside."

Jessie squatted in the clump of bushes Juno had chosen for a blind and stared out at the junction of the gravel road and the narrow lane that provided access to the property. A red, SUV with personalized license plates crept along the road; what Grandma Grace called redneck music drifted from the open windows. "You're right," Jessie whispered as they rolled past heading toward the game preserve. "It's like they can't see a way in."

"And this is the third time they've driven by." Kim frowned. "I don't understand it."

"Unless they're looking for other exits," Juno said as she duck walked closer. "Or a way to come in without us seeing them. It's what I'd do…if I was looking for someone who didn't want to be found."

Kim nodded. "But that would mean coming in through the woods and from what Jenny says, Kenneth is a city boy through and through."

"So, what do we do now?" Jessie pushed herself backward and tucked her knees up to her chest; Ian slipped in to take her place.

"We watch and we wait," Juno said, "It takes them about twenty minutes to make the round trip from here. If they don't come back in that amount of time, we'll assume they're coming through the woods and we'll track them with the girls; make sure they don't find what they're looking for." She grinned at her partner.

Kim reached forward and scratched behind Cagney's ear; Jessie hadn't noticed the dogs sprawled in the shadows until that moment. "It won't be hard to nudge them in the right direction, will it girl?" Cagney chuffed and her tail thudded twice against the ground.

"So what we need is for everyone…"

"Here they come," Ian warned and all eyes turned toward the road; the Rover was moving faster now and sailed past them as though all of the beasts of the forest were on its tail.

Kim smirked. "Looks like someone didn't find what he was looking for."

"Now what?" Jessie moved her knees in tighter, forcing herself not to panic. How were they supposed to convince Kenneth that he was barking up the wrong tree if he refused to confront them?

Juno stared at the empty road for a moment then turned herself around to face Jessie. "Do you have your phone and the keys to the van?"

"I have Cali's phone," Ian said as he pulled the bright red case from his jacket pocket; he handed it to Jessie.

"And the keys?" Juno asked. Jessie pulled a blue, key fob from her pocket and held it up with trembling fingers. Juno smiled. "Good. Now phone Jake. Cali said they were going to pull off the highway at some derelict gas station. Ask him to keep an eye out for that SUV. The 'Manly 1' plates should be a dead giveaway."

Jessie frowned. "So you think they're headed back to Winnipeg…"

"Or they're on their way into Gimli."

"But why?" Jessie looked down at the phone. "They were right here. Why would they just leave?"

"That's what you and I are going to try and find out. Hope you like bar food." Juno smiled at Kim and the blond woman nodded.

"Bar food?"

"Where else would a bunch of angry men go to drown their sorrows…or find their courage?" Juno chuckled. "Now make that call. Okay."

Lee turned in her seat at the bow of the red canoe and stowed her paddle. She suspected that this fishing trip was more than just a way to assess JoJo's skills, but Maggie had been playing her cards pretty close to her chest lately so there was no way to be certain.

She waited for her friend to drop the red and white lure into the water then folded her arms across her knees and leaned forward. "My feet are wet, Maggie. I don't have a pole so I'm obviously not here to fish and my student of many years sits in silence while the weight of the world rests heavily on her shoulders." She stiffened her spine as she caught the look in Maggie's eyes; there was confusion in those blue depths and a deep sense of longing that seemed to resonate with the life around her…but not quite. "So, why am I here, my friend?"

Maggie gave her a vague smile. "Can you feel her, Lee? When I woke up this morning, it was like she was resting just beneath my skin and then the feeling was gone and I couldn't get it back" She waved vaguely toward the other canoe. "She talks to Sophia…tells her all will be well…and she's made her presence known to many, if not all, of the young people, but when I reach out to her there is a wall of silence between us that I can't get past. I thought…I thought perhaps you could help me break that wall down."

"You talk about the spirit of this place; that which Kaylyn calls the Earth Mother and Tilly's people know as the Source?" Lee raised an eyebrow. "The one whose pedigree has caused so much dissension these past few days?"

Maggie nodded, but the look of confusion only intensified.

"The entity who speaks to Sophia and reveals herself to those who welcome her in has been here since the beginning of time, Maggie, and her essence resides in all of us…we are one and the same, and we are everywhere; connected for all time. She has always been inside of you and, for some reason, this morning she made herself known to you in a way you could understand."

"But I don't understand." Maggie took a deep breath and struggled to center herself. "There was a time when the dance brought me closer to her when I could feel her moving with me…"

Lee grinned. "Exactly. You opened yourself to the possibility without reservation and the connection was completed."

"Then why can't I do that now?"

"Have you danced lately? Have you walked in the forest just because it's there? Have you stood under the stars and listened to them sing? Or have you given yourself over to fear and worry and the pressure of trying to be everything to everyone?" Lee watched Maggie open her mouth to protest and shook her head. "Take some time for yourself, Maggie. Join my students and I for tai chi at sunset. Enjoy the beauty that surrounds us. Open yourself to the possibility, and you'll find your way." She smiled and nodded toward the faint ripples in the water. "Now, are you going to bring that fish in, or shall I?"

Maggie blinked and reached for the pole just before it slid out of the boat. Light danced across the water. *I remember.*

Kim took Jessie's empty chair in the circle; Ian sat down on the ground at her feet.

"What's going on?" Grace demanded. "Why are Jessie and Juno leaving? Is Kenneth here?"

"He was…well, not exactly here…" Ian looked up at Kim. "Maybe you should tell them."

Kim smiled. "Sure, kid."

"Tell us what?" Robert frowned at his son.

"That Kenneth has been here and gone," Kim said. "But we don't know where he's gone or whether he's coming back." She went on to tell them about the red Rover's frequent trips up and down the road and the possible reasons they'd discussed for Kenneth's odd behavior. "Juno and Jessie are taking the van into Gimli to see if they can figure out what's going on."

"And how are they planning on doing that," Caroline asked.

Ian giggled then pressed his hand to his mouth. Kim shook her head at her nephew and leaned back in the chair. "It's quite possible that Kenneth and his crew are going to be looking for a place to eat. If Juno and Jessie get close enough, they may hear something useful."

"The best-laid plans…" Grace said with a sigh. "So what are we supposed to do until Jess and Juno get back?"

"I could eat," Ian said. He looked at his mom with pleading eyes.

Lisa smiled. "That sounds like a good idea. I've been looking forward to checking out these…" She raised her eyes to Kim. "What do you call them?"

"MRE's" Kim stood up glad to no longer be the center of attention. "The extra crate is in the quonsie. I'll bring it over…"

"No need of that," Grace said, "We should stretch our legs anyway, and maybe we can get some work done while we're there."

"Sounds good to me," Robert said as he stood up and folded his chair. Everyone else followed suit.

"I'll go tell the others." Ian headed toward the makeshift soccer field while Robert led the way toward the Quonset huts.

"So we're not considering the possibility that they actually couldn't find our road," Megan asked as she and Kim plowed through the combination of dead grass and new shoots.

Kim glanced down at the tiny Grandmother; she didn't know her well enough to determine if she was serious or not. "Do you think that's the case?"

Megan grinned up at her and shrugged. "I'm just saying."

Lunch seemed to be over for hours when Lisa looked up from the container of odds and ends she was sorting to see her sister striding across the meadow with Jessie and Juno at her side.

"They're back," Ian yelled as he took off at a run.

Lisa closed the box and handed it to Robert. "Put this away for me, please. I need to go wrangle our son or the rest of us will be waiting until midnight to hear the news."

"Did you find them?" Ian demanded as he skidded to a stop in front of his aunts; Juno took a step back and frowned. "Did they go to a bar? What was it like? What did they say? What…"

"Yes to your first question," Kim looked up and smiled as her sister approached then returned her attention to Ian. "As for the rest of it, you'll have to wait to hear the answers along with everyone else."

"But…"

Lisa cleared her throat to get her son's attention. "Uh…hi, mom." Ian gave her his brightest smile. "I was just…"

"Trying to get the inside scoop," Lisa smiled apologetically in Jessie's direction then shook her head at her son. "You heard what Kim said. You'll just have to wait." Ian sighed, gave his aunts a long-suffering stare then turned and trudged back toward the Quonsets.

"Sorry about that," Lisa said as she turned toward Jessie, "I take it you have news for us."

She tilted her head to the side and waited expectantly.

Kim nudged Juno and grinned at Jessie over her sister's head. "Now you know where Ian gets it from."

Lisa rolled her eyes and Jessie smiled. "A simple yes would have been enough for me." Lisa turned on her heels not even looking at her sister as she followed in her son's footsteps. "Come on. There are a lot of anxious people wanting to hear your news. Let's not keep them waiting."

Ian was standing just inside the big doors quietly talking to Wanda as they approached. Lisa knew that she and Ian would need to discuss what had just happened eventually but now wasn't the time. Sometimes she longed for the familiar routine of their past life and the family discussions around the dinner table. She sighed as Ian made an obvious effort to avoid her eyes; maybe when all this upheaval because of Kenneth was over, the inventory was done and the yurts were up, they'd be able to set aside some time each day just to talk.

"Juno. Jessie. Glad you're back." Grandmother Grace walked out of the Quonset hut followed by Robert and Caroline. "Just give us a minute to get everyone together…"

"Actually, Grandmother, we need the entire camp to hear what we have to say…including everyone down at the barn," Jessie said and Juno nodded.

Lisa felt the intense curiosity she shared with her youngest son raise its ugly head; she chewed at the corner of her lip as she forced it back into a fragile state of quiescence and stepped forward. "Do you think that's safe?"

Juno nodded. "Kenneth won't be back anytime soon…"

"You're certain of that," Grace demanded.

"We are, Grandmother," Jessie smiled at the old woman.

Grace tugged at her blue cap and squared her shoulders. "That's good enough for me. Alright everyone," The grandmother said in what Lisa assumed was her best parade voice, "Gather around. We've got work to do. Campfire tonight and we need to let everyone know."

"I'll let Grandma Maggie know," Wanda said as she knelt down to tighten her boot laces.

"And I'll go with her and set up the fire pit," Ian gave his mother a sideways glance; Lisa smiled and nodded, relieved by even this small acknowledgment. A moment later, her son followed Wanda toward the game trail at a slow jog.

"I'll phone Kaylyn and let her know to get things packed up," Juno glanced at the young people hovering by the door. "They're going to need help getting everything back to camp though."

Kwasi stepped forward. "I will go with the others who already know the way." Four of the young people came to stand at Kwasi's side.

"I'll take Wanda's place," Cali said moving up beside Mel.

"And the rest of us can tidy up here," Lisa moved to stand beside her husband.

"Maybe someone should give Jake the all clear…"

"Already done, Robert," Kim smiled at her brother-in-law. "Juno and I are going to keep an eye out for them…just in case."

Grace frowned. "Just in case what?"

Kim exchanged a panicked glance with Juno. "Just in case they need help," Juno said.

"Alright then." The grandmother didn't look completely convinced by that answer and Lisa couldn't blame her; there was obviously something important her sister wasn't telling them, but Grace let it go and clapped her hands together. "Let's get to it. We have a lot to do here and we don't have much time before dark."

Chapter Twenty-Six

"What are you cooking, Grandmother? Smells…great."

Maggie glanced over her shoulder at the sound of her granddaughter's voice. Wanda stood just inside the cookhouse door; her face was flushed and her chest heaved as she struggled to catch her breath. Maggie frowned and continued to stir the contents of the oversized kettle; there was only one reason she could think of that would bring the child here in such a state. "Has Kenneth finally shown up?"

Wanda straightened and took a deep breath. "He did…well kinda…and then he left. That's all I really know," she said apologetically then glanced toward the pot. "Is there fish in that stew?"

Maggie scooped a small portion into a bowl and set it on the work table as she mulled over what she'd just heard; had Kenneth been here or not. "Come sit down and tell me why you're here looking like the Hounds of the Baskerville are on your heels."

Wanda grinned. "I actually know that one, Grandmother. Conan Doyle, right?" She sank into one of Tilly's wooden chairs and pulled the steaming bowl toward her. Maggie waited patiently while Wanda took the first bite. "This is delicious." She looked up from beneath her bangs. "Did JoJo catch this?"

"Well actually, it was a combined effort, but I'm glad you like it." Maggie smiled. "So…"

Wanda swallowed another mouthful of stew. "So Kenneth left without coming in and Momjay and Juno went into town and found him and his friends. When they came back they said they needed to tell the whole camp their news. I'm supposed to let you know that we're having a campfire tonight; then I'm supposed to let everyone else in the main camp know."

"And the others?"

"Momjay phoned Momkay to tell her they needed to come back. Kwasi and some of the other gatherers are going down to help with their stuff. They caught up to Ian and me on the trail. Cali said Kim and Juno are waiting for Grandpa Jake and his ripples."

"His ripples. Why aren't I surprised?" Maggie shook her head. More mouths to feed. More need for beds they didn't have. How was she supposed to relax when everything kept spiraling out of control? "It's a good thing the pot's full," she said as she stood up to give it a stir.

Wanda noisily scraped at the bottom of her bowl. "I better go," she said as Maggie turned back to face her. "Any idea where Jo and Billie are? I thought maybe they could help me find everyone else who stayed in camp."

"They're with Grandma Lee by the fire pit. She's teaching the little ones the first movements of Tai Chi." Maggie smiled wistfully. "Maybe it's time we all got back to that."

Wanda nodded. "Maybe you're right, Grandmother." She stood up, washed her dish in the bucket of soapy water then paused to give Maggie a peck on the cheek. "Thanks for the soup, Grandmother. I should get going. Maybe we can even get some of the tents switched back."

Maggie sighed. "And maybe, while you're at it, you can find a space for Jake's ripples…at least for the night."

"The people from the barn just came in," Lee said as she strode into the cook tent just before dark followed by two of her students. "Bao and Ji will take the soup pot down to the fire pit. Is there anything else that needs to go while we're here?"

Maggie smiled at the young men hovering at Lee's side then took a final glance around the makeshift kitchen. "I think we're good. I'll just…"

"Grandma Maggie." Jessie ducked through the open flap and pulled Kaylyn in behind her. She bowed to Lee and her two assistants then glanced toward the back table. There was a hint of panic in her voice. "I'm sorry to intrude. I know you're busy, but I need to speak with you when you have a moment?"

"We'll just get the pot and get out of your way," Lee said, sharing a concerned glance with Maggie as she nudged the boys toward the stove. "Good to have you back, Granddaughter." Lee gave Kaylyn's hand a squeeze as she waited then nodded to Jessie and followed Bao and Ji out the door carrying the heavy container between them.

Maggie sighed. "Come sit down." She headed toward the ornate table without a backward glance and sank into the chair closest to the stove. It seemed that her long day was about to get even longer. "What's this about?" she asked as her oldest granddaughters sat down on the other side of the table.

"I need your help, Grandmother," Jessie said without preamble, "I don't know how I'm going to convince everyone out there that our little lane just disappeared this morning…for almost two hours." Jessie glanced sideways at the look of astonishment on Kaylyn's face then closed her eyes and sighed.

"Especially when you're not certain that you believe it yourself," Maggie said into the silence; for some reason she couldn't fathom, she wasn't at all surprised by Jessie's news…maybe because she so desperately wanted it to be true.

Jessie raised her head and nodded. "When we found Kenneth and his buddies at the bar in Gimli, Juno got us a seat close enough to overhear everything that they said…not that they were trying to keep their voices down." She sighed. "Long story short, they didn't come in to look for Jenny and Brit because they couldn't find us, but when Juno and I got back, the lane was there clear as day just like it always is."

"That's it." Kaylyn smacked her hand on the table making Maggie jump. "That's what Tilly meant." She looked up and smiled apologetically. "Sorry. It was kind of a weird night and I'll tell you all about it when there's time, but the important thing is that Tilly had a dream…at least that's what she called it." Kaylyn ran her fingers through her hair and stifled a yawn. Jessie frowned and chewed at the corner of her lips; she looked as impatient for Kaylyn to continue as Maggie was. "Tilly said she was standing on the gravel road," Kaylyn continued, "looking toward our lane when the air shimmered and the lane disappeared behind a wall of trees. She said it was like a mirage only more solid; then a voice said 'it is done,' the dream ended and all that was left behind apparently was Tilly's understanding that her home was now secure."

Maggie took a deep breath, sought that place of calm buried at the center of her core, and felt the scattered thoughts of the past few hours come together like the pieces of a jigsaw puzzle…a gift of clarity for her daughter's child. "So, I'm just going to lay all these cards right out on the table," Maggie said as Kaylyn finished speaking. Jessie shook herself and turned toward the sound of her grandmother's voice.

"I spent most of today stirring the pot and wrestling with everything that has been happening over the past weeks while I let my mind drift," Maggie continued, "trying to make some sense of it all: Chloe's awakening, Earth Song's meltdown, the young people finding solace in the forest and a new sense of purpose, the slow, and sometimes painful awakening of hearts and minds to the remarkable potential of this place we now call home," She squared her shoulders, not daring to look at either of her granddaughters. "And the thing is, it really doesn't make any sense…not until you fully give yourself over to the fact that the impossible has already happened; that we're all here, living in this incredible forest because a woman who could see the future gifted us with a prophecy."

Maggie raised her head and smiled. "After that, it's easier to accept that the spirit we have found here is not a figment of our imaginations; that she has been waiting for us and is actually an intrinsic part of that prophecy…" She took a deep breath. "And may even have influenced its creation."

"Wow." Kaylyn stared at Maggie wide-eyed for a moment, then she smiled and nodded. "It makes sense…a mother fearing for her wayward children, trying to protect them from total decimation by the only means open to her."

Jessie locked eyes with her partner as Kaylyn turned toward her. "Do you really believe that?" Then Jessie ducked her head and sighed. "Of course, you do."

Kaylyn squeezed her partner's hand. "Just think about it for a moment, Love." She said softly. "This forest isn't just some random piece of property; it's beautiful and unspoiled and it's a part of her…part of the Earth Mother…just like you and I and everything else that exists. That solar flare will wreak havoc with a large portion of humanity and nothing can stop it. Is it such a leap to believe that she chose some of the pieces of herself and tucked them away for safe-keeping? And before you ask, I have no idea how she made those choices, but I'd like to think she did."

"Okay. I'll give you that," Jessie took a deep breath, "And after spending time with the gatherers, I can even believe it…mostly."

Kaylyn smiled. "I know. I saw you in the grove surrounded by all those young people. Remember? I watched you when you found your center and reached out to her; the look of peace and contentment on your face was enough to tell me that you'd found her."

"You were watching me?"

"I was." Kaylyn smiled. "I do that a lot actually."

Jessie blushed then turned her attention back to Maggie; Kaylyn stifled a giggle which Jessie chose to ignore. "Even if that's all true, Grandmother, how does it help me? How do I convince everyone out there that they're safe? They know what's at stake if Kenneth comes back and most of them aren't going to believe that our little lane disappeared this morning because...because the spirit of this place was protecting us."

"Are you certain of that, Jess?" Maggie didn't wait for an answer as the dinner bell rang for the third and final time. "Earth Song's meltdown, as difficult as it was for everyone, has been a catalyst for much thought and consideration these past few days. You may have more allies in this than you imagine. Just tell them the truth as you know it." Maggie followed Kaylyn to her feet then held her hand out to Jessie. "It'll be okay, Jess," Maggie said softly and Kaylyn nodded. "You've got this."

"Kenneth's buddies have decided that coming here was a wild goose chase and they're not interested in coming back; even if Kenneth decides to come alone, which I doubt he'll do being the coward that he is..." Jessie watched as Jenny hugged her daughter tight and whispered something in her ear that Brit obviously agreed with. "...he won't find us. We're safe here and now it's time to turn our minds to other things...to creating a home we can all be proud of."

"So what you're saying is that Tilly's dream wasn't a dream at all," Chloe reiterated; she sat in her chair beside the fire, her face a mask of flickering shadows. The sun had fully set while Jessie spoke, but not even the children seemed to notice the encroaching darkness. "That the...Earth Mother...was sending us a message, telling us that she'd denied Kenneth entry to this place to keep us safe."

Jessie squeezed Kaylyn's hand. "That's right," Jessie said trying to sound as confident as she felt about the conclusions she'd drawn from her talk with Maggie. She'd fully expected some form of denial from her listeners, especially from Tilly when she'd used the old woman's dream as verification of Kenneth's inability to find them and what that meant for the future, but Tilly, like Chloe and everyone else, had chosen to remain silent until this moment.

"What other explanation could there be for everything that happened this morning?"

"There isn't one," Kaylyn said from Jessie's side. She stood up and looked around the circle; Jessie watched as heads bobbed and the first hints of a smile dimpled many a cheek. "I think that most, if not all of you, know in your hearts that everything we've heard here tonight is true; we are loved and we are protected…"

"They're here!" Wanda paused halfway to her feet, ducked her head, and blushed; a ripple of laughter made its way around the circle. "Sorry, Momkay, but the girls are back and that means that Grandpa Jake and the others can't be far behind."

Kaylyn smiled at her daughter as Juno and Kim walked out of the forest. "Apology accepted. I think we've said all that needs to be said tonight. Now go."

"I think Grandma Maggie was right about our allies." Jessie squeezed Kaylyn's hand as Wanda dashed away and the circle dissolved around them. "No one seems too disturbed by what was said here tonight…even Tilly."

Kaylyn grinned at Jessie; her eyes twinkled in the light of the dying fire. "Maggie's seldom wrong about these things. As for Tilly, I think she's a changed woman after last night. Now, will you come on?" She reached down and pulled Jessie to her feet. "I've been waiting two days to find out the second part of Jake's secret."

"You and everyone else." Jessie lunged for Trin as she scurried past. "Whoa. Slow down, Little One. It's too dark out to move that quickly. You're going to break a leg."

Trin shook her head and pointed frantically down the beach to where dark shadows emerged from the forest.

"I know. Grandpa Jake made them your responsibility." Jessie said sensing the tension in her youngest daughter's body as she nodded. Jessie took a second look at the shadows then loosened her grip on Trin's fingers; Jake wouldn't have given this task to Trin if he thought it was unsafe. "Just slow down. Okay?" Trin nodded and pulled her hand away. Jessie smiled as the tiny body seemed to glide over the sand at a slightly more sedate pace.

"Alpacas. Really, Jake, whatever could have possessed you?" Maggie handed the old man a bowl of stew and lowered herself to a nearby chair. It had taken almost an hour for the novelty to wear off enough to extricate the animals from their admirers and send the alpaca and their caregivers on their way; Trin and Kaylyn had gone with them and the circle around the campfire had slowly dwindled to a mere handful. "And to give Trin that much responsibility…"

"I've been watching her with the dogs and that kitten of Cali's; that little girl has more animal sense in her little finger than anyone else in this camp, except maybe the pilots." Jake grinned. "You saw how Trin had those huge beasties wrapped around that finger the moment they set eyes on her; Bertha said she'd never seen anything like it." He raised his eyebrows and shrugged. "Besides, Kaylyn and Jess didn't seem too upset about it."

"I wouldn't be too certain about that." Maggie shook her head as Jake shoveled soup into his mouth, totally unconcerned by her warning. "So, have you given any thought to where Bertha and her children are going to sleep…especially when the yurts go up? We're now short four bunks."

Jake peered at her over his upraised spoonful of fish then lowered it back to the bowl untouched. "Zeke and I already have that covered," He nodded as Maggie narrowed her eyes. "The grandmothers aren't the only ones with those handy little pension checks. How do you think we bought the lumber for the barn and our other additions to the camp?"

Jake's eyes became thoughtful. "You know, I had my doubts about this whole thing at first. I couldn't imagine any of us surviving out here for very long once everything shuts down, but all that's changed somehow, and I don't really know why." Maggie smiled to herself, but before she could attempt to enlighten him, Jake looked up and waved his spoon. "Come to think of it, Maggie, it's too bad we hadn't done this years ago when those checks first started coming in: pooled our resources, found a place like this to settle…the whole kit-and-caboodle of us, built a sustainable legacy for the youngsters. It certainly would have made everything easier considering what we're facing now."

He raised his head and caught her eye. "You know, Zeke and I are just trying to even the odds the best we can…like providing a way to dry fish now JoJo has found a way to catch them." He cocked his head. "I'm assuming it was Jo."

"Her and her crew," Maggie said.

"In those canoes, the pilots brought in?"

Maggie nodded.

"Good. Then I guess we'd better get that smokehouse built."

"And the alpacas…" Maggie said trying to steer the conversation back to their most pressing concerns.

"A little milk. A little cheese. A lot of wool. And four more good people to make our community stronger," Jake said as he took another spoonful of stew and smiled at her. "And if the food runs out some winter…" He shrugged the rest of that thought away and she didn't pursue it.

"That's all well and good," Maggie said. "But how are we going to feed them when the snow comes?"

"We'll hay the meadow down by the Quonsets in the fall. Bertha says that Alpaca don't eat much compared to goats or cows and with all hands on deck we shouldn't have any problems," Jake smiled in an attempt to reassure her. "We already bought a dozen scythes and spools of cord to tie the sheaths with, so we'll be fine."

Maggie shook her head and sighed; at least the old men's hearts were in the right place. "Then I guess I'm going to need to set the girls to doing some research."

Jake nodded. "You do that, Maggie."

"I call first dibs on the wool," Mae said from where she'd been sitting quietly behind Maggie. She smiled as both Jake and Maggie turned her way. "I couldn't help but overhear."

"Jenna mentioned that you're a weaver," Maggie said.

"That I am and because Mark and Andrew decided to…" She shrugged. "…use their own initiative, shall we say, when packing up the house, my spinning wheel and my looms are down at the Quonsets."

"There you go, Maggie." Jake grinned as she turned to look at him. "Warm hats and mittens. Liners for our boots. Maybe even a sweater or two. Can't go wrong with that and if a little girl gets to find her niche…well, where's the harm?"

Maggie shook her head and sighed. *What's done is done. No sense arguing.* She filled her ladle and held it up. "You want some more stew, Old Man?"

"That about does it," Zeke dumped the last of the feed bags into the manger as Kwasi and Bao filled the trough with fresh water. "You coming, Trin?"

Trin smiled up from where she lounged against a young, grey, female called Rosie and shook her head. Kaylyn smiled from her perch on the wall of the pen as the Old Man struggled with the refusal. "It's okay, Zeke. Trin and I are staying the night, so I'll keep an eye on her." Kaylyn watched her youngest daughter reach up and scratch her current backrest behind the ear; Kat gave her head a gentle shake. "Not that she needs keeping an eye on."

Zeke smiled and nodded. "Then I'll take the volunteers back to camp…see if I can help Jake smooth things over with the grandmothers."

"Well, good luck with that. Things have been pretty hectic around here since the two of you just up and left; they're going to take a lot of convincing, I imagine, before they let you off the hook for this one."

Zeke sighed as he closed the stall door then turned to peer at Trin through the slats; the little girl had her eyes closed and her ear pressed to the alpaca's side; a soft rumble drifted across the stall. "Is Rosie purring?" Kaylyn asked as she leaned closer; a shadow flitted across her right eye.

"Humming actually." Kaylyn looked down at the short, brown hair woman suddenly standing beside her. Bertha smiled. "Seems Jake was right about your daughter; Rosie really likes her and if Rosie likes her, the rest will too."

Kaylyn watched as the other four occupants of the female pen finished at the feeder and ambled over to lie down next to Rosie and Trin.

Zeke smiled. "Well, I guess we'll be going. Have a good night. We'll be back bright and early to get things sorted." He quickly gathered his volunteers together including Kim and Juno and their girls, waved goodbye to Kaylyn and Bertha, and stepped out into the night.

"He's a good man…they both are," Bertha said as she watched Zeke leave. Then she looked at Kaylyn and smiled. "You said something about supper." She frowned as she looked around the barn and shrugged. "We should probably have brought some of our supplies with us from the truck, but the animals come first, so anything you can spare will do."

"Well, have I got a treat for you," Kaylyn said as she took one more look at her daughter then wiped the frown from her face and jumped down to join Bertha. It was obvious that Jake and Zeke hadn't let their ripples know exactly what they were getting into…which was typical; the grandfathers danced to the beat of a different drummer and often didn't get things quite right, though she knew that their hearts were always in the right place. "Hope you like spaghetti and meatballs."

Bertha frowned as no other information was forthcoming then followed Kaylyn into the space set aside for winter storage. Bertha's children looked up from the cards spread out between them then quickly put the cards into piles and stowed them away in their knapsacks.

"I'm hungry," the youngest boy said as he turned to face Bertha; a swath of brown hair fell across his forehead and he pushed it aside revealing a pair of bright eyes the same shade of green as his mother's. He appeared to be about eight years old. "And Aron ate the last of my cheese balls."

An older version of his brother scooted forward. "You gave them to me, Henry. Don't say you didn't."

"But you didn't have to eat them all."

"Well, I have something for you that's much better than cheese balls." Kaylyn pointed to the green crate tucked away in the far corner as all eyes turned toward her. "Kyle, do you think you could bring that box over here?"

Fifteen-year-old Kyle glanced at his mother then nodded and scrambled to his feet. He was back a minute later with the unused ration packs. "Now we're going to do some magic," Kaylyn said as she opened the box. She glanced up at Bertha. "Could you tell Trin it's time for Spaghetti?"

"I really thought you were joking," Bertha said as she wiped spaghetti sauce from her chin with a tissue from her pocket. "But that was delicious."

"We don't eat like this very often…hardly ever actually." Kaylyn smiled as Trin sucked a dangling noodle into her mouth and Henry giggled. "I guess you could call them our emergency supplies…and there aren't many of them left."

Bertha looked down at the empty bag in her hand. "Maybe you shouldn't have…"

"Hey. It's share and share alike out here." Kaylyn smiled at Bertha then glanced toward the children as they explored the remaining contents of their MREs; there'd be a dessert in there, some bread or crackers…maybe even a candy bar. "Besides, your boys deserve a treat after all the work they did today."

Bertha gave her a wistful smile at the sound of the children's excited giggles. "I appreciate that. They're good kids and treats have been in short supply around our house since their father died; Tim was a better farmer than he was a businessman and the past couple of years have been hard." She drew a deep breath and her shoulders slumped. "If it hadn't been for Jake, we would have gone under a long time ago…" She glanced over at the sleeping animals. "I figured this might be a way I could pay him back and it's not like we would have had a home much longer with the unpaid taxes."

Kaylyn nodded. She has been right all along; in their haste to fill their barn, the grandfathers had neglected to share the more important details of life at Dragon's Flare. "Well, you have a home here now…you and your children." She leaned her arms on her knees and smiled. "So how much did Jake tell you about us?"

Bertha shrugged. "Not much. He came by a few months back and started talking about prophecies and solar flares. He said that he and a group of friends were working on creating a safe place and he wanted the kids and I to be a part of it."

"And what did you tell him?"

Bertha sighed and ran her fingers of her left hand through her hair. "You have to understand, I've known Jake most of my life. He was my father's best friend and when my dad died, he kind of stepped in and took his place for a while; I love him, but he's always kinda been out there, you know."

"So when he started talking about prophecies and solar flares, you didn't know what to think." Kaylyn smiled as Bertha nodded.

"But I didn't want to hurt his feelings, so I told him I'd think about it. He was disappointed, but he said it was fine, to take all the time I needed since the prophecy gave you a year to prepare." Bertha shrugged. "I didn't think much more about it after that until he and Zeke showed up on my soon-to-be-repossessed doorstep saying the timeline had changed and we needed to come now."

"And you did," Kaylyn said as she watched Bertha struggle with the outcome of that visit.

"He built us a barn, Kaylyn." The words came out almost as a sob. "We'd sold off most of the herd by then, but Rosie and the others in that pen…they're special and now we have somewhere to keep them safe. My kids and I are good workers and we don't need much; we'll earn our keep."

Kaylyn made a note to sic Grandma Maggie on Jake for his bumbling and proceeded to fill a wide-eyed Bertha in on everything the grandfathers had neglected to tell her about their new home…including how special their relationship with the land was. She figured that Bertha and her children would hear about the events of the past few days sooner or later and she wanted to make certain that they had the whole picture.

"I don't know what to say," Bertha whispered when Kaylyn was done speaking. "It's not like I've never thought about those things; there were places on our farm that just felt special, but I could never put a name to the feeling; as to the rest of it…" She raised her head and smiled. "…my boys and I would be honored to be part of this family."

"I thought you'd all be asleep by now." Four pairs of slightly rheumy eyes peered up at her as Maggie pushed her way into the tent she shared with Kathleen, Grace, Megan, and Matibi.

"We thought we'd wait for you," Kathleen said as she swung her legs over the edge of her cot and sat up, "Since Meg saw you drag Jake away as soon as the hubbub broke up, we figured you'd be awhile, but it's probably better for us to process today's events sooner rather than later."

Maggie shrugged and sank heavily to her cot. "I don't know if that's even possible for me right now. It's been a long day and talking to Jake kinda put the cap on it."

"Let me guess," Matibi said from the far corner. "Jake thinks the alpaca is the greatest thing since sliced bread."

Maggie sighed; Mat never could take a hint. "That's right and Mae would probably agree with him."

Matibi frowned. "Why?"

"She's a weaver, and apparently, she has all of her equipment here thanks to Mark and Andrew." Maggie tucked her pillow in her lap and leaned on it "She's quite excited actually, but I don't know if this is just going to cause problems with Tilly." She frowned. "Though Tilly was awfully quiet this evening."

Megan giggled. "Apparently, she's had an epiphany."

"What makes you say that?"

"Because she was here, Maggie, wanting to apologize." Kathleen nodded as Maggie stared at her wide-eyed; that was the last thing she'd expected to hear. "She said she'd been a stubborn old fool, but she couldn't deny what happened last night and she hoped that we'd give her the opportunity to redeem herself."

Maggie scratched at the back of her neck. "And you believed her."

"We all did." Kathleen smiled. "Even Grace."

"With reservations," Grace shrugged. "But it can't hurt to wait and see. If she is sincere, it'll make all of our lives a whole lot easier…especially with all the work that needs to be done around here…preferably sooner rather than later."

Maggie nodded. "I agree…"

"We need to set up a council," Matibi said without preamble, "Just a temporary one for now with young, old, and not-so-old members; just until we get ourselves organized then we can revisit it."

Maggie sighed. "And this is what you've been doing while I was making sure Jake didn't have any more surprises up his sleeve."

"You heard our granddaughter." Grace frowned. "How did she put it 'We're safe here and now it's time…'"

"…to turn our minds to other things." Megan grinned "…to creating a home we can all be proud of. So what do you say, Maggie? We thought tomorrow morning would be as good a time as any to have the vote. It shouldn't take us long to figure out the best way to go about it."

"So we're just going to force this on everyone."

"Of course not, Maggie. You know us better than that." Kathleen sounded indignant and she had a right to be.

"Of course, I do. I don't know what I was thinking." Maggie shook her head and sighed. "And I suppose no one will mind us taking the initiative if it gets things moving ahead."

Megan grinned. "That's the spirit, Maggie. Now here's what we need to do…"

Chapter Twenty-Seven

"That's the last of the sixteen-footers, Cali." Greg sank to the chair across the table, pulled a red handkerchief from his pocket, and mopped his brow with it; the weather had turned hot over the past week and the building crews were feeling it the most. "Robert's taking his crew down to the lake to get cleaned up…no sense opening another crate this late in the day."

Cali smiled up from her ledger. "That's seven yurts in nine days. That's amazing. I'll let Mel's team know they have another one to set up tomorrow then we'll get Jake and Zeke in there to install the woodstove. At the rate you guys are going we'll be right on track to have everyone permanently housed by the end of June."

"Good thing too." Greg looked down at the soggy square of cloth in his hand. "If it gets much hotter we'll only be able to work up there half days. Wouldn't want anyone keeling over from heat exhaustion."

"I'll make a note of that." Cali scribbled a reminder at the bottom of the page then smiled as the old man tucked the bandana into his back pocket. "I'll make certain to bring it up at supper tonight…find out whether the building crew is noticing any ill effects."

"You do that," Greg said as he pushed himself to his feet. He stood with his hands on the table for a moment as he caught his balance then turned toward the door. "Think I'll go take a nice long swim, put on some clean clothes…" He grinned at her over his shoulder. "Maybe talk Maggie out of a cup of that black tea she's been hoarding."

Cali smiled back. "Well, good luck with that, but I wouldn't hold my breath, if I were you."

Greg laughed then disappeared out the door as Jenna walked in carrying four, white sacs; she set them on the prep table just as Wanda followed her inside with two sacks of her own. "Looks like you had a good day," Cali said as they refilled their canteens then ambled over and sat down. They both wore the safari hats the grandmothers had bought for them, long-sleeved t-shirts and blue jeans tucked into their boots. "How were the ticks?"

"Not bad at all actually. The cedar spray that Chloe made for us seems to work really well." Wanda raised her arm and sniffed. "Makes us smell pretty good too."

Jenna grinned at Wanda's antics then took off her hat and rolled up her sleeves. "It's awfully warm in here. How do you stand it?" Cali shrugged; at least she was out of the direct sun. Jenna frowned across the table. "You're coming out with us tomorrow, right?"

Cali nodded. "Kwasi's in charge of the ledger tomorrow. The building crew is going to be starting on the twenty-foot yurts and the inventory crew will be bringing in their tallies for him to record, so facing a few ticks doesn't seem so bad."

"I know this council business is right up your alley, Cal." Wanda folded her arms on the table "But it'll be good for you to get into the woods for a while…make contact, breath some fresh air…shake out the cobwebs." She grinned, glanced over her shoulder then wiggled her eyebrows at Cali. "That sounds like the cooking crew. Guess you're free now. How about a swim? Jen made some more of her lavender hydrosol and I need someone to help me wash my hair."

"Momkay and Lisa are going to be talking about hair tonight at supper." Cali nodded as Wanda and Jenna's brows furrowed into identical frowns. "Apparently, they're going to suggest that everyone with long hair gets it cut." She shrugged. "You have to admit that short hair is easier to keep clean and tick free…"

"But Momkay would never cut her hair," Wanda protested. Cali raised her eyebrows and chin-pointed to the other end of the tent. Wanda looked over her shoulder and shook her head in denial as Kaylyn stepped inside. "I don't believe it. She's always been so proud of her hair."

"I know," Cali said with a twinge of sadness, "But she said she couldn't ask anyone else to do something she wouldn't do herself."

"You were there?" Wanda asked as she dragged her eyes away from the other end of the room.

"Since she was sitting right at the end of this table, yeah, I was there." Cali sighed remembering the sadness in her mother's eyes. "Grandma Kate must have asked her a dozen times whether she was certain before she finally went to get her scissors."

"Looks like Kaylyn wasn't the only one to get a haircut," Jenna whispered as Maggie and Trin walked into the tent.

"Hey. I didn't have anything to do with it." Cali threw her hands up as Wanda stared at her accusingly. "Grandma Maggie is a fully grown woman and Trin just plunked herself down in that chair and wouldn't move until Grandma Kate complied."

"I know it wasn't your fault, Cal." Wanda pushed an escaped lock of hair behind her ear. "It's just that they…they look so different."

Cali muffled a giggle. "Grandma Maggie thinks it makes her look twenty years younger."

"The inventory is finally complete." Grace slammed the black, coil notebook shut with a satisfying thwack and slid it into the messenger bag she'd found in a box of odds and ends. "So how does the list look?"

"We still have a lot of purchases that need to be made," Caroline said, "I just hope there's enough money to cover it."

"I just hope we can find everything we need close to home," Megan said from her perch on an empty deck box. "Gimli has two big grocery stores, so the extra food won't be any problem, but I don't know about the rest."

Hanna joined Megan on her box. "We'll just have to do the best we can. Between the second-hand store and the hardware stores, we should be able to find most of it."

"There are a lot of little stores too if I remember correctly. We can scour the town and see what we come up with," Grace tugged at her blue beret. "I'm sure it'll be fine."

"Then we should go tomorrow." Meg stood up and stretched. "Sooner begun. Sooner done. Right? Oh…" She turned to Caroline. "Maggie asked if we could add those black mats people put inside their doors. She said it will cut down on the dirt being tracked in."

Caroline nodded and added the mats to the list. "Boot trays would also be helpful."

Grace huffed out a breath and sat down. "If we're going tomorrow, we should leave early so we're back when the gatherers get in. We're going to need them to cart the stuff down here and stow it away until it's time to outfit the yurts and get a proper kitchen set up."

Caroline nodded. "I'll talk to Jenna when we get back. Get them to meet us around three. That should give them time to get everything put away before supper."

Megan glanced around the Quonset and sighed. "It's going to take weeks to get the stuff we need for the winter from here down to the camp."

Grace nodded. "You're right, but it can't be helped. At least we'll have the entire summer to do it…flare or no flare."

"I know." Megan shrugged. "It's just going to be a lot of hard work for the young people."

Caroline grinned. "Maybe not as hard as you think. Greg says that the garden center in town sells wagons like the ones we already have except bigger and Jake and Zeke are going to purchase five more when they go in to get the fencing for the alpaca. They'll bring them back in one of the trucks we left in there."

Grace closed her eyes and sighed. "They've never really been team players those two…always going off on their own tangent."

Megan giggled. "Made doing group seminars with them very interesting."

"So you've known them since university." Caroline cocked an eyebrow. "You've been friends for a long time then."

Grace chuffed. "You could say that."

Jessie wasn't surprised to find Kaylyn sitting cross-legged on her cot staring at the wall. She hadn't seen her partner since this morning, but she'd heard about the haircut through the grapevine and figured that Kaylyn would need some time to come to terms with what she'd done. "Grandma Maggie said I'd find you here." She waited for Kaylyn to change her focus and smiled. "Looks good, by the way."

Kaylyn's hand rose to the back of her neck. "Do you really think so?"

Jessie nodded. She sat down on the edge of her cot and braced her arms on her thighs. "You look as beautiful as always…and I'm not just saying that."

"Flatterer." Kaylyn smiled and swung her legs over the side of the cot. "Lisa's right, it's going to be a lot easier to keep it clean, but it's going to take some getting used to."

"That's what Maggie said." Jessie tilted her head as images of her grandmother flashed through her mind. "You know, I don't remember a time when Maggie didn't have that braid. I'm surprised she gave it up so easily."

"Oh, it wasn't easy for her at all…for either of us." Kaylyn pursed her lips and sighed. "But it was necessary and at least something good came out of it." She reached into the bag at her feet, pulled out what looked like a thin rope, and passed it across the space between them.

Jessie held the offering up to the light from the single window; the braid was tricolored and felt rough beneath her fingers. "This is your hair…"

Kaylyn smiled. "And Maggie's and Trin's—the three generations of our family. I thought…"

She drew a deep breath and caught Jessie's eyes. "I thought it would go nicely with the spirals Aunt Alice left for the girls. You do still have them, don't you?"

Jessie blinked. It had been a long time since she'd thought about that blue box. She nodded and looked down at the tricolored braid resting on her palm. "So you think it's time we gave them to the girls."

"I do," Kaylyn said softly. "I did a little research a while back and the double spiral is a very ancient symbol. It's been found etched into stones all over the world. It's thought to represent birth, death, and rebirth in some cultures; in others, it's a symbol of feminine power, the consciousness of nature, or a journey to the source." She caught Jessie's eye and shrugged. "Considering everything that's happened since we started on this journey, I have to believe that Alice had a good reason for leaving those pins to our children." She sighed and looked away. "But we'll never find out what that reason is if you just keep them squirreled away."

"And if there is no reason?"

"Then they'll have a piece of their family to carry around with them." Kaylyn slipped the braid out of Jessie's fingers and put it back in the bag. A smile twitched at the corners of her lips. "If you agree, I'll ask Mae for help. She does jewelry, among other things, and she might have the clasps and toggles in the stuff Mark and Andrew brought in to help put the necklaces together."

Jessie saw the ill-concealed excitement in Kaylyn's eyes and sighed. She reached for the knapsack tucked under the bed and felt a weight she hadn't realized she carried lift from her shoulders. "Then I guess it's time."

Kathleen dried her hands on the tea towel draped over her shoulder and dug her cell phone from her sweater pocket; she'd never been certain how she felt about the beeping that heralded every incoming message; it was annoying and not very helpful as far as she could tell, but the girls seemed to think they were an essential part of keeping in touch and who was she to argue...especially this late in the game. "I've got a text for you, Maggie. It's from Mildred."

"Just like clockwork." Maggie handed her stirring duties over to Mae and reached for the phone. "Every Monday without fail." She mock-frowned at Kathleen and raised an eyebrow. "It is Monday, isn't it?"

Kathleen smiled at the seniors' humor. "Yep. It says so right in the left-hand corner of the screen. So what does our indefatigable house manager have to say?"

Maggie peered down at the tiny screen and cleared her throat. She says, *"We went on a nature walk today. The children love to collect pretty rocks and bits of wood; we display them on the window ledges. Today, Byron brought a baby garter snake home in his pocket. We made a terrarium for it in a pickle jar. I want to thank you again, Maggie, for allowing the children and I to have this time together. I'll let you know when we find a permanent residence. Sincerely, Mildred Shute."* Maggie sniffed, closed the cover on the phone, and handed it back to Kathleen.

"Sounds like those children are having a great time," Mae said, "You did good letting them have your house."

"But I should have done more. I should have..."

"Not helping, Maggie." Kathleen slipped the phone back into her pocket. "You did everything you could for those children, short of endangering our granddaughters' future, and Mildred will fight like a momma bear to keep them safe...and maybe she'll even succeed."

And maybe she won't. "You're right," Maggie said as she took the spoon from Mae. "I just wish there was a way..."

"We all do," Kathleen said as she started to pile the tin bowls and cups into the wagon Mark had brought down to them. "Now let's get finished up here. I'll take the dishes down to the fire pit and send some of the youngsters up to carry the pots. Good thing pine tree tea tastes as good warm as it does hot because Lisa wants everyone to get a good dose of vitamin c tonight."

Maggie gave the pot a final stir, but Kathleen could tell that her heart wasn't in it. "Those cattail roots JoJo brought in with the last stringer of fish seem to have added a bit of a tang to the stew," Maggie said, "I hope everyone likes it."

"Won't matter if they don't." Mae grinned. "Even the little ones have figured out that it's better to have the food in your belly than on your plate. They'll get used to it."

"You're right." Maggie puffed out a breath that made her bangs ruffle and gave the pot a final stir. "Just give me a sec and I'll join you, Katie," she said as she wrestled the lid into place. "I need to make certain that Jake hasn't forgotten about the beds for our new arrivals. We'll be moving into the yurts soon and I don't want Bertha and her boys to be without a proper place to sleep…especially when they were so uncertain about their acceptance here when they first arrived."

Kathleen snorted then covered it with a laugh. "Can you blame them with Jake bragging about all the milk and cheese we were going to be able to add to our menu? I'm glad Bertha finally felt confident enough to speak up and set him straight. It's a shame that the alpaca isn't dairy animals, but we'll still have an abundance of wool and Hanna is ecstatic about the manure for her garden. Then there's the emergency meat supply…"

"Let's not go there," Maggie said as Kathleen stopped beside the fire pit and waved Wanda and Cali over, "It would break Trin's heart if that were to happen."

Kathleen met her friend's eyes and saw the resignation and the sadness that comes with fearing the inevitable. "And if it does, we'll all be there for her."

Maggie nodded. "I know, but let's hope it never comes to that. That little girl has had enough heartbreak in her short life; she certainly doesn't need anymore."

Caroline still couldn't understand how she had ended up as a member of Dragon's Flare's first official council, but here she was waiting to guide tonight's meeting and report on her committee's progress with the inventory. Not that she minded the added responsibility; Dragon's Flare had given her a new lease on life and she was more than grateful for that; besides, it was good to feel useful again.

She smiled as she took another mouthful of tonight's version of fish stew and savored the unique flavor as she chewed on a bit of cattail root. The gatherers and the fisherfolk were doing an amazing job of keeping everyone fed and she was quite proud of Mel for the role she was playing in that. She glanced over to where her young charge sat with a group of her new friends talking animatedly to Jenna; it was good to see Melanie coming into her own now that she was among people who genuinely cared about her and respected her intelligence.

"It is time." Mark stood with his hand in the air as the narrow line of pink over the trees faded to black and everyone turned his way. Caroline felt a shiver run down her spine as dozens of voices were instantly raised in song:

Day is done, gone the sun.
From the forest, from the lake, from the sky.
All is well, safely rest, She is nigh.

Caroline sighed as the tune ended in peaceful and lingering silence. Mel had found that tune in an old children's book and adapted it to suit her budding understanding of their relationship to the spirit of this place. It was, without a doubt, a stirringly beautiful way to greet the night.

She blinked moisture from her eyes and stood up. "That was lovely." She raised her head and nodded across the fire. "Thank you. Now on to this evening's business…but first I'd like to commend the gatherers, the fisherfolk and our amazing cooks for the delicious meal; who would have thought cattails could be so tasty." That brought a scattering of laughter and a mock glare from Cali as she cuddled her cat carrier to her chest. Caroline smiled. "Now on to business," she said as she glanced down at the wrinkled paper in her hand. "The inventory is complete and the final list of purchases needs to be attended to as soon as possible. The committee will be going into Gimli tomorrow to start that process." She looked to her right. "Kaylyn, may we use your van."

Kaylyn smiled and nodded. "Of course."

"Then we'll leave as soon as it's light out. Are there any questions?" Caroline waited for a count of ten then went on to the next item on her list; best to keep things moving along. "Does the building committee have anything to report?"

"Just that we'll be starting on the twenty-footers tomorrow," Greg said from his seat beside Mark.

Cali raised her hand and Caroline acknowledged her. "There's some concern about the recent heat wave and I wanted to know if the builders are experiencing any adverse effects."

"Well, the smell isn't too pleasant." Mark grinned and waited for the laughter to die down. "But I think we're doing okay for now."

"An extra jug or two of water would be helpful," Andrew said. "But besides that, we're fine."

"We'll boil an extra pot tonight," Kathleen said as Cali turned toward her. "It'll be ready for pickup in the morning."

Cali nodded. "Thank you, Grandmother."

"Does the food committee have anything to report?" Caroline glanced at Maggie.

Maggie received a head shake from both Jenna and JoJo: she smiled. "Not at this time."

"And the education and training committee?"

Grandma Lee stood up and bowed to Caroline who returned the gesture. "The littles are progressing well with their lessons. The slates that Cali brought in are perfect for them to practice their numbers and letters. I would ask that some of the children's books be brought out of storage as soon as possible so we can make better progress with their reading." She paused and smiled at the children beside her. "My older students have found a perfect place for the archers to practice and are constructing a backstop in their free time. Hopefully, we'll be ready to begin training as soon as our current tasks are complete."

"Yes!" Billie grinned then ducked her head as all eyes turned toward her.

Grandma Lee smiled. "That is the end of my report."

Caroline returned the grandmother's bow and turned to Kaylyn and Lisa. "I guess you're up."

Cali zipped the tent door shut and plunked herself down on her cot. She'd known that Momjay and Lisa's proposal wasn't going to be popular with some people, but she'd never expected it to turn into a shouting match. "Who would have thought Mark was so attached to his hair," she said as she kicked off her boots.

"That's a good one, Cali." Jenna giggled as she lay down and pulled the blanket up to her chin. "Attached to his hair."

Cali scowled. "You know what I mean; I don't think I've ever seen him that upset."

"I have…a few times" Jenna shrugged. "Usually when Tilly expected him to do something he didn't agree with; he never had any choice but to fall into line since she'd make his life miserable if he didn't."

"But no one here is going to force him to do it." Cali protested.

Jenna rolled onto her side facing Cali. "You know that and I know that…and eventually Mark will know that too, but it's going to take some time."

Cali shivered remembering the harshness in Mark's voice and the sick feeling it invoked in the pit of her stomach. "Well, I hope that it happens sooner rather than later."

Jenna nodded. "Yeah, me too."

Cali leaned forward and pulled the blanket over her shoulders. "So was it awful living at Earth Song? I mean they all seem like basically good people." She thought about that for a moment then shrugged. "But sometimes good people can do bad things."

"They were never anything but kind to me, Cal…even Tilly, but she knew my grandmother and thought very highly of her, so maybe that helped." Jenna shrugged one shoulder and smiled. "And now that all that stuff about Helka's theory and Tilly's promise has been sorted and Tilly is trying so hard to make amends, Mark will come around; we just need to give him time."

Cali grinned. "You really like him, don't you?"

"He's been the big brother I never had." Jenna narrowed her eyes. "And don't you go imagining anything else."

Cali chuckled. "Wouldn't dream of it." She ducked as a pillow sailed toward her head.

"Make certain that you don't. I…"

"Cali, you in there?"

Cali recognized that voice. "Be right there, Grandmother." She tossed the pillow back to Jenna then got up to open the flap. Grace smiled then brushed past her and into the tent. "We were just getting ready for bed," Cali said as she closed the flap.

Grace smiled. "Well, that's good because sunrise comes pretty early this time of year."

"Sunrise, Grandmother?" Cali frowned; the only people who got up that early were the cooks.

Grace lowered herself to the foot of Cali's cot. "The inventory committee's been talking and…well…some of us aren't really up to a full-day shopping spree." She cleared her throat and sighed. "Myself included. So we'd like the two of you and some of the other youngsters to take our place…if you're willing."

Cali tamped down her excitement and nodded seriously. It had taken a lot for the grandmother to make this request and she needed to respect that. "Of course, Grandmother."

"That goes ditto for me," Jenna said as she swung her legs over the side of the bed. "But I'll have to tell the gatherers…"

"Ian will take care of that in the morning," Grace said, "His mother has already talked to him about it. Wanda will also be coming with you along with Mark, Kwasi, Kaylyn, and Juno. Juno will bring the Jeep back if it's needed."

"Sounds good," Jenna said with a very serious nod then she smiled. "And thank you for the opportunity, Grandmother, we won't let you down."

Grace nodded and stood up. "Kim will be around to wake you up then she and the dogs will escort you to the van. You'll get breakfast in town." She made her way toward the door. "Now get to sleep. You have a big day ahead of you."

"Breakfast in a restaurant." Jenna sighed and flopped back on her cot as Cali closed the flap. "I think I've died and gone to heaven."

Chapter Twenty-Eight

The restaurant they found was just past the hospital and offered a full breakfast for less than seven dollars. Wanda forced herself to eat slowly, savoring every bite as Momjay split them into two teams and gave them their assignments. She wondered if they could sneak some bread in with the groceries; she really missed her toast in the morning.

"There are two large grocery stores in town, so each team will take one of them," Kaylyn said around a mouthful of egg; Wanda was glad Grandma Maggie wasn't here to see that. "I know the committee thought that one vehicle would be enough…" She looked up and caught Juno's eye. "What do you think?"

"Two will make things easier and faster," Juno said, "And the jeep is just two blocks from here. It won't take a minute to go get it when we're done."

Kaylyn smiled. "Good. So we'll start with the two grocery stores and the two, large hardware stores then we'll meet back here for lunch."

Jenna's mouth fell open. "We get lunch too."

Cali giggled as Mark raised an eyebrow in Jenna's direction. "Still got that hallow leg I see." Mark grinned and took a swallow of his orange juice. Wanda caught just a hint of the blush staining Jenna's cheeks as she ducked her head; she'd have to ask Cali about that when they got back to camp since her sister seemed to know something she didn't.

Kaylyn just smiled and looked down at her list. "You'll be looking for dried beans, peas and lentils, rice, oatmeal, powdered potatoes and milk, pastas, and anything else that has a long shelf life, won't freeze, and can feed sixty people. Each team has a thousand dollars to spend on food, so use it wisely."

"A thousand dollars." Kwasi looked stunned. "That is a very large amount of money."

"Not when you're trying to feed sixty people for the winter." Juno smiled at the young man. "That's why what you kids do is so important. Without the food you bring in, well…" She shrugged. "…to put it bluntly, we'd probably starve this winter."

"Then it is time we learn to hunt," Kwasi said, "We will need the extra meat when the store food runs out."

Juno nodded. "You're right and archery lessons will start as soon as the yurts are completed. Kim and I will also be teaching tracking and concealment skills and Jake and Bertha will be showing everyone how to clean and skin their kills."

Wanda shuddered. She knew in her head that meat would be their staple food in the winter, but she'd never really thought about what role she'd play in putting that meat on the table. "So we will all be expected to become hunters," she said softly, "because I don't think I can do that."

"There may come a time when you have no alternative." Juno raised sad eyes to meet Wanda's. "Would you let your family starve instead?"

"No, but…" She thought about the deer she'd seen with its gentle eyes and quivering nose. It had been beautiful and brave and made no attempt to run away when it saw her. She shook her head; if need be, she'd give up everything, even the earth mother's blessing, to feed her family for another day. She just hoped that, somehow, she'd be forgiven if that day ever came. "There is no but, is there?" she said softly.

Wanda felt a hand on her shoulder and looked up. "That's a discussion for another day," Kaylyn said gently. Then she smiled. "Right now we have things to do and places to be. You up for it?" Wanda forced a smile and nodded.

"It's a good thing Juno has her jeep here, or some of us would be walking home," Wanda said as she shoved the last of the drying racks into the back seat of the van. It had taken almost the whole day and a considerable amount of creativity to finally cross every item, or a reasonable facsimile, off their list; the food was easy, but washbowls and jugs were replaced with salad bowls and tea kettles and clothes racks and shower curtains in a variety of bright colors would take the place of privacy screens…and who knew why Grandma Hanna wanted twenty extra-large, plastic garbage pails. "I guess all that's left is Grandma Hanna's seed potatoes."

"And all the kale, cabbage, and Brussels sprout seeds they have in stock," Jenna said as she shut the door and leaned against it. "Something about a fall planting. I guess they're going to use the wood from the crates and the soil from the toilet holes to make raised beds between the yurts. I guess the builders have already volunteered to do that."

"You girls ready to go?" Kaylyn appeared around the front of the jeep with a large bag in her hand; it looked heavy.

"I'll just take the trolley back," Jenna said as she grabbed the handle and headed for the door.

Wanda turned to Kaylyn and nodded toward the bag. "What's that, Momkay?"

Kaylyn smiled. "Odds and ends: hooks, wire, nails, screws. Just things we might need while we're getting everything set up." She handed the bag to Wanda. "So where are we off to next?"

"The garden center and that's practical across the streets." Wanda tucked the bag into the back seat with the boxes then climbed in beside Kaylyn. "We're supposed to meet Juno there." She scooted over so Jenna could climb in beside her.

"This has been a very weird day," Jenna said as she fastened her seatbelt. "It's like we've entered some sort of parallel universe; everyone just going about their business without a care in the world. It gives me a funny feeling in my stomach."

"Yeah. I know what you mean." Wanda gave Jenna a one-arm hug; she'd been so excited about today, but nothing about their impromptu shopping spree had felt right. She looked out the window at the people leaving the store without a care in the world then turned to Kaylyn. *We don't belong in this world anymore.* "Momjay."

"What is it, Love?"

"After the garden center, maybe we could just go home." Wanda turned to Jenna. "What do you say?"

"No ice cream?"

Wanda shook her head. "No ice cream."

Jenna smiled. "Fine with me."

"Then home it is," Kaylyn said as she pulled up beside the garden center and cut the engine. "As soon as we get Hanna's seeds."

It took five days to move everything from the vehicles to the ridge, but gradually each yurt was fully equipped with most of the things its inhabitants would need to stay safe and comfortable once they moved in. Cali sat beside Wanda in the doorway of the second twenty-footer while the builders finished removing the twenty-four-footer from its crate. "I guess they're going to put Grandma Hanna and her family in there," she said. "It'll give the little ones a bit of extra room to move around in if they can't go outside."

"I've heard there's going to be a sign-up sheet to give people a chance to choose their bunkmates." Wanda raised a beringed eyebrow in Cali's direction.

The young councilor laughed. "Not very subtle, sister-mine. And yes, the sheet should be up by now, but there are some stipulations like elders get bottom bunks. I talked to them yesterday and they've already been penciled in."

Wanda nodded. "Well, that makes sense and I guess I wouldn't mind sharing with the grandmothers as long as I'm not the only young person, but I can't speak for everyone else."

"I don't think we'll have any problems." Cali shrugged. "I guess we'll just have to wait and see."

Wanda stood up and smoothed the wrinkles from the knees of her jeans. "I'm going to wash up. I promised the cooks that I'd help move things down to the fire pit before supper and Grandma Grace will want to know that the vehicles are cleaned out." She ran her fingers through her hair and sighed. "I hope we have everything we need because I don't want to do that again."

Cali frowned. "But you always loved shopping."

"I know, but it's different now. Jenna says it's like being in an alternative universe." Wanda shrugged. "I'm just glad I don't have to go out there anymore…even if I do need to learn to hunt."

Cali saw the hurt and the near panic in Wanda's eyes. "We may all need to learn to hunt, but that doesn't mean we'll all be hunters," She gripped Wanda's shoulder. "Just like we're not all gatherers or fisherfolk. So I wouldn't worry about it, if I were you; who'd bring in all those lovely, fresh veggies if you were running around the woods chasing deer."

Wanda grinned. "Thanks, Cal. That makes me feel a lot better."

Cali gave Wanda's shoulder a gentle squeeze then let go. "Any time."

"So…are you coming?" Wanda said as she stepped away. "Chloe just gave me a new batch of her lavender infusion. I'll share if you're good."

"Please. I'm always good." Cali raised both eyebrows and Wanda giggled. "Just give me a few minutes, okay? Trin is taking care of Mouser today, and I just want to check in with them."

Wanda smiled. "I'll get our towels and meet you down at the lake then. We should have just enough time for a good wash and a change of clothes before I have to be at the kitchen." Wanda tucked a stray piece of hair behind her ear and started down the path. Cali took a final glance at the builders struggling with a second crate then turned and followed.

"So the twenty-four-footer should be up by the end of the day tomorrow," Grace said as she dried another plate and added it to the pile. "Sounds awfully fast to me."

"Greg says it's possible." Maggie handed Grace another plate. "They got it uncrated and the platform laid out before they quit for the day." She smiled as she dunked another dirty dish into the bucket of soapy water. "I think they're looking forward to getting out of the tents as much as everyone else." She handed the dish to Grace. "That's the last one."

"Well, thank goodness for that." Grace stacked the plate, wound up the tiny flashlight her granddaughters had given her then turned off the lantern; someday the battery would die out and she wasn't certain what they'd do after that, but that was a problem for another day.

Maggie stood in the doorway with her own flashlight in her hand. "It looks like the others have headed off to bed," She secured the flap then followed Grace past the dying embers of this evening's fire. Cagney and Lacey stopped to give them both a sniff and receive a pat before continuing on their rounds. "Those dogs are a gift," she said as they entered their tent.

"No argument here," Grace said, "And when Kim and Juno have the pups trained our camp will be as secure as it can be."

Matibi's laugh came from the far corner. "Those pups haven't even been born yet."

"I know that, but Juno says it should be any day now." Grace sat down on her cot and untied her boots. "I guess she and Kim have already made a nest for them down at the barn; they'll be safe there until they're old enough to fend for themselves."

"Oh, Trin will love that," Kathleen rolled onto her side and propped her head on her hand. "She's already laid claim to every animal around here with the exception of Cali's cat. I can just imagine what going to happen when it's time to choose the pups trainers."

Maggie laughed. "I'm sure Kim and Juno will be able to handle it." She undressed, pulled on the t-shirt and sweat pants she wore to bed, and crawled under the covers before she turned off the light. "Sweet dreams everyone."

"Sweet dreams."

"What the hell is that?"

Maggie cracked one eye open and then the other as Grace turned on her light. "Sounds like the dinner bell, Gracey."

"It's four o'clock in the morning."

"Well, whatever time it is, someone obviously wants to get our attention." Kathleen stood up and shoved her feet into her boots. "Best get a move on ladies."

"Take your bear spray," Maggie said as she pulled on her sweater and leaned down to tie her boots. "We have no idea what's going on out there."

"Someone's lit the fire," Megan said as she stuck her head out the door then looked back over her shoulder. "You guys ready?"

"As ready as I'll ever be." Grace pulled the flap back all the way and stepped out onto the verge. Maggie secured the flap behind them. They were halfway to the fire when the bell stopped ringing and the sound of worried voices took its place.

"Is that Kwasi?" Kathleen pointed to the tall figure standing before the fire waving them forward. "I wonder what…oh, no. Didn't Greg say Kwasi and his brother were monitoring the sun's activity tonight?"

"Shit." Megan huffed as everyone turned to stare at her. "Any of you got a better word."

"It has begun." Kwasi's voice boomed out over the now-silent crowd. "Three websites are tracking a solar flare bigger than any in recorded history they say. They estimate seventeen to twenty hours before the corona reaches earth."

Robert stepped forward. "Have the alerts gone out?"

Kwasi turned to his brother who was still monitoring the phone; Ibo shook his head. "No alerts."

Robert nodded and wrapped his arm around Lisa's shoulder.

"So what do we do now?" Megan moved up beside Grace clutching her blanket around her shoulders.

"We thank the mother for keeping us safe," Kathleen said, "Then we go back to bed. Dawn comes early and we have work to do."

"She's right." Maggie yawned and by the time they were up, she'd be gone.

Chapter Twenty-Nine

"Good morning."

Maggie pressed her hand to her chest and turned toward the voice. "Juno. You scared me half to death. What are you doing out here?"

"Patrolling." Juno leaned against the bumper of Kaylyn's van and folded her arms across her chest. "Gotta keep the girls in shape...especially now." She narrowed her eyes and Maggie tried not to flinch. "And you?"

Maggie forced a smile and reached for the door handle. "Let's just say I'm on a rescue mission and leave it at that, shall we?"

"'Fraid I can't do that, Maggie." Before she could blink, Juno was standing at her side; strong fingers gently prying her hand from the latch. "That flare is heading this way any time now; even Greg admits that the seventeen to twenty-hour estimate could be way off. If I let you get into this van, you may not be coming back and I can't let that happen." There was a hint of pleading in Juno's voice. "We need you 'here,' Maggie..."

"And right now, six little children with no family except each other need me more." Maggie squared her shoulders and glanced sternly at their entwined hands; she sincerely liked this young woman who had seen so much conflict and death in her short life and still had the capacity to care so deeply for others, but Maggie couldn't let that deter her. "You'll have to use force to stop me, Juno," she said softly, "And I don't think you want to do that."

Juno's eyes looked sad as she shook her head. "I would never do that to you, but if you won't stay here where you're safe, then I'm coming with you." She let her hand fall to her side and gestured the dogs to her with a flick of her wrist. "You'll need my help to keep those kids safe if the flare hits before we get back." She avoided Maggie's eyes as she squatted beside Cagney and whispered in the Shepard's ear. Maggie kept her hand firmly on the door handle trying to convince herself that she wasn't as relieved as she felt by

Juno's offer and failing dismally. A moment later, both dogs barked a farewell and headed back to camp. "I'll drive," Juno said as she stood up.

Maggie pulled the keys from her pocket and held them out. "Thanks for this," she said as she dropped them into Juno's hand and made her way around the van to the passenger side.

"So where exactly are we going?" Juno turned the key in the ignition and the engine stuttered to life.

"Winnipeg."

"Of course, we are." Juno sighed and looked down at the gas gauge. "Well, I hope you have some of that pension money left because, right now, we're running on fumes."

Juno pulled up to the only available pump at the gas station on the outskirts of Gimli and cut the engine. "I need to give Kim a call. Let her know what we're up to," she said as she flipped her cell phone open. "Maybe you could get us a coffee, while we're waiting."

Maggie grinned. "Right after I use the bathroom. It's been so long since I've used a flush toilet I hope I haven't forgotten how."

"Strangely enough, that can happen." Juno laughed as Maggie did a double take then shook her head and crawled out of the van. Juno pressed the send button; Kim's voice came over the line almost instantaneously.

The girls delivered your message. I assume you're in the van since it's gone.

"I am and so is Maggie."

Kathleen came looking for her this morning...said she was on the breakfast crew. They're starting to get really concerned.

"Well, you can tell them she's with me...or I'm with her." Juno sighed. "This wasn't my idea, but I couldn't force her to stay and I couldn't let her come out here alone."

Juno, what's going on? If that flare hits before you get back, you'll be walking home and the trek from Gimli may be too much for someone of Maggie's age...especially in this heat.

Juno winced. "Well here's the thing, Kimmy…"

What felt like an eternity later, Juno groaned and snapped her phone shut as Maggie slid into the van. This was shaping up to be the worst day of Juno's life and she'd had some doozies in her time. "Kim is furious." She said through clenched teeth. "The whole camp has been looking for you since you didn't show up to make breakfast and once they find out where you…we…are going, they're going to be frantic until we get back." *If we get back.*

"Can't be helped," Maggie said matter-of-factly. "If I could have brought those children here before now, I would have, but I couldn't take the chance with my granddaughters' futures." She passed Juno an extra-large cup of coffee and smiled. "Cream. No sugar. Just the way you like it…I hope."

Juno closed her eyes and sighed before accepting the offering; she needed to stay calm and focused if they were going to make it through this. "That's good," she said as she swallowed a mouthful of the dark, creamy liquid; coffee was definitely one of the things she would miss in the years to come. She glanced sideways as she slid the cup into its designated holder; for a moment she could see the anguish and uncertainty in the old woman's eyes; then Maggie blinked and all that remained of her pain was an overriding sense of grim determination.

"I hope half a tank will get us there and back," Maggie said as she stowed her cup and pulled her seat belt over her shoulder.

"It should. It isn't really that far." *If you're not walking.* Juno turned the key, eased on the gas as the engine purred to life, and turned onto the highway. "Now why don't you tell me about these children you're so set on rescuing. Not that I blame you. If there was a way to rescue them all…" She shrugged. She'd learned to accept the inevitable a long time ago. "But there isn't, is there?"

"Nope, but we should rescue the ones we can, don't you think, and now that social services won't be able to mess with my granddaughters even if they did find out what's going on, I need to get those children out of Dodge. They're staying at my house right now, so that's the easy part…I know exactly where they are."

"At your house."

"With their house manager." Maggie sighed and sank back against her seat. "It's a group home right now and the kids are all around Trin's age. Their social worker is a good person; she's the one who arranged for Jessie and Kat to become foster parents, but sometimes she gets overwhelmed and that's how the children ended up living at my place…they had nowhere else to go and Andy wanted to keep them together since they were already attached to each other."

"But just because it's your house, doesn't mean we can just walk in and steal them away."

"Never intended to," Maggie said, "That's why I borrowed Cali's phone. It's got all kinds of information on it about the solar flare." She raised her head and stared thoughtfully out the window. "You know, I don't think most people know about it yet. There must have been a dozen people in that convenience store and not one of them said anything about it. Shouldn't there be some sort of alert going out by now?"

Juno had been involved in enough full-scale emergencies to know exactly why no warning had been given. "As soon as the powers that be are safe and secure in their bunkers or their summer houses or where ever they think they can ride this out," she said with as little emotion she could manage, "they'll issue their alert and not a moment beforehand. That way, when people start to panic—and they will—the self-appointed essential personnel will be safely out of it."

Maggie shook her head in disbelief. "I can't believe that."

"It's happened before, Maggie, more times than you want to know." She pulled into the right lane as they entered the divided highway. "Not to sound callous, but it just might work in our favor this time if we can get in and out before the panic starts in earnest."

Maggie sat up straight and grabbed her coffee; her lips were pursed and her eyes were filled with resolve. She gave Juno a nod. "Then I guess we need to make the best of a bad situation. Turn left at the first lights then right on Main Street."

It felt strange to be knocking on the door of the house she'd lived in her entire life, but it was the polite thing to do and she didn't want to ruffle any feathers at this stage of the game. The door opened against the chain and a pair of bright, blue eyes peered up at her from hip level. Maggie smiled at the little boy with corn-colored hair.

"Byron, come away from there. You know better than that." The eyes blinked and disappeared as the chain was released and the door opened. "Maggie. Andy said you were coming."

Maggie smiled. "Hi, Mildred. May we come in?"

"Of course." The short, brunette stepped aside and Juno followed Maggie into the front hall. "The kids are all out back…with the exception of Byron." Mildred smiled. "I don't know how he does it, but he seems to know someone's at the door before they even have a chance to knock."

"Sounds like our Trin," Maggie smiled back then turned to Juno. "Juno this is Mildred…the woman I was telling you about. Mildred…Juno."

Mildred stuck out her hand and Juno accepted the gesture. "Nice to meet you."

"So is Andy here yet?" Maggie glanced into the kitchen as she kicked off her running shoes; she'd come prepared if walking was involved.

"She just called. She said she's on her way…should be here in five minutes." Mildred followed Maggie's eyes then turned on her heels and led them into the kitchen; the room was as spotless as the day Maggie had left it. "Come sit down. I just put on some tea."

"Whoa. Now, this is a kitchen," Juno said as they followed Mildred to the table. "My Grandma had a kitchen like this. She used to be able to fit our entire family into it plus the neighbors. Good times. Too bad…" She shook her head and reached for her cup.

Maggie glanced sideways at Juno. She'd never seen this side of the young pilot before; she seldom talked about herself and never about her past. "So, Mildred," Maggie said as Juno's eyes roved around the room. "I've really enjoyed your messages. Sounds like the children are doing well."

Mildred's face lit up. "They are. They're thriving now that they're getting proper food and lots of TLC. Three of them will be ready to start school in the fall. We even have a line on a house. We should be able to move in…"

"Mildred? Millie?"

"In the kitchen, Andy." Mildred got up and filled the fourth cup with tea.

Maggie shared a determined look with Juno and squared her shoulders as Andy walked into the room. "Sorry, I'm late." The young social worker took the seat across from Juno. "Hi. I'm Andy."

"Juno."

Andy nodded to Juno then turned her attention to Maggie. "So, how are the girls? Enjoying their introduction to the great outdoors, I hope."

Maggie flinched and hoped no one noticed. Then she took a deep breath and steadied herself. "We don't have time to beat around the bush, Andy," she said, "So I'm just going to give you the down and dirty version and you can believe me or not."

Andy's eyes grew wide as she leaned across the table. "What's this all about? Did something happen to one of the girls?"

"Of course not," Maggie said indignantly. This was going to be much harder than she'd thought. "The children have been learning a great deal about life in the forest, but we never went to any of the parks we listed." She took a deep breath as Andy continued to stare at her. "The truth is we've been spending our time in the middle of a forest preparing for the advent of a very large solar flare…one that will inevitably change the world as we know it."

"This solar flare." Juno held up Cali's cell phone; her voice was calm and matter of fact. "The corona is scheduled to reach us in…" She glanced at the clock over the stove. "Nine hours, give or take, and when it does, it will shut down everything for the foreseeable future: the internet, all means of communications, transportation, the power grid…"

"She's joking." Mildred raised wide frightened eyes from the picture in front of her. "Right, Maggie."

Maggie shook her head. "Sorry, but everything Juno just said is true. Believe it or not, it's up to you; we won't force you to come with us, but we have a place where the two of you and the little ones can be safe. We have fresh water, warm housing, a good supply of wild foods, and lots of intelligent dedicated people to make it work." She stood up before either of them could say anything. "There are a few things I need from the Nan Cave. Look through the information on Cali's phone. Give Jessie a call if you need verification, but do it quickly. We need to be out of here inside the hour."

"Or sooner," Juno said, "I wouldn't want to be on the road with six children when the flare hits." With that, Juno turned on her heels and followed Maggie out of the room.

"So this is the Nan Cave," Juno leaned forward as Maggie removed the padlock and pushed the door open. "Cali told us about it. She said the forest makes her think of home because it smells just like this room."

Maggie smiled. "I suppose it does: a little cedar, a hint of sage and lavender. I used to toss them in the fire to help everyone relax." She took a deep breath, capturing the memory then picked up a cardboard box from the end of the desk. "I have some things to pick up that I should have brought with me the first time around." She pointed to her great-grandmother's eight tea tables and their trolleys in the far corner; now Mat would have a place for her teeth and Cali would have a writing desk. "Including those. The trolleys are on wheels, so if you could just roll them out to the front door…"

Juno nodded and Maggie carried the box over to her shelf of family memorabilia; the special photo albums went in first followed by her grandmother's journal, her father's pipe, her mother's pearl necklace, and a lock of her daughter's hair—the stuff of endless stories around the fire in the past; maybe she'd revive the tradition, make storytelling a part of campfire nights. She smiled at the thought and had just closed the cardboard flaps when Mildred ran into the room.

"Maggie, that solar flare you were talking about…an alert just came up on that phone you gave us." Mildred wrapped her arms around her chest as Maggie turned toward her. "Andy says we're coming with you…if you'll still have us." She shrugged. "My husband died a while back; these kids are my family now and I want them safe, so does Andy. She's bringing the kids inside right now."

"I heard the alert as I was going by the kitchen," Juno said as she came up behind Mildred. "Did it give a time estimate?"

Mildred looked like a deer caught in the headlights. "F…four hours." She winced. "On the outside."

"Damn. It must be picking up speed somehow. I didn't think that was possible." Juno ran her fingers through her hair then took a deep breath. "Okay. Here's what we're going to do." She turned to Maggie. "I'll pack up any food I can find. You and Mildred get the children's belongings. Don't forget their winter gear and if any of them have a favorite toy, make sure you bring it. We don't want a repetition of what happened with Trin."

"What happened with Trin?"

"I'll tell you later, Mildred." Maggie shared a smile with Juno and grabbed Millie's hand. "Right now we have work to do."

"I want everyone out to the truck in fifteen minutes," Juno said as she picked up Maggie's box. "We need to be halfway home by the time people figure out that the warning isn't a test."

Andy met Maggie and Mildred in the hall leading to the stairs with a handful of green bags. "We'll take those," Maggie said as she held out her hand. "Maybe you can help Juno pack the food while you're keeping an eye on the kids."

Andy raised a dark eyebrow then nodded. She handed Maggie the bags and headed toward the kitchen "Don't forget the hall closet," she called over her shoulder. "They're going to need those snowsuits."

"I'd almost forgotten about them," Mildred said as they climbed the stairs, "Some sporting goods store donated a couple of dozen really expensive snowsuits to the group homes and each of my kids got one. Apparently, the owner developed a soft spot for foster children recently."

Maggie didn't even need to wonder how that had happened; she'd been right there while her granddaughters charmed the owner of the hunting and camping goods store with their negotiating skills and their generosity. The discount he'd given them had been more than magnanimous and everyone at camp would be warm this winter because of it. *Go figure.* "Well, at least that's one thing we won't need to worry about," Maggie said as she stopped at the first room and handed Mildred four bags. "We should take the pillows and blankets too. If you'll do this room, I'll get the next one."

Mildred nodded. "I'll be as quick as I can," she said as she pushed the door open.

"We can't all fit in there." Andy stood on the front stoop holding Byron's hand while the other children peered out from behind her. "And even if we could there aren't enough seat belts. The children will need their booster seats…"

"We're not going on a Sunday drive," Juno growled then she took a deep breath and steadied herself as Andy took a step back. "Look, it's going to get crazy out there and we can't take the chance of being separated. We may not make it all the way back to camp before the flare hits and the children will need all of us to watch out for them if we end up having to walk."

"She's right, Andy. Trust me. We're stronger together." Maggie stepped out beside the young social worker holding the hands of two little girls in matching pink hoodies. "Now let's get the children buckled in as best we can." She started down the stairs. "You know, when I was a kid I don't think the cars even had seatbelts and I'm glad." She chuckled. "It would have been awfully boring sitting in one place for the whole ride."

Mildred laughed and followed Maggie down the stairs. "I can remember sleeping in the back window of my grandfather's big, old Oldsmobile when he drove us to the cottage. I was about six at the time."

Andy looked at both of the older women as though they'd lost their minds. Juno tensed for another round. "You're missing one," she said as she locked eyes with Andy. "I'll take Byron. You go find…"

Andy blinked. "Kale…his name is Kale and he should just be finishing up in the bathroom."

With that, she nudged Byron toward Juno and turned on her heels. "We'll be out in a minute."

"I'll take him," Mildred said as she reached for the little boy's hand. "You'll have to forgive, Andy. She does everything by the book; it's good for the children's welfare, but it doesn't leave much leeway for situations like this. It's going to be hard for her when she has to throw that book out the window for good."

"I'll keep that in mind." Juno nodded her thanks, let go of Byron's hand, and turned toward the back of the van. It had taken some creative packing to get all the various bags and boxes tucked away and she really had to bring the hatch down hard to close it. It felt good to release some of the tension that was slowly building up inside; these people were in her care whether they liked it or not and she refused to let any harm come to them no matter how bullheaded they might be.

"The children are all belted in." Maggie smiled at Juno as she made her way around the vehicle. "I'll just squeeze myself in and then we'll be ready to go. Never thought I'd see the day when I'd be glad that Kaylyn bought this monstrosity. Goes to show how wrong a person can be sometimes."

Juno grimaced at the grandmother's not-so-cryptic remark and eased herself into the driver's seat beside Maggie. "We need to take the shortest way to the number eight," she said as she backed out of the drive. "Hopefully, we'll be out of the city before things get too bad."

Maggie let out a long sigh then pulled her eyes away from the house and pointed to the right. "Take the second left then go left again at the lights. We'll go up to Arlington; if people are panicking, they'll want to stock up and Arlington has far fewer stores than McPhillips. We'll have to cut left at Leila though to get onto the highway. That'll take us straight north."

Juno blocked out the sound of laughing voices and the occasional squeal from the back seat and focused all her attention on the task at hand. Traffic was slower than Juno liked, but Maggie was right; they didn't hit any real problems until they turned into the shopping district.

"We'll never get out of here," Andy said from Maggie's right. Juno gripped the wheel tighter and ignored the comment; not getting out of here wasn't an option. She watched a trickle of cars take a right at the street ahead and turned to follow them. Andy gasped. "What are you doing? This isn't the way."

"Andy, let the woman drive," Maggie snapped; Juno would have hugged the grandmother if she didn't have both hands on the wheel. "We're moving and we're still going north. That's better than the alternative."

Juno glanced at the dashboard clock and clenched her jaw; less than three hours according to the latest estimates and they still had almost a hundred kilometers to go. She brushed that thought away and kept her eyes on the rear-view mirror as she followed the car ahead of her; the lineup of cars behind her had grown in the past few minutes. A red SUV sped past her, jockeying for position and she eased off the gas to let it pass.

"People are starting to get anxious," Maggie said as two more cars squealed past. She leaned forward as they rolled through the next intersection then pointed to the left. "I think we need to turn at the next street. It should get us onto the highway. There should even be light there if I remember correctly."

Juno saw the car ahead of her veer left at the stop sign, pumped her brakes, and followed; less than a minute later they were on the highway heading north in fits and starts toward the perimeter. She looked at the clock and tried not to groan; at the speed they were going, there was no way they were going to make it.

"One more set of lights then the pace should pick up." Maggie patted Juno's knee. "You're doing great, Granddaughter. Just hang in there."

Juno allowed herself to smile. "Did you just call me, Granddaughter?"

The old woman chuckled. "I guess I did."

"That sign we just passed said it's eleven kilometers to Gimli." Andy leaned across Maggie. "That means we're almost there. Right?"

Juno kept her eyes fixed on the road ahead. The traffic had been keeping a slow, but steady, pace since they'd passed the turnoff for Selkirk and they'd been able to make up some of the time they'd lost, but they weren't out of the woods yet. "The camp is thirty-seven kilometers past Gimli and most of that's a gravel road."

"But we can still make it?" Mildred said from the back seat.

Juno eyed the clock and shrugged. "If the last time estimates were right."

"You kids want to hear some music?" Maggie glanced at Juno as cheers came from the back seat then pressed the 'on' button for the disc player. There was a warning in Maggie's eyes; little pitchers had big ears. Juno nodded as the familiar refrains of the Teddybears' Picnic filled the van.

"This is my favorite," a child's voice said above the music then broke into song. Everyone in the van hummed or sang along, including Juno. Maggie glanced up at her and smiled.

It wasn't until they passed the signs leading into Gimli that the outside world reasserted itself. The gas station was packed with people jockeying for position at the pumps, and Juno allowed herself a moment to feel sorry for their wasted effort; in less than an hour, those vehicles wouldn't be going anywhere ever again. "Maggie, you got that phone handy?" Juno waited as the grandmother dug through her pockets; she'd have to stop the car to dig her own phone from her back pocket and she didn't want to waste the time if she didn't have to.

"Found it," Maggie said after an anxious minute.

Juno heaved a sigh of relief. "You need to phone Kim. Tell her we just passed Gimli. Make sure she knows we have six little ones with us."

Maggie nodded and relayed the message. "They'll be watching for us," she said as the call ended. "She also said a few other things I won't repeat in front of the children."

"I'm sure she did."

"Who's Kim?" Andy asked. It was the first time she'd actually spoken to anyone since they left Winnipeg.

Juno glanced at the young social worker and thought she saw the shimmer of tears in her eyes. Perhaps she should cut Andy some slack; it wasn't every day that a social worker had to make instantaneous life and death decisions for the children in her care…especially when those decisions were contrary to every rule in her well dog-eared book. "Kim's my partner and she's not very happy with me right now."

Maggie chuckled. "She would have done the same thing if she'd been in your shoes. Just remind her of that when we get back. Now put the pedal to the metal as they used to say in my day; times a wasting."

Juno watched the gas gauge ease toward empty as she managed to coax a little more speed from the aging vehicle. She eased on the brake as they approached the turnoff to the system of gravel roads that would ultimately lead them to the camp; bits of rock spewed from beneath their wheels as a fine mist of sand and silt made the rear-view mirrors useless. "Keep your eye open for the first turnoff, Maggie. I missed it last time I came this way."

The old woman pointed. "It's just past that big, old oak tree…the one with no leaves. Do you see it?" Juno nodded. "Just be careful when you make the turn. I think that's where Kenneth went off the road." Andy gasped but didn't comment. "The ditches there are pretty steep."

Juno halved her speed and eased around the corner.

"We must be close, right?" Andy peered out the front window at the encroaching forest; the shimmer in her eyes was gone and she sounded more curious than frightened.

Juno glanced at the clock then tore her eyes away. It didn't matter what the clock said; they'd either make it or they wouldn't. "We're still about fifteen klicks out, but at least that distance is manageable if we need to walk."

"Maybe for us," Andy said. "But the children…"

"Will be fine," Maggie pointed. "Next left."

Juno took the indicated turn; she was grateful for the grandmother's powers of observation. Kim usually drove when they left the camp and Juno had gotten lost twice when she and Jessie made their trip into town. They didn't have time for that kind of miscalculation today. She heard Mildred talking softly to the children, telling them a story about a magical forest. *If she only knew.*

Chapter Thirty

Juno handed each of the adults a knapsack, pulled her own on over her shoulder, and closed the hatch.

"What's in here?" Maggie groaned as she struggled with the second shoulder strap of the paisley knapsack Juno had given her. "Feels like a ton of bricks."

"There's a container of water, a box of granola bars, a bottle of juice, and a flashlight in each bag." Juno reaches over and helped Maggie settle the load on her back. "I found the knapsacks hanging up in the mudroom."

Mildred smiled. "The children like to wear them when we go on our walks." She hooked her thumbs under the straps. "So how are we going to do this?"

"By putting one foot in front of the other," Maggie said as she nodded her thanks to Juno.

Andy startled as some small animal rattled the bushes on the side of the road. "Maybe we should stay here overnight and get an early start in the morning. I wouldn't want to run into a bear or something in the dark."

Maggie pulled a can of bear spray from her jacket pocket. "If we do just squirt this in his face and if that doesn't work, Juno will take care of it." She reached around and patted the middle of Juno's back then raised her eyes to the young pilot and winked. "Some of us are more observant than others. Don't worry. I won't say anything." She turned to Mildred and Andy. "If we stay here, it just means the others will have farther to walk and…"

"So you think someone else is coming?" Andy's eyes darted up and down the road. "Who?"

"Kim will have organized a rescue party; they would have left when the flare hit and we weren't back," Juno said, "If we don't meet them at least partway, we'll all be stuck here for the night."

Andy drew a deep breath, clutched the bear spray in her fist, and nodded. "Then I guess we'd better get the children." Mildred nodded and opened the back door.

Byron stuck his head out and blinked. "Is this the magic forest, Millie?"

"It sure is, Bud." She took his hand and helped him out of the van then guided each of the children out behind him. Juno grinned at the chocolate smudges on their fingers and cheeks; now she knew why it had been so quiet back there for the last few kilometers. "I'll take Byron and Kale," Mildred took the two boys by the hand and turned to Juno.

Maggie stepped forward. "I'll take the two girls…"

"Jill and Angela," Andy said.

Maggie smiled at the young woman. "I'll take Jill and Angela. That leaves one each for you and Juno. That way you'll each have a hand free…just in case."

"Just in case…" Andy's eyes grew wide. Then she nodded and reached out her hand to the little black-haired girl and the redheaded boy standing behind Mildred. "Amber, you come with me. Seth, you go with Juno." Seth squinted his eyes and looked around.

"That's me, Seth." Juno extended her hand. "I'm Juno. Want to take a walk in the magic forest with me." Seth nodded his head vigorously and reached for her hand. Juno closed the door and checked that it was locked; probably a wasted effort considering what had just happened, but it made her feel better.

"Everybody ready," Mildred said and six little heads nodded. She smiled at Juno then started off down the road. "If you go into the woods tonight…"

Kim looked down at her cell phone as her hand tingled and the screen went blank. She glanced at the windup watch on her wrist; at least it was still working. "That's it people; we're officially on our own now."

"Seems almost anticlimactic," Robert observed from Kim's right.

"Out here maybe, but elsewhere…" She shook her head to dislodge that thought; she had a rescue mission to get underway. She stood and turned to the people behind her. "Okay. Listen up. By my estimates, they're between eight and twelve klicks out and it's going to be dark in four hours, so put your packs in the wagons and let's move out."

"Don't be too upset with Juno," Jessie said as she came up beside Kim. "My grandmother is a force of nature when she wants to be. Juno didn't stand a chance."

"I kinda figured that out." Kim smiled and glanced sideways at Jessie. "Given who her grandchildren are, she'd have to be."

"You've got that right." Jessie grinned then changed the subject. "So...do you think we'll reach them before dark? Those little ones are going to be awfully frightened if we don't."

"Maggie's there and two of their workers..."

"Did Juno give you their names?"

Kim shook her head. "Junie just said she and Maggie had backup if worse came to worse...and I guess it did."

"Hey. Twelve kilometers isn't so bad and, with the kids in the wagons, we should be able to make good time coming back." Jessie nodded thoughtfully. "Juno and Maggie have saved eight more people from harm today and we get to help them; I think that's a pretty auspicious way to herald the end of the world as we know it. Don't you?"

Kim sighed thinking about her partner acting as a shepherd to six children, one old lady, and two unknowns—an easy assignment for someone who'd helped rescue dozens of civilians from war-torn villages, but these weren't civilians—they were family the moment they got into that van and, for a long time, Juno hadn't had much of that in her life; it would tear her apart if anything bad happened to them. "As long as we get them all back in one piece."

Jessie nodded. "We will."

"Okay, people, step it up." Kim glanced over her shoulder as the people trailing behind her lengthened their stride. They were taking all eight wagons with them including the five new ones the grandfathers had brought in two days ago. Kim wished that Jake hadn't taken the truck and trailer into town this morning on some mysterious errand and run the tank dry getting back; that vehicle could have gotten them closer to the van before the flare hit. "Left. Right. Left..."

Jessie watched the shadows lengthen as they moved briskly along the road. She'd raked her brain all day searching for the signs she must have missed, but there had been no outward indication that her grandmother was about to risk her life to save the children staying at her childhood home. Jessie had seen the tears in Maggie's eyes when everyone finished commenting on their incredible luck and their hopes for the future, but every adult in the circle had shed a tear or two for all those left behind including herself and beyond that, there was nothing. Maggie had made her way to bed along with everyone else after the initial shock of Kwasi's announcement had worn off and, in the morning, she was just gone.

"I think my grandmother decided to do this the moment she offered Mildred the house," Jessie said suddenly, "I can't be certain, mind you, but my gut tells me I'm right. That's why she wasn't more upset than she was last night; she already had a plan."

Kim nodded. "You're probably right, but it doesn't help us now. I'm just glad…"

"Shh." Jessie's hand shot up and the line behind them staggered to a halt; Kim frowned at her. "Just listen," Jessie said as her ears tracked the sound. "Do you hear that? It sounds like…"

"…singing." Kim smiled and turned on her heels. "Everyone. We're close, so let's step it up, and maybe we can get those little ones back to camp before dark."

Wanda stood right behind Jessie with her eyes closed and her head tilted to the side. Then she laughed. "It sounds like the Teddy Bears Picnic."

Chapter Thirty-One

"Here are the blankets you wanted, Grandmother. Hua and Mel should be along shortly with the sheets and pillows." Cali dropped the makeshift bundle at Megan's feet then crossed her ankles and sat down; her breath came in short, hard pants as she nodded toward the bulging sheet. "They're really beautiful…"

"Warm too." Megan smiled as she pulled the sheet aside. "Trappers used to trade for them and turn them into coats. I saw the finished product in a museum once; looked as good as new."

"So…you're giving them to the little ones Grandma Maggie went to pick up."

Megan nodded and her face lit up. "I thought it would be a nice way to welcome them to the family and my husband would have approved. He gave them to me…one a year from our first anniversary right up to the year he died; said they'd come in handy someday." Then she shrugged. "Besides, the children aren't likely to have brought much with them and the nights are still chilly."

"And the extra blanket?" Cali cocked her head to the side. "There are only six children coming in tonight, but you asked for seven blankets."

Megan grinned. "The extra one is for Trin of course. She can be quite persuasive with Sophia's help. I guess she convinced Kaylyn that one of the extra bunks in the twenty-four-footer should be hers since the new kids would need someone to show them the ropes."

Cali giggled. "That should be interesting."

"That's what Kaylyn said." Megan shook her head and smiled. "But I guess Sophia has volunteered to help out for the first while, so Kaylyn gave your sister the go-ahead on the condition that she paid attention to Mildred and did everything she was told."

And good luck with that. Cali smiled and changed the subject. "I asked Mark how they'd managed to buy five sets of bunks in Gimli this morning when Jake had to go all the way to Selkirk to get the ones for Bertha and her children. You know what he said." She watched the elder slowly shake her head. "He said 'Jake has his ways.' Now, what the heck does that mean?"

There was a flicker of something akin to panic in Megan's eyes; then it was gone, but Cali wouldn't forget what she'd seen. "I think it means that we should just be glad that no one will be sleeping on the ground this winter and let it go at that." Megan leaned down and retied the bundle. "Now help me get this up the hill. There's still a lot to be done if we're going to move everyone into the yurts after the feast."

They followed a line of builders carrying camp-cots up the path to the rise. Grandma Maggie would be grateful to those who had given up their bunks for the children; she'd probably had too much on her mind just getting the children home to worry about what would happen once they got here. *Or maybe she just knew that things would be taken care of somehow.*

"There you are," Mel said as she and Hua caught up to them; they both carried two large bundles and looked as tired as she felt. "The rescue party just left, so I guess the corona has entered earth's orbit."

Cali reached into her pocket and pulled out her phone; a frisson of something akin to fear trickled down her spine and she pushed it angrily aside as she opened the cover and pressed the button to turn the phone on. She'd known this moment was coming for weeks; she should be used to the idea by now. "Nothing," she said as she stared at the empty screen.

"How close do you think they got before the van stopped running?" Hua asked as they turned toward the north side of the ridge and the large yurt designated this morning for the children Maggie was bringing in; a slightly smaller yurt to the left of it would house Hanna and her grandchildren.

"I heard Kim tell Robert twelve klicks may be less," Mel said. "She thinks they should be able to get the children back here before dark, but she's not sure."

"They'll be here." Megan grinned as she pulled open the door. "I can feel it in my bones. Tonight, we celebrate becoming one with the forest; no more gimmicks and gadgets—just us and the mother of us all and those children are a big part of that. Of course, they'll be here; she wouldn't have it any other way."

"I believe you are right, Grandmother," Hua said softly.

Megan shrugged. "I'm just saying."

"They're here Grandmothers," JoJo skidded to a halt just inside the cookhouse door. "Wow. That smells amazing. What is it?"

"Macaroni with ground rabbit, wild onions, and tomato sauce," Matibi grinned. "Since we're celebrating our future tonight, we thought we'd pull out all the stops." She pointed toward the deck benches in the corner by the north wall. "You'd be surprised at what's in those boxes. You, young people, have been doing such a good job feeding us that we almost forgot that they were there."

JoJo ducked her head at the compliment and tried not to blush. "Billie says she can hear the kids on the path. Momkay said to tell you that most of the tents have been taken down and the yurts are ready for occupation. She thought it was important for you to know that."

"And she was right," Grace said as she ladled the sauce into the macaroni then reversed the process. "It means it's time for us to finish up here. We're going to need people to take everything out to the fire pit, including the water jug and the cups."

"I'll go find some people to help and I'll be right back." JoJo took another sniff of the delicious aroma and darted out the door.

She and Ian and Sam and most of Grandma Lee's students had spent the day collecting wood for tonight's fire, helping to take down tents and setting up the supper circle with the elder's chairs and a variety of logs for the younger folk as Grandma Megan called them. She stopped for a moment to admire their handiwork then snagged Mark on his way by. "The grandmothers need help with the pots."

Mark nodded. "Andrew and the others are washing up down at the lake. I'll go get them." He gave her a thumbs-up before he turned away. "Good job today."

She returned the gesture. "You too." She headed back to the cook tent and filled three reusable grocery bags with plates and mugs and sporks. "Mark went to get Andrew to help with the pots. Should I ring the bell?"

"I think that would be a great idea," Grandma Kathleen said as she helped Grandma Grace put the lids on the pots and move them off the stove. "We don't want supper to get cold, do we?"

"No, we do not." Jo smiled, picked up the bags, and headed out the door. A moment later, the sound of the dinner bell rang out over the clearing just as the wagons delivered their cargo. JoJo sighed with satisfaction; all things considered it had been a good day.

Jessie smiled as Kaylyn took her hand and led her toward a brightly colored chair. "Does this mean I'm an elder now?" Jessie quipped.

Kaylyn grinned over her shoulder. "You were born old, Jess. This is just a sign of appreciation from the people who love you best." She waited for Jessie to sit down then took the chair beside her. "The girls used the last of the money on their cards. They asked Jake to pick the chairs up when he went to get the beds for Bertha and her boys. I guess they even managed to buy a few extras." She pointed to where Mildred smiled gratefully as Billie guided her toward a chair.

"I wonder how long it will take for Millie to realize what an honor she's just been given," Jessie said as she leaned her head back and closed her eyes. "This feels amazing. I haven't walked that far since…" She chuckled. "Since forever, I guess."

"Well, it looks like everyone came through relatively in one piece…even Maggie."

Jessie opened her eyes and sat up; the grandmother was sitting across the fire surrounded by her peers. "I doubt she'll be able to walk tomorrow, but she didn't falter…not once the whole way back. She's really an amazing woman, you know."

Kaylyn giggled. "That's not what you said this morning when you found out where she'd gone." She glanced over Jessie's shoulder and smiled.

"Hope you're hungry, Momjay." A steaming bowl appeared in front of Jessie. "The cooks made a special meal to commemorate everything that happened today."

Jessie's stomach rumbled right on cue as she reached up and took the bowl. "Thanks, Cali. It smells wonderful. And tell your sisters thank you for the chair; it's much appreciated."

Cali grinned and ducked her head. "Glad you like it." Then she handed Kaylyn a second bowl, tossed a "see you later" over her shoulder, and scurried away.

Jessie shoveled a spoonful of macaroni into her mouth and chewed thoughtfully as she watched the activity around the fire. The six children they'd escorted in today had each found a welcoming lap and were busily filling their empty stomachs with no signs of lingering distress as Trin kept a watchful eye on them and made certain they had enough to eat. There were smiles everywhere she looked and even Andy, who had chosen a spot beside Mildred and Juno, seemed more relaxed though she never took her eyes off of the children. All around Jessie, people ate and talked and laughed as the sun sank toward the trees, the sky darkened and her family prepared to greet the first night of an uncertain future.

Mark stood with a fist in the air, but before he could speak, a clear, high voice rang out through the sudden silence, "Look, everyone. The rainbows are dancing."

And so mote it be.